The Bear Slayer

Ormstunga Saga: Book 4

Donovan Cook

Book Cover by Rafael Andres

First edition 2025
Paperback ISBN 978-1-0683908-0-7
Hardback ISBN 978-1-0683908-1-4
Ebook ISBN 978-1-8383008-9-0

donovancook.net

To Joey, our lovable and crazy Frenchie

Chapter 1

The smell of death filled the air. The sickly sweet scent of blood from the wounds of his prey made his mouth salivate even as his heart still raced in his chest. The sun shone brightly through the branches of the trees, but the only sounds which he heard over the rustling leaves were the ravens. Telling him to hurry so they could feast. He ignored them, as he always did. He would take his time and enjoy every bite as he fed on the corpse of his prey.

He was about to take a bite when his ears pricked. A noise amongst the trees that did not belong. One that was familiar, yet he knew it was not a friend. He stopped and listened, tilting his head while sniffing the air. But he couldn't smell anything over the blood of his prey. He turned to where the noise came from, not wanting it to be what he suspected. Placing one foot in front of the next, he crept towards the sound, his racing heart drowning out the sounds of the ravens. But then he realised that they too had gone silent when a new noise reached his ears. This one louder than the first and coming from the other side of the clearing. He turned his head towards the new sound and frowned when the trees that were there only a few heartbeats ago were gone. And so was his prey. Nothing remained of it, not even its blood. The only thing that remained was the scent of death in the air, only now it was stronger. Darkness had replaced the trees and ravens. A darkness he had hoped never to see again because he knew it meant one thing. A growl escaped from his throat as he bared his teeth at the darkness, a warning to whatever may be hiding there and waiting to pounce as soon as he turned his back. He was not a pup any more. The darkness did not frighten him as it once did.

He sensed movement behind him and turned, his legs crouched and ready to launch himself at his foe. But there was no giant troll or cloaked figure. All that faced him was a snake, its scales green and glistening in the darkness. He scowled at the snake as she coiled up on herself and hissed at him and growled. But instead of being frightened away, the snake launched at him. He jumped back with a yelp, not expecting the attack, but she had missed as she intended to. He knew that if she wanted to hurt him, then she would have done. Another rumbling behind him made him look over his shoulder, but again, he saw only the darkness. He turned back to the snake to ask her what she wanted, but she was gone.

His fur stood on end as he scanned the darkness, searching for any sign of the snake, but he was alone. Just as he had been before. Even the larger presence was gone, but the fingers of fear were gripping his heart as he wondered why she had come to him again after so long. He already knew the answer to that, though, because her presence meant only one thing.

Death.

Winter AD 845, Jelling, Denmark

The boy froze as he stared at the tall warrior wearing an old bearskin cloak, ignoring his broad shoulders and slim arms. It wasn't the warrior's brynja under the warrior's cloak or his sword with the golden hilt that caught the boy's attention. Neither was it the scowl on the young warrior's face or the way his fists were clenched. It was the ugly scars on his face that frightened the boy. Three long lines, paler than the rest of the warrior's sun-darkened face, which started near his right eye and went all the way down his face to his mouth. The warrior's thin beard, with a braid in the centre, grew in patches around the scar which pulled the skin tight and gave the warrior an almost lopsided look. His light-coloured hair was long and worn loose, as if the warrior was trying to hide the scars with it, but the wind kept blowing it away from his face.

The boy's friends called out to him, eager to carry on with the game they were playing, but the boy had forgotten all about that. He had forgotten about everything as he gaped at the warrior who stopped in front of him. Angry eyes, the same colour as the blade of a sword, stared at the boy, and when the warrior growled, the boy screamed as he turned and fled back to the safety of his home.

Ulf sighed as he watched the boy run away as if being chased by wolves. He knew he shouldn't have scared the boy like that, but he had got irritated at the way he was staring at him. Even if he understood why. The scars on his face, given to him by a large brown bear in a forest in Southern Norway. Near where he had grown up on his uncle's farm, but could never return to. That was where he had earned his by-name, Bear-Slayer. That had been four winters ago, and no one had called him that since he had left Norway. Now he was just Ulf. He sighed again and made his way to the market while doing his best to ignore the stares as people of Jelling gaped at his face. The large town was where the king of Denmark had his hall, although Ulf ignored the large mead hall in the centre of the town and surrounded by small wooden longhouses which were built too close together, leaving only thin paths for those who lived here to move around. It was packed and stuffy behind the large wooden walls of Jelling, made even worse by the endless smoke from the many houses filling the sky. Ulf hated it here and missed the openness of his uncle's farm, but he could never go back to that. Not any more.

Ulf knew, though, it wasn't the boy's staring or being in Jelling that had irritated him as he wrapped his cloak around him to hide from the winter cold. It was the dream he had the night before. His hand went to the Mjöllnir pendant around his neck, the ivory worn smooth with time and his fingers. So smooth that the swirling patterns were barely noticeable. Ulf used to have dreams like that all the time once, dreams filled with blood and death, and had been told they were messages from the gods. He never knew if that was true, but his dreams had been silent since he had been banished from Norway. Until now, and that worried him.

'Took you long enough,' a voice barked at Ulf, stopping him in his tracks. Ulf blinked as he glanced around him at the busy market square and wondered how he had got there. People jostled with each other as they tried to see what traders from across Midgard offered, some haggling with stubborn traders or arguing over who saw something first. It sounded like standing in the middle of a large waterfall, but Ulf found some comfort in all the noise. 'You should have been here long ago! Where were you?' Ulf glared at Tormod, a trader and a Dane, and a miserable bastard, but then he took a deep breath to calm himself. Tormod and his brother, Ingolfr, had taken Ulf in when he had nowhere to go and provided Ulf with food and silver so he could buy new clothes when he needed them. In return, Ulf helped to load their ship and protected them from bandits when they travelled. The brothers liked the effect that Ulf had on people, and it was not just the scars on his face. It was also the anger in Ulf's eyes that made people feel nervous around him. But that anger had also caused them many problems as Ulf was prone to lashing out and had been in more fights than he should have been in. Ulf had thought that his anger would leave him when he had killed those responsible for the deaths of his family, but it had never gone away. Instead, his anger festered inside of him, growing stronger every day until he could no longer hold it in. Ulf had hoped to leave the life of a warrior behind him, just like his uncle had. But he wasn't so sure any more. 'Well?'

Ulf shook his head to clear it. 'I had business to take care of.'

'What business can you have here?' Tormod raised an eyebrow at Ulf.

'Leave the young man, Tormod.' Ingolfr, a small and thin man, walked to the trader and clapped him on the shoulder. 'Jelling is a strange place if you have never been here before, and the gods know it's easy to lose track while wandering the streets.'

Tormod scowled at his brother, who was shorter than him. 'Ulf has been here many times since we took him in.'

Ulf said nothing as he gripped the hilt of Ormstunga, the cursed sword that had been in his family for generations. He could still remember the first time he laid eyes on the double-edged sword, with its name engraved on the blade, as a young boy. Just before his father went off to fight his last battle. On the golden half circle pommel of Ormstunga, Jörmungandr encircled the Valknut, just like the giant serpent circled Midgard. Her grip was made of dark red wood and had a gold ring in the middle while the guard, also made of gold, had two intertwining fire-breathing serpents engraved on it. Written in runes on these serpents were the words which were seared into Ulf's memory. *I am from a place of darkness. Do not draw me in the light of the sun.*

Ulf had been raised by his uncle and aunt on their small farm, but as he grew older, his anger at the gods for taking both his parents away from him only grew stronger. Like flames feeding on dry wood. But the gods did not appreciate Ulf's anger towards them and had sent a giant man called Griml to kill his family. That monster was dead, killed by Ulf, but Ulf had been banished from Norway soon after, when he had learnt the truth about his father's death.

Ulf had left his fate in the hands of the gods after that. Something he had never done before. He had gone to the land of the Swedes and the Geats. Lands he had raided with men he once called friends. It was there that Ulf had met Ingolfr, who took him in and gave him work on his ship, even though Ulf knew little about sailing. Ingolfr's brother, though, had not been so keen on Ulf joining them at first. That was until he saw the effect Ulf's scars had on people.

Ulf had tried to learn how to be a trader from the two brothers, but they soon discovered that Ulf did not have the patience or the skills required for that life. His temper often got in the way while haggling with others and they'd be forced to leave markets sooner than what the brothers had wanted to. That was when Tormod had decided that Ulf would be better used as their muscle and not a trader. So Ulf wore his brynja and Ormstunga. He wore the arm rings he had earned from the few raids he had been on, and he glared at any person who looked like they might be a threat to the brothers. Which to Ulf was everyone.

'Leave Ulf, brother. Can't you see he is troubled?'

Tormod grunted. 'Ulf is always troubled. That is his problem.'

Ingolfr moved closer to Ulf and put a hand on his shoulder. 'Ignore Tormod. The gods know he has always been far too serious. I suggest you go for a walk, Ulf. Clear your mind of your troubles. But come back when the sun goes down. Tomorrow we leave for Hedeby and we need to pack tonight.'

Ulf nodded and forced himself to let go of Ormstunga. He noticed how Tormod's eyes lit up as he glanced at the sword, but was used to that as well. Tormod had already offered him a small fortune for the sword, but Ulf could never sell her. Tyr would be furious with him if he did, and Ulf did not want to anger the god of war. No, Ormstunga would stay with Ulf until he died, and then he would be buried with it. Ulf was determined to be the last of his line to be cursed by the blade, which, according to legend, was made from a sliver of Jörmungandr's tongue. 'Thank you,' Ulf said and turned to leave.

'And remember,' Tormod called out to him. 'One more fight and you are on your own.'

Ulf clenched his fists as he glanced at Tormod over his shoulder. But he knew he couldn't be angry at the trader for that. It was his temper that had strained their relationship. After the last fight Ulf had got into, one that had cost the brothers dearly as Ulf had broken a few stalls and wares of other traders, they had warned him they would part ways with him if he ever got into another fight. Ulf forced himself to unclench his fists and thought about the dream he had the night before. As he walked away from the market in search of a place where he could get some ale, he felt a familiar sensation he had not felt since he had left Norway. A tingling in his spine which told him that someone was watching him.

Ulf gripped the Mjöllnir pendant around his neck because he was certain now that the gods wanted something from him.

Chapter 2

Ulf left the tavern he had spent most of the day in and saw that the sun was already setting. He cursed the short winter days and knew that the brothers would be angry with him. He had lost track of time as he sat in the tavern, staring at the same cup he had ordered when he had first walked in. Ulf did not like drinking, just like he had not enjoyed the atmosphere in the tavern. It had been too cheerful and too loud as warriors drank and sang songs. It reminded Ulf of a different time. A time when he was surrounded by men he had thought of as friends. But that felt like a long time ago, like a different life.

The streets around the tavern were quiet as most people were in their homes, sitting around the hearth fires as they shared meals with their families. Only a few people were still out, and Ulf ignored them as he pulled his cloak around his shoulders to stay warm and made his way to the market, hoping the brothers were still there. His shoulders hunched and head lowered against the cold, Ulf had lost himself in his thoughts again when he bumped into a group of warriors.

'Watch it, you pig!' one man shouted.

Ulf turned and shoved the man, not noticing the other warriors around him.

The red-headed warrior, about the same height as Ulf, but older and thicker-limbed, grabbed Ulf by his tunic and pulled him in close. 'You have a death wish, do you?' The man glared at Ulf, who only glared back as he fought to calm himself, because Ulf knew he could not get into a fight with this warrior. And not because of the other warriors around him, but because of Tormod and Ingolfr. They had done much for him, and he did not want to let them down.

'All quiet now,' one warrior behind the man said, and the others laughed.

'Aye, not so brave. Come, Ragnar, leave the boy and let's go.'

Ragnar, the name rang in Ulf's head. The name of the man who had killed Ulf's father. The flames of Ulf's anger exploded in the pit of his stomach and before he could stop himself, Ulf headbutted the older warrior.

The man staggered backwards, but before Ulf could do anything else, one of the other warriors struck Ulf in the side of the head. White light flashed in Ulf's head as his legs buckled underneath him, but he stayed on his feet, only to be punched by the second warrior again. This time Ulf collapsed, scuffing his knee in the dirt, but his anger refused to allow him to stay on the ground. Ulf growled as he struggled to his feet, his head still spinning, while the surrounding warriors laughed at him. He wiped the blood from his mouth before removing his cloak from his shoulders.

'I think he wants more,' one of the warriors said, as Ragnar, the red-headed man he had headbutted, wiped the blood from his nose with the back of his hand.

'You're not very clever, are you, boy?' Ragnar asked.

Ulf responded by charging at the older warrior, who dodged Ulf's punch while the others just laughed. Ragnar kneed Ulf in the stomach and pushed him to the ground, but just like before, Ulf struggled to his feet, although this time he was not as steady as before as he struggled to catch his breath.

'Just stay down, boy,' one of the others said, a man who looked older than Ragnar but had light-coloured hair.

'I'm not a boy,' Ulf growled, which was true. He was almost twenty-two winters old, or so he thought, and that everyone still called him a boy only fed his anger.

'Then what are you, a girl?' The warriors laughed as one of them said this.

Ulf screamed and launched himself at Ragnar again. He swung high with his right hand, which Ragnar blocked, but then brought his left up and punched Ragnar on the chin, his speed catching the older warrior by surprise. Ragnar's head snapped up, and he staggered backwards as the surrounding warriors fell silent. Ulf rushed forward, not wanting to give the older warrior a chance to recover, and caught him with a hook to the temple, which made Ragnar's knees wobble, but then the older warrior somehow swatted Ulf's next strike away. He grabbed Ulf by his tunic and kneed him in the stomach again, but this time, he didn't let go as he drove his elbow into the back of Ulf's head. Stars erupted in Ulf's vision and before he could recover, the warrior pulled him up and punched him in the face. Ulf's legs gave way and he collapsed in a heap, only to be kicked in the back and then in the side as he twisted in pain.

'That's enough, Ragnar. I think the boy has learnt his lesson,' the older man with the light-coloured hair said, and the kicking stopped.

Ulf lay on the ground, his body burning from the pain. He tried to feed on his anger as he attempted to get up again, but his anger had left him and all Ulf felt was pain and the disappointment of knowing he had let Ingolfr and Tormod down again.

He sensed Ragnar leaning over him. 'You better leave my town, boy. The gods know that if I see you again, then you're a dead man.'

Again, Ulf tried to get to his feet. He groaned as he got himself up to his knees, which only made the others laugh again.

'I think he wants more, Ragnar,' one warrior said.

'Aye, but that's a pretty sword he's got there,' another added.

'So it is,' Ragnar said, and Ulf could hear the curiosity in his voice. He resisted the urge to grab the hilt of Ormstunga and thanked the gods he had not drunk that much in the tavern. Otherwise, he might have done and then the brothers would be forced to leave Jelling. 'I wonder how such a shit fighter can afford a sword like that?' The others laughed again as Ulf gritted his teeth. He forced himself to his feet and for the first time studied the group of Danish warriors. The man called Ragnar looked nothing like the Ragnar Ulf had known before. This Ragnar was older, although his hair was also red, and his tunic, now covered in blood from his bleeding nose, looked like it belonged to a man of wealth. So did the gold-hilted sax-knife tucked into the fine leather belt around his waist. Beside this Ragnar stood the man with light-coloured hair, and he, too, wore a fine tunic with new looking leather boots. In the dim light of the early night, Ulf noticed that the man had bleached his hair as some warriors liked to do. Ulf heard the gods laughing at him because he knew then that these Danes were important. Ingolfr's warning rang in his head, and Ulf knew he needed to get away from there. He mumbled an apology and made to turn when Ragnar said, 'I think that sword would be enough to compensate me for the attack.' Again, the warriors laughed, and Ulf clenched his fists as he felt the embers of his anger stir. 'Give me the sword, boy. You obviously don't deserve it.'

'Aye, the gods only know how he got it,' one of the warriors said.

'Probably stole it,' another added.

'Did you steal it?' the older man beside Ragnar asked and Ulf shook his head.

'It belonged to my father and his father before him.' Ulf resisted the urge to grip Ormstunga, but he could sense her talking to him. Telling him to free her and to kill these bastards who wanted to take her from him. Ulf glanced at the sky. The sun had been replaced by the moon and the stars, and Ulf felt his fingers twitch.

'I think you should leave, boy. Get out of Jelling before there is more trouble for you and the traders you came with,' the older man said, and Ulf raised his eyebrows at him.

'What traders?' Ragnar asked, glancing at the man.

'Tormod and Ingolfr. I recognise him now. It's hard to forget those scars. I saw them together in the market the other day.' The older man looked at Ulf again. 'Get going, boy. Before Ragnar changes his mind.'

'Not without giving me that sword.'

Ulf glared at Ragnar. 'You don't want this sword.'

Ragnar laughed, and so did the men behind him. 'And why, in Odin's name, would I not want that sword?' A few of the warriors behind Ragnar stepped forward, and Ulf felt his heart racing. He cursed himself for lashing out because he was certain that someone was going to die and prayed that it would not be him. Ulf had once believed that he was blessed by Odin. That he could not die until he had avenged his family. But he had done that, and he doubted Odin had any more reason to keep Ulf alive.

'The sword is cursed.'

'Cursed?' Ragnar struggled to keep the smile from his face as the warriors behind him laughed. Although Ulf noticed how more than one of them rubbed the Mjöllnir pendants they wore around their necks.

'Is this true?' the older warrior asked and Ulf nodded, but he did not want to tell them why. Not that the older warrior asked as he turned to Ragnar. 'It'll be a bad omen to take a cursed sword from another, Ragnar. Let the boy go and let's go get some ale. My throat is dry after all this talking.'

Ragnar glanced at the older man as he rubbed the hilt of his sword. He took a deep breath and nodded, but before Ulf could be relieved, he said. 'I'm still owed mangæld for your attack on me, boy. So I'll be seeing those traders tomorrow. And you better be gone by then if you know what's good for you.' With that, they all turned and left, leaving Ulf gaping at their backs as his heart thudded in his chest. He had hoped that Tormod and Ingolfr would not get involved in this.

Ulf cursed himself and his temper. He had thought that it would leave him once he had avenged his family. He had given himself to the gods and followed the path he had thought they had laid out for him, but his anger was still there and now it had ruined everything for him. Ulf felt the winter wind pick up and shivered when he thought he heard his name whispered in it. The hair on the back of his neck stood up and his heart raced as he scanned the dark streets and houses around him. The last time Ulf had felt that sensation, she was there. Watching him. Luring him like a fish to do her bidding, or the bidding of the gods. Ulf had hoped he would never see her again as his hand went to the Mjöllnir around his neck. He wanted to call out her name, but then stopped himself, as if saying it would curse him even more. With a last glance at the moon, Ulf decided not to go to the market as he turned and walked back to the room the brothers had got for him as fast as his trembling legs would take him.

***

'You got into another fight! By the gods, Ulf! Can't you stay out of trouble?' Tormod jabbed a finger at Ulf, his face red as spit landed on Ulf's bruised face.

'Well, if the gods are kind, then this might not be connected to us,' Ingolfr said, his shoulders lowered. He glanced at Ulf and shook his head.

Ulf looked at his feet, not knowing what to say. He had hoped they wouldn't know about the fight he had the night before, even though they would have noticed the bruises on his face and his cut lip. But even in a large town like Jelling, gossip spread faster than fire and word had reached the brothers of a fight the night before. And when they saw his face that morning, the brothers knew that he was involved.

'Who did you fight this time?' Tormod asked.

Ulf hesitated. He did not want to tell them, but he knew he could not hide that from the brothers. They would find out soon anyway. 'A man called Ragnar. He wanted to take my sword.' Ulf decided not to mention that he only wanted the sword after the fight.

'Well, you should have just given it to him! In the four winters you have been with us, I have not once seen you use it anyway!' Tormod threw his hands into the air as Ulf bit back his anger.

'The sword is cursed.'

'Aye, so you keep saying.' Tormod shook his head, and then his face paled as he looked at something behind Ulf. 'By Thor, please don't tell me that is the Ragnar you fought?'

'Oh Ulf,' Ingolfr said, as Ulf glanced behind him and saw Ragnar and the older man with the bleached hair walking among the market stalls while a group of armoured warriors followed them. Both men wore furs around their shoulders and had thick golden chains around their necks. They were dressed in fine tunics and Ulf was certain that thick golden rings covered their fingers. Ragnar's face was bruised, but not as badly as Ulf's. His eyes were dark though, and Ulf knew that if Ragnar spotted him here, then he would be hanged. Ulf rubbed the old hanging scar around his neck. He had been hanged once before when he had been accused of killing the first woman he had ever loved, but then the branch of the tree broke and Ulf lived. Many had believed that Odin had saved Ulf, and Ulf had often wondered the same after that, but he still didn't know. All Ulf knew was that he doubted Odin would do the same again.

'You've really fucked up now, Ulf. Not even the gods can help you now,' Tormod said with a frustrated shake of his head. 'And worse still, you've fucked us as well. After everything we did for you. We took you in and fed you. We gave you a chance to make something of yourself, and this is how you thank us. By fighting one of the most important men in Denmark.'

'Oh Ulf,' Ingolfr repeated with a shake of his head.

Ulf's hands trembled, but he knew Tormod was right. He had the chance to be something other than a warrior. To not have to feel the fear of the shield wall again. But perhaps that was where Ulf was meant to be. His father had been a warrior and so had his father, and his father before him. All the way back to Tyr, the god of war. But Ulf was not the warrior his father had been, or any of his ancestors. 'I will leave before he sees me.'

'Doubt it makes any difference to us. If he is here, then it means he knows you worked for us.' Tormod hawked and spat as Ulf noticed how he said worked and not work.

'Go to your room, Ulf. Collect your things and leave Jelling. Perhaps even Denmark. Jarl Ragnar is not a man you want to anger,' Ingolfr said, not looking at Ulf. 'We'll clean up your mess, but this will be the last time.'

Ulf nodded as he swallowed back his anger. But this time, it was at himself for not being able to control his temper. 'Where will I go?'

'You can go back to Norway,' Tormod said, his eyes fixed on Jarl Ragnar.

Ulf nodded but knew he couldn't. He had never told the brothers that he had been banished from Norway. They only traded in Denmark and occasionally Sweden. 'Thank you for everything you have done for me,' Ulf said. 'I am sorry I've let you down.'

'You let yourself down, Ulf.' Tormod sighed. 'But then, you were always meant to be a warrior. Not a trader. We were all foolish for thinking we could change you. And now it will probably cost us everything.'

'A wolf is meant to be a wolf. He can never be a pet.' Ingolfr smiled at him, and Ulf hated himself for letting them down. Especially Ingolfr. 'May the gods be with you, Ulf Bjørnson.'

Ulf took a deep breath. 'And you both.'

Tormod nodded. 'Now get out of here before Jarl Ragnar sees you. And Ulf,' he said before Ulf left. 'I hope you find what you are looking for.'

Me too, Ulf thought as he lowered his head and made his way to the room in a tavern near the market square. *But first, I need to work out what that is.*

Chapter 3

Jarl Knut rubbed his eyes, wishing the morning sun wasn't so bright and regretting drinking so much the night before. *Although the night had its amusements*, he thought as he glanced at his younger cousin with the fresh bruise on his face. Ragnar had always been an arrogant bastard, and Knut had to admit that he had enjoyed watching the ugly young warrior punch him in the face. And not just once. Few in Denmark would have the courage to do that, not even Knut himself, and that was what had made it so much better. Ragnar had never expected it. None of them had, and afterwards, when Jarl Knut had returned to the hall provided to him by the king, he had drunk even more as he spent the night laughing about it. Jarl Knut had his own lands to the north, where he had his hall and town, but like many other jarls, he had been summoned to Jelling by the king of Denmark. The king had wanted the jarls to stop raiding the Frankish kingdoms to the south, but so far, all the talk had been about organising a large raid instead. Jarl Knut had been one of the voices behind this. He was tired of watching the Norse jarls and kings grow rich from raiding the Frankish kingdoms while they were forced to travel further west to raid.

Knut glared at the traders as they shouted at anyone who walked past their stalls. Their loud voices were like hammers pounding his already fragile head, and he wondered why they had to be so loud. Perhaps if they spoke normally, then they wouldn't have to shout to be heard over each other. It was one of the many reasons Jarl Knut never came to the markets. If he needed something, then he would send one of his thralls to buy it for him. But this morning, he knew he had to be there when Ragnar confronted the brothers about the young man who had attacked him.

'What are you smiling about?' Jarl Ragnar barked at him when Knut remembered the shock on Ragnar's face when the young man had punched him. Even Ragnar's hirdmen glared at Knut, but he knew they were embarrassed that their jarl had been attacked in front of them.

'Just thinking what a fine day the gods have blessed us with,' Knut lied. 'There they are.' He pointed to the two brothers when he spotted their stall. Knut didn't know Tormod very well but disliked the man. Tormod was crude and had no respect for those better than him. Men who took up spears and swords and fought their enemies. Instead, Tormod paid others to do that for him. Ingolfr, though, Knut knew well. He had fought for Knut once, and when he had earned enough to buy his own ship, he left. Never mind the oath he had sworn to Knut. Knut smiled again as he wondered if he could take that ship from them. Their man attacked a jarl, after all. But then he remembered the sword the young warrior had carried and knew that he wanted that more than the brothers' ship. And that it was cursed made him desire it even more. It was the same as how a married woman was more desirable to him than an unmarried woman.

'I hope for their sake that trade has been good for them because they'll be paying a hefty price.' Ragnar glanced at the warrior walking behind him, one of his hirdmen. 'Have your men found the bastard yet?'

The warrior shook his head. 'They searched all night. There's no sign of him. They told me about a strange woman lurking about, though, and muttering something to them.'

Jarl Knut raised an eyebrow at the warrior, who towered over him. 'Your men are afraid of women now?'

The warriors bristled at Jarl Knut, but he kept quiet as they reached the brothers.

'Jarl Ragnar, Jarl Knut,' Ingolfr greeted them with his best trader's smile. The man had learnt it well, Knut had thought. It almost made him feel as if Ingolfr thought of them as his dearest of friends, which was the opposite of the scowl on his brother's face.

'Ingolfr,' Jarl Knut said and then glared at Tormod, who pretended to be busy readjusting the wares on their stall. Jarl Knut glanced at the trinkets. Jewellery made from gold and silver. Some with delicate carvings on them, while others looked like a child made them. A large amber pendant caught his eye, and Jarl Knut wondered if his wife would like that. But then she had many such necklaces already. Tormod saw him staring at the pendant and moved it ever so slightly, as if making Jarl Knut aware that he knew what he was thinking.

'That will look very nice on Lady Borghild.' Ingolfr picked up the necklace and handed it to Knut. 'A gift for the lady.'

Jarl Knut saw how Tormod glared at his brother, and even though he was about to decline the gift because he knew Ingolfr was only giving it because he hoped it would soften their resolve, he took it just to annoy Tormod. 'Thank you, Ingolfr. I'm sure she'll be thrilled with it.' *She'll most likely put it in her chest with the many other amber necklaces and forget about it*, he thought and then looked around the stall.

'Is there anything we can help you with?' Tormod said, scowling at them.

'You have a young warrior who works for you,' Jarl Ragnar said. 'A man with a scared face and a sword with a gold hilt. Where is he?'

The two brothers glanced at each other and Knut saw that they already knew what this was about. Which meant the ugly bastard was already gone.

'He's no longer with us,' Ingolfr said while rubbing his hands in front of him. The man might have been a warrior once, but he had lost that spark, and Jarl Knut almost hated him for it.

'He was causing too many problems. Always scaring customers off with his face and his mood. And besides, we can't afford to feed him any more. Trade has been difficult,' Tormod said before any of them could say anything.

Jarl Ragnar glanced at Knut, who shrugged. He had hoped the young man would still be here. That way, he might have got his hands on his sword, but now Knut had to think of another way to get it. He had spent the entire night dreaming about the sword and knew he would not be satisfied until it was his. The only thing he wanted more was the crown of Denmark, but his other cousin refused to die so that he could take it.

'Is that so?' Jarl Ragnar said, his jaw muscles working under his beard. And Knut understood why. The scarred warrior had humiliated Ragnar in front of his warriors, and like most proud men, Ragnar could not let him get away with that.

'If the young man is gone, then you will have to compensate Jarl Ragnar.'

'What for?' Tormod asked, his eyebrow raised, but Knut was sure they already knew.

'Your man gave Jarl Ragnar that bruise on his face.' Knut had to fight hard not to smile as Ragnar glared at him. 'He assaulted the jarl and needs to pay mangæld for that.'

'The gods know we regret the actions of Ulf. He has always been hot-tempered,' Ingolfr said, using his best trader's voice to calm the situation. 'But Ulf is no longer with us and he is responsible for his own actions.'

Jarl Ragnar turned his glare to the brothers, who shrunk away from the violence in his eyes. 'I don't care that he is no longer with you. Last night I was told he is your man, so as far as I'm concerned, it is your responsibility.'

'Bastard is probably hiding in Jelling somewhere,' one warrior said. 'Waiting for us to leave before he comes back to you.'

Tormod shook his head. 'If I see Ulf again, then I'll castrate the bastard for all the trouble he has caused us.'

Knut almost believed the man, but he didn't want to leave empty-handed. Not with his head pounding the way it was from all the ale he had drunk. He should still have been under the furs with his favourite thrall. 'If he is not here, then you will have to pay mangæld to Jarl Ragnar.'

The brothers' eyes widened and Ingolfr said, 'But we can't afford that.'

'Then you should control your man better,' Jarl Ragnar said, his brow creased. 'You will give me whatever you have earned and then you leave Jelling. If I see you in this square again, I will take everything you have and hang you both.'

Ingolfr's face paled, while his brother's turned red. 'You will leave us with nothing? You can't do that. We paid our taxes to the king to trade here freely.'

Jarl Knut clenched his fist as he stepped towards Tormod. The other traders around them, and the people of Jelling, all stopped and stared as they tried to work out what was going on. 'Be glad I don't take your ship as well. You are free to trade in Denmark, just not in Jelling or anywhere I am.'

Tormod looked like he was about to protest again and Knut wanted him to, because then he would have a proper reason to take their ship, but then Ingolfr put a hand on his shoulder and pulled him back.

'Of course. Allow us some time to pack up and we will leave.'

Ragnar nodded and Jarl Knut felt his irritation grow at not getting what he wanted. And what he wanted was the bastard's sword.

'My man will stay here to make sure you do that. You can give the mangæld to him and he will pass it on to me.' With that, Jarl Ragnar turned and left, leaving Jarl Knut standing there like a fool. Knut gritted his teeth as he glared at the back of his younger cousin's head.

He turned his attention back to the brothers. 'This Ulf. Where did he go?'

Tormod scrutinised him for a few heartbeats before he responded, 'Only the Norns know. We told him to leave, and that's what he did.'

Knut grunted and then looked at Ingolfr. 'I told you you were a fool when you left my services to become a trader.'

Ingolfr shrugged. 'I was tired of all the bloodshed, Jarl Knut. I suppose you will be sending men to find Ulf?' Knut didn't respond, so Ingolfr said, 'He's a good man, young Ulf. He just struggles with his temper. So I ask you to let him be. We will pay the mangæld and do what Jarl Ragnar wants.'

'Aye, but it's not what I want.' Knut turned and walked away, leaving the brothers to frown at each other.

He made his way back to his hall and grabbed a jug of ale, hoping it would wash his irritation away. 'Hallr!'

'Jarl?' Hallr said when he walked into the hall.

'You remember the young bastard that punched Ragnar?'

Hallr smiled. 'Aye, never seen anyone dumb enough to do that.'

'Well, I want his sword.'

Hallr raised an eyebrow. 'But he said it was cursed.'

Knut glared at the warrior. 'Your mother was cursed the day she pushed you out. I want that sword and you will get it for me.'

Hallr scratched the back of his neck. 'But Jarl, Jelling is a large town. We might not find him.'

'He is not in Jelling any more. The bastard took my advice and left.'

'So how do we find him, then?'

Knut sighed and wondered why Hallr was one of his best men. 'You've hunted before, haven't you, Hallr?'

'Aye.' Hallr frowned at him.

'So, go hunting. There are only so many roads out of Jelling. Take thirty men and split them into small groups. Have them spread out and the group that brings me the sword will be richly rewarded.'

Hallr smiled at the mention of a reward. 'And the ugly bastard?'

Knut shrugged. 'Kill him for all I care.' As he said the words, Knut felt icy fingers stroking the back of his neck. He shuddered and turned, but there was no one in his hall other than him and Hallr. Even the thralls were out. But then his eyes caught something outside his hall. A short woman with dark hair and wearing deer hide as a dress. She had something that looked like dried snakeskin around her neck as she stood there, her mouth moving as if she was saying something, but Knut could not hear her words. She was too far away.

'Jarl?' Hallr asked and Knut looked at the warrior. 'What's the matter?'

Knut shook his head and looked outside his hall again, but the woman was gone. So was the strange feeling at the back of his neck. 'Nothing. Now go.'

'Aye, Jarl.' Hallr left the hall and Knut stood there, staring at the door and rubbing the back of his neck as he wondered who the woman was.

Chapter 4

Ulf pulled his bearskin cloak tighter around his shoulders as he tried to hide from the cold, his father's old Dane axe strapped to his back and Ormstunga by his waist, and again cursed himself for not being able to control his temper. He had a bed, warm food and, more importantly, a purpose. Now he was trudging around in the Danish countryside, with nowhere to hide from the winter winds. It had been five days since he had left Jelling and Ulf did not know where he was going. He did not know Denmark that well and had decided to do what he had done when he had been banished from Norway. He followed the path of a raven, hoping that the gods would guide him to somewhere where he could at least wait out the winter. Then in the spring, he could find himself some work. Perhaps he would look for a jarl who needed more warriors. *A wolf is meant to be a wolf*, Ingolfr's words rang in his head and Ulf had decided that he was tired of resisting what he was. He was a wolf. A warrior. Tyr's blood ran in his veins and the longer he resisted that, the harder it became for him to control his temper. First, though, he had to find a place with a warm fire and food, at least until the winter was over. Then he would find a jarl he could offer his services to.

Ulf hunched his shoulders as he tried to hide his face from the wind and was grateful that it wasn't snowing. But that did not make it any better, as the day before it had rained and Ulf's bearskin cloak was still wet because he could not dry it overnight. The cloak was old and tattered, but Ulf did not want to get rid of it. It was the fur of the bear that had given him the scars on his face, and he somehow felt comforted with its weight on his shoulders.

He walked for two more days, often hiding from the wind behind a large tree or a boulder, which seemed out of place. Like a giant had thrown it from the mountains in Norway. Perhaps at Thor. In his time with the brothers, Ulf had not once seen anything like the mountains in the north of Norway. Not that he had seen those, either. Denmark was flatter than Norway. There were many rugged hills across the landscape with patches of forests or farmsteads in the valleys between them, and occasionally he would see a small village. Ulf had ventured into the villages at first, hoping to find somewhere to stay, but the way people avoided him made him realise no one was going to offer him a place by their hearth fire, so now he avoided them.

His stomach growled, which reminded him he had not eaten that morning. Ulf had run out of the food he had bought from the last village, with the hack silver the brothers had given him the day before, and prayed that he would find somewhere to get more soon. He had come across a farmstead that morning, but if anyone was there, they had decided not to open their door to him. No matter how hard he had knocked. Although he couldn't blame them. He was a lonely warrior wrapped in an old bearskin cloak and with a large Dane axe strapped to his back. Perhaps they thought he meant to harm them. Just like the giant stranger who had arrived on his uncle's farm on a warm summer's day four winters ago. Griml Troll-Face. The bastard who killed his uncle, aunt and their two daughters, but not before raping his aunt. Ulf's hand went to the scar on his side that he got that day. He had been arrogant and believed he could defeat a man that size when he should have taken his aunt and cousins to the forest and hidden there until the ugly bastard had left. Ulf had almost died that day and would have done if it had not been for the old forest man and Vidar. The silent boy who had become like a brother to him. Vidar had also been killed by Griml, as had many others, but Ulf had finally got his vengeance when he killed Griml with his uncle's one-handed axe. But that had not taken the pain of their loss away and he missed them every day.

Ulf sensed someone behind him, but it was not the same as the feeling he had got in Jelling. There was no shiver down his spine, and neither did the hairs on the back of his neck stand up. But he sensed trouble as he turned and saw six warriors standing there, all of them grinning at him. He glanced at the sky, trying to spot the raven that usually appeared when there was trouble, as if it had been sent by Odin to watch him. But there was no raven, only the few birds that were brave enough to stay in Denmark during the winter months. Although where the other birds went, he didn't know.

'That's a nice axe you have there,' one of the warriors said, his hand twitching as he gripped his one-handed axe.

'And that cloak looks very warm,' another said. The six men all had brynjas and weapons in their hands, but none of them had any shields or helmets. Ulf was glad for that, although his helmet was in the pouch he had slung over his shoulder, and Ulf doubted these men would give him the time to put it on. He glanced behind the men and saw another standing further back with horses. Turning his attention back to the warriors in front of him, Ulf tried to see if he recognised any of them from the night he fought Ragnar because he was sure that was who had sent them.

'It's not warm,' Ulf said. 'It got wet yesterday.'

The second man raised an eyebrow. 'Then why didn't you dry it?'

Ulf shrugged and used the moment to take a step away from the six men. They all looked like experienced warriors and worse than that, they looked like men who enjoyed killing. Some men fought because they had to. They fought to defend their loved ones or to provide them with food. Others fought because they enjoyed the violence and killing. Ulf had never understood where he stood. At times, he believed he fought to defend others, but when the voices of his ancestors took over, there was no better feeling for him than slaughtering his enemies. Although, Ulf had not heard those voices in a long time. Not since he was banished from Norway.

'Why does that matter? Our jarl wants that pretty sword of yours. And I'll take that axe on your back.' The leader of the group grinned, and Ulf knew he had been right as he prayed that Tormod and Ingolfr were spared from Ragnar's anger.

'What happened to your face?' another of the warriors asked, which caused the leader to glare at him.

Ulf's hand went to Ormstunga under the bearskin cloak. 'This bear attacked me.'

'You killed it?' the same man asked again, glancing at the others.

'Aye.' Ulf noticed how the warriors moved closer and felt Ormstunga sing as he gripped her hilt. It was like the sword sensed the danger and wanted to taste the blood of the men who threatened him. Before he could free her from the scabbard, though, the clouds parted and the sun shone brightly above them. Ulf cursed and let go of the sword.

'You really think you can fight us?' The leader of the warriors grinned, and the others laughed.

Ulf glared at the men as they spread out and realised they had done this before. For a moment, Ulf wondered why Ragnar was so eager to get hold of Ormstunga. Surely the man was rich enough to buy any sword he wanted, and Ulf had told him it was cursed. But then he dismissed the thought. It didn't matter. What mattered was that he could not hope to defeat them. The wet cloak weighed him down, which meant he would not be able to move as fast as he could. He guessed he could use the Dane axe, but Ulf had never practised with it. He only kept it because, like Ormstunga, it had belonged to his father and it helped frighten bandits away who were tempted to rob the brothers.

Ulf eyed the men as his hands trembled. 'I don't want any trouble. Just let me go on my way and tell Ragnar you couldn't find me.'

The leader laughed. 'Don't you worry. You won't be any trouble.' He glanced at the man beside him, a man about the same height as Ulf, but thinner. 'Kill him.'

The man grinned. 'With pleasure.' He lifted his axe and took a few steps towards Ulf, who backed away and took the Dane axe from his back. Ulf glanced at the sun again and wondered why Thor had parted the clouds. Perhaps he was bored and hoped this fight would entertain him. But Ulf would have preferred to use

Ormstunga, as he gripped the unfamiliar Dane axe in two hands. 'I always wanted a cloak made from bear fur.'

The man roared and charged at Ulf, who stepped aside, but before he could bring the axe around, the warrior turned and punched at him with the head of his axe. Ulf deflected the blow with the haft of his axe and sensed movement behind him, but couldn't turn in time as something struck his back. He staggered forward, his back arched in pain, and Ulf was glad he was wearing his brynja under the bearskin cloak as he turned and buried the Dane axe in the neck of the man who had stabbed him with his sword. The warrior's eyes widened as Ulf pulled the axe out and blood squirted out of his neck. His hands trembled and for a moment, Ulf forgot about the remaining five men as he stared at the first person he had killed since he had left Norway. His blood thudded in his ears, but the whispers he normally heard when his battle lust kicked in remained silent.

'He killed Leif!' one of the men shouted, which snapped Ulf out of his stupor. He turned and kicked the man behind him, who was still too stunned by the death of his companion to react, between the legs and before the man even hit the ground, Ulf ran.

'Get the bastard!' the leader of the group screamed, and Ulf glanced over his shoulder to see their leader and another warrior going for the horses as the other three ran after him. As the wind rushed past his ears, he thought he heard the gods laughing at him, and Ulf cursed them for the first time in many winters. He had trusted his fate to them and they had led him to his death. Ulf refused to die in a field in Denmark, though, just like he refused to be killed by these bastards. Unfortunately, they outnumbered him, and with the sun still out, he could not use Ormstunga. And

Ulf doubted he could kill the men chasing him without the sword of his ancestors in his hand.

The Dane axe gripped in one hand and the other holding the sack that carried his few belongings, Ulf ran towards the forest he saw in the distance, hoping that he could lose them amongst the trees. He glanced over his shoulder and cursed when he saw the warriors were gaining on him. He cursed again as he realised they would catch him before he could reach the forest, and then his heart skipped as his foot caught on something and he tumbled to the ground. His shoulder struck a stone, which numbed his arm and made him drop his sack, but Ulf could not think of that as he rolled to his knees in time to deflect the sword of the first warrior to reach him. He pulled his sax-knife out of its scabbard and stabbed the man in the leg before he jumped to his feet and stabbed him in the neck. Before the others could catch up, Ulf turned and ran, leaving his sack behind and hoping that the death of another of their comrades would stop them, or at least slow them down. His hopes were soon dashed when he heard the leader scream.

'You're gonna die for that, you coward! Run faster, you bastards! Get him!'

Ulf lowered his head and ran as fast as his long legs could take him and soon reached the trees, but when he looked behind him, he saw the remaining warriors were not far behind. He prayed to Thor for protection and asked the thunder god to hide the sun. Because Ulf was certain he would die if the sun stayed out.

The three on horseback were forced to dismount, and they waited for the others to catch up. There were still five of them, as the one who had stayed back with the horses had joined in.

'Odin knows you're gonna pay for that, you ugly bastard!' the leader shouted. 'Those were good men you killed!'

Ulf took a deep breath as he hid behind a tree. He knew he couldn't stay where he was and glanced up at the branches. But then Ulf dismissed that idea. He could never climb the tree before the others found him. In the silence among the trees, he heard the other warriors sneaking up on him and knew he had to move.

'There he is!' one warrior said as Ulf pushed himself off the tree and ran as fast as he could. He heard the others give chase and gripped the axe tight as he ducked below a low-hanging branch.

'Don't let him get away!' the leader shouted, which worried Ulf because he sounded closer than Ulf had thought he was. But the men hunting him were not weighed down by a fur cloak.

Ulf cried out as something struck his shoulder and sent him tumbling forward. He rolled over as soon as he hit the ground and caught sight of the one-handed axe lying on the forest floor as he realised he couldn't move his right arm. Panic gripped him then, but he had no time to let it affect him as the leader of the warriors reached him. The man swung a fist at him and Ulf instinctively ducked under the punch, but then the warrior followed up with a knee in Ulf's chest. Ulf grunted as the wind was knocked out of him and, out of the corner of his eye, saw another warrior stab his sword at him. Ulf brought the Dane axe up, having to use it with one hand, and deflected the sword before the leader of the group punched him in the face. The other warriors had caught up, but stood back as their leader and the other warrior circled Ulf, like wolves about to kill their wounded prey. Ulf flexed his right hand and was glad that he could move his fingers. That meant that the axe that had struck his shoulder had not broken anything and that feeling was returning to his arm. But the sun still shone brightly through the trees, which meant that Ormstunga had to stay in her scabbard.

'By Odin, why did you have to make this so difficult?' The leader glared at Ulf as he picked up his axe from the ground. Ulf struggled to his feet and backed away from the men. 'All you had to do was let Leif kill you and then we would be on our way back to Jelling.'

Ulf hawked and spat. 'I told Ragnar the sword is cursed. It'll only bring him bad luck.'

The leader shrugged. 'Not my problem.'

'How is the sword cursed?' the warrior to Ulf's left asked and as his hand went to the Mjöllnir pendant around his neck, Ulf gripped his Dane axe with both hands and swung it at him. The warrior could do nothing as the axe cut through his arm and buried itself in his chest, killing him before he could make a sound. The remaining warriors, enraged by the death of another of their group, screamed at Ulf before they charged. With no other option, Ulf let go of the axe before he turned and pulled Ormstunga from her scabbard, ignoring his own warning as the blade glinted in the sunlight. He sliced the neck of the leader open before the man could react to what was happening, drenching Ulf in blood and blinding him.

'Bastard! That was my brother!' one of the remaining men shouted before he tackled Ulf to the ground while he struggled to clear the blood from his eyes. Ulf's heart thudded hard in his chest as he did his best to keep hold of Ormstunga while the man punched him in the face, but finally, the voices started waking up as he felt the familiar grip of his ancestors' sword in his hand.

He turned the blade and stabbed up. There was a moment of resistance before Ormstunga found a weak point in the man's brynja and tore through his lungs. The warrior spat more blood in Ulf's face before he pushed him over and struggled to his feet. For a moment, Ulf had forgotten about the other two warriors as he wiped the blood from his face, and when he opened his eyes, he saw them glaring at him.

Ulf gritted his teeth as he tightened the grip on Ormstunga's hilt. He barely had enough time to worry about the curse as the two warriors attacked at the same time. He ducked under the attack of the first warrior, but felt the man's sword catch his bearskin cloak as the second warrior struck Ulf in the head with the side of his axe. Ulf's head snapped to the side and his vision blurred as the voices in his ears left, and he did all he could not to let go of Ormstunga. Shaking his head to clear it, he struggled to regain his balance when the first warrior attacked him again. Somehow, Ulf batted his sword away with Ormstunga, but he struggled to move his right arm and worried that the axe the leader of the group had thrown at him had done more damage than he had first realised. The second warrior rushed in and chopped his axe at Ulf, who could only jump out of the way before he turned and ran.

'Get back here!' one of the warriors shouted as Ulf shifted Ormstunga to his left hand because he doubted he could hold on to the sword for much longer with his right hand. He had to forget about his father's Dane axe, which was lying on the ground behind him. But Ulf as fled, he doubted it mattered whcther he still had the axe or not. He had drawn Ormstunga in direct sunlight, and Ulf knew he was going to die because of it.

Chapter 5

A raven cried out from the trees above as Ulf ran from the remaining two warriors. Odin was watching him. Ulf was certain of that. He had drawn Ormstunga in direct sunlight, but he had no choice. If the sword had stayed in her scabbard, then he would have been dead already. Although Ulf doubted the gods would care about that. He had been warned. The runes carved on Ormstunga's guard told him not to draw the blade in direct sunlight. And now the gods were watching him, waiting to punish him for ignoring the curse.

Over his ragged breath, Ulf heard his pursuers. He heard them shouting after him, threatening to torture him before they killed him. His right shoulder burnt from the axe that had been thrown at him, while his vision blurred from the blow to his head. Ormstunga was still in his left hand, her blade too bloody to be put back in her scabbard. Not that Ulf had the time or the thought of doing that. He might still need her. There were only two warriors left. He had fought those odds before and had won. But his ancestors had been with him. Now their voices were silent, and he was injured. Ulf stopped and leaned against a tree, catching his breath as he tried to work out which way to go. He knew he could not fight these men. He was injured and exhausted, so his only hope was to lose them amongst the trees.

'There he is!' the shout came from behind and without looking, Ulf groaned as he pushed himself off the tree and ran.

Something struck Ulf from the side, knocking him to the ground. For a heartbeat, Ulf thought it was a bear when he caught sight of the large shadow. Then he saw it was one of his pursuers, who had been closer than he had realised.

'Time to die, you bastard coward!' The warrior stabbed down with his sword, and Ulf rolled out of the way in time to avoid being skewered. He swung Ormstunga at the man's leg and felt her keen blade slicing through the man's muscles. The warrior cried out as he dropped to one knee and Ulf struggled to his feet, but before he could think of killing the man, the other warrior arrived and swung his axe at Ulf's head. Ulf swayed out of the way and stumbled backwards, the sudden movement disorientating him, but that saved his life as he avoided the follow up strike as well. He fell against a tree and dropped to his knees when he saw the axe coming for his head. Over the blood pumping in his ears and the raven crying from the branches above, Ulf heard the axe bite into the tree trunk. Ulf stabbed up with Ormstunga, hoping to kill the warrior before he could free his axe, but he was too exhausted and not used to using his left arm, so the sword failed to break through the man's brynja. The blow still hurt the warrior, though, as he grunted and staggered backwards, leaving his axe in the tree.

Ulf struggled to his feet, swaying as if he had drunk too much ale, and glared at the warrior. He was about to attack the man when the raven cried out again. Ulf glanced to his side and saw the sword Dane on his feet again, his leg bloody from where Ulf had cut him, and stabbing his sword at him. He twisted and felt the man's sword scraping along his brynja. He punched the man in the side of the head with the pommel of Ormstunga just before the other Dane tackled him to the ground. Before Ulf could get his hands up to protect himself, the man punched him in the face. Blood from his nose ran to the back of his throat, choking Ulf. Ulf's heart was racing as he spat out as much of the blood as he could, while the warrior wrapped his hands around Ulf's throat and squeezed.

Ulf had a flashback from the last time someone had him in this position, but this time Ulf could not angle Ormstunga to stab at the man's side, so instead he aimed for the man's head. The angle was still not good and Ulf ended up striking the man with the side of Ormstunga's blade. She sliced his cheek open, and the man cried out as he let go of Ulf and rolled off him. Ulf turned and spat the blood out from the back of his throat before he struggled to his feet. His head spun and his right shoulder ached, forcing Ulf to lean against the tree as he glared at the two Danes. The sword Dane was struggling to his feet as well, and Ulf saw how he tightened the grip on his sword, even as he had to lean on his good leg. The other Dane also got to his feet, the blood from the cut to his cheek soaking into his beard.

'Just let me go,' Ulf said. 'You don't want this sword.'

The sword Dane hawked and spat. 'It's got nothing to do with the sword now. You killed my friends.'

'All you had to do was die and let us take that fucking sword. But you Norse bastards were always too dumb to know what's good for you.'

Ulf took a deep breath to clear his head as the two Danes crept closer. The one with the axe had his sax-knife in his hand now, as his axe was still in the tree. Ulf glanced at it and wondered if he could reach it before the two warriors attacked him, but doubted it. He was exhausted and could barely see straight. And even if he reached it before the two Danes got to him, he doubted he had the strength left to free it from the tree. So instead, he looked the other way.

'Don't even think of running. You stay there so we can kill you.'

'Fuck you,' Ulf said and pushed himself off the tree and ran. He gripped Ormstunga tightly in his left hand so that he didn't drop her as he heard the two Danes curse and set off after him. *Tyr, help me.* He prayed as he ran out of the trees and into an open area. Ahead of him, he saw a river and knew that the gods had abandoned him. Tyr, the god he had been told was his ancestor, had turned his back on Ulf. All because he drew Ormstunga in direct sunlight.

'You got nowhere left to run,' one of the Danes shouted. Ulf glanced over his shoulder and saw it was the one with the cut to his cheek. The other Dane, the one Ulf had cut in the leg, was not far behind, but he was struggling to keep up with them. Ulf cursed and made his way to the edge of the river and then cursed again when he saw it was moving too fast for him to cross. He turned as he heard the Dane roar behind him, and just avoided the man's sax-knife. Ormstunga came alive, or so it seemed, as the blade shot up and stabbed the Dane through the neck. The warrior's eyes widened as he choked on the sword in his throat, and it took all of Ulf's strength to free her. But as soon as he did, the other warrior crashed into him and they both fell into the freezing river. Ulf gasped in shock as the icy water gripped him, but he had no time to think about that as the remaining Dane punched him and forced his head under the water. He fought against the man's grip, but had no strength left to fight as the water numbed him. For a moment, Ulf wondered if he would go to Valhalla if he drowned in a river. He knew those who drowned at sea went to Ran's hall under the waves, but no one had ever told him what happened to warriors who drowned in rivers.

As the river dragged them along, they bumped into something hard which caused the warrior to loosen his grip on Ulf, who got his head above the water. He took a deep gulp of air before the Dane grabbed him again. Ulf elbowed the man in the face, but the warrior refused to let go of him, just like Ulf refused to let go of Ormstunga. He remembered the sword still in his hand and struck the warrior in the face with the pommel. The man's head snapped back and disappeared under the water, and Ulf used his legs to push himself away from the Dane. But the bearskin cloak he was wearing had been caught in the grip of the icy river and was dragging Ulf down. Ulf struggled to free himself from the cloak and if he hadn't been so cold from the water, he would have laughed at the irony of being killed by the fur of the bear that had scarred his face. He swallowed a mouthful of water; the coldness burning his insides as Ulf fought to keep his head above the water, but it was a fight he was losing and Ulf knew it. Ulf's vision darkened and soon his lungs were burning as he struggled to get air into them. But he kept on fighting. Ulf had faced armies and giants, and he refused to die in an icy river in Denmark. The current was too strong for him, though, and there was nothing Ulf could do as the water gripped him for the last time and dragged him under. Just before his vision went dark, Ulf looked at the sword of his ancestors, still in his left hand, and thought he could hear her whisper to him.

You should not have drawn me in direct sunlight. I warned you.

***

He felt the snake slither over his body and opened his eyes to find it staring at him, its tongue flicking out as it tasted his fear. But he was not afraid of the snake. He had seen her enough times to know that she was not a threat to him. No, not her, but what she presented. Death and destruction. He had hoped never to see her again, but here she was. Curled up on his naked body. Or his corpse. He wasn't really sure.

The ground he lay on felt cold and wet, and his nostrils were filled with the sickly sweet smell of death. In the darkness beyond his view of the snake on his chest, he sensed something else. Something far larger than he could imagine, but also something he recognised.

I warned you. The words reached his ears, and he trembled with fear.

Where am I? He wanted to ask, but the words could not come out. His mouth was filled with water and no matter how hard he tried, he could not spit it out.

I warned you, and you didn't listen. Now you belong to me. Just like they do. The words came to him again.

I had no choice, he wanted to say, but again, the words refused to come out. He tried to push himself up, but the snake on his chest weighed him down. He looked at her and saw her shake her head. Then he noticed something else. A cloaked figure on the edge of his vision. Someone he had not seen in a long time. Help me, he tried to get the words out again but failed as a giant serpent head loomed over the cloaked figure.

I warned you. The words burnt his ears, and he wanted to scream. The snake on his chest slithered closer to his face and curled up under his chin as she faced the giant serpent.

It is not his time; she seemed to say, and the giant serpent pulled her lips back to reveal fangs as long as the mast of a warship, their whiteness almost blinding him before she turned and disappeared in the darkness.

'No, it is not,' the cloaked figure said as a scream pierced the darkness.

***

A woman's scream woke Ulf from his dream, and he groaned as he opened his eyes. Pain tore through his body, his headache almost blinding him and as he turned towards where the scream had come from, he cried out as hot pain seared his right shoulder blade. Ulf squeezed his eyes shut, willing the headache to go away, but they snapped open when the woman screamed again. Another noise, like furniture being knocked over, made him ignore the pain as he focused on where he was. The room he was in was unfamiliar to him and he turned his head towards the door as if he expected someone from his past to walk in. Ormstunga lay by his side, her blade still unsheathed, and as Ulf struggled to understand where he was, another scream made him grab the sword of his ancestors as he jumped to his feet and rushed towards the door. Ulf's head spun, and he felt the bile reach the back of his throat, but Ulf did his best to ignore that, along with the pain that made it difficult for him to move. A woman was in danger and Ulf refused to let his pain stop him from helping her. Just like he had been unable to help his aunt and cousins when their farm was attacked. The memory of that day ignited the flames of his anger, which spread through his body and dulled the aches that prevented him from moving properly.

With Ormstunga in his left hand, Ulf pushed the door open and saw the inside of a farmhouse as the smell of animals and stale furs reached his nose. He ignored the upturned table and benches, and the small hearth fire, as well as the dead goat nearby, as he glared at the two men, with rusted axes in their hands, who were about to attack an old man lying on the floor. The men, their clothing dirty and torn, looked like they spent more time sleeping under the stars than under a roof. Their unruly beards and long hair covered dirty faces and a grimace from one man showed a mouth full of rotten teeth.

'What the—' One man looked up and gaped at him.

Ulf saw two women, one old enough to be his grandmother and the other much younger, although her face was hidden as she tried to protect the old woman from the outlaws.

A third man walked into the farmhouse and stopped as he, too, gaped at Ulf. 'Who's he, and by Thor's cock, why is he naked?'

Ulf frowned and looked down to see that he was naked. But he had no time to wonder about that as the three men crept closer towards him.

'That's a pretty sword he has there. Odin knows that would earn us a fair bit of gold.' One outlaw leered at Ormstunga as if the sword was a pretty young thrall.

Ulf wobbled as he struggled to keep his balance. His head still spun, and he worried he might vomit. He was sure the only reason he was still on his feet was because his anger at the outlaws and the memory of Griml attacking his family's farm were preventing him from giving in to the pain that wrecked his body. 'Leave this place,' he said through gritted teeth, which only made the outlaws laugh.

'Or what? You gonna kill us with that sword?'

'Which one?' another outlaw asked. 'The one in his hand or the one between his legs?'

The others laughed as one of the men wiped a tear from his eye. 'Looks more like a knife to me.'

Ulf tightened his grip on Ormstunga's hilt as he felt her trembling in his hand. It was like she too remembered the attack on his uncle's farm and wanted Ulf to kill these bastards for thinking they could attack those weaker than them. The men came closer, still laughing, and Ulf took a deep breath. His body was weak and the fact that he was naked did not help, but he refused to let these bastards kill the old man and rape the women. He glanced at the three outlaws as they came closer and almost smiled when he saw how close they were to each other. Ulf waited another few heartbeats, Ormstunga trembling in his hand, or perhaps that was just his hand trembling, and when the nearest man was close enough, he attacked. His body protested, but Ulf did his best to block the pain from his mind and stabbed the outlaw through the chest before the man even realised what was happening.

'By the gods!' one of the remaining two outlaws screamed, his eyes wide as he watched Ulf pull his sword out of his companion's chest and swing it towards his head. The man lifted his axe to block Ormstunga, but his grip was weak and the axe flew from his hand as soon as Ormstunga struck it. Her tip sliced the man's cheek open, but before Ulf could kill him, the third outlaw struck his right shoulder with the flat of his axe. White hot pain tore through Ulf and he cried out as he dropped to his knees. The voices of his ancestors screamed in his ears and Ulf, having learnt a long time ago to listen to them, rolled out of the way before the outlaw could kill him.

The man with the cut cheek picked up a knife and rushed at Ulf, who jumped to his feet, but the sudden movement made his head swim. He dropped to his knees again, doing all he could to keep hold of Ormstunga and not vomit. Through blurred vision, he saw the man come at him and stabbed up with his sword. The outlaw ran into Ormstunga, almost forcing her out of Ulf's hand as he grunted. Ulf's vision cleared, and he saw the man frown at the sword in his stomach before he dropped to the ground, his eyes pleading for Ulf to help him. Ulf freed his sword from the man's stomach and thanked the gods that these men were not warriors as he turned to face the last man.

'I told you to leave.'

The man glanced around him with wide eyes, but the only way out was behind Ulf. His face paled when he saw that, and he dropped his axe as he begged Ulf. 'Please, let me go. I swear by Odin I will leave these people alone. I will leave Denmark and go far away. Please, I beg you.'

Ulf glared at the man as he dropped to his knees. He gripped Ormstunga as he remembered seeing his uncle's farm after he had recovered from his injuries. All that had been left of it were blackened posts and ashes, as the bastard who had attacked his family had burnt it with his aunt and cousins still inside. The heat from his anger raced through his limbs, and Ulf clenched his jaw. 'It's too late for that now.'

Before the man could utter another word, Ulf sliced his neck open and stood there as the outlaw's blood sprayed over him, quenching his rage and bringing all the pain back. Ulf did not move, though. He just stood there and glared at the bastard as he died.

'Inga, are you alright?' the old man's voice broke Ulf from his spell and he looked toward where the two women were.

The younger woman looked up and instead of gratitude, her narrow face was contorted in hatred as she glared at him. Ulf's heart stopped when he remembered the first time he had seen her in a market town in the north of Denmark. As his vision blurred and the room went black around him, Ulf remembered her name and muttered it before the darkness took him again.

'Eldrid.'

Chapter 6

Eldrid wiped the blood off Ulf's chest, her hands trembling as she stared at his face and the three long scars which ran down the right side. A face she had prayed never to see again. The face of the man who had ruined her life.

Eldrid had been the daughter of a jarl in Sweden, a man who had lived by the sword and who had made a name for himself in the shield wall. Her father had not been the most powerful jarl in Sweden, but he was respected and feared. And Ulf had killed him. Ulf Bear-Slayer, a name she doubted she would ever forget, just like she would never forget his face, especially his eyes. As grey as the blade of a sword and filled with an anger that made her shiver when she thought about it. And now, because of Ulf, she was a thrall forced to cook and clean for an old family in Denmark. But Inga and Asketill had been good to her. Inga almost treated her like a daughter and Eldrid thanked the gods that Asketill was too old to use her. Unlike the bastards that had sold her to the old folks.

She dipped the cloth in a bucket of bloody water and stared at the many scars that covered his body. More than she had expected Ulf to have.

'You know him then?' the old woman's voice said behind Eldrid and made her jump. She took a deep breath to calm her nerves, still shaky after the attack that morning, and nodded. 'I thought as much.' Inga smiled when Eldrid gaped at her. 'I saw it in your face when you first found him by the river.'

Again, Eldrid took a deep breath and stared at Ulf's face. Even in his sleep, he looked angry. Like he was fighting something in his dreams. 'He killed my father.'

Inga raised an eyebrow as she brought a bucket with clean water. 'And you sit here and clean him. I'd have thought you'd cut his throat the first chance you got. Although, I thank the gods you didn't.'

'Because he also saved me from a fate much worse than this.'

'A fate worse than being a thrall?' Inga shook her head as if she could not imagine such a thing, but then she had never met Griml.

'My father had betrothed me to someone more beast than man. A monster even the gods would be afraid of.'

Inga nodded as if she understood, but Eldrid knew she couldn't. Inga had been lucky to marry a man who treated her well and took care of her. That was why she was here. Inga was getting too old to do many of the things that needed to be done on the farm and since all their children were dead, Asketill had sold some animals to buy her a thrall. And Eldrid was that thrall.

'He killed the man? This monster?'

Eldrid shook her head. 'He kidnapped me. Him and his friends. All so they could lure Griml away from his army.'

Inga gasped, and when Eldrid looked at her, she saw her pale face. 'Griml Jotun?'

Eldrid nodded. 'You've heard of him?'

Inga swallowed before she responded. 'Heard he was some sea king. Came out of nowhere and took over a market town in the north of Denmark. But then he just disappeared.'

'He chased the men who had kidnapped me. There was a battle against a jarl in the south of Norway. Ulf fought for his son, and it was the son's idea. My father's men told me it was a mighty battle.' Eldrid closed her eyes and remembered watching Ulf and his friends return from that battle. It was the first time she had seen anything other than anger in Ulf's eyes. And then she remembered the young boy without a voice who had not returned. She never knew what had happened to him.

'Ulf?'

Eldrid nodded again as Ulf stirred at the mention of his name, but he did not wake. 'That is his name. Ulf Bear-Slayer.'

'Bear-Slayer?'

'They say he killed a bear with his bare hands.'

Inga barked a laugh. 'I pray to the gods that he was at least wearing some clothes when he fought the bear.'

Eldrid's eyes went to Ulf's lower half, now covered by some furs after she was forced to clean him. Something she had not enjoyed. She couldn't help but smile as she pictured Ulf fighting a bear naked, like he had the bastards that had attacked them that morning. The three men had appeared out of nowhere and forced their way into the farmhouse. Asketill had done his best to defend them, but he was too old and not a warrior. Eldrid looked at the bruise on Inga's face where one of the men had struck her when she had tried to protect Eldrid from the lust in their eyes. That was before Ulf had barged into the room, his eyes dazed and barely able to stand straight.

'Why did he kill your father?' Inga asked and Eldrid's mind went back to the holmgang in the market town where Griml had made himself a king. *Because of me,* Eldrid thought but did not say.

'My father challenged him to a holmgang. Claimed Ulf had dishonoured him. The fight was only meant to be to first blood, but Ulf broke my father's skull with his shield and he died some time later.'

Inga grunted as her hand went to the pendant she wore around her neck. 'And now he appears as if sent by the gods and saves your life again. I'm an old woman and don't understand much, but it seems the Norns have decided that your lives are intertwined. The gods wanted this to happen.'

Eldrid wanted to be angry at Inga for her words, but she couldn't. She had sensed the same when she had found his body by the river, frozen and blue, but as much as she wanted to, she could not just leave him there to die. Or kill him with the sword still gripped in his hand.

'He must be some warrior,' Inga said as she glanced at Ulf's sword. Eldrid followed her gaze and stared at the golden pommel, with the valknut, three triangles linked together, surrounded by a serpent, and felt a shiver run down her spine when she read the warning engraved on the guard. The first time she had seen that sword was when she had first met Griml. The memory of that day still made the bile in her stomach threaten to erupt. But she had never understood why Griml carried the sword, because it was too small for his giant hands. Later she had learnt that the sword belonged to Ulf and that Griml had taken it after he had killed Ulf's family.

'Not really,' Eldrid said as she thought about the holmgang that killed her father. Even she could tell that Ulf lacked the skill to be a warrior. But that had been a long time ago, and all the scars on his body told her he had fought in many battles since then.

'He beat your father, and those bastards that attacked us today.'

Eldrid nodded. 'He got lucky against my father. And those men,' she could barely say the word, 'weren't warriors.' She sighed. 'But you are right. He did kill them, even in the state he is in.'

'What do you think happened to him?' Asketill asked, and both women jumped as they had not heard him enter. He held a hand up in apology as his wife glared at him, but Eldrid's eyes were still fixed on the sword.

'I think it's best we don't know, but whatever is it, the gods know he is lucky to still be alive.'

***

Ulf groaned as he opened his eyes and saw only darkness around him. At first, he thought he was in a dream again, but there was no sign of the snake or the cloaked figure that usually came to him in his dreams. He frowned as he tried to understand where he was when he sensed a presence near him. His hand went to his side, and he felt Ormstunga lying there, which calmed his racing heart. If the sword was there, then this was not a dream. Ormstunga never came to his dreams. Ulf frowned at the darkness around him and sighed when he realised it was night again.

Ulf tried sitting up, but the pain in his right shoulder made it impossible, and he worried he might never use his right arm again.

But it felt like he had been lying down for too long and besides, he was desperate for a piss. So Ulf gritted his teeth and forced himself to sit up. As Ulf waited for the pain in his shoulder to subside, he peered into the darkness and wondered about the presence he had sensed, but then decided it must have been his imagination.

He struggled to his feet and took deep breaths as he steadied himself when he sensed movement near him. Ulf turned to grab his sword, the movement too sudden for his body, and he just stifled the scream before it came out of his mouth. Holding his breath, he waited a few heartbeats, but nothing came out of the darkness, apart from the memories of what had happened earlier that day and seeing her again. Ulf closed his eyes and thought back to the first time he had seen her long, thin body and her serious expression. The way she had moved, like she glided over the ground and when she had smiled at the trader, Ulf had forgotten everything around him. And then he remembered the last time he had seen Eldrid. On the ship with her father's men and sailing away from Thorgilsstad after the battle against Griml. Ulf had later learnt that her ship had never reached Sweden.

He let go of the breath he was holding and took Ormstunga, feeling comforted by her hilt in his hand. Ulf was about to sneak out of the house when he realised he was still naked. But it was too dark for him to see anything, so instead, he grabbed the furs he had been sleeping under and wrapped them around him, before he snuck out of the house, being careful not to trip over anything or anyone. Somewhere in the farmhouse, he heard someone snoring and remembered the old man who had been on the ground when he had barged into the main room.

Ulf moved as silently as his aching body would let him, and once outside, he gasped at the coldness of the air. Even so, he savoured it as it filled his lungs. Ulf had believed he was going to die when he fell into the river, and he thanked the gods that he still lived as he glanced at the moon in the cloudless sky. He wrapped the furs around him as the cold started to bite and knew that he should go back in the house, but Ulf just dropped to the ground and sat there, staring at the moon as it moved across the sky in the winter night. His breath clouded in front of him and he shivered as the cold crept in under the furs, but it numbed the pains of his injuries, so Ulf stayed where he was. If he was going to die, he would have done so when the men sent by Ragnar attacked him and when he had drawn Ormstunga in the sunlight. Odin wanted him to live. Ulf was certain of that and he wondered if it had anything to do with Eldrid, who was sleeping in the house behind him.

***

Eldrid had watched Ulf's silhouette as he sat and looked around the room he was in. She had gripped the knife in her hand and pictured plunging it into his chest, but she knew she would never do it. The thought had come to her after her conversation with Inga, which had left her frightened. If the gods had decided that their lives were linked, then she knew she had to unlink them. Even if it meant angering the gods. What was the worst they could do? Her family were dead and she was a thrall. But as she crept into the room and stood over Ulf's sleeping form, she thought about how he had saved her from Griml and the outlaws earlier that day, and she could not kill him.

Instead, Eldrid sat on a chair in the corner and watched him sleep until he woke up. She held her breath as he struggled to his feet and wondered how he had found himself on his own in Denmark. The last time she had seen him, Ulf had friends and a place to live. He had earned himself a reputation after what he had done in the battle against Griml. And yet, here he was, in Denmark. Battered and bruised with fresh wounds and on his own. Perhaps he was not as blessed as she thought he was, and perhaps that was the real reason she could not kill him.

When Ulf suddenly turned, as if he had heard something, her heart had stopped, afraid that he had noticed her sitting there. She prayed to the gods that he hadn't and sighed with relief when he took his sword and left the room. Eldrid was not sure what she would say to him if they had to speak, but she knew the moment would come soon when she had to face the man that had killed her father, but had also saved her life.

She had stood and watched as he went outside with nothing more than the furs he took with him and wondered where he was going. For a moment, she hoped he would sneak off into the darkness and that Inga was wrong. But she knew that if Ulf did that, then he would die of the cold. Eldrid had considered going after him, but then decided against it. If Ulf wanted to freeze to death, then that was his choice and had nothing to do with her. So she had gone back to her corner and lay down on the furs where she slept. Before she closed her eyes, Eldrid prayed to the gods and asked them to send Ulf far from here, because she was certain his presence would lead to only more death.

CHAPTER 7

'YOU STILL HERE THEN?' The old man's voice woke Ulf, who blinked the sleep away and frowned at the surrounding land. There were hills in the distance and behind the hills he saw thin trails of smoke reaching up to the clouds.

'Where am I?' Ulf glanced over his shoulder at the old man, who, like him, was wrapped in an old fur cloak. His skin was rough, and a fresh bruise covered his heavily lined face around his left eye.

The old man chewed on something as he scanned his lands before he hawked and spat. 'On land farmed by me and my father before me, and his before him.'

Ulf nodded, not sure what else he had expected the old man to say. He turned his attention back to the landscape and saw no other farmsteads nearby. Like his uncle's farm, this one was isolated. To one side was a small field, where he guessed they grew the food they needed, but there were no signs of animals other than the one goat the outlaws had killed. 'How did I get here?'

The old man stayed where he was. 'The girl found you by the river, not far from here. Thought you were dead at first, but then you muttered some words and gripped that sword of yours like your life depended on it.' Ulf looked at Ormstunga in his hand and thought of the dream he had before he heard the screams as the old man came closer. 'Had to get the lads from Randolf's farm to carry you here, as you were too heavy for me and the girl. They tried to take that sword of yours, but couldn't free it from your grip.' The old man laughed. 'One of them wanted to break your hand, but the girl warned them not to. I wondered about that, but now I guess I know why.'

'Eldrid is your thrall?'

The old man frowned at him for a few heartbeats, as if wondering why Ulf had asked that. 'Aye.'

'Where did you find her?'

Again, the old man frowned at him. 'At the market.'

Ulf sighed and then wondered if it was worth asking the next question, but decided it wasn't. The old man probably didn't know where the traders got Eldrid from.

'She said you killed her father.'

Ulf looked up at the morning sun and wrapped the furs around him. At some point during the night, he had fallen asleep as he stared at the stars and he thanked Tyr that it was a dreamless sleep. His headache was gone, but he still felt the dull pain in his shoulder and hoped the axe had not broken anything. He flexed his fingers on his right hand, but knew that they could move meant nothing. Then his mind went back to the holmgang against the older Swedish jarl he had fought so many winters ago. 'I didn't kill him,' Ulf said, but even he didn't believe his own words. 'When we left, he was still alive.'

'You landed the blow that killed him,' a woman's voice said behind him, and Ulf turned to get to his feet, but his body was stiff from the cold and injuries. He just managed to keep the cloak wrapped around him when he remembered he still wore nothing under it. 'He might not have died when the blow landed, but you still killed him.'

'Where you going?' the old man asked when Eldrid walked off.

'The river to get water.'

The old man nodded. 'Just don't bring back any more bodies.' He laughed to himself before he turned to Ulf. 'Come, let's find you something to wear. You can't go around naked all the time.'

A while later, Ulf grimaced as he chewed on the grainy porridge Inga had given him for the morning meal. More than once, he had to spit a stone out and wondered if he would have any teeth left by the time he finished eating. He glanced at the old man and saw that most of his teeth were missing and thought he understood why. The trousers and tunic he was given fit badly and were so itchy, he wouldn't be surprised if his body was full of lice bites. The trousers were too loose and too short and the tunic had one sleeve longer than the other. Ulf winced as he bit another stone and had to take deep breaths not to scream and upset his hosts.

They did not have much, especially not anything worth stealing, but they had given what clothes they could and food. Asketill, the old man, had tried to ask Ulf where he was from and asked about the raids he had been on, but Ulf did not want to talk about any of that. Instead, he wanted to talk to Eldrid. To find out how she had ended up here, but she had not returned from the river yet. Ulf worried about that, but the old folks weren't too concerned.

'She sometimes just sits there. Only the gods know why,' Inga said when he asked about it.

He had finished his porridge by the time Eldrid returned, carrying a bucket filled to the brim. Ulf jumped to his feet to help her, but her glare told him to back off. He knew she could be dangerous as his hand went to the small mark on his neck where she had tried to stab him.

The rest of the day was one of the most challenging in Ulf's life. Icy rain prevented him from going outside, which meant he was stuck inside where the atmosphere almost suffocated him. Ulf had to wrap himself in foul-smelling furs as there wasn't enough wood to keep the hearth fire going, but that didn't seem to bother the old folks. Asketill spent the day telling Ulf of his past, of how he had been a warrior before age took his skill away, only for Inga to say he never had any skill, while she and Eldrid spent the day doing different chores. Ulf tried his best not to stare at Eldrid as she moved around the small farmhouse and was sure that he could feel her eyes on him on more than one occasion. The only thing Ulf was glad about was that he could move his right arm more, which meant the injury wasn't too serious, but he knew it would be a while before he could use his arm to wield Ormstunga. At least it was winter now, which meant he would not have to.

As the day wore on, the old folks fell asleep, leaving Ulf and Eldrid alone. Ulf tried to summon the courage to talk to Eldrid, but every time he walked her way, her glare made him turn around. After a while, though, as Ulf stood by the door and stared at the heavy winter rain, he decided he had enough. He took a deep breath and turned, only to find Eldrid standing behind him. They stared at each other for a few heartbeats; her glaring at him more than staring, and Ulf had to resist the temptation to grip the Mjöllnir pendant around his neck.

Clearing his throat, Ulf said, 'Thank you.'

Eldrid raised an eyebrow at him. 'For what?'

'Asketill told me it was you who found me.'

Eldrid laughed, causing Inga to grunt in her sleep, but the old woman's eyes stayed closed. 'Aye, a cruel trick by the gods for me to find the man who took everything from me. Even crueller that I could not find the strength to just leave you there.'

Ulf nodded, not knowing what to say to that. He rubbed the back of his neck as he fought to keep eye contact with Eldrid. 'I...I'm sorry about your father. I didn't want to fight him. I—'

'It doesn't matter what you wanted. You still did, and you killed him.' Her hands balled into fists, and Ulf wondered if she would strike him. Then he wondered what he would do if she did. Tears ran down her cheeks as she said, 'You killed my father and ruined my life. Because of you, I am a thrall to these—,' she pointed behind her, but couldn't finish her sentence. Instead, she turned away from him. 'I wanted you to be dead when I found you. I prayed to the gods that you had drowned, but you still lived. Gods, all I wanted to do then was to stick your head under the water and hold you there until you stopped breathing, but I couldn't.'

Ulf blinked as she told him this and glanced at the open door behind him again. He wondered if he should just leave this place. But then he looked at Eldrid again. 'Why didn't you leave me there? The cold would have killed me.'

Eldrid looked away from him. 'I couldn't. For a reason only the gods know, I felt like I had to help you. So I ran back here and told them about you.'

Ulf felt compelled to reach out to her but then thought better of it. 'Thank you,' he said again.

Eldrid laughed as she turned to face him again. 'Well, I guess we're even now. I saved your life, and then you saved me from those outlaws.'

Ulf remembered the three men he had fought the day before. He looked around and, for the first time, he wondered where their bodies were. He saw the reddened patches on the ground where he had killed them, but there was no sign of the three men. 'Who were they?'

'Bastards who deserved what they got. We'd heard that outlaws had come to the area and were attacking farmsteads, especially isolated ones like this, but Asketill didn't think they'd come here. Nothing worth stealing, he had said.' She shuddered, and Ulf wondered if she was thinking about what they would have done to her after they killed the old folks.

'How did you get here? Last time I saw you, your father's men were taking you back to Sweden.'

Eldrid wrapped her arms around herself as she looked away from him. For a long time, she just stood like that, and Ulf thought she wasn't going to say anything. Over her shoulder, he saw Inga staring at them and wondered how long the old woman had been awake. 'We were almost home,' Eldrid said at last. 'I could even see the land from the prow of my father's ship. And then they attacked us.'

'Who?' Ulf frowned.

Eldrid shrugged. 'Pirates. They appeared out of nowhere, like demons from the seas. We tried to outrun them, but their ships were faster and they caught us before we could reach the safety of land. My father's men fought like gods, but in the end, there were too many pirates and they killed everyone.'

'And they sold you as a thrall.'

Anger flashed in Eldrid's eyes, similar to what Ulf imagined others saw in his. 'They did more than that to me. At first, I prayed to the gods. To Odin, Thor, Frigg, even Loki. I prayed to them all, asking to be saved, but those prayers fell on deaf ears. I prayed to them again, asking to die. But still, the gods ignored me. I blamed you and your friends. Ulf Bear-Slayer and Snorri Thorgilsson. Two names I would never forget.'

'We saved you from Griml,' Ulf tried to defend himself, but knew from the look on Eldrid's face that he had said the wrong thing, even before she struck him. Ulf fought the urge to rub his cheek where she had slapped him.

'You didn't save me! You kidnapped me after you killed my father! You took me away from him as he lay on his deathbed, all so that you could draw Griml away from his army. And for what? Your revenge! My father died alone. He died alone because of your vengeance.' Eldrid lifted her hand to slap him again, and Ulf almost wanted her to do it. Because she was right. But then she lowered her hand and glared at him. 'So tell me this, Ulf Bear-Slayer, was it all worth it? Taking me away from my father and causing me to become a thrall. Was it all worth your revenge? All those who died. And for what? You didn't even kill Griml that day!'

Ulf flinched as she spat the words at him and wished she had struck him instead. *Was it all worth it?* It was a question he constantly struggled with, especially because of everything he had lost. Snorri and his mother had warned him against his quest for revenge. They had told him to live his life. Not to seek the death of another. But Ulf had never been good at listening to others. He took a deep breath as he thought of all those who had died because of his revenge.

'And where is Griml now? Do you even know? Is that why you are in Denmark? To hunt him down?' Eldrid continued, her blazing eyes boring into him.

Ulf looked at her, his hand twitching for the hilt of Ormstunga, back in her scabbard by the furs Ulf had slept on. Even after his death, Griml still haunted him. 'Dead,' Ulf said, and Eldrid's eyes widened.

'Dead?'

Ulf nodded. 'I killed him in Francia.' *After he and your brother plotted to kill me and my friends*, Ulf thought, but didn't say. She didn't need to know that he had also killed her brother. Not yet. 'Griml was like those men who attacked you yesterday. Only worse. He killed my uncle and raped my aunt. And when he was done with them, he burnt their farmhouse down on top of them. I don't even know if they were still alive when he did it. My aunt and my cousins. But Vidar is not the only friend I lost in my hunt for vengeance. I lost more than you could ever imagine.'

Eldrid stared at Ulf for a while, as some of the fire in her eyes disappeared, and then she asked. 'So, Ulf Bear-Slayer, was it worth it?'

It was Ulf's turn to stare at the woman he had fallen for so many winters ago and who he thought he would never see again. He took a deep breath as a raven cried out somewhere outside.

'I don't know.'

Chapter 8

Ulf grunted as he stabbed Ormstunga at his imaginary foe, the blade still in her scabbard as the sun shone through the clouds. He held the sword there for a few heartbeats and listened to the approaching footsteps. He knew it was Eldrid before she spoke and wondered why she had come to him.

The worst of the winter was gone, along with the Yuletide and the winter solstice, and the days were slowly getting warmer and longer. Spring was approaching, and so was the time for Ulf to leave. His shoulder had healed, and Ulf used every moment of daylight to train and strengthen it again. He also trained with Ormstunga with his left arm so that he was as comfortable with the blade in that hand as with the right. In the past, Ulf had used a one-handed axe in his left hand. That was when he was at his deadliest, but now he had no axe. Even his father's Dane axe was gone, lost in the forest while he was fighting for his life.

He had spent much of the winter on his own, contemplating his next steps, but had struggled to stay calm with all the inactivity. The old folks allowed him to spend the winter on their farmstead and, in return, he helped where he could. It reminded him of his youth on his uncle's farm, and Ulf found he enjoyed the work around the farmstead. Until he remembered what had happened to his family. He and Eldrid spoke little during the winter, though, but he often looked up to find her eyes on him, her expression unreadable.

'She likes you,' Asketill had said one night with a grin in his grey beard.

'She wanted to kill me,' Ulf responded as he poked at the hearth fire.

Asketill laughed. 'Aye, that's how you know she likes you.'

Ulf had raised an eyebrow at the old man, thinking that Loki had stolen his wits. 'You make no sense, old man.'

'When you lived as long as I have, you realise nothing makes sense. Sometimes I wonder if even the gods know what they are doing.' Asketill stroked his beard as he stared into the flames.

Ulf shook his head to chase the memory of that conversation away and thought of another woman whose presence he had not felt all winter. And that worried him more and more every day. He had felt her watching him in Jelling, but since he had woken on this farm, there was nothing, and Ulf didn't know what that meant.

'Who are you fighting this time?' Eldrid's voice broke him from his thoughts and he turned to see her serious expression on him.

'Myself,' Ulf said, not knowing what else to respond.

Eldrid scrutinised him for a few heartbeats and then glanced at his sword. 'Why is your sword still in its scabbard?'

Ulf glanced at Ormstunga and then squinted at the sun. 'It's bad luck to draw her blade in sunlight.'

A small smile played on Eldrid's lips. 'The words on her guard?' Ulf nodded, and she shook her head. 'You men are too superstitious. What bad luck can a sword bring?'

Ulf scowled as he thought of his fight against the men Ragnar had sent after him. 'Why do you think you found me in the river?' Eldrid frowned at him, and Ulf told her about his fight with Jarl Ragnar's men and how he had fallen into the river. It was the first time they really spoke, and he was surprised that she listened to everything he told her, not once interrupting him or looking away as if she didn't care.

'And you think it's all because of the sword?'

Ulf nodded. 'Ormstunga is cursed.'

She shook her head at him again. 'Then why not get rid of the sword? Throw it into the deepest sea.'

Ulf thought he could feel Ormstunga's anger at Eldrid's words, or perhaps that was just his heart racing. 'To do that would anger Tyr. Ormstunga's curse is mine to bear, as it was my father's before me, and I must carry it to my death.'

Eldrid sighed and crossed her arms. 'So now what for Ulf Bear-Slayer?' Ulf frowned at her. 'Winter is almost over and you've recovered from your injuries. There's no need for you to stay here. You know that as well as the gods do.'

'You want me to go?'

He saw the spark in her eyes and realised she still blamed him for what had happened to her. 'I never wanted you here in the first place.'

Ulf turned and scanned the horizon, taking in the flat landscape and the hills in the distance, just so he didn't have to look at the anger in her eyes. 'I guess I'll go to another town, perhaps find a jarl in need of more warriors.'

Eldrid nodded, as if she expected that answer. 'So you want to go ruin the lives of others? Like all warriors, just out for death and glory.'

'You don't know me,' Ulf said, although he knew that was a weak argument.

'I know a warrior when I see one. Blood and violence run in your veins, Ulf Bear-Slayer. Why do you think you keep getting into fights wherever you go? The gods are showing you who you are, and the longer you ignore them, the worse they'll make it for you.' Ulf's face darkened because he knew she was right, even if he didn't want to admit it. When Ulf was still a boy, he wanted to be a warrior. To be better than his father had been. But after standing in the shield wall and watching his friends die, Ulf had done his best to avoid that life. 'My father was the same. He hated not being able to fight his enemies, and when he had none, he'd go looking for some.' Ulf raised an eyebrow at that and wanted to ask a question he knew better than to ask. Eldrid was talking to him and he didn't want to ruin it by bringing up the fact that he had killed her father. 'You are a warrior, even if you're not a good one.' Eldrid turned and left him staring into the space where she had been standing only moments before, her words in his mind. And not just hers, but Ingolfr's as well. *A wolf is meant to be a wolf.*

Ulf spent the next few days brooding over what Eldrid had said, which had left him in a foul mood. Something Asketill seemed not to notice when he returned from visiting one of the nearby farmsteads. The old man greeted him cheerfully and told him of the folks he had visited. It had been their sons who had helped bring Ulf to their farmhouse after Eldrid had found him, he had told Ulf, who didn't really care as he watched Eldrid work. She looked as miserable as he felt and not for the first time; he wished there was a way to free her from being a thrall. But apart from killing the old folks, he had no other way of doing that. The hacksilver Ingolfr had given him was gone, most likely taken by the river spirits, and the only other wealth he had was the arm rings he wore. But Ulf knew they would not be enough to buy her freedom. That left him with only one choice. To go raiding. Lost in his thoughts, Ulf ignored Asketill until the old man said something that caught his ear.

'What was that?' he asked Asketill, who frowned at him.

'What was what?' the old man scratched his head.

'What did you say about a raid?' Ulf noticed how Eldrid looked up from her task.

'They're saying there's a big raid,' Asketill said. 'To West Francia. Many of the jarls had pressured the king into allowing them to raid the Frankish kingdoms.'

Ulf's heart raced as he thought about it. Francia was rich. Everyone knew that, and he had seen that for himself when he raided the Frankish kingdoms with Snorri and the men of the Sae-Ulfr. All he needed was to do one raid. One summer and he could earn enough to buy Eldrid from the old folks and free her. Maybe even have enough left so she could return to Sweden. Although he wasn't sure what she would return to. Her family was dead. Ulf had killed two of them, and he knew her mother had died. Her brother had told him that. 'When does this raid start?'

Asketill raised an eyebrow at Ulf. 'You want to go on this raid?'

'I might,' Ulf responded.

'Why?'

Ulf took a calming breath as he tried to think of a good reason, because he didn't want to tell Asketill that he wanted to free Eldrid.

'It's Ulf's business, not yours,' Inga said before Ulf could respond and gave him a look, which made him think she knew his reasons. Ulf couldn't help but glance at Eldrid and was surprised to see that she wasn't where she had been before. He looked around the farmhouse, but couldn't see her anywhere.

'In the spring, I think.' Asketill frowned at his wife. 'But I'm not sure. Randolf didn't really know, but he told me that Jelling is very busy as the jarls from all over Denmark have gone there to prepare for the raid. They say warriors are sleeping outside in the cold because there is nowhere for them to sleep.' Asketill laughed. 'Ah, the gods only know that if I was still a young man, I'd have gone with.'

'It's a good thing you aren't then,' Inga said with a scowl. 'The gods know you'd probably trip over your own feet and skewer yourself with your own spear.'

Asketill returned his wife's scowl and then turned his attention back to Ulf. 'Ignore her. I was a great warrior in my youth. Men spoke my name with fear.'

Ulf sighed. He had heard Asketill say the same thing many times during the winter months. 'How far is Jelling from here?' Ulf had never thought about how close they were to Jelling because he was determined never to go back to that place. He wondered if the gods were laughing at him now.

'Four days' walk, south-east. Randolf's oldest is leaving in two days.'

'Thorir is also going?' Inga interrupted her husband, who nodded.

'Aye. The young ones today don't want to be farmers any more. Their heads are filled with tales of mighty battles and glory, so they all want to be warriors. Just like Ulf here and me.'

Inga shook her head at her husband as Ulf thought about it. He decided it might be a better idea to travel with this Thorir. That way, he could avoid those in Jelling who might still remember him. As Ragnar's warning came to him, he thought of another question. 'Who's leading the raid? The king?'

Asketill laughed. 'Gods, no. The king won't want the Frankish kings to know that he is behind the raid. No, a cousin of his is leading the raid.' The old man scratched his thin hair as he tried to remember the name. 'Ah yes, now I remember who is leading the raid. Jarl Ragnar.'

Chapter 9

'Jarl Ragnar?' Ulf's eyes widened as he remembered the man he had fought that night in Denmark. The man who had told him to leave Jelling and to never come back. The man who had sent others after him.

'What's the matter with you?' Inga asked as she and her husband scowled at Ulf. 'You know Jarl Ragnar?'

Ulf shook his head, not wanting to tell them the truth. 'I've heard his name.'

Asketill barked a laugh. 'Who hasn't? Even Odin knows his name.' Outside, a raven cried out, which sent a shiver down Ulf's spine, and judging by the way Inga gripped the Mjöllnir pendant around her neck, she felt just as uncomfortable as he did.

'Don't say things like that. You'll anger the gods. We've had enough trouble already,' she berated Asketill, who dismissed her words with a wave of his hand. But Ulf knew that was not what the raven was warning them about. The raven was telling him not to go to Jelling. Not to go on this raid, but Ulf had no choice. Eldrid was a thrall because of him, and it was his duty to free her from that.

'I need to prepare my things,' Ulf said and went to his sleeping corner as Inga told Asketill off. He pulled the furs he had been sleeping on to one side and stared at his brynja. That was all that Ulf had left. That and Ormstunga. Everything else had been lost as he had fought for his life not so long ago. Even his father's Dane axe and his helmet. The bearskin cloak was gone as well, lost to the river while he was fighting against it. Ulf sighed and knew that he'd need to find a second weapon. Ormstunga's curse meant she could not be his only weapon when he stood in a shield wall because if the sun was out, then he couldn't use her. Then he looked at his brynja. He had not touched it since he had woken up here and it showed. The brynja was covered in rust and mud from the river, and Ulf knew it would take him a long time to clean it, as he tried not to think about the warriors who had attacked him.

'Here,' Asketill said behind him, and Ulf turned to see him holding a one-handed axe. Ulf frowned as he looked at the axe in the old man's hands, its edge dull and with a few rusted spots on the axe head. 'It belonged to my son. He wanted to be a warrior. Had to sell a cow to afford that axe for him, but he died before he got to use it. Illness took him. Perhaps you can find some use for it, even with that sword of yours.' Ulf thought of refusing, but the sadness in the old man's eyes made him change his mind.

'Thank you,' Ulf said, as he took the axe and inspected it. Despite its condition, the axe felt like a quality weapon and under the dirt and rust, he thought he could see a pattern engraved into the iron. Ulf was surprised the old man only had to sell one cow for it.

Ulf spent the next few days cleaning his brynja and the axe. Both were scrubbed clean, the brynja to get rid of the dirt and the rust, and the axe was sharpened. Ulf had stared at the serpent engraved on the axe head, which reminded him of the snake in his dream, and couldn't decide if it was a good omen or not. The snake had protected him in the dream, but he knew who she represented and that frightened him.

Eldrid had barely spoken to him during those days and Ulf wasn't sure if it was because she didn't want him to go on the raid, or because she couldn't wait for him to leave. But when the day came to leave, Ulf was more nervous than he thought he'd be.

'I know why you are doing this, and even the gods think it's dumb,' Eldrid said as the son of Randolf arrived. He had two horses with him, the one he was riding and another he was leading by the reins. Ulf frowned at her, but said nothing as he rubbed his hands on his trousers to dry the sweat off them. 'You really think that I will forgive you if you buy my freedom?'

Ulf shrugged. 'I'm not doing this for your forgiveness.'

Eldrid crossed her arms. 'Then why are you? Why does my fate matter so much to you?'

Ulf watched Thorir approach as he thought about her question. 'Because you were right. You are here because of me and I want to make it right.'

'Why? So that you can feel better about yourself?'

Ulf frowned at her and wondered if that was not really the reason. 'Because you deserve better than being a thrall,' he said, which only made Eldrid laugh.

'Ulf Bear-Slayer, you don't know what I deserve.' She sighed. 'Just don't get yourself killed. I have enough people haunting my dreams. And I don't want to see your ugly face every night when I try to sleep.'

Before Ulf could respond, she turned and walked off, leaving him to shake his head. He wondered if he could ever do something good in her eyes. Ulf pushed the thoughts out of his mind and scrutinised Thorir. The bóndi was shorter than him and looked like he had never used an axe for something other than chopping trees. Thorir was about the same age as Ulf, or perhaps older, and Ulf wondered why he had never left to be a warrior before as the man grinned at him.

'It's good to see you have recovered. The gods know we thought you were dead,' Thorir said, and Ulf nodded as he introduced himself.

Ulf heard footsteps behind him. For a moment, he hoped it was Eldrid and was almost disappointed when it was Asketill and Inga.

'You take care of that boy,' Inga said to him, a tear in her eye. 'Make sure he comes back home.' Ulf could only nod. He had been in enough battles to know there was nothing he could do to guarantee that. It was up to the Norns, and the sisters of fate had already decided if Thorir would return or not. Just like they had already decided his fate. 'And you look after yourself too, Ulf.' She reached up and patted him on the cheek, which surprised him.

'I...I...' Ulf started, but didn't know what to say.

'See, you've embarrassed him now.' Asketill grinned for a moment, but then his face turned serious. 'But I agree with her, Ulf. You make sure you return. Eldrid will be waiting for you.'

Ulf glanced towards the farmhouse and doubted that Asketill spoke the truth, but part of him wanted to believe the old man. He took one of the golden arm rings from his wrist and gave it to Asketill, who raised an eyebrow at him. 'For your hospitality.'

'Nonsense, you don't have to,' Inga said, even as Asketill grabbed the arm ring from his hand, like a starving child would a loaf of bread. Inga scowled at her husband. 'The gods insist we open our doors to those in need.'

'And I insist. I would have died if not for you.'

'And we would have died if not for you,' Inga said, grabbed the arm ring from her husband and gave it back to Ulf. 'The gods would be angry if we take this from you. You can repay us for the hospitality by bringing Thorir back to his parents. They need him around the farm.' Ulf nodded and was about to leave when Inga said, 'You are always welcome here, Ulf. I'm sure even Eldrid would say the same.'

This time, Ulf smiled. 'Thank you, Inga and Asketill.' He mounted the horse Thorir had brought for him as Asketill shouted,

'And you need to bring a lot of gold if you want to buy her freedom!'

***

'By the gods, I've never seen Jelling so busy, not even during the festivals.' Thorir gaped as they stared at the countless warriors hanging around in the streets of Jelling. Ulf's nose crinkled at the stench of the large town as he hoped that the many warriors would make it easier for him to hide from Jarl Ragnar, whose warning kept ringing in his ears. *You better leave my town, boy. The gods know that if I see you again, then you're a dead man.* Although that warning was almost drowned out by what sounded like a thousand voices competing with each other to be heard. Ulf was not used to the smell and the sound of a busy town any more, not after spending the winter on a farm surrounded only by fields and birds.

It had taken them three days to get to Jelling, and not long after they had left Asketill's farmstead, they joined others who were travelling towards Jelling to take part in the raid. Most were farmers, like Thorir, but some were warriors. There was even a minor jarl with a handful of warriors, but the man was boastful and judging by the lack of good armour his warriors had, Ulf decided it was best not to ask this jarl if they could join his small force.

'So where do we go, Ulf Bear-Slayer?' Thorir asked as they walked the streets and tried not to bump into anyone. Asketill had told the bóndi that that was Ulf's by-name after he had heard Eldrid say it. But it was different when Eldrid used it. Her mocking tone almost made it better, but the blind admiration in Thorir's voice only irritated him. Ulf did not feel like he was someone to be admired. Not when he was lucky to still be alive.

'How would I know?' Ulf looked towards where he knew the market would be and wondered if Ingolfr and Tormod were there. He had often wondered what had happened to them after he had left Jelling before the winter and had prayed that the brothers would one day forgive him.

'You're the warrior. You must know someone who needs strong warriors,' Thorir said as he flexed his arms at some passing women who barely looked his way.

'I don't know anyone in Jelling,' Ulf said, which wasn't a lie. 'We walk around and keep our ears open. Perhaps we will hear something that might help us.'

Thorir frowned at Ulf but said nothing as they spent the day walking around the busy town and avoiding the market and the large hall in the centre of the town where Ulf thought Jarl Ragnar might be. But Thorir was right. They needed to find a jarl in need of some warriors, someone with a few rowing benches empty on his ship.

The sun was setting and the two of them were on their way to the stables where their horses were when Ulf sensed movement behind them. He grabbed the hilt of Ormstunga, glad that it was cloudy, but before he could turn, Ulf heard.

'By Odin. Look who is dumb enough to return to Jelling.'

Ulf turned, his lips curled and his hand still on the hilt of Ormstunga as he glared at the old warrior with the bleached hair facing him. Ulf's heart skipped a beat when he recognised the man from the night he had fought Jarl Ragnar. He had been the one who had convinced Jarl Ragnar to let Ulf leave Jelling with Ormstunga. But he had also told Ragnar about Tormod and Ingolfr. A woman nearby grabbed her son and dragged him away as Thorir jumped back, his face pale at Ulf's sudden reaction and the group of warriors facing them.

'You were told not to come back to Jelling,' the old warrior said, his eyes flicking to the hilt of Ormstunga, but the friendly smile on his face left Ulf confused. So did the fact that none of his warriors looked like they were getting ready to attack. That still didn't stop some of the townspeople from stopping and staring.

Ulf let go of the sword and took a deep breath to calm his racing heart. 'I don't want any trouble.' Thorir scowled at Ulf, who ignored the bóndi as he kept his eyes on the old jarl and the warriors behind him.

'Then why are you in Jelling?' the old warrior asked.

Ulf hesitated for a moment. 'I heard about the raid.'

'The raid?' The man raised an eyebrow as he glanced at the warriors behind him, which made Ulf wonder if he too wasn't a jarl. 'And what about the raid?'

Ulf looked around him and saw how most people were avoiding the group, but some could not help but glance in their direction. Thorir had taken a step away from Ulf, as if he was trying to distance himself, but Ulf couldn't blame the man. If there was a fight, then it was best if he ran away instead of trying to fight. 'We want to join.'

'We?' The old warrior glanced at Thorir, who stood straight and puffed his chest out. Something which only made the warriors behind the man laugh. 'And who is your friend? I don't recognise him.'

'My name is Thorir Randolfson,' Thorir said, making his voice deeper than what it naturally was.

'You ever fought in a battle before, Thorir Randolfson?'

Thorir shook his head. 'But I've fought some bandits before. Bastards who tried to steal my father's goats.'

The old warrior turned his attention to Ulf again. 'If Jarl Ragnar finds out that you are in Jelling, then he will not be happy.'

Ulf clenched his teeth as his anger threatened to erupt as he remembered the men he had fought soon after leaving Jelling. 'What's he going to do? Send more men after me?'

The old warrior smiled as he glanced at Ormstunga on Ulf's waist. 'Aye, we wondered what had happened to those men.'

'What *did* happen to them?' one of the warriors asked.

Ulf glared at the man. 'Their corpses fed the ravens and the wolves. Although two of them fed the fish in the river.'

The warrior bristled at that, but he kept quiet as he glared at Ulf.

The old warrior raised a hand to calm the bristling warrior, which again made Ulf think he was a jarl. That and the rich clothing he was wearing. 'What's your name?'

Ulf thought about not answering, but then said, 'Ulf Bjørnson.'

'Well then, Ulf Bjørnson and Thorir Randolfson. I am Jarl Knut, cousin of King Horik. Seek me out in the morning in my camp outside Jelling. I know of someone who could use warriors of your quality.'

'Jarl Knut, are you sure that's a good idea?' the same warrior as before asked. 'Jarl Ragnar—'

'Jarl Ragnar does not need to know about Ulf's return. So you will not tell him. Besides, we could do with a warrior as skilled as Ulf here.' Jarl Knut turned to Ulf, and Ulf wondered at the spark he saw in the man's eyes. 'I bid you two a good night, but I have a meeting with the king.'

Before they left, Ulf asked. 'The traders, Ingolfr and Tormod, what happened to them?'

Jarl Knut stroked his beard as he seemed to think about it. 'Jarl Ragnar made them pay the mangæld owed to him and told them to leave Jelling.'

Ulf frowned as he struggled to believe Jarl Knut as Thorir turned to him.

'What was all that about? Why did Jarl Ragnar tell you to leave and never come back?'

Ulf sighed. 'Because the last time I was here, I got into a fight with him.'

Thorir's eyes widened. 'By Thor! What were you thinking?'

'I wasn't, and I didn't know who he was then.'

'Would it have made a difference?' Thorir raised an eyebrow at Ulf, who scratched his head.

'Probably not,' Ulf admitted.

'And Jarl Ragnar told you not to come back to Jelling?'

'Aye, said he'd kill me if I did.'

Thorir threw his arms up in the air. 'Thor's balls! And now he'll probably kill me because I came with you.' He started pacing around, his eyes darting towards every shadow as if he expected someone to jump out and slaughter them. 'Why didn't you tell me? And what about the warriors he sent after you? Is that why you were in the river?'

Ulf took a deep breath to calm his anger, but it wasn't Jarl Knut who had angered him. If anything, the jarl had just left Ulf confused. It was Thorir's fear. The man wanted to go on a raid, and yet the thought of a fight made him more frightened than an injured deer facing a pack of wolves. Ulf turned and walked towards the stables. He wanted to sleep and then the following day, he would seek out Jarl Knut, because the only way to free Eldrid was to go on this raid and get rich. But as Ulf walked away from the nervous Thorir, he felt the hairs on the back of his neck stand on end. He stopped and scanned the shadows as he sensed her presence. His hand went to the axe, and he rubbed the serpent pattern on the axe head.

'Where are you? I know you're here,' Ulf said through clenched teeth, but there was no response.

'Who are you talking to?' Thorir asked, looking even more frightened than before as he, too, scanned the shadows.

'No one,' Ulf said, even as he felt her eyes on him. Ulf resisted the urge to grip the Mjöllnir pendant around his neck because he knew that if she was watching him again, then it could only mean one thing. Death was coming, and he could only pray that it wasn't his. Not until he had freed Eldrid.

Chapter 10

'Are you sure that was a good idea, Jarl?' Hallr asked after they left the scarred warrior and the bóndi. The warrior looked thinner than before, but he still had the same fire in his sword-grey eyes. And he still had the sword. Over the winter, Knut had almost forgotten about it, as well as the men that had disappeared, but seeing the sword made his desire for it burn again. But Knut knew that he needed to wait. He had other problems to deal with. Problems this Ulf Bjørnson might solve for him.

'Is what a good idea?' Knut asked Hallr just to distract himself from his thoughts.

'To invite that bastard to join your army. He killed—'

'I know who he killed!' Jarl Knut said, his heart racing as he remembered the men he had sent after Ulf. Of the thirty men he had sent out to hunt the young warrior, six had never returned. A few days later, Knut had sent more men to search for them, but they were never found. Some had suggested they had fled Denmark and had gone north to Norway or east to Sweden, but Knut knew those men wouldn't do that. They had been some of his most loyal warriors. 'We underestimated this Ulf.'

'If the others find out it was him—'

Again, Knut interrupted Hallr. 'Nobody will find out!' He glared at his hirdmen as they stood around him. 'Nobody will find out. Do you understand?' All the warriors nodded, but Hallr's face darkened and Knut understood why. A man who had been like a brother to him had been one of those six warriors and his disappearance had hit Hallr hard. Jarl Knut put a hand on Hallr's shoulder, a warrior he had known since he was a boy. 'When the time is right, you can do what you want with him and his bóndi friend. But not yet. And besides, he will not be part of my army.' Jarl Knut smiled as a plan formed in his head. One that will solve all of his problems. He turned to another of his men. 'Find Jarl Hakon. Ask him to join me for a drink in my tent.' The warrior frowned at first, but then left to do what Knut had asked. Jarl Hakon was one of Knut's closest allies, but only because he was not a Dane. The man was from Sygnafylki, a small kingdom in the north of Norway, but had been on many raids with Knut. Jarl Hakon spent more time in Denmark than in Norway because he had had a falling out with his king.

'When the time is right for what?' Hallr asked with a raised eyebrow as they made their way back to Knut's camp outside the town. Knut refused to stay in the house King Horik had offered him. Not after the king had stabbed him in the back.

When word had come that the raid to Francia would start soon, Knut had rushed to Jelling and expected to be named as the leader of the raid. He was the king's oldest cousin and the one who had pushed the hardest for the raid. For a long time, King Horik had refused to raid the Franks because of a treaty he had signed with their now dead emperor. And even after the bastard had died, Horik still refused to send his ships, while men from Norway, men like Jarl Hakon, got rich from raiding those fertile lands. Lands where gold grew on trees, Knut had been told by Jarl Hakon. And when he finally agreed to send a fleet, he decided that Jarl Ragnar should lead it.

Jarl Knut ignored his men as he entered his camp, which was sprawled out near Jelling, and walked to his large tent in the centre of the camp. He had brought ten ships with him, four hundred warriors, and their camp was the largest of all the jarls who had come for the raid. All the jarls apart from Ragnar.

Hundreds of tents and campfires surrounded him and the noise of so many men and the smoke from their campfires made his head hurt, but at least he didn't have to make sure that his warriors did what they were supposed to. Hallr and his other hirdmen did that for him. Knut did not like to waste time dealing with his army, making sure they had what they needed and training them. Just like he rarely fought in battles himself. He paid his warriors to do that for him, and he paid them well. His men were richly rewarded for their deeds and harshly punished if they failed him. Knut had always believed he would have been a better king than Horik, but the Norns had decided that his cousin should wear the crown.

Brooding, he walked into his tent and did not see the other man sitting on the stool and drinking his ale.

'Took you long enough. Was beginning to think the dwarfs had taken you to their world.'

Knut turned, his hand gripping his sword as he glared at the man. 'Hakon! What, in Odin's name, are you doing here?' Knut thought about flogging the bastards who were supposed to be guarding his tent, but they knew Jarl Hakon well enough to know that he was no threat to their jarl. Jarl Knut's tent was well furnished with the same luxuries he had in his hall. There was a large bed with furs for him to sleep on, as well as three beautiful thralls to keep him entertained. Furs were thrown on the ground around his bed and his war chest, and standing in the corner of his tent was a large barrel with his best ale, which had been opened by his guest.

Jarl Hakon, who was taller and broader than Knut, took another sip of his ale. 'You asked me to come.'

Knut rubbed his forehead. 'Aye, I did. But I didn't think you'd be here so soon.'

Jarl Hakon shrugged. 'I was on my way anyway when your man found me.' Hakon frowned at Knut's creased brow. 'Who pissed in your ale?'

'You mean the ale you are drinking?'

Hakon looked at his cup. 'I thought it tasted strange.' He took another drink and Knut shook his head. There was something wrong with the Norse. Perhaps that was why they were such fierce warriors. 'Are you still brooding because your king decided Jarl Ragnar should lead this raid?'

'I should be the one to lead this bloody raid, not him!'

Hakon shrugged, which only annoyed Knut even more. 'Does it really matter? The gods know you will come back far richer than before. Rich enough to raise an army three times the size of your cousin's and then you can be the new king of Denmark.'

'Of course it matters!' His face went red, annoyed that they were having this conversation again. 'For generations to come, the sagas will tell of how Ragnar raided the West Franks and crushed their armies in the name of our gods.'

Hakon drank more from his cup. 'The sagas are full of shit. No one listens to them.'

'Everyone listens to them!' Knut slammed his fist on the table in his tent, but Hakon barely reacted. 'It should be my name they talk of, not his! I am older than Ragnar! I have more battle experience! The gods know I should be the one to lead this raid!' Knut paced around the tent, his arms waving in the air as he ranted. All the while, Hakon just signalled for one thrall to refill his cup and drank more ale.

'Perhaps your king doesn't trust you.'

Knut turned to Hakon, his nostrils flared. 'Doesn't trust me? And he trusts that bastard? Ragnar is also plotting to take the throne from Horik. The gods know it as well as I do. And this raid will mean that men will flock to him and forget about me.'

Hakon shrugged as if none of this was important. 'So what are you going to do?'

Knut stopped and glanced around his tent. A smile spread across his face as he thought of the plan he had come up with. The one the gods had given him. 'Ragnar will not return from this raid alive. And I know just how we are going to do that.'

'We?' Hakon raised an eyebrow.

'Aye, Hakon. We. Help me in this and when I become king of Denmark, then I will help you become king of Sygnafylki.'

Hakon stared at him for a few heartbeats and then said, 'How do we do it?'

Knut rubbed his beard as he tried to find the right words to explain his plan to Hakon, who, although a great warrior, was not very smart. 'Do you remember the young man I told you about? The one who bruised Ragnar's face.'

'Aye,' Hakon nodded.

'He's back in Jelling and he wants to join the raid.'

'So?'

'So, he will join your army. We—'

'Why my army? I have enough men.'

Knut raised an eyebrow at Hakon and wondered why he had to explain things as if he was talking to a child. 'Because we need to keep him close so that we use him to kill Ragnar. And he can't be part of my army because he killed six of my men.'

'You don't know that he killed your men.'

Knut grunted. 'We don't know that he did not not kill them. And besides, that is not important. Some of my men believe he did and they'll want revenge.'

Hakon nodded as he understood, but Knut doubted he did or cared. 'How will we use him?'

Knut smiled. 'He thinks Ragnar sent the men after him, and I think we can use that. If we goad him enough and make him think Ragnar is the one at fault, then, gods willing, he will kill my cousin and I can take charge of the fleet.'

'And how do we goad him?'

Knut shrugged. 'I'll think of something.'

Hakon rubbed his beard as he thought of it. 'Ragnar is a great warrior. What if this man doesn't bite, or can't kill your cousin?'

Again, Knut shrugged. 'Then we'll have to think of something else.'

Hakon nodded as he thought about it. 'So, why my army?' he asked again and Knut sighed as he wondered if the Norse man was doing this just to irritate him.

'I already told you. And because he is Norse, like you. Also, I don't like looking at his face. It makes me feel uncomfortable.'

Hakon raised an eyebrow. 'What's wrong with his face?'

'It looks like some beast clawed half his face off. It's unsettling to look at.' Knut used his fingers to imitate the three scar lines on Ulf's face.

Hakon sat up straight for the first time since Knut walked into his tent. 'Like a beast clawed his face? Three lines that run down his face?' Hakon scowled, which made Knut nervous.

'Aye. What is it?'

'I need to see this warrior.'

'You know him?'

Hakon shook his head and smiled. 'No, but I might know of him. And if he is who I think he might be, then the gods have blessed you.'

'Why?' Knut frowned at Hakon.

'Because this warrior has many names back in Norway and one of them is Jarl-Killer.'

Chapter 11

Ulf woke early the next day and prepared himself for the meeting with Jarl Knut. He combed and braided his hair and then combed his beard and worked in a thin braid in the middle of it. After slipping his brynja on and tying his belt around his waist, Ulf adjusted Ormstunga and the axe so that they were comfortable. He put his two remaining arm rings on his wrists. He had to use the third arm ring to pay the stables owner so they could sleep in the stables. It wasn't comfortable and smelt of horse shit, but it was the only place they could find. All other accommodation in Jelling had been taken by others waiting to go on the raid. Ulf wrapped his new cloak that Inga had made for him around his shoulders and took a deep breath before he made to leave the stables.

'Where are you going?' Thorir asked as he sat up and rubbed the sleep from his eyes.

'You go home. Go back to your father's farm and live, Thorir,' Ulf said and left the stables. He eyed the grey clouds and wondered how much longer they'd have to wait for summer. Ulf had had enough of the cold winter and longed to feel the warmth of the sun.

Thorir chased after him, even as he struggled with his cloak. 'What do you mean, go home?'

Ulf sighed. 'You are no warrior and the battleground is no place for a bóndi.'

Thorir grabbed Ulf by his shoulder and turned him around so they were facing each other. Ulf clenched his fists and glared at Thorir as he dug his fingers into Ulf's shoulder. Even through the brynja and the cloak, Ulf could feel the man's strength. 'I am not just a bóndi. I can also be a warrior. You just want to get all the glory so that Eldrid lifts her dress for you.' Ulf felt his anger ignite in the pit of his stomach and had to fight the urge to punch Thorir in the face. But then Thorir's face paled and he let go of Ulf. 'Forgive me, Ulf. I did not...' Thorir looked at his feet. 'I can't go back. My entire life, I wanted to be more than a farmer, a bóndi. I wanted to be a warrior, like the ones you hear about in the sagas.'

Ulf's anger vanished as he remembered wanting the same when he was just a child. But Thorir was not a child. He was older than Ulf and should know that the sagas only ever talked of the few who survived, and never of the many who had died. Of the warriors who prayed for mercy as their tears soaked their beards and their blood soaked the battleground. Ulf glanced at Thorir's one-handed axe and wondered if it had ever tasted the blood of another person. 'Don't believe the sagas, Thorir. They only lie to you. The shield wall is not a place you want to be.' Even as Ulf said that, he remembered how Snorri and his men loved nothing more than fighting in the shield wall. How they had relished the clash of shields and sounds of their enemies dying. But Thorir was not Snorri. And neither was Ulf.

'But there won't be any shield walls,' Thorir said with a conviction that Ulf didn't understand. 'The Franks will run when they see us coming. Not even their god can protect them. Asketill told me many stories of when he was a warrior. He told me how the Christians just ran when they saw our ships.'

Ulf wanted to tell Thorir that Asketill had never been on a raid. The old man might have told many stories, but Ulf could see in Asketill's eyes that he had never taken the life of another man. But then Ulf sighed as he decided it was not his responsibility to correct the man. If Thorir wanted to believe the old man's tales, then that was his problem. 'Aye,' he said as he turned and walked away.

'So where do we find this jarl?'

'Jarl Knut?' Ulf raised an eyebrow as he wondered the same. 'He said he has a camp outside the town, so we just need to find out which camp is his.' *And avoid Ragnar or any of his men*, Ulf thought as they walked through the busy streets of Jelling. Ulf had always been amazed by the amount of people who lived here and had often wondered why. He always felt suffocated when they came to large towns like Jelling and had realised a long time ago that he preferred living on a farmstead. Although, Ulf knew that life was not for him.

It didn't take them long before they found Jarl Knut's camp. The first person they asked pointed them to the largest camp outside the town walls and before it was time for the morning meal, Ulf and Thorir were walking towards the large tent in the centre of the camp. Ulf felt all the Danish warriors stare at him, their eyes squinted and mouths twitching as they scrutinised him and Thorir. Some of them pointed at Ulf and laughed while others only glared, but unlike Thorir who was almost trembling, Ulf barely blinked at it. He was used to this kind of scrutiny. People always stared at him because of the scars on his face, and Ormstunga always attracted plenty of attention because of her golden hilt. So

Ulf ignored the warriors as he stopped in front of the tent of Jarl Knut.

'What do you bastards want?' the warrior standing in front of the tent asked and Ulf recognised him as one of the warriors that were with Jarl Knut the day before.

'Jarl Knut is expecting us.'

The warrior raised an eyebrow, and Ulf sensed the other warriors circling behind him. 'Is he now?'

'Ulf?' Thorir said, his fear obvious in his voice.

Ulf sighed and wondered why he hadn't thought that this might be a trap. Why else would Jarl Knut tell him to find him? The jarl was a friend of Jarl Ragnar, or at least that was what Ulf believed. He had been there that night. Ulf's hand went to his axe as he glanced at the sun in the sky. There were a few clouds, but not enough to allow him to draw Ormstunga. 'We don't want any trouble. Jarl Knut told us he might know someone who could use our services and told us to come to him.'

'Jarl Knut didn't tell me anything about that.' The warrior took a step towards Ulf, who refused to back down. The man might have been older than Ulf and had fought more battles, but Ulf was still taller than him and had fought enough battles not to be threatened by him. Even if his oath to Odin was the only reason he had survived those battles, and that oath was no longer valid. But still, Ulf refused to back down as he wondered what the man's problem was. The warrior was there when Jarl Knut had told them to come to his camp.

Thorir pulled on Ulf's cloak. 'Maybe we should leave, Ulf.'

'You should listen to your friend,' the warrior said, and Ulf shook his head.

'I'm not going anywhere until I see Jarl Knut.'

The other warriors came closer and Ulf heard a few of them laughing, but he couldn't just walk away as his ancestors stirred in his ears. He gripped the head of the axe, waiting for the warrior to make the first move, when someone came out of the tent.

'What, in Odin's name, is going on here?'

The warrior in front of the tent kept his eyes on Ulf as he answered. 'This ugly bastard said the jarl told him to come talk to him.'

'You know the jarl did, Hallr. So let the ugly bastard and his friend in.'

The warrior grinned at Ulf. 'I was just having a bit of fun.'

Ulf gritted his teeth and ignored the laughing warrior as he tried to walk past him. But then the warrior put his hand on Ulf's chest and Ulf fought hard not to kill him.

'Not with that pretty sword of yours, or the axe,' Hallr said. 'No weapons in the tent.'

Ulf clenched his fists as Thorir handed his axe and sax-knife over. He knew it was the custom to leave weapons outside a jarl's hall or tent, but he didn't want to leave Ormstunga in the care of people he didn't know. Especially not with the glint he saw in the man's eyes as he glanced at Ormstunga.

'No,' Ulf said.

'What do you mean, no?' The warrior glared at him. 'I said no weapons in the tent.'

'And I'm not leaving my sword with you.'

Hallr took a step towards Ulf. 'Think you're a tough guy just because you have a pretty sword?'

'They say he killed a bear with his hands tied behind his back,' Thorir said, which only made the warriors laugh.

'No wonder his face is all messed up. Probably not the only thing the bear messed up,' the warrior guarding the tent said as the others laughed.

Ulf glared at Thorir, who shrugged an apology at him, and took deep breaths to stop his anger from taking over. Already the voices of his ancestors were whispering in his ears, telling him to slaughter everyone. To take his axe and to bury it in the man's skull.

'I think you made the bear fucker angry,' someone said, which only made the warriors laugh even more. Even Thorir smiled as the voices got louder.

'He can't be a bear fucker, because the bear fucked hi—'

Hallr barely finished the last word before Ulf punched him. All his anger went into the punch that caught the man in the mouth and knocked one of his teeth out. Before Hallr landed on the ground, the others rushed at Ulf. He ducked under one punch, spreading his legs wide so he could get lower than the shorter man, and blocked another before someone kicked his legs out from under him. Ulf landed hard, but rolled to his feet before the warrior could stomp on his face, and punched the man in the face. Ulf turned to face the others when he was grabbed from behind.

'Let go of me!' he screamed as Thorir backed away from the group of warriors approaching him.

'Today you die for what you did to our friends,' someone whispered in his ears. Ulf barely heard the words over the sound of his blood pumping in his ears. He roared as he stomped on the foot of one warrior holding him, but before Ulf could take advantage of his free hand, another punched him in the stomach with the head of his axe. Ulf grunted and would have dropped to his knees if it hadn't been for the other warrior holding him. His ears rang as he was punched in the face again, which silenced the voices of his ancestors, and there was nothing he could do as the others piled in on him.

He clenched his jaw as punches landed all over his body and, for a moment, he forgot about Thorir as he struggled to free his hands so that he could protect his face.

'Enough!' a voice boomed over everything, like thunder on a clear day, and the punches stopped. 'Let go of him.'

The warriors holding on to Ulf let go, and he dropped to the ground. He spat blood out of his mouth and then wiped it clean with his cloak before he struggled to his feet.

'Stay down, Ulf,' Thorir pleaded, but Ulf ignored him. He refused to stay down. If these bastards wanted to kill him, then they would have to fight him for it. He pulled the one-handed axe from his belt and glared at the surrounding warriors, even as he struggled to stand straight.

'Who's first?' he asked and then frowned as Jarl Knut laughed.

'See, I told you the bastard has a lot of fight in him.'

Ulf turned and glared at Jarl Knut, still believing this was some kind of trap. He frowned at the man standing beside the jarl, at least a head taller and a few winters younger, as he tucked his thumbs into his belt and scrutinised Ulf and the few warriors on the ground.

'Aye, he's got fight.' The man's eyes lingered on Ulf's scars, which annoyed him. Ulf tightened the grip on his axe and glanced at Jarl Knut's warriors around him, many of them looking like they were about to jump him again. 'But can he be relied on? My warriors are disciplined. They fight as one. This one seems to want to fight everyone.'

Jarl Knut laughed again. 'Aye, the gods know he's got to learn to deal with his anger. And his fighting needs to be worked on a bit. But he's fast. Caught Jarl Ragnar by surprise and not many manage that.'

The man raised an eyebrow and Ulf gritted his teeth as they spoke about him, as if he was some priced bull. Then he wondered if he was a bull to be bred or to be sacrificed to the gods. The hairs on the back of his neck tingled at the thought, and Ulf couldn't help but wonder if she was here, watching him. But there was no sign of her and when he turned his attention back to Jarl Knut and the other man, he saw they were both frowning at him.

'Bastard just attacked us.' Hallr got back to his feet, his mouth and beard covered in blood. 'Should be hanged.'

Ulf growled at the man, who only glared back at him.

'No one just attacks you, Hallr.'

'But he did,' another said. 'His friend as well.'

Ulf glanced over his shoulder at Thorir and frowned at his swollen eye and bloodied grin. Perhaps he had misjudged the bóndi. He turned his attention back to Jarl Knut. 'Your man laid a hand on me. He's lucky he still has that hand.'

'I was only doing what the jarl told me to do.' The man looked at his jarl. 'Knocked my tooth out, the bastard.'

Jarl Knut glared at the rest of his warriors, who looked away from his glare, even the one whose tooth Ulf had knocked out. Ulf wondered who Jarl Knut was for his men to fear him so much. 'I might be old, but the gods have not taken my hearing from me yet. Jarl Hakon and I heard everything that was said.'

'And you did nothing to stop it?' Ulf asked, surprising himself.

Jarl Knut shrugged. 'I thought it would be a good chance to show Jarl Hakon how you fight.'

Jarl Hakon smiled as Jarl Knut said the words and again, Ulf felt the hairs standing on end on the back of his neck. His hand went to Ormstunga's hilt, and he wondered what danger the volva was trying to warn him about.

Chapter 12

'By Thor! Who are these two bastards?' an old warrior asked as Jarl Hakon took Ulf and Thorir to his camp not far from Jarl Knut's. Ulf eyed the old man, his face covered in more scars than Ulf had on his entire body and his left hand missing, while Thorir was staring wide-eyed at the camp they were in. Like Jarl Knut's camp, tents were put up wherever the warriors could find a spot and campfires dotted between them. The warriors all looked like they had not stopped fighting since the day they first learnt to walk and many of them sported fresh scars, which made Ulf think they had recently been in a battle.

'This one,' Jarl Hakon pointed at Ulf, 'is the one they claimed killed Griml Troll-Face.' Ulf raised his eyebrows at Jarl Hakon as many of the surrounding warriors gasped and gaped at him.

'Thor's balls, that can't be true!'

'Aye, he's too skinny to have killed that giant turd!' another added. Ulf glanced at his arms. He had lost much weight during the winter, as the old folks didn't have much to feed him, but he still would not have called himself skinny.

'Who is Griml Troll-Face?' Thorir asked, frowning at Ulf.

'Griml Troll-Face was a vicious bastard who killed his jarl, my brother and everyone we sent after him,' Jarl Hakon said.

'Griml is also the bastard that took my hand!' the old man said. 'I prayed many nights, begging Odin to send Griml back north so I could deal with him. And you tell me this ugly bastard is the one that killed him?'

Jarl Hakon nodded, a smile on his face. 'You all heard the story. A group of warriors led by a young scar-faced warrior and how that warrior used one of Thor's lightning bolts to kill Griml.'

'I used my uncle's axe to kill him, not a lightning bolt.' Ulf gritted his teeth as he remembered that fight. But it was not hard to. He dreamt of it most nights. 'And I didn't lead the group. Snorri Thorgilsson did.'

'Aye, Jarl Snorri,' Jarl Hakon said, and Ulf frowned. It was strange to hear him addressed like that, even though Ulf knew Snorri had become jarl of Thorgilsstad. 'We also heard how you killed his father.'

Again, the warriors around Ulf gaped at him and even Thorir stared at him, his mouth open in shock. 'You killed a jarl? By the gods, no wonder you are cursed,' the bóndi said, and many of the warriors rubbed the hilts of their swords or the Mjöllnir pendants around their necks.

'You brought a cursed warrior into our camp? Have you lost your wits, Hakon?' the old man said.

Ulf wanted to explain that he had killed Snorri's father by mistake. He had only defended himself from the jarl's attack, but he knew these men would not care about that. He had killed a jarl and perhaps Thorir was right. Perhaps he was cursed because of it.

Jarl Hakon shrugged, his smile still on his face. 'I brought a warrior of renown into our camp. I also brought a warrior who gave

Ragnar a bruised face.' Again, the surrounding warriors gasped as they stared at him.

The old man nodded, but his creased eyebrow showed he was still unconvinced. 'And who is the Dane?'

'My name is Thorir Randolfson, and I am going to be a great warrior. Just like Ulf Bear-Slayer, here.' Thorir puffed his chest out, which caused some warriors to laugh and Ulf to shake his head. *You don't want to be like me*, he thought, but kept to himself.

The old man shook his head and glared at Jarl Hakon. 'This is why you shouldn't be allowed to go off by yourself, Hakon. You make dumb decisions.' Jarl Hakon laughed as the old man turned and walked away.

'Don't mind old Ragnvald. He's been bitter ever since he lost his hand.' Jarl Hakon gripped Ulf by the shoulder. 'Now come, let's find you somewhere to sleep.' He led them to the edge of the camp as Ulf wondered who the old man was and why he spoke the way he did to Jarl Hakon. And more importantly, why the jarl allowed him to do it?

'You are from Norway?' Thorir asked as they walked past warriors sitting by their tents, some of them cleaning and sharpening weapons, while others slept in the afternoon sun. It was the same as every camp Ulf had been in and he realised he missed sharing these quiet moments with Snorri and his friends.

'Aye, from the north. A land of mountains and fjords. Nothing to do there but to fight and fuck.' Jarl Hakon laughed at his own words as Thorir gaped at him.

'So why are you here? In Denmark?' Ulf asked as he glanced at the Norse warriors around him.

Jarl Hakon shrugged. 'Jarl Knut and I go back many winters. I was visiting his hall when he received word of the raid, so I joined.' The jarl stopped and looked at Ulf. 'I heard you raided West Francia before.'

Ulf nodded as Thorir gaped at him again. He wished the bóndi would stop doing that before Loki used his magic to make sure that his face stayed that way. 'We joined with a jarl from Denmark, who joined up with another.'

Jarl Hakon clapped him on the shoulder and walked on. 'Good. The gods know it would be useful to have someone who knows the land when we are there.'

Ulf frowned at the jarl as Thorir stared at him.

'You raided West Francia?' Ulf nodded, but said nothing as he followed the jarl. 'By the gods, you must tell me about it.'

'I'd rather not,' Ulf said.

'You can put your tent and your belongings here. Tomorrow, old Ragnvald will run some drills with some of the men, so make sure you are there.' He pointed to an empty spot near the edge of his camp, before he turned and walked away, leaving Ulf and Thorir staring at his back.

'We don't have a tent,' Thorir said.

'Aye, we don't.' Ulf rubbed his head and then glanced behind him as he felt that familiar feeling again. 'Follow me,' Ulf said as he walked back to Jelling.

'Where are we going?'

'To find a tent and you some armour.'

'A brynja, like yours?' Thorir's eyes lit up like a young man seeing a woman naked for the first time, and Ulf shook his head.

'Can't afford a brynja. You'll have to make do with a leather jerkin.'

'How did you get your brynja?'

'Took it off a warrior I killed,' Ulf responded, which was only half true. Snorri had given it to him, after taking it off a warrior Ulf had killed.

They walked in silence after that until they reached the market which looked the same as the last time Ulf had been there, but the noise of the traders competing for customers bothered him more than it had before. Townspeople were all jostling with each other to get to the stalls and buy the products they wanted before they disappeared. They cleared a path for Ulf when they saw his glare and bruised face, made worse by the scars on his face. The glare might have been because of his headache, an aftereffect from the fight he had earlier, or it was because he was nervous about running into Tormod and Ingolfr. Ulf would rather avoid them than let them see him fresh after another fight. Thorir, his also bruised face, did not help, and Ulf wondered if he should have left the man back in the camp. But in the end, there was no sign of the trader brothers, which made Ulf even more nervous. Ulf prayed to Thor that nothing bad had happened to them. He bought a tent for him and Thorir and a leather jerkin for the bóndi with the last of his arm rings, but he had promised Inga that he would look after Thorir. Something Ulf had never been good at, but he was determined to try.

As they left the market square, Ulf caught a movement in the corner of his eye. He wasn't sure why that movement made him stop in his tracks, especially as the market square was filled with people moving around. But something about the dark hair he caught sight of made him shiver. His hand went to his axe, and he turned to Thorir, who was carrying everything he had bought.

'Wait here.' Ulf walked away before Thorir could respond. He didn't know where he was going, and just walked in the direction he thought the dark hair went. Ulf, his hand still on his axe, turned a corner and braced himself as if he expected her to be standing there. He sighed with relief when all he saw was the people of Jelling frowning at him. A boy pointed at him and said something to his mother and when his mother looked up and saw the scars on Ulf's face, she dragged her son away. Ulf stood there for a few heartbeats, scanning the street for any sign of whatever it had been that had caught his attention before. Deciding that it must have been his imagination, Ulf turned and went back to Thorir.

'What was that?'

'Nothing,' Ulf said, resisting the urge to rub the Mjöllnir pendant around his neck. He rubbed the iron head of his axe, though, and hoped that that would be enough to chase the evil he felt around him away.

***

For the next few days, Ragnvald worked them hard. Denmark was shaking off winter's grip, but the days were still short, and the old bastard made them run drills from sunrise to sunset. He seemed to enjoy pushing Ulf past his limits and Ulf often wondered what he had done to upset Ragnvald.

Thorir had not fared much better. The stocky man might have been used to hard work on the farm, but the life of a warrior was a different type of hard work. One his body was not used to. The first day, he had puked up his morning meal after Ragnvald had made them run laps around the camp until they collapsed, and in the evening, he had been too exhausted to eat. The next day had been much the same, only this time, they had to run wearing their armour. Ulf was glad that he was already used to the weight of his brynja, but it was still difficult. After that, it was weapons training. Thorir had struggled with that. Like Ulf, he was not a natural warrior, but Ulf at least had mentors who had treated him better. Ragnvald often shouted abuse at them and encouraged Jarl Hakon's men to be extra violent, something they all relished.

'By Odin, why do I have to suffer because the old bastard hates you,' Thorir had complained after the fourth day, as he rubbed his bruised arm where he had been struck by one of Hakon's men.

Ulf shrugged. 'I told you to go home.'

Thorir smiled. 'And I told you I can't. I promised old Inga I'd take care of you.'

Ulf raised an eyebrow at the bóndi and wondered if he was being serious, but then guessed the man was. Inga had been kind to him and Ulf had thought it was because he had saved her life, but now wondered if it was not more than that. 'I'm not the one Inga needs to worry about. And besides, I also don't know why Ragnvald hates me.'

The following morning, Ulf and Thorir were on their way to the training ground when they saw most of Jarl Hakon's men grouped together. The way they were smiling at Ulf made him nervous, and it seemed that Thorir felt the same.

'Why do I feel like a goat about to be slaughtered?'

The group parted and Ulf saw Ragnvald and Jarl Hakon standing in the centre of the group, both looking grim, and Ragnvald with his sword in his hand. 'Because I think we are goats about to be slaughtered.' And the idea angered Ulf. He was no goat. He was a wolf, and another was threatening him.

They stopped in front of Jarl Hakon and Ragnvald. Ulf glanced over his shoulder as Jarl Hakon's men closed up behind them.

'What's going on?' he asked Jarl Hakon, his hands already trembling.

Jarl Hakon stared at him and Thorir for a moment, his face creased as he judged them. 'Tomorrow we sail for West Francia. Over two hundred ships, I am told.' Someone whistled at that, and even Ulf raised an eyebrow at that number. 'I need to make sure that you two are good enough to join my army and fight under my banner.'

'You invited us to join your army, and now you want to test us?' Ulf asked, his anger growing with every heartbeat.

'I did not invite you. Jarl Knut suggested I take you. I know you gave Ragnar a bruise, and you killed some of his men. But they are all Danes and the Danes can't fight. Not the way we Norse do.' Jarl Hakon smiled at Thorir, who bristled at his words. Even Ulf thought that was unfair. Thorir had done well over the last few days, even though he was not a warrior.

He glanced at Ragnvald, who was rolling his neck. 'And we have to fight him?'

Ragnvald shook his head. 'Not the Dane. Only you.' Some of the men laughed, and again, Ulf wondered why Ragnvald hated him. He glanced at the sky and saw thick clouds covered the sun, but had already decided that Ormstunga would stay in her scabbard. She would demand death, and Ulf did not want to kill the old fool. Just to make sure, he unbuckled the sword from his waist and handed it to Thorir.

'Whatever you do, do not draw her blade.'

Thorir stared at the sword as if it was a draugr come to eat him as he nodded at Ulf.

'When I beat you, I get that pretty sword of yours,' Ragnvald said.

'You don't want that sword.' Ulf took his axe from his belt. Ulf had tied a leather strap around the hilt so that he had a better grip of the axe. The last thing he wanted was for the axe to slip from his sweaty hand while fighting. He glared at the one-handed warrior as he swung his sword in wide arcs. 'This has nothing do to with testing us for the raid, does it?'

Ragnvald shook his head as Jarl Hakon moved out of the way and his men formed a circle around them. 'Odin knows I've been watching you closely over the last few days and I still can't see how you defeated Griml. So I decided to test you for myself.'

'This is about Griml?' Ulf frowned, wondering why the giant troll still haunted him, even after his death.

'This is about what was taken from me!' Ragnvald attacked even as the words came out of his mouth. The old man moved faster than Ulf had expected, but he still dodged out of the way of Ragnvald's sword as he stabbed at Ulf's stomach. Ulf saw an opening where he could bury his axe in the back of Ragnvald's neck, but decided not to take it as he stepped back.

'What did I take away from you?'

Ragnvald turned and swiped his sword at Ulf's face. Ulf stepped back again, using his speed to stay out of the reach of

Ragnvald's sword. 'Stop talking and fight!' He stabbed at Ulf, who twisted out of the way and kept his axe low.

'What did I take from you?' Ulf asked again. Ragnvald roared at him and made to stab high with his sword. As Ulf ducked to avoid the blow he thought was coming, Ragnvald kicked him in the face. Hakon's men cheered as Ulf staggered back, his vision blurred from the kick. At that moment, he realised he had never asked what the rules of this fight were and panic gripped him when he sensed the old warrior charging at him. Ulf dropped to his knees and felt Ragnvald's sword swing over his head. He punched out with his axe, more in desperation than wanting to fight, but the axe missed. Ulf's vision cleared in time for him to see Ragnvald stab at him and he avoided the sword as it came for his chest. The voices of his ancestors started whispering in his ears, and Ulf did his best to ignore them as he deflected another stab with his axe. Out of instinct, he punched Ragnvald in his exposed side, but the old man's brynja hurt his fist more than the punch seemed to hurt him.

'That all you got?' Ragnvald said. 'And you claim you killed Griml Troll-Face!' He swung his sword again, a backhanded swing that caught Ulf by surprise and if it hadn't been for Ulf's brynja, then he might have died there. But instead, the edge of Ragnvald's sword scraped along his chest and sent him back a few steps. Ulf resisted the urge to clutch his chest because of the pain and twisted out of the way of Ragnvald's sword as the older warrior attacked again. 'Griml would have eaten you alive!'

Ulf's anger started taking hold of him, making it harder to ignore the voices of his ancestors. He knew that if he gave into them, then he might kill the old bastard. But if he ignored them, then he might die. And he still didn't know why Ragnvald hated him so much. He kicked the back of Ragnvald's leg and, as the old warrior dropped to his knee, Ulf struck him on the side of his head with his elbow. Ragnvald's head snapped to the side and Thorir shouted in support, but was quickly silenced by the glares from Jarl Hakon's men as Ulf turned to the jarl. 'By Tyr, stop this!'

Jarl Hakon only shook his head as he watched them, his face as cold as a frozen river.

Ragnvald stood up and shook his head. 'I'm disappointed in you, Bear-Slayer. The bear you killed was probably already dead as well.' Some warriors laughed as Ulf backed away. He tightened his grip on his axe and tried to think of a way out of this, but knew there was none. Ragnvald wanted to hurt him, and Ulf couldn't understand why. 'So how did you kill Griml, Ulf Bear-Slayer? How did you kill him if you can barely handle a one-handed old man like me?' Again, Jarl Hakon's warriors laughed as Ulf glanced at Thorir. The Dane's face was pale as he watched the fight and Ulf hoped they would at least let him go.

'I didn't fight him on my own. I could never defeat him on my own. No matter how many times I tried,' Ulf said, hoping that would make Ragnvald back off. But the old warrior used it to goad him even more.

'So others did all the fighting, and you snuck up behind Griml, stabbed him in the back with that pretty sword of yours.'

'No,' Ulf said as the voices got louder in his ears, almost drowning out the cheering of Jarl Hakon's warriors.

Ragnvald hawked and spat. 'You're a coward, Ulf Bear-Slayer. And I don't sail with cowards.'

'I am no coward!' Ulf glared at the old warrior. 'I fought Griml! More than once! What have you done?' Ragnvald raised an eyebrow at him. 'I killed Griml. I avenged my family while you hid away!'

Ragnvald smiled. 'Fine. Now that you are angry, let's see what you can do.' Before Ulf could respond, he charged at him.

Ulf stepped out of the way of his sword and raised his axe to take his other hand, but then pulled back as he fought to control his anger. Ragnvald turned and sliced his sword at Ulf's stomach, but Ulf jumped back and the blade missed. The old warrior kept attacking Ulf as those watching went quiet, but Ulf avoided each stab, each cut of Ragnvald's sword, and not once tried to fight back. His pace, fuelled by his anger, was too much for the Ragnvald, who was soon breathing heavily as he tried to get to Ulf. But Ulf was getting fed up with this, and that he still didn't know if this fight was only to first blood or to death, only made him angrier.

'Fight me, you bastard!' Ragnvald roared, also unable to control his anger, but still Jarl Hakon did not stop the fight. 'Did you run away like this when Griml killed your family?'

Ulf stopped and for a moment saw nothing but the family he had lost, and not just them, but all the friends who had been killed by Griml. The axe fell from his hand as he staggered backward, the words landing a harder blow than Ragnvald's sword. Ragnvald must have sensed his moment and attacked, and if it wasn't for Thorir's cry of alarm, then Ulf might not have seen it. He stepped out of the way of Ragnvald's sword and punched the old warrior in the side of his head. Ragnvald staggered sideways and there was nothing he could do as Ulf followed up with another punch. Ulf barely heard Ragnvald's nose crunch before he kicked him in the chest and sent the older man flying onto his back. Before Ragnvald could get to his feet, Ulf jumped on him and punched again and again. Hands grabbed him from behind, but Ulf shook them off and kept on punching the old warrior. 'What did I do to you?' Ulf roared between punches as Jarl Hakon's men struggled to get him off the old man. 'Why do you hate me? Why?' Ulf grabbed Ragnvald by his brynja. 'Why do you hate me? What did I do to you?'

Someone struck Ulf on the side of his head, which allowed the others to grab Ulf and drag him away from Ragnvald. But before he let go of the old man, Ulf heard him say, 'You killed my son. You killed Griml.'

Chapter 13

He stopped, shoulders hunched and fur raised. He didn't know why he stopped, but something made him do it. He scanned his surroundings but saw only the darkness. Still only the darkness. He had lost track of how long he had walked or when his paws started bleeding, but still there was only the darkness. And worse, he wasn't alone. Not this time. She was here, following him. Watching him. He did not need to see her to know that. He could sense her presence in the darkness. Like a blade at his throat. But what frightened him more was the other presence he felt. This one similar, but far larger. Behind him, beside him and even above him.

He sniffed the air, more out of habit than expectation, and frowned when he smelt something other than death in the air. He looked around, but still saw nothing. He turned around, trying to find the snake, but as before, he could not see her. Even the cloaked figure was nowhere, but he forgot about them as he sniffed the air again and tried to make sense of this new smell. Salty air. He frowned as he tried to work out what that meant when something touched his paw. He yelped as he jumped back, but then sniffed the air again. Still, he could smell the salt in the air. And then there was a new noise, one he had not heard in a long time. Or at least it felt like that as he listened to the sound of waves crashing against rocks.

Cautiously, he took a step forward and felt his paw touch the water. He took a step back, not understanding what was going on or where he was. Was this a trap? Would he drown if he went into the water? It was her domain, after all. The giant serpent that watched him, that waited for him to make another mistake like he had before. Was she luring him there?

He shook his head. I don't want to go there. Not again.

Then don't. The response came from the darkness.

He frowned, wondering who responded to him. But I have to. She needs me.

No, she doesn't. Turn and go back. Only death waits for you there.

He growled at the words and felt his body tremble with rage. Death waits for me everywhere. Why is this different?

He waited for a response, but none came. All he heard were the sounds of the waves. He turned around, glaring into the darkness. Where are you? What do you want from me?

Laughter broke through the waves creasing against the stones, a loud sound that rung in his ears and chased his anger away.

Only death waits for you there.

***

Ulf opened his eyes and stared at the sail as it bulged in the wind. Above the sail, clouds filled the sky and seabirds circled, their calls echoing off the seawater as it crashed against the hull of Jarl Hakon's ship. He took a deep breath, willing the sea air to chase the remnants of the dream away, before he sat up and looked around him. Warriors were doing much the same as him. Some were sleeping while others sat in groups and told stories and sharpened weapons. Beside Ulf, Thorir gripped the side of the ship, his eyes wide as he stared at the sea surrounding him. Thorir had never sailed before and screamed with joy when a whale broke through the surface of the water the day before.

Ulf stood up and stretched, his legs adjusting to the motion of the ship so he wouldn't fall over, while looking at Jarl Hakon's other ship sailing beside them. Ragnvald was on that ship, staring at him, and Ulf felt his anger reignite. It had been three days since the fight with the old man, and his words still rang in his ears. Ragnvald was Griml's father. He was the father of the man who had killed his family and friends. And he hated Ulf for killing his son. Or did he? Ulf still didn't understand what Ragnvald wanted. He turned to where Jarl Hakon stood by the stern of the ship, the steering oar in his hand. Jarl Hakon waved at him, and Ulf decided it was time to get some answers. Some of the warriors glared at Ulf as he walked past them, either not happy with the fact that he beat Ragnvald or with how he beat him. Ulf didn't know and didn't care. He never wanted to fight the old man, but Ragnvald had pushed him until he had no choice. Other warriors clapped him on the shoulder and smiled at him. Many of them even offered him some of their food and ale. Thorir had enjoyed the extra attention, though, as if Ulf's victory had been his as well. That was why Ragnvald was not on the same ship as Jarl Hakon. Ulf guessed the jarl didn't want any more problems.

'Njörd blesses us today.' Jarl Hakon smiled when Ulf reached him. 'Good winds, so we don't have to row and no sun to burn our skin. Couldn't ask for better weather.'

Ulf nodded as he scanned the surrounding ships. More than two hundred, he had been told, and even though it was not the first time he had seen a fleet this large, it still took his breath away. He didn't even try to work out how many warriors there were, but guessed it must have been more than the number of fish in the seas. Jarls from all over Denmark and even some from Norway had added their ships and warriors to this raid, and Ulf felt sorry for the people of West Francia. Many of them hated the Norse and the Danes, Ulf knew that, but he also knew there were many who were just trying to survive and provide for their families. 'Why did you let Ragnvald attack me like that?'

Jarl Hakon's face went serious as he stared at his other ship where Ragnvald stood watching them. 'It was his right. You killed his son.'

Ulf clenched his fists. Jarl Hakon had avoided him since the fight, as had Ragnvald, although he had avoided the old man as well. Ulf had been surprised when he was told that he and Thorir would sail on the jarl's ship and not his other one. 'His son slaughtered my family and stole my father's sword. He sacrificed my friend to Odin.'

'He also killed my brother and my niece. As well as many people I called friends,' Jarl Hakon said to him. 'The gods know I am very aware of what Griml was, but Ragnvald is his father and has a right to challenge you for killing his son.'

Ulf shook his head, unable to understand anything that Jarl Hakon was saying. 'Why do you let the father of the man who killed your family sail with you? Even more, you let him tell you what to do.'

Anger flashed in Jarl Hakon's eyes, but then he took a deep breath and watched the sea bird for a few heartbeats. 'The father is not like the son, and the son is not like the father. Odin is as dark as the night sky, while Baldur shone as brightly as the sun. They were father and son, yet they were very different from each other. Ragnvald taught me how to fight and how to be a man. He is more like a father to me than my own father was.' Jarl Hakon pulled on the steering oar as Ulf thought about his words.

'But Griml was still his son.'

'Aye, and not a day has gone by since he attacked my brother that Ragnvald has not been ashamed of what his son did. He tried to stop him that day and Griml took his hand.'

Ulf's brows creased as he stared at Ragnvald again. 'Then why is he angry at me for killing his son?'

Again, Jarl Hakon did not respond straight away, and when he did, it was not what Ulf had expected. 'Tell me about the fight against Griml.'

Ulf glanced at him and thought about refusing. It was not a day that he wanted to relive. He had done his best to forget about that battle and everything that had happened since. But then he shrugged to himself and told Jarl Hakon what he remembered. Which was everything, because despite his best efforts to forget, Ulf remembered every moment of the day when he killed Griml. When he was done, Jarl Hakon nodded and then looked at Ragnvald on the other ship.

'Sounds like a fight the gods would have enjoyed.' He waited for Ulf to say something, but Ulf didn't know what to say to that. He knew the gods had enjoyed that fight because they had made sure it had happened. 'Ragnvald doesn't hate you because you killed his son. He hates you because you took that from him.'

Ulf widened his eyes as he stared at Jarl Hakon. 'He wanted to kill his own son?'

Jarl Hakon smiled, but it was not a happy smile. 'Ragnvald had disowned Griml after that day, but he still saw it as his responsibility to make him pay for the crimes he had committed.'

'Then why didn't he?'

'Because we couldn't find him. We had sent many men after him and most of them ended up dead and others we never found. We heard rumours of a sea king in the north of Denmark called Griml Jotun, but by the time we got there, he was already gone. Then we heard of the battle in the south of Norway, but we could find no sign of the troll after that.' Jarl Hakon glanced at Ulf. 'That was until we heard about his death in Francia.'

'How did you hear about it?' Ulf asked as he followed the path of a seabird.

'We were in Denmark when the remnants of his army returned. They told us. Also told us many other strange stories, and many seemed to involve a young warrior with scars matching yours.'

Ulf looked at Jarl Hakon. 'So you told Jarl Knut about me?'

Jarl Hakon shook his head. 'We heard you were banished from Norway by King Halfdan of Vestfold, although you could have come north. His laws only apply in his region, not ours. But then you just vanished and there were no more tales of the young scar-faced warrior who kills bears and giant trolls.' Ulf nodded, but said nothing. Unlike Denmark, Norway wasn't ruled by one king, but was instead made up of small kingdoms and ruled by self-made kings. Although Ulf knew that anyone with more than a hundred warriors could call himself king, but those men never lived long. There was always someone with a larger army who wanted their land. Ulf followed the seabirds again and wondered if he would live long enough to see Norway united under one king, like Denmark was. Would he even want to? The reason the Norse were better warriors than the Danes was because when they weren't out raiding other lands, they were fighting each other on behalf of their so-called kings.

Ulf looked towards the front of the fleet, to where Jarl Ragnar's ship was. The leader of this enormous pack of sea wolves hunting an unexpecting prey to the west. Jarl Ragnar would have been a king in Norway, and a powerful one at that, with the men he had and all the other jarls he could bring together. But in Denmark, he was just a jarl. Ulf frowned as he wondered if King Halfdan would have accepted that fate. He turned his attention back to Jarl Hakon, who was staring at the sea as he steered his ship. 'Ragnvald will not let this go, will he?'

Jarl Hakon glanced at Ulf with a smile on his face. 'Only the Norns really know what Ragnvald will do. But not only did you kill his son and take away from him what he believed would have restored his honour, you also humiliated him in front of all the men.' Jarl Hakon shook his head. 'No, Ulf Bear-Slayer. I doubt Ragnvald will let this go. If I were you, I'd keep my distance from him.'

Ulf looked up at the seabirds circling about him, their cries sounding more like mocking laughter with every heartbeat as he wondered how he was supposed to avoid the old bastard when they were going to stand in the shield wall together.

Chapter 14

'Is that it?' Thorir asked as they stared at the mouth of the large river.

They had sailed for many days, around the tip of Denmark and across the North Sea. They sailed past Britain, an island full of wealthy kingdoms and rich lands, and then they sailed around the coast of the Frankish kingdom until they reached this river. The journey had not been pleasant, and Ulf often wondered why Jarl Ragnar wanted to set off for the raid when winter had not passed yet. Ulf knew that most jarls waited until spring or early summer before they started raiding. Many of the men who went raiding were bóndi, like Thorir, and needed to plant their crops first before they could leave their farms. Although, Ulf sensed that was changing, even in Denmark, as more men and women decided to be full-time warriors. The risks were higher, but so were the rewards.

Njörd had blessed them with good winds and little rain, but the sun lacked the warmth of the summer, which meant that most of the warriors had spent their time wrapped in their cloaks and huddled together for warmth. The cold did not seem to bother Jarl Hakon, or many of his men, but then Ulf had heard that the north of Norway was colder than Denmark. A land of mountains and frost, where Thor fought the ice giants whenever he got bored.

'You raided here before?' Thorir asked when Ulf didn't respond to his first question.

Ulf nodded, but said nothing as he stared at the mouth of the river and remembered what had happened the last time he had sailed up it. It was by a large walled city up this river where he had killed Eldrid's brother, when he had attacked Snorri's men after pretending to be a friend. Even though it was four winters ago, the memory still burnt bright in Ulf's mind, and he felt his heart racing.

'You never talk about it.' Thorir frowned at him. 'The other warriors told me many stories of their past raids and battles, but you never say anything about it.' Ulf raised an eyebrow at the bóndi. Unlike Ulf, who had kept to himself, Thorir had befriended some warriors on the ship and would often sit with them. Ulf had been happy about that, though, because Thorir's constant questions and boasting were starting to annoy him. The bóndi knew nothing about the shield wall, or of what it felt like to watch a man's life leave his eyes, but yet he kept insisting that he would be a great warrior. 'Some of the men think that you're not really such a good warrior. That you only got lucky against Ragnvald.'

Ulf rubbed the hilt of Ormstunga with his thumb as he remembered the many times he had been lucky in the past. The many times he would have died, should have died, if his luck had not saved him. Someone had once told him that what some might think of as luck, others would call being blessed by the gods. He tried to remember if it was the volva who had said that to him as he glanced at Thorir, who was staring at him, and shrugged. 'They can believe what they want.'

Thorir shook his head. 'By Odin, I don't understand you, Ulf. We're about to raid one of the richest kingdoms on Midgard, fight against people who would rather pray to their god than lift a weapon to defend themselves, and yet you look as if a troll stole your favourite cow.'

Ulf felt the thud in his chest at the mention of a troll as his mind went to Griml and glared at Thorir. 'We are going there to kill people like you, Thorir. People who work hard, day after day, to feed their families. People who already have to give most of what they have to those more powerful than them, just like your family have to pay landskyld to the king. Those are the people who will fall to our blades. Not the Frankish kings or their nobles. People like your father, your mother and your sister. Those are the people we will attack and kill. Those are the women who will be raped and then sold as thralls.' *Just like Eldrid*, he thought. Ulf turned and walked away from Thorir, leaving him gaping, but Ulf doubted his words would sink in. Thorir wanted to be a warrior because he believed there was a greater honour in that than living off the land and growing your own food to feed your family. Just like he had once done.

Ulf walked back to his spot on the ship and sat down, taking his axe from his belt and the whetstone from his pouch. And as he dragged the whetstone along the already sharp edge of the axe, he felt someone staring at him. He looked up and saw Ragnvald glaring at him from Jarl Hakon's second ship and, for the first time in many winters, wished he was back in Thorgilsstad. He missed the wise words of Snorri's mother, who always seemed to know how he felt or what he was thinking. Ulf wondered if she hated him for killing her husband, but then shook his head to chase the thought away.

'Signal!' one warrior shouted and Jarl Hakon nodded as he turned the ship, his second ship doing the same, as they followed four ships that broke away from the fleet. Ulf recognised the ship leading the break-away group as Jarl Ragnar's and his heart raced as he tried to work out what was happening.

'We're going to introduce ourselves to the locals,' Jarl Hakon said when he saw Ulf's frown. 'The raid starts now! We will fill our ship with more gold and thralls than what even the gods would know what to do with! Odin favours us, the gods favour us!'

The men on the ship cheered, some of them stomping their feet on the deck of the ship. Ulf noticed how Thorir cheered with them, his arm around the shoulders of another warrior, and ground his teeth.

'The Bear-Slayer does not seem happy,' Jarl Hakon said to some men nearby, who laughed. 'I would have thought a warrior of your renown would relish a chance to fight those who wish to see the end of our gods and our way of life.'

Ulf glanced at Jarl Hakon as he grinned at him. This was not the first time he had heard those words, and he was certain that Jarl Hakon wouldn't be the last person to use them as an excuse to raid the Christian lands. Some warriors did it for the plunder, so they could provide for their families, while others did it for the love of the fight and to make a name for themselves. Ulf was certain there were many who did it because they believed the Christian god was a threat to their gods, although Ulf doubted he really was. 'The gods of Asgard are too powerful for one god or his followers to deal with,' Ulf said as he wondered what Jarl Hakon's motivations really were. He doubted it was because he cared so much about what happened to Odin, Frigg and Thor, and the rest of the gods.

'They say he sacrificed his own son for his people,' one warrior said, and Ulf glanced at the man with a shaved head.

'Odin sacrificed himself,' Ulf countered. 'Not Baldur or Thor. Himself.'

'Aye, for himself. The Christian god did it for his people,' Jarl Hakon said, smiling.

'But we gained from that sacrifice. What did the Christians get?'

Everyone around Ulf shrugged as Jarl Hakon laughed. 'Who knew the Bear-Slayer was so clever? The Christians believe they got salvation, that their so-called sins were forgiven.'

'Aye, so now they feel better about committing new ones,' one warrior said.

'The Christians care too much about their sins and their afterlife, that is why they are all so sour. Perhaps Ulf is a Christian,' another said, and everyone laughed, even Thorir, who had joined them. Ulf gritted his teeth and then saw Jarl Hakon scrutinise him.

'I am no Christian. I am a descendant of Tyr.'

'Well then, it looks like you will get a chance to show us what a descendant of Tyr can do.' Jarl Hakon was staring at something over Ulf's shoulder. Ulf looked behind him and saw a large town on the bank of the river. Already church bells were ringing and Ulf imagined the townspeople grabbing their most important possessions. Jewellery passed on by parents or silver earned from backbreaking work, fleeing the town for the safety of nearby forts or forests. Men would grab whatever weapons they had at hand, usually old spears or the axes they use for cutting wood. Ulf imagined a town this size had warriors there to defend the town, but then he guessed most of them would be in the fort behind the town, the one many of the townspeople were fleeing towards. The fort was most likely built to protect the coast from raiders, and the town had grown around it. There were no town walls and most of the houses on the edge of the town had fields where the people grew their own food. Ulf growled at the idea of fighting farmers and old men, and even though the sun was not out, had already decided that Ormstunga would stay in her scabbard.

'This is it,' Thorir beamed. 'By Odin, I need to piss. Why do I need to piss now?' The warriors around laughed as Ulf took the shield he had been given. He took his axe and scratched three long lines in the blue and black paint, the colours of Jarl Hakon, ignoring all the glances he got from the others. 'Why did you do that? Do I need to?' Thorir frowned at him, and Ulf just shook his head. He didn't really know why he did that. Perhaps it reminded him of a time when he had fought alongside men who were friends and who he could trust.

Frankish men, armed with axes and spears, were running towards the banks of the river as the ships approached. The Norse warriors roared with a fury that made the ships tremble and Ulf admired the defenders for standing the ground. He tried to work out how many there were, but it was hard for him to tell. Ulf looked at the six ships around him, with roughly thirty men on each ship. They outnumbered the Franks, but Ulf was certain that the church bells would warn the nearby fort of their attack and that the warriors in the fort would rush out to send the Danes back to their ships.

The first of Ragnar's ships, with Jarl Ragnar by the prow, sword in hand, beached on the riverbank near the town, and before she stopped, Jarl Ragnar and his warriors jumped overboard and charged at the Franks. The warriors on Jarl Hakon's ships cheered as Jarl Ragnar's men crashed into the defenders and the first blood of this raid was spilled. Jarl Hakon's ship changed course under his feet and Ulf saw some warriors reef the sail to slow the ship down. He turned to Thorir, who was staring wide-eyed at the battle on the riverbank. 'Keep your shield up and stay close to me. And remember, Thorir, even a bóndi can kill a great warrior. All he needs is luck.'

'For the gods!' Jarl Hakon shouted as his ship hit the riverbank, his second ship not far behind. The Norse warriors roared as they jumped over the side of the ship and stormed at the Franks, who were fighting for their lives.

Ulf took a deep breath as he followed Jarl Hakon's men. He did not want to spill the blood of those who were only trying to protect their homes, but he knew he could not avoid the fight as much as he wanted to. Ulf had a reputation, one he didn't want, but one he had to maintain. And not for him, but for those who came before him and those who would come after him. He glanced at Thorir, who was running near him, his face pale and shield held in front of him. Ulf understood his fear. He still remembered his first battle against a group of pirates. Right until he killed his first man. After that, the battle was a blur in his mind.

As they neared the town, a group of Franks wearing thick woollen tunics and armed with spears rushed at them, screaming what Ulf guessed were curses. Ulf lifted his shield and blocked the spear of the first man to reach him, and hacked into his leg with his axe. The Frank cried out as he collapsed, but Ulf had already forgotten about him as he moved onto the next Frank and punched the man with the rim of his shield. The Frank's head snapped back, his mouth a bloodied mess, when Thorir rushed in and buried his axe in the man's neck. Blood sprayed over Thorir as he screamed loud enough for even the gods in Asgard to hear him. He pulled his axe free and stormed at another Frank, who dropped his spear and fled, while Ulf killed the remaining Frank.

'By Thor, they were right. The Franks are cowards!' Thorir said, his voice loud and eyes wild with excitement.

Ulf glanced at the men they had killed. 'These men weren't warriors.' He hawked and spat, and walked away before Thorir could say anything. In the distance, he saw that Jarl Ragnar, wearing furry breeches, and his men had entered the town and wondered what the leader of the fleet would do if he saw Ulf here. He pushed the idea from his mind as he followed Jarl Hakon and his warriors. Thorir was beside him again, licking his lips as his blood lust seemed to have taken hold of him. Before they reached the town, though, a horn blew, and they all turned to see Frankish warriors leaving the fort and rushing towards the town.

'This is it, boys. The real fight begins now!' Jarl Hakon shouted. 'Let's show these Danes how to fight!' The Norse warriors cheered, Thorir amongst them even though he was a Dane. Ragnvald stepped forward, a sword in his right hand, but no shield because he couldn't carry one.

'Skjaldborg!'

The Norse warriors rushed towards the road between the fort and the town and formed a shield wall before the Frankish warriors could reach them.

'Stay behind me,' Ulf said to Thorir as he forced his way into the front rank of the shield wall. Jarl Hakon and Ragnvald both glanced at him, and the jarl smiled as Ragnvald shook his head. But Ulf didn't care what they thought. He had fought in many shield walls and had always been in the front row. That was his place. Thorir nodded and Ulf wished the Dane had a spear and not just his axe, but there was no time to worry about that now as the Norse warriors locked their shields together. The thunderous noise woke the voices of Ulf's ancestors in his ears and as the Frankish warriors rushed at them, their weapons and armour glinting in the dull daylight, he gave into them and his anger. Anger that had built up over a long period. Anger at Jarl Ragnar for sending men to kill him and Eldrid for blaming him for her fate. And at the Norns for deciding that was to be her fate. Ulf didn't hear the roar of the Frankish warriors because of the blood rushing in his ears. All he saw were the snarls on their faces and the fear in their eyes.

He lifted his shield to block the spear aimed at his head, before he stepped forward and punched the Frank in the face with the head of his axe. The Frank crumbled to the ground as Ulf stepped back into the safety of the shield wall. The warrior beside him killed another Frank, spraying them both with blood, before he had to duck behind his own shield as a spear came for his head. Ulf hacked at the spear holder's hand, chopping it off at the wrist, and as the Frank gaped at his missing hand, the man next to Ulf stabbed him in the neck with his sword. The Frank died with Norse steel in his throat, but before he dropped to the ground, Ulf felt a sudden weight on his shoulders as Thorir tried to jump over him to hack at the warrior facing Ulf. Thorir's weight drove Ulf to his knees, and he screamed at the Dane. The Frank facing Ulf blocked Thorir's attack with his shield and then smiled at Ulf before he stabbed at his face with his sword. Ulf, unable to move because Thorir had pinned him down, got his shield up to block the blow before he chopped his axe at the man's leg. The Frank cried out as Ulf's axe bit into his leg, cutting the flesh and breaking the bones, before he collapsed and dragged both Ulf and Thorir down with him. One of the Norse warriors killed a Frank as he tried to stab Thorir in the back and Ulf had to jump to his feet and shoulder barge another as he tried to do the same. But this caused the break in the Norse shield wall and left Ulf isolated and surrounded by the Franks.

His ancestors roared in Ulf's ears as he did all he could not to get skewered by Frankish spears, all the while trying to protect Thorir, who was still grappling with the Frank on the ground. He lifted his shield to block a spear, but could do nothing as another Frank struck him in the face with the hilt of his sword. Ulf's vision blurred, and he struggled to stay on his feet as the ground spun around him. He sensed movement near him and ducked behind his shield before he felt something strike it, the blow hard enough to drive him to his knees and for the shield to fall from his hand. Ulf looked up at the large Frank looming over him, an ugly grin on his face as he lifted his large two-handed axe. Ulf knew there was nothing he could do and cursed the gods as a voice whispered in his ears.

Only death waits for you there.

Chapter 15

Ulf watched as the large axe came down, its movement so slow that it felt like he could live a lifetime before it split his skull. The voices of his ancestors roared in his ears, telling him to move, to use his axe to deflect the blow, but there was nothing Ulf could do. Nothing would stop the Frank from killing him here and he cursed the Norns for his fate. But then someone fell on top of Ulf, knocking him over, and instead of the axe being buried in his head, Ulf felt it thud into the body on top of him. He watched, wide-eyed, as Ragnvald stabbed the large Frank under the arm, his sword finding a gap in the Frank's armour and tearing through his lungs. The Frank's eyes bulged, and he muttered something before Ragnvald pulled his sword free and kicked the dying man to the ground.

'Our fight is not done yet, Bear-Slayer. Only I get to kill you.' Ulf just stared at the old one-handed warrior as he charged at another Frank, before he shook his head to clear it. He picked up his shield and got to his feet while scanning the battleground around him. The Franks had broken and many of them were fleeing back to the fort, although Ulf could already see that was a bad idea as Ragnar's forces stormed the fort. The ground was littered with the dead, most of them Franks, but Ulf saw a few Norse men amongst them as the familiar stench of death filled his nostrils. And then he remembered Thorir.

Ulf's heart raced as he searched for the Dane and sighed with relief when he saw the man sitting next to the Frank he had killed, his face pale and his beard soaked in blood and vomit. His leather jerkin was the same, and Ulf recognised the blank stare on Thorir's face. He had seen it many times in those who faced death for the first time. Ulf's anger at Thorir disappeared as the breeze blew over him and he made his way to the Dane. Ignoring the glances the other Norse men were giving him, he held a hand out for Thorir.

'Still want to be a warrior?'

Thorir blinked a few times before he looked at Ulf. But instead of responding, he turned and vomited again.

'Not everyone is made to be a warrior,' Jarl Hakon said from behind Ulf, who turned and was surprised to see Jarl Knut with him, although the Danish jarl, with his clean brynja, looked like he didn't take part in the battle.

'It's his first battle,' Ulf said, irritated with Jarl Hakon's words even if he agreed with them. But he had sworn to Inga that he would look after the bóndi, and Ulf was determined to do that. He heard the gods' laughter in the calls of the ravens circling above them, but resisted the urge to grip the Mjöllnir pendant around his neck.

'Aye, and he almost got you killed,' Jarl Hakon said.

Jarl Knut laughed. 'But the gods ensured that the Bear-Slayer is still with us.' He glanced at Jarl Hakon and Ulf wondered about the smile the two jarls gave each other.

'Ragnvald saved me, not the gods.' Ulf turned and helped Thorir to his feet, doing his best to ignore the stares of the jarls on his back. 'Come Thorir, let's get you cleaned up.'

They made their way back to the river and Thorir vomited again as they walked past and over the dead. The stench of death already filled their nostrils and reminded Ulf of the dream he had had recently, something which sent a shiver down his spine. But luckily for him, Thorir was too caught up in his own misery to notice. The Dane couldn't keep his eyes off the mutilated bodies at their feet, many of them with missing limbs or their innards spread out around them. Ulf was glad it wasn't the middle of summer, because the heat would have made the stench worse than it already was. Thorir, though, was not used to it and his face turned greener than the new leaves which were appearing on the trees near the river.

'Ho...how d...do you do it?' Thorir managed to get the question out, and Ulf raised an eyebrow at him. 'How do you deal with the fear?'

Ulf sighed as they reached the river. Many of the injured were being carried back to the ships and tended to, even while the Danes were fighting to get into the fort near the town. But Ulf had no wish to go back to the battle. He had spilled enough blood and knew he couldn't stomach what would happen to the women and girls once Ragnar's army got into the fort. The men were lucky, as most of them would be killed, although Ulf knew some would be tortured. Those young enough would be kept alive so they could be sold as thralls, something Ulf had never agreed with, even if he saw the necessity of it. But the women and girls. Their fate would be far crueller than they deserved, and Ulf had often wondered why Frigg or Freya did nothing to protect them. He thought of Eldrid and of what had happened to her, which only made him more determined to free her. Ulf looked at Thorir, who had his head in the river, as he was trying to drown himself, and thought about how boastful the man had been before. 'Some try to ignore it,' he said when Thorir pulled his head out of the water. Most of the blood and vomit had been washed off, but Ulf could still see some of his morning meal in his beard. 'Others drink it away.'

'And you?'

Ulf glanced at his trembling hands. Something that happened after every battle. 'I use it to keep myself alive.'

Thorir frowned at him and then he nodded as he lay down. His face was still pale and Ulf knew that once the battle lust fully wore off, then the Dane would sleep like a bear through winter. He almost felt envious of that, because Ulf rarely slept like that. His dreams didn't allow him to. But perhaps Thorir would be the same. Many warriors had nightmares about past battles. He sighed as he sat down next to Thorir and cleaned his axe in the river.

'You almost got me killed. I told you to stay behind me.'

Thorir opened his eyes and Ulf saw the shame in them. 'I...' He looked away when he couldn't find the right words.

Ulf patted Thorir on the chest. 'You live, and so do I. We should thank the gods for that,' *Or Ragnvald*, Ulf thought. He wondered why the old bastard had saved him. Surely his death would have been what Ragnvald wanted. Ulf cleaned himself as he remembered Ragnvald's words to him after he had saved his life. The hairs on the back of his neck stood on end again and Ulf found himself scanning the area, but knew she couldn't be here.

'Ulf?' Thorir asked him and Ulf frowned at him. 'You look like you saw a draugr.'

Worse than a draugr, Ulf thought, and then shook his head. 'No, just thinking that I need to keep a close eye on Ragnvald.'

'Why?' Thorir's brow furrowed. 'He saved you. Even I saw that.'

'Aye, he did,' Ulf said, as his hand went to the Mjöllnir pendant around his neck. 'But the gods know he did that so he could kill me himself.'

'Because you killed his son? Some of the men told me about it,' Thorir explained when Ulf raised an eyebrow at him.

'Aye.'

'But why? They told me what this Griml did. Why would Ragnvald want to kill you because of that?'

Ulf shrugged as he watched the ravens and crows start their feast on the dead. 'I don't know.'

Thorir fell silent and stared at the river as the water flowed past them. After a while, he took a deep breath. 'Eldrid told me not to go with you.'

'She did?' Ulf raised an eyebrow.

Thorir nodded. 'She said you were cursed, just like that sword of yours. Said that the gods were punishing you.'

Ulf's hands trembled as he watched a pair of ravens fighting over a corpse. He thought of Odin's two ravens and wondered if they still watched him like they used to. 'She's right. People I care for either die or live long enough to hate me.'

Thorir sat up and smiled at Ulf. 'It's a good thing you don't care about me then.'

Ulf shook his head. 'Especially not after I almost died because of you.'

'Forgive me. I got carried away.' Thorir looked away from Ulf, who sighed and got to his feet.

'Next time, don't jump over the man in front of you in the shield wall. Wait for your time.'

Thorir nodded and then said something, but Ulf didn't hear the words as he watched Jarl Ragnar and Jarl Knut walking back to their ships. Both of them had large grins on their faces. Jarl Ragnar's brynja shone red with the blood of the Franks and the lower half of his face was also covered in blood. Ulf held his breath as Jarl Ragnar went to the river and cleaned himself up. He was about to look Ulf's way when Jarl Knut stepped between them and pointed at something in the distance. Jarl Ragnar nodded before the two men walked away.

'By Loki, that was close,' Thorir said and Ulf could only nod. 'What do you think he would have done if he saw you?'

Ulf shrugged, not wanting to think about it. 'Come, let's get you better weapons.'

'Where?' Thorir scratched his head.

Ulf pointed towards the field of dead, the air thick with ravens, crows and other carrion birds, whose cries drowned out all other noises. He was sure that by nightfall, wolves and foxes would join the feast and that by sunrise, there won't be much of the Franks left to be buried. 'The dead Franks don't need their weapons any more. Their heaven is a place of peace, or so they say.'

They walked among the dead, Thorir's face pale again and Ulf hoped the bóndi wouldn't vomit as they searched the dead for anything of value. Ulf and Thorir weren't the only ones. Many of the Danes and Norse were doing the same, although some of them were searching for dead comrades who they took back to the ships.

'What will they do with them?' Thorir asked between deep breaths.

Ulf pulled a golden ring from the finger of one dead Frank before he responded. 'Clean them and make sure they have all their weapons. Then they will find a good spot somewhere and bury them so the men can find their way to Valhalla.'

'Even if they're buried in Francia?' Thorir scratched his head and Ulf shrugged as he continued to walk amongst the dead. He didn't really know the answer to that, and if he was honest, it wasn't something he wanted to think about. They spent the rest of the day in silence. Ulf kept his head low as if he was searching for something worth taking, but in truth he was doing it so he didn't have to look at the town or the fort. Otherwise, he would be thinking about what was happening in there as thick smoke drifted towards the clouds. Thorir had found himself a few finger rings, which had brought the colour back to his face. At one point, Ulf saw a dead Dane with two arm rings on each arm. He had been tempted to take them, to replace the ones he had used to buy supplies, but then he decided against it. The man needed to look his best in Valhalla, and arm rings had to be earned. He could only take them if he had killed the man, not if the Dane had died fighting in the same shield wall as himself. Apart from the few rings and a belt buckle, Ulf had taken nothing else from the dead Franks.

As the sun made its descent, a horn blew and Ulf sighed with relief. It was time to head back to the ships and rejoin the fleet, something Ulf was eager to do because it was easier to hide from

Jarl Ragnar amongst thousands of men than it was on the field amongst the dead. That had been another reason he had avoided the town and the fort. Jarl Ragnar was in one of them, and Ulf knew the gods would make sure Ragnar saw him. Especially if Odin or Loki were bored and needed entertainment. Ulf could only hope that this small battle would be enough for the All-Father, and he would not decide to amuse himself at Ulf's expense. Thorir and Ulf made their way back to the ships, where many of the Norse warriors eyed Thorir's new sword and Ragnvald glared at them.

Ulf ignored them all as he watched the captives being loaded onto the ships. Thorir stood beside him, a frown also on his face.

'I've seen the thrall markets in Jelling many times, but I never really thought about where they came from.'

'Aye,' was all Ulf could say, and then he walked away.

'There he is, the Bear-Slayer,' Jarl Hakon said when he saw Ulf. Ragnvald grunted beside him and Ulf wondered if he should thank the old man for saving him, but then decided against it. Ragnvald would only ridicule him.

Which he did anyway when Ulf was near them. 'I expected more from you. Thought you'd kill all the Franks with that pretty sword of yours. Not sit on your knees and beg for your life.'

Ulf gritted his teeth as he fought to stop the flames of his anger from igniting in the pit of his stomach. He had fought and he had killed. That he had ended up on his knees was not his fault. A few of the Norse warriors laughed, but some didn't. Ulf guessed they were the ones who had stood near him in the shield wall and saw what had happened.

'Perhaps next time, you stand in the second row of the shield wall,' Jarl Hakon said.

Ulf turned and glared at the jarl. 'I stand in the first row.'

'You don't deserve to be in the first row,' Ragnvald said as he took a step towards Ulf. 'That is where the real warriors fight.'

Ulf clenched his fists as Thorir put a hand on his shoulder and tried to pull him away. But Ulf shrugged him off. 'I beat you in your little holmgang, old man. So if I don't deserve to stand in the front row, then neither do you.' The warriors all gasped as Ragnvald's face turned red and Jarl Hakon laughed.

'By the gods. The Bear-Slayer has balls bigger than the thunder god.' He gripped Ragnvald by the shoulder and pulled him away. 'Come, Ragnvald. We're all tired from the fight. Ulf fought well, and so did the Dane.'

Ragnvald spat at Ulf's feet before he turned and walked away, leaving Ulf glaring at his back. He felt his fingertips dig into the palms of his hands as he continued to clench his fists. Ulf was just about to turn and walk away when he heard Jarl Ragnar's voice behind him.

'What, in Odin's name, is he doing here?'

Ulf turned and saw the leader of the fleet, the man who had told him to leave Jelling, staring at him, his nostrils flared as the vein in his forehead bulged. In the silence of the men around him, Ulf heard the gods laugh and knew that Odin was not done with him yet.

Chapter 16

'I TOLD YOU TO leave Jelling,' Jarl Ragnar said to Ulf through gritted teeth. 'And yet, here I find you in my army.'

Ulf glanced at Jarl Knut behind Jarl Ragnar and wondered why the man wasn't saying anything. 'We're not in Jelling.'

Jarl Ragnar glared at Ulf as many of the men, including Thorir, stepped away from him. Everything around them seemed to disappear as they glared at each other, both men clenching their jaws and fists. Ulf was still worked up from his confrontation with Ragnvald and even though he knew he should have backed off, he couldn't. The voices of his ancestors refused to let him. His hand itched for the feel of Ormstunga, especially after he noticed how Jarl Ragnar glanced at her.

Jarl Ragnar growled at Ulf, who didn't hear the whispers of the surrounding warriors, some of them making bets on whether Jarl Ragnar would kill him. All he heard was the thudding of his heart in his ears. And then there was a fluttering of wings and the call of a raven, which broke both Ulf and Jarl Ragnar from their glares as they looked at the large black bird sitting on the mast of Jarl Hakon's ship.

Jarl Knut cleared his throat, and Ragnar glared at him. 'Ragnar, enough blood has been spilled today. Ulf has apologised for attacking you, and the traders paid the mangæld. He fights for Jarl Hakon now.'

'And how does he come to fight for Jarl Hakon? A man you are close to.'

'He approached me outside Jelling, and I saw no reason for him not to join my forces. An extra warrior never hurt anyone.' Jarl Hakon said, and Ulf wondered why he was lying to Jarl Ragnar.

'This man insulted my honour.'

'An if I had known, then I would have hanged him myself, Jarl Ragnar. But I didn't know. And besides, Ulf Bear-Slayer is a warrior of great renown back in Norway. Tales of his deeds are told even in the North where my hall is.'

Ulf watched as Jarl Ragnar's jaw muscles worked hard under his beard. He kept his hand away from the hilt of Ormstunga, but his back straight and head high. He refused to cower in front of Jarl Ragnar, no matter who the man was.

Jarl Ragnar glared at the Norse jarl. 'He is your responsibility, Jarl Hakon. If he sets one foot wrong, then I will blood eagle you myself.'

Jarl Hakon nodded as many of the men gripped their Mjöllnir pendants. Ulf had heard tales of the Blood Eagle, although he doubted anyone had really used it on another man. It seemed impractical to him and he wondered if the gods would really want a sacrifice like that. But then he remembered how cruel the gods could be and decided they most likely would. 'I understand. Ragnvald will keep a close eye on him,' Jarl Hakon said.

Jarl Ragnar nodded and then glared at Ulf. 'When you die, that sword of yours is mine.'

'Odin doesn't want me to die. So I'll hang on to my sword,' Ulf retorted, and Jarl Ragnar grunted before he turned and walked away. Jarl Knut stood there for a moment and smiled at Ulf, before he glanced at Jarl Hakon and followed Jarl Ragnar.

'Why does everyone want your sword?' Thorir asked when Jarl Ragnar was out of earshot.

Ulf glanced at him. 'You wanted to take it from me as well.'

Thorir paled. 'Aye, but I changed my mind. Besides, I have my own sword now.'

Ulf turned and saw Jarl Hakon staring at him. 'If I were you, Bear-Slayer, then I'd watch my back. Ragnar is not a man you anger. Not even the king of Denmark dares to do that.' Many of the men nodded at that as Ulf frowned. But before he could say anything, Jarl Hakon turned to his men. 'Get everything loaded. We leave soon.'

Ulf stood there, confused, as Jarl Hakon's men loaded the last of the captives and their plunder onto the jarl's ships. He glanced at the raven, still on the mast, and wondered what Odin was planning for him now, and why the one-eyed god had to interfere in his life again. Ulf had thought that Odin was done with him, but still the All-Father watched him. And not just Odin, Ulf thought as he felt the familiar feeling of somebody watching him. He scanned the riverbank and the trees but saw no sign of the volva.

'Ulf?' Thorir asked and Ulf blinked at him. Thorir frowned and then said, 'It's time to go.'

Ulf nodded when he saw the others were already taking their places on the ships. Jarl Ragnar's ships, as well as Jarl Knut's, had already pushed away from the riverbanks and the men were preparing the oars so they could row back to the rest of the fleet.

Ulf almost groaned at the thought of rowing as he followed Thorir onto the ship. He felt Ragnvald glaring at him from Jarl Hakon's other ship as they were handed their oars and then Ulf forgot about him. He gripped the oar in his hands, feeling the groves worn out by other hands, and took a deep breath as he tried to calm his racing heart. The volva was out there somewhere and Ulf knew it was only a matter of time before she would reveal herself. But he couldn't help but wonder what part she played in Odin's game.

As they rowed up the river, Ulf saw the devastation left behind along the riverbank by the rest of the fleet. Even Thorir gaped as he tried to row in time with those around him, but occasionally he was too focused on the burnt farmsteads and villages, with black smoke filling the sky around them. Corpses lay strewn out along the river, mostly men who had fought to protect their homes and women. In a few places, the Danish warships were still there, their men cheering at Jarl Ragnar's ship as they rowed past.

'Still excited about the raid?' Ulf couldn't help but ask Thorir as he rowed. Thorir stayed silent, his head fixed on the back of the man in front of him as if he had not heard Ulf. But Ulf knew he had, even while Jarl Hakon's men were singing songs about Thor fighting the giants and Odin hanging himself on the great tree. Ulf sighed and decided there was no point in harassing Thorir. The man wanted to make a name for himself and now he had to deal with the ugly side of the raids, the parts the sagas rarely told you about.

They rowed for a while, with Jarl Hakon's men still singing their songs, when a horn blew from Jarl Ragnar's ship. In the dying light of the day, Ulf could see Ragnar's ship veering towards the river when he glanced over his shoulder.

'What's happening?' Thorir asked, the first time he had spoken since they started rowing. Ulf could hear the tiredness in the man's voice and was surprised he was keeping up with the others. But then, Thorir was used to working hard on his father's farm.

'We're stopping for the night,' one man said. 'And thank the gods, I'm exhausted.' The others laughed and teased the man, who was one of the older warriors in Jarl Hakon's army, but he took it on his chin and carried on rowing until the ship changed course and the order was given to lift the oars so they wouldn't hit the riverbank and break.

Ulf sighed with relief and, like many of the men, stood and stretched his back after the oars had been shipped and the ship tied to a nearby tree, so the river wouldn't take it away. But his relief was short-lived when Jarl Hakon walked past him and said, 'You and the bóndi have first watch, so you might as well stay on the ship.'

Others laughed as Ulf groaned and Thorir frowned.

'First watch?' the bóndi asked.

'Aye. It means we have to sit here and watch the thralls, while everyone else gets to drink the ale they took from the town and sleep.'

This time Thorir groaned and Ulf wondered if Jarl Hakon was punishing him or keeping him out of Ragnvald's way. *Or perhaps out of Jarl Ragnar's,* he wondered as he watched the men build a temporary camp and start the many campfires to cook their meals.

'Why this river?' Thorir asked Ulf a while later when the full moon was up and the men were celebrating the day's raids. Ulf frowned at him. 'We passed many large rivers along the way, so I was wondering why Jarl Ragnar chose this river.'

Ulf shrugged. 'Why did Odin give his right eye and not his left?' he asked instead, and then smiled when Thorir's brow creased. 'Just like Odin had his reason, so does Ragnar and I don't care either way.' All he cared about was making enough to free Eldrid.

They sat in silence as the moon disappeared behind thick clouds. Thorir frowned for most of the time and after a while he smiled and said, 'Odin gave his right eye because it was his favourite eye.'

This time, Ulf frowned. 'Then why not give the left eye?'

'Well, it's like my father sacrificing his favourite bull to the gods to make sure we get a good harvest,' Thorir explained with a grin. 'Odin had to give his favourite eye to get the knowledge he was after.'

Ulf shrugged and guessed Thorir had a point. 'So Ragnar chose this river because it is his favourite?'

'Jarl Ragnar chose this river because of what lies at the end of it,' a voice said behind them, and both Ulf and Thorir jumped to their feet, although only Ulf had his axe in his hand. Jarl Knut stood there, smiling at them with a jug in his hand. 'I thought you'd like some ale. Jarl Hakon told me you fought well today.'

Ulf scowled at the Danish jarl. 'He told me something different.'

Jarl Knut waved Ulf's words away with his free hand and handed the jug of ale to Thorir, who took a deep gulp and burped, before he wiped his mouth clean.

'Not bad stuff. Mother's is better, though.'

'What lies at the end of the river?' Ulf asked, ignoring Thorir.

'A large city wealthier than Asgard. Or so they say.'

'Wealthier than Asgard?' Thorir repeated, his eyes wide, and Jarl Knut nodded.

'So they say.' Jarl Knut turned to Ulf, who was scrutinising him. 'Before you ask, I came to warn you, Bear-Slayer.'

'Warn me?' Ulf resisted the urge to rub the Mjöllnir pendant around his neck, but his right hand went to the hilt of Ormstunga.

Jarl Knut nodded. 'Aye. Ragnar is furious. Says your presence mocks him, makes him look weak.'

'My presence has nothing to do with him.'

Jarl Knut nodded again. 'I'm sure the gods will know that's the truth, but he feels otherwise. And he still lusts after that sword of yours.'

Ulf raised an eyebrow at Jarl Knut. 'Why are you telling me this?'

'To warn you. I fear Ragnar might do something foolish.'

'Like send men after me?'

'Like sending more men than last time. He wants to punish you for what you did, and he wants your sword. And Odin knows Ragnar is as stubborn as Thor. If he wants something, he gets it.' Thorir burped again and Jarl Knut smiled. 'That's all I wanted to say. You enjoy the ale, I'm sure Jarl Hakon will send men to relieve you soon.'

Ulf doubted that would happen, but kept his thoughts to himself. 'Thank you, Jarl Knut.'

Still smiling, Jarl Knut nodded and left the ship, but not before eyeing one of the captives. A pretty woman with a cut lip and bruised eye. She tried to shuffle away from him, but had nowhere to go.

'By Loki, that was strange,' Thorir said before he took another drink of the ale Jarl Knut had brought them. He offered it to Ulf, who shook his head. The conversation with the Danish jarl had left him feeling uneasy, and he doubted ale would make him feel any better.

'Aye, that was.'

They sat in silence for a long while, Ulf staring at the full moon as it fought hard to be seen through the clouds and Thorir with his eyes fixed on the pretty captive Jarl Knut had looked at.

Feeling frustrated, Ulf got to his feet and wrapped his cloak around him.

'By the gods, you gave me a fright,' Thorir said, his hand on his chest as if he was trying to calm his heart. Ulf realised the bóndi had fallen asleep, but then didn't blame the man. They had fought a battle and rowed upriver, and now Jarl Hakon expected them to watch the captives all night long instead of sending someone to relieve them.

'I need a piss,' Ulf lied. He just wanted to get away from the captives and the ship. Even Thorir's presence was annoying him, and he needed to be on his own for a while. 'Make sure you stay awake.'

Thorir nodded, but then made himself even more comfortable. Ulf shook his head and left the ship. He stood on the riverbank for a moment and then walked to the nearby trees. There, he stood amongst the trees and closed his eyes as he breathed in the scent of fresh leaves and wet ground. Forests always calmed him. It didn't matter if the forests were in Norway or in Francia, but breathing in the earthy aromas made it feel like Freya had placed a soothing hand on his face and his anger would just fade away.

'That's not all Freya would do with that hand of hers,' a woman's voice said behind him. Ulf's heart jumped in his chest and he turned towards the voice, Ormstunga in his hand, her blade singing as he pulled her out of her scabbard. But when Ulf saw who it was, he knew that if any blood was going to be spilled, it would be his as he gaped at the short woman wearing a deerskin dress and with twigs and bones in her hair. The familiar dried snakeskin around her neck made him shiver, as did the blackened gums that greeted him as she smiled. Somewhere amongst the trees, an owl hooted, which sent a shiver down his spine and made the volva smile even more. 'I hear she is quite talented with those hands of hers.'

'Wh...what are y...you doing here?' Ulf asked, as he tried to calm his nerves. He should have known that Skadi would sneak out of the shadows and scare him, because she enjoyed toying with him as much as the gods did.

The volva's eyes went to the sword in his hand. 'I see someone is very happy to see me.' She gave him a mischievous smile, and Ulf felt his cheeks go red as he put Ormstunga away. He took a deep breath and straightened his back, certain that he had nothing to fear from the volva. 'You don't seem too surprised to see me, young wolf. Although you are not so young any more.'

'I knew you were coming. You've been in my dreams again, although I guess you knew that already,' he explained when the volva raised an eyebrow at him. Skadi glanced at the bright moon, which broke through the clouds.

'Odin has his eye on you again, young wolf.'

'And you are here to make sure he gets what he wants?' Ulf also glanced at the full moon, which looked like a giant eye, and wondered if that was Odin staring at him.

Skadi shook her head. 'I am here to make sure you live.'

Ulf's brow creased. 'What do you mean?'

Skadi walked around him and he felt her eyes on him as she scrutinised him. He wanted to turn to face her, but it felt like his feet refused to obey him. 'A young and lonely wolf joins a pack of wolves. Some wolves see him as a threat, while others want to use him. And worse, he brought a dog with him. A dog that wants to be a wolf, but doesn't have the same bite.' Skadi stood in front of him again, the smile replaced by a glare that made Ulf shiver. He never understood why she was frightening. He was an experienced warrior who had survived many battles, on land and sea, and yet he was frightened of a woman shorter than him. Perhaps it was because she spoke for the gods and did their bidding. Or because he understood what she would do to get what she wanted. Skadi had used Griml to get to Ulf, and she had used him as a blade to get her own revenge on Snorri's father and mother, her own sister, for the death of her daughter. Skadi had used Ulf, although he never understood how, but she had directed his anger towards Thorgils, Snorri's father. That was why Ulf had killed the jarl. He had always believed it was an accident, but now, as he stared into the dark eyes of Skadi, he wasn't so sure. 'The question, young wolf, is who dies first?'

'Who are you talking to?' Ragnvald's voice made Ulf turn, and he saw the old warrior stepping out from behind a tree. His face creased in anger.

'I...' Ulf turned to Skadi, but she was gone. It was as if she had never been there, not even her footprints on the soft soil of the forest remained. Ulf shook his head and knew he shouldn't be surprised. This was not the first time she had done something like this, and he was certain it wouldn't be the last. 'Nobody,' Ulf said and attempted to walk past Ragnvald so he could return to the ship.

Ragnvald grabbed Ulf's brynja and stopped him from walking past him. 'Don't lie to me. I heard you talking to someone.'

Ulf fought his anger, not wanting to kill the old bastard under Odin's eye. 'I wasn't talking to anyone.' He pulled himself free and went back to the ship, where he found Thorir snoring away. Ulf was tempted to kick the bóndi awake, but then decided not to. Instead, he sat down and stared at the moon as his conversation with Skadi rang in his ears. He was certain that he was the young wolf and Thorir the dog, but he didn't understand who the others were. Ulf sighed as he leaned his head against the side of the ship's hull. He had hoped that he had been imagining her presence, but now he knew she was really there and that frightened him more than any shield wall ever could.

Chapter 17

Ragnar walked back to his tent as the full moon sat high in the sky, his vision blurred from the ale he had been drinking with Knut and the other jarls. The men were in good spirits and the gods knew they deserved to be. The raid had started better than he could have imagined, and so far, the information the traders had given him about this river had been accurate.

The towns and farmsteads they had attacked had provided them with plenty of plunder and captives, enough to make him one of the richest men in Denmark, but Ragnar knew there was more to come. He licked his lips at the prospects of attacking more settlements until they reached their target. Paris. A large city with so much wealth that even the gods were jealous of it, or so Ragnar had been told. He had raided these lands before, many winters ago, before his cousin, the king, made an agreement with the Frankish kings and the raiding had to stop. But Ragnar had never seen a city with as much gold and silver as he had been told Paris had. Not to mention all the churches that surrounded the city. And the current situation in the new Frankish kingdoms had made them ripe for the plucking. Like a sweet virgin ready for a good fucking. Only Francia wasn't a virgin. She was a well-protected beauty, but her husband had turned his attention away and men like Ragnar had come to plunder her.

Ragnar took another gulp of ale from the jug he was carrying as he greeted some of his warriors. His hirdmen weren't far behind him, but Ragnar felt he had nothing to worry about. Nobody would be foolish enough to attack him. He had spent many winters building his reputation as one of the most feared warriors in Denmark. But just as the smile from that thought crossed his lips, he sensed movement behind him.

Ragnar turned and caught the blurry movement as someone rushed at him. The full moon glinted off a metal object in the attacker's hand, and even though he was drunk from the ale, Ragnar had enough sense to twist out of the way and felt the knife scrape along his brynja. His attacker moved fast and before Ragnar could grab his arm, he jumped out of reach and launched at Ragnar again, this time aiming for his face. Ragnar ducked under the knife, the movement making his head spin, but his warrior instinct was driving him on and he punched the man in the side. That was when he saw the golden hilt of the man's sword. He reached out to grab the sword when his attacker elbowed him in the side of his head, driving Ragnar to his knees and making him drop the jug of ale. Ragnar grunted as his head spun from ale and the blow, and braced himself for the killing blow when there were shouts of alarm. The attacker hesitated and Ragnar tried to see his face, but the coward had covered it with a cloth and all Ragnar saw were dark eyes glaring at him before his attacker turned and fled.

'Jarl Ragnar? What happened?' one of Ragnar's hirdmen asked as he rushed to Ragnar's side.

Ragnar got to his feet and grabbed his hirdman by his brynja as the others arrived, all of them frowning. 'What happened?' Ragnar snarled at his hirdman. 'I was attacked by a coward hiding in the shadows like a snake!'

The warrior's eyes widened, perhaps thinking about what might happen to him for failing to protect his jarl. He stammered, struggling to get the words out when Knut and the Norse jarl arrived.

'By the gods, what is all the commotion about?' Knut said with an eyebrow raised at Ragnar, who let go of his hirdman.

'That bastard, the Bear-Slayer. Where is he?' Ragnar asked Jarl Hakon, who scratched his beard.

'He's on one of my ships, guarding the captives. Why?'

Ragnar frowned as he remembered the golden hilt of his attacker's sword. He knew there were many men who had swords with golden hilt, by Odin, even he had two such swords. But there was only one warrior with a sword like that who had attacked him before and who had reason to attack him again. Ragnar glared at Jarl Knut. 'He just tried to kill me.'

***

Rough hands woke Ulf from his sleep. A dreamless sleep he craved so much and, thinking that the ship was under attack, he reached for the hilt of Ormstunga. Before he could grip his sword, though, someone punched him in the side of the head while others grabbed his arms.

'Ulf, what's going on?' Thorir shouted as he too was grabbed by warriors.

Ulf's anger erupted from the pit of his stomach and he kicked one of the men attacking him in the groin. The warrior's eyes bulged and when he bent over, Ulf kicked him in the face. Feeling one of the men holding him relaxing his grip, Ulf pulled his hand free and punched the other in the face. The man's head snapped to the side and he let go of Ulf, who pushed the first man over the side of the ship and into the river. Before the warrior's screams were stopped by the water, Ulf's hand went to Ormstunga. The moon was still out, which meant Ulf did not have to worry about the curse of his ancestors' sword.

'Let go of Thorir,' Ulf said as he freed Ormstunga from her scabbard.

The warriors holding on to the bóndi hesitated as they glanced at each other, and Ulf used the moment to see what was happening on the ship and the riverbank. He did not recognise any of the men as Jarl Hakon's warriors and there was no sign of attack other than the men who had grabbed him and Thorir.

'Enough of this. Ulf, put your sword away. Odin knows you've caused enough problems as it is.' Jarl Knut's words made Ulf frown, and he took a step back when the jarl climbed aboard the ship. The men holding Thorir let go of him when Jarl Knut gave the order, but then they drew their own weapons and faced Ulf. Thorir looked pale as he stared at Ulf, who shook his head. He did not understand what was going on, but he didn't want Thorir to die because of it.

'What problems have I caused?' Ulf asked and wondered if Ragnvald had told him and Jarl Hakon about what he had seen in the forest. Although Ulf doubted the one-handed warrior saw anything. Skadi was very good at hiding her tracks. So good that Ulf had often wondered if she was real or just part of his dreams.

'When I warned you about Ragnar, Ulf, I didn't think you'd be dumb enough to attack him,' Jarl Knut said.

'Attack Jarl Ragnar?' Ulf's brow creased, and he glanced at Thorir, who looked as confused as he was. Jarl Hakon joined them, with Ragnvald and some of his warriors behind him. Again, Ulf wondered if the old bastard was behind any of this. He couldn't defeat Ulf in his little holmgang, so now he had to get others to do that for him. But then why save him during the battle earlier that day? None of this made any sense to Ulf, and he looked at Jarl Knut again. 'I didn't attack Jarl Ragnar.'

'The gods know I want to believe you, Ulf. But Jarl Ragnar was attacked and his attacker had a sword with a golden hilt. Just like yours.'

Ulf looked at Ormstunga and wished he had kept her in her scabbard. 'Many warriors here have swords with golden hilts. Why does he think it was me?'

Jarl Knut nodded as if he thought Ulf had made a good point. 'Jarl Hakon says you were supposed to be guarding the ship and the captives. Is that what you were doing?'

Ulf hesitated as he glanced at Ragnvald behind Jarl Knut, but before he could say anything, Thorir stepped forward.

'Aye, he was here the entire night.'

Jarl Knut and Jarl Hakon raised an eyebrow at Thorir. 'Are you sure? Remember, if you lie for him, then you will also be guilty of the attack.'

Thorir nodded. 'As the gods are my witnesses. Ulf was here the entire night. He fell asleep after drinking some of the ale you brought us, Jarl Knut. You know the Norse. Can't hold their drinks.' There were some growls from the Norse warriors, but Jarl Knut smiled, as did Jarl Hakon. Ulf glanced at Ragnvald again as he expected him to say something. But the old warrior stayed silent as he glared at Ulf.

'If you lie, then you know the gods will punish you.' Jarl Knut looked at Thorir, who nodded to show that he understood.

'Ulf never left the ship.'

Jarl Knut stared at Thorir for a few more heartbeats as Ulf waited for Ragnvald to tell them he had seen Ulf amongst the trees. But then Jarl Knut smiled and wiped his forehead.

'By the gods, I'm glad to hear that. I hated to think that the Bear-Slayer would attack a man from the shadows. I will tell Jarl Ragnar it couldn't have been you, but I warn you, Ulf. Jarl Ragnar will still believe it was you, no matter what I say.'

Ulf nodded, even as he still struggled to understand what was happening. He wondered for a moment if Skadi was behind the attack. She had done the same before, but he couldn't understand why she would do that. Just like he still didn't understand why she was here or what she had warned him about.

They stood in silence for a while when Jarl Hakon said, 'We should inform Jarl Ragnar and then perhaps start a search for the person who attacked him.' He turned his attention to Ulf and Thorir. 'And I'll deal with the two of you for falling asleep when you were supposed to be guarding the captives.'

'Don't be too hard on them, Hakon. You can't expect them to stay awake the entire night, not after fighting the Franks and rowing for half the day. You should have sent someone to relieve them,' Jarl Knut said.

Jarl Hakon smiled as he glanced at the jug of ale emptied by Thorir. Ulf wondered about that as the jarl said, 'Aye, I guess you are right. I was too busy celebrating that I forgot to do that.'

As everyone left the ship, Ragnvald hung back and glared at Ulf, who again wondered why he had said nothing. His hand went to the Mjöllnir pendant around his neck as he worried about what game the gods were playing with him. When they were on their own, he turned to the bóndi. 'Why did you lie? They'll cut your tongue out if they find out.'

Thorir shrugged as he picked up the jug and shook it to make sure that it was empty. 'I promised—'

'If you tell me you promised Inga that you'd look after me one more time, then by Loki, I'll cut your tongue out.'

Thorir smiled, but then he went serious and stared at the camp on the riverbank. 'Someone attacked Jarl Ragnar?' He then looked at Ulf, who got irritated at the bóndi for the suspicion in his eyes.

'If you think I attacked him, then why did you protect me?' Thorir opened his mouth, but Ulf silenced him with a glare. 'Don't say it. And no, I didn't attack Jarl Ragnar.'

'You attacked him before, and Jarl Knut said he was still angry at you for it.'

Ulf rubbed the hilt of Ormstunga, now back in her scabbard, as he wondered about that. 'Aye, he did, but I don't understand why.'

'To protect you?'

Ulf shrugged, but couldn't see that either. 'Why would he want to protect me? I'm nobody to him.'

This time, Thorir shrugged. 'Only gods will really know what is going on.'

Ulf glanced at the moon as it sat low on the horizon. That was what was bothering him. The gods would know because they were behind whatever was going on.

***

'Your man failed,' Jarl Hakon said, but there was no judgement in his voice and that annoyed Knut even more. He clenched his fists, but said nothing as he cursed the gods. People had claimed for a long time that the gods favoured Ragnar. That was the reason King Horik had chosen the bastard to lead the raid. It was also the reason Knut was certain that Ragnar would make a move for the throne of Denmark as soon he returned. A throne that should be his. 'Ragnar will have his guard up now. It'll be harder to get to him again.'

'I know!' Knut hissed at him and then took deep breaths to calm himself. During the feast, he had done his best to make sure Ragnar drank more than he usually did, hoping that it would make it easier for Hallr to kill him. But Hallr had still failed. They walked in silence, both men sullen, as Hakon's one-handed warrior followed not far behind. Knut never understood why Hakon kept the old man nearby. His best days were behind him and Knut had been told that his son was responsible for the massacre where Hakon's son had died. All because of a woman.

The mood around the camp was as dark as the night sky as word had spread about the attack on Ragnar. Knut knew that many of the men would be furious that someone had tried to kill their jarl, a man favoured by the gods, and he hoped they wouldn't find out that the Bear-Slayer was the man blamed for the attack. Ragnar wouldn't say anything. He would want to play it down, but Knut knew how warriors liked to talk. They were worse than the women they left behind in their halls. There was no such thing as a secret in an army. Everyone knew everything, even important things they should not know. That was why Knut and Hakon worked hard to keep their plan amongst themselves. Not even Ragnvald knew about it, or so Knut hoped.

When they returned to his tent, they found Hallr waiting for them. The golden-hilted sword Knut had lent him was gone, hidden most likely so that others won't find it. 'What happened?' he barked at Hallr, who rubbed his side and moved gingerly.

'Forgive me, Jarl. Ragnar must have heard me approach. He turned before I could stab him and then his hirdmen arrived. I had to flee.'

Jarl Hakon walked into the tent, leaving his one-handed man outside. 'It'll be harder now,' he said again and Knut sighed.

He filled a cup with ale and drank from it while he thought about his next steps. Hakon was right. Ragnar would have his guard up now, so it would be harder to get to him. Their only option was to kill him during a battle. But Knut knew Ragnar would avoid pitched battles. Unless he was certain of an easy victory. That was their way and what had made them so successful at raiding the Christian kingdoms. Why fight a large battle and lose most of your men when you could run and return later when the enemy thought they had won? Knut turned to Hakon. 'Is your man certain Ulf never left the ship?'

Hakon shrugged. 'Ulf left for a piss, but that was it.'

'So the bóndi lied.' Knut rubbed his beard, trying to work out if he could use that.

'Does it really matter now? If we hang Ulf now for trying to kill Ragnar, then our plan will fail. Ulf needs to be here and alive so we could blame him for the attack,' Hakon said, which was the same thing Knut was thinking.

They fell silent as Knut thought about what to do next. Hallr lifted his brynja and tunic, and Knut saw the red mark on his pale skin, while Hakon helped himself to Knut's ale.

'Perhaps we could encourage the Bear-Slayer to attack Jarl Ragnar,' Hallr said as he prodded the red mark on his ribs. Knut raised an eyebrow at him and Hallr explained. 'He has a short temper. You saw that yourself when he attacked me for no reason.' Hakon laughed at that and Hallr glared at him, but then he continued. 'If we can give him a reason to really hate Jarl Ragnar, then perhaps he will kill him.'

'But you failed to kill Ragnar while he was drunk,' Hakon said, a mischievous smile on his face. 'Are you saying that Ulf is a better warrior than you? That he can kill Ragnar when you failed to?'

Hallr bristled and clenched his fists, forcing Knut to step in between the two men. He glared at Hakon, who only smiled back, and wondered why the Norse always had to start fights. Then he looked at Hallr.

'That is not a bad idea, Hallr. But how do we do that?'

'Make him think Jarl Ragnar wants to kill him. Or kill the bóndi and make him think Jarl Ragnar was behind it.'

Hakon smiled. 'That might work. And we make sure that Ulf is near Ragnar during any fight. That way, he might be encouraged to stick that pretty sword of his in Ragnar's back.'

'You'll have to make sure it's a cloudy day then,' Hakon said as he drank more ale.

'Why?'

'Ulf thinks his sword is cursed, so he never fights with it while the sun is out. Only when it is dark or cloudy.'

'Why?' Knut asked again.

'Only the gods really know, but that's what he believes.'

'He can always use his axe or his sax-knife,' Hallr said. 'Doesn't have to be the sword.'

'It doesn't matter. By the gods, why do you have to make this more complicated?' Knut sighed before he turned to Hakon. 'Can you find a way for the Bear-Slayer to think that Ragnar is trying to kill him?'

Hakon smiled. 'Aye, I'll think of something.'

'Good. If the gods are with us, then Ragnar will be dead before we reach Paris.'

As he spoke the words, an icy breeze suddenly entered his tent and Knut remembered the strange woman he had seen in Jelling before the raid started and a shiver ran down his spine.

CHAPTER 18

ULF SCOWLED AT THE dark smoke as it twisted and turned on its way to the sky to join ranks with the dark clouds already there. The smoke reminded Ulf of a snake slithering along the ground as he glanced to where Jarl Ragnar, wearing the furry breeches he liked to wear when he fought, stood with the other jarls. It had been many days since Jarl Ragnar had been attacked, and Ulf had done his best to avoid the leader of the fleet. But that had not been easy. Jarl Knut was close to Ragnar, and Jarl Hakon was close to Jarl Knut. So where Jarl Ragnar went, so did Jarl Hakon, which meant so did Ulf.

'That was easier than I thought it would be,' Thorir said beside him, and some of the men laughed.

Ulf turned his attention back to the burning farmstead and grunted. They had left the riverside camp two days before and had continued to travel upriver. Along the way, small groups broke off and raided along the riverbank, bringing back with them more plunder and captives. Livestock and ale were taken as well, which meant the men got to eat and drink well, something which kept everyone in good spirits. Even as rain lashed down on them for a few days. 'Aye,' Ulf said and looked at Jarl Ragnar again. The leader of the fleet was glaring at him as Jarl Knut whispered something in his ear. But Ulf didn't care. All he cared about was surviving this raid, something he had not really thought about until Skadi had come to him. Ulf had not sensed her presence since that night, and neither had she come to him in his dreams. He worried about what that meant and glanced at Thorir. *The dog pretending to be a wolf.*

Thorir started talking to some of Jarl Hakon's men, many of whom had befriended the bóndi, and would often invite him to their fire for a drink. Not Ulf, though. No one invited him, which Ulf was happy about. He did not need these men to be his friends, because when the raid was over and they returned to Denmark, he would part ways with them.

'You didn't do much fighting, Bear-Slayer,' one man said, the disdain clear in his voice.

Ulf raised his eyebrow at the warrior, who looked like he had only seen twenty two winters, like Ulf. 'I only fight warriors, not farmers and old men.' Ulf hawked and spat, before he walked away, leaving the warriors glaring at him.

'You should try harder to be friends with them,' Thorir said as he followed Ulf. 'They're good guys, for Norsemen.' He glanced at Ulf, as if expecting Ulf to bite, but Ulf stayed silent. 'The gods only know where Jarl Ragnar will keep all the captives. I don't think there is any space left on any of the ships.'

Ulf sighed. He knew what Thorir was doing, just as Thorir knew there was plenty of space on the ships. But the bóndi had a point. They had travelled far upriver and would soon need to find a place where they could protect the plunder and captives. The ships weren't the safest option, as they could easily be attacked and sunk, which meant all the plunder would be gone. He also wondered why the king of the West Franks had not sent an army to stop them yet. Surely he must have heard about Ragnar's fleet and the attacks along the river.

A few days later, one of the questions was answered when Jarl Ragnar decided to build a camp on a large island in the middle of the river. The island was large enough to hold most of the fleet, but more importantly, it could only be approached by boat, which meant it would be easy to defend. Especially with the wall Jarl Ragnar wanted built around the camp.

Many of the men had complained when they were sent out to the nearby forest to cut trees down for the defensive wall. Ulf, though, was glad to get away from the large fleet. Since the attack on Jarl Ragnar, it felt like everyone was watching him, and Ulf was tired from constantly looking over his shoulder.

Ulf stretched his back and wiped the sweat from his brow. He and Thorir were with a group of men from Jarl Hakon's army, the few who were less hostile to Ulf than the rest, chopping down trees. The men were joking and talking about the battles they had fought on the raid, often making fun of each other. Thorir was in the thick of the conversation and was often the butt of the jokes, but the Dane didn't seem to mind. He was so eager to be a warrior that he was willing to let the men make fun of him if it meant they saw him as one of their own. But Ulf knew they didn't. Warriors did not like others pretending to be like them. These men were killers. Hard men who faced death more than any man should and they resented those who believed they could show up with a spear or axe and fight in a shield wall. But they tolerated Thorir, something that made Ulf nervous.

He frowned as one man clapped Thorir on the back and was about to turn back to the tree he had been chopping, when he heard a noise behind him. Ulf's heart skipped as he recognised the sound and ducked, and as he stared at the arrow in the tree where his head had been a heartbeat ago, he thanked whichever ancestor or god had warned him. The other warriors cried out in alarm and they all turned in the direction the arrow had come from, their axes ready and their teeth bared. Ulf jumped to his feet and scanned the trees, but saw nothing out of the ordinary.

'That's an arrow,' Thorir said, his face pale as he stared at the arrow in the tree. Ulf ignored the Dane as he wished he had his shield with him. From the nervous twitching of their fingers, Ulf guessed the other warriors felt the same. He had faced arrows on the battlefield before, and nothing scared him more. A sword or spear you saw coming and could stop with your shield. But arrows killed many before they even knew of the threat, even while they hid behind their shields.

'Franks?' one man asked, his eyes darting amongst the shadows cast by the trees.

'With only one arrow and aimed at the Bear-Slayer?' another asked, and Ulf glanced behind him at the arrow.

'Someone tried to kill me?'

'Brave and clever. No wonder the gods favour him,' Hjalmar, the oldest of the group, said as he walked to the arrow and pulled it out of the tree. He scrutinized it and then glanced at Thorir. 'It's Danish.'

'How do you know?' Ulf frowned at the arrow in the warrior's hand.

Hjalmar shrugged. 'I've been around long enough to know the difference.'

'You did try to kill Jarl Ragnar,' another added, and Ulf turned to the man, his brows creased.

'If I wanted to kill Jarl Ragnar, I'd face him in the open. Not hide in the shadows.'

Hjalmar shook his head. 'Well, the gods know that someone just tried to put an arrow through your eye and I'm guessing it was because of the attack on Jarl Ragnar.'

Ulf raised an eyebrow. 'Why? If Ragnar really believes that I attacked him, then why not just hang me?' But as Ulf said the words, he remembered the men Ragnar had sent after him before the winter. He turned back towards the tree again and wondered if the old warrior was right. That Jarl Ragnar wanted him dead. And then another thought came to him. 'How do we know that someone really attacked Jarl Ragnar?'

The others took a step back from him, as if he had just fallen in dog shit, and Ulf regretted asking the question out loud.

'You saying that the jarl lied?' Thorir asked while scratching his head.

Ulf shook his head. 'No... I don't know what I'm saying. Perhaps I'm just rattled by the arrow,' Ulf lied, but the thought made him frown. They only had Jarl Ragnar's word that he had been attacked, just like the others only had Thorir's word that Ulf never left the ship. Something which Ulf and Thorir both knew was a lie. And not just them, but Ragnvald, as well. So how did he know Ragnar spoke the truth? *Some are threatened by the young wolf.* The volva's words came to him and Ulf wondered if Ragnar was threatened by him. But then he shook his head to chase the thought away. Jarl Ragnar was a mighty warrior and had the blood of kings in his veins. Ulf was nobody, at least he believed so anyway.

Hjalmar had decided they should return to the camp after that and as they made their way back, the others kept their distance from Ulf. He was a marked man, which was as good as being cursed by the gods, and no man wanted to be near a marked man. But Thorir either did not care about it or did not understand as he walked by Ulf's side, telling him stories from his father's farm. Ulf ignored him, though, as he thought about the arrow that almost killed him. He wasn't sure if the arrow came from a Danish bow, but only because he did not know how to tell the difference. To him, an arrow was an arrow, and he hated all of them. He also couldn't understand why Jarl Ragnar would send someone to kill him like that. Surely it would have been easier to have someone stab him in the back during a battle. The thought sent a shiver down Ulf's spine and he wished he had never had that thought. That was the way his father had been killed, and Ulf's heart raced at the thought that he might die the same way.

Ulf stopped and stared at the camp being built around him. His brows creased as he wondered how many of these men would do that. *All of them*. The voice whispered in his ears, and Ulf wondered where it came from. But it was right. None of these men, neither the Danes nor the Norsemen, were his friends or owed him anything. To them, he was just another warrior who had joined the raid to make himself rich. And one less warrior meant more plunder for them.

'Ulf?' Thorir asked as Ulf scrutinised the camp, his fingers rubbing the hilt of Ormstunga. The island was large enough for most of the men to stay on, and while some were busy building a wooden wall around the camp, others were erecting their tents and starting fires. Sounds of wood being chopped filled the air, drowning out the cries of the many captives who had been put in cages that were built as soon as they had arrived on the island. The warriors laughed and joked. Some sang songs as they worked and Ulf had even heard a few make bets on who could chop the most trees. Most of the five thousand men were busy doing something as Ragnar wanted the camp to be built as quickly as possible. They still expected the king of West Francia or a local lord to send an army to deal with them, but apart from the warriors who had protected the towns they had raided, there had been none.

Ragnar's tent was in the centre of the camp. It was larger than the others and stood proud, like a jarl's hall with two banners on either side flapping in the wind. Ulf stared at the ravens on Jarl Ragnar's banners and wondered why most men chose the scavenging birds as their symbols. Perhaps it was because ravens were associated with Odin and the jarls hoped it would bring them luck. As Ulf watched the tent, he saw Jarl Knut leave with a scowl on his face. Jarl Hakon came out soon after, and the two of them lowered their heads as they spoke to each other. Jarl Knut looked back towards Jarl Ragnar's tent and shook his head before he turned around and saw Ulf watching them. He said something to Jarl Hakon, who looked Ulf's way and waved him over.

'What do they want?' Thorir asked, and Ulf wondered the same.

'Go get our tent set up and I'll go find out. And don't say anything about the arrow,' Ulf said, ignoring the frown on Thorir's face.

'But the others might have done already.'

Ulf shook his head. 'No, they'll keep quiet about it.' Ulf hoped that was true. He did not want word to spread that someone had tried to kill him, because he worried it might encourage others to do the same.

He walked towards the two jarls, who greeted him warmly. Ulf nodded his greeting and glanced at Jarl Ragnar's tent behind them, still wondering what the two men were talking about.

'Jarl Ragnar is planning his attack on Paris.' Jarl Knut smiled. 'It will be an attack worthy of the gods and will make us all richer than Fafnir.'

Ulf raised an eyebrow at Jarl Knut. The look on his face when he had come out of the tent suggested he had not liked what had been said inside the tent, but Ulf decided not to say anything about it. He did not want to get involved with whatever dispute there might have been. All he wanted was to make enough to free Eldrid. 'When does he plan to attack?'

'He is waiting,' Jarl Knut said, and Ulf sensed the frustration in his voice. Perhaps that was what he and Jarl Hakon were discussing.

'Waiting for what?'

'The Christians have an important celebration coming up and Jarl Ragnar wants to attack Paris while they celebrate. He believes the Christians won't expect an attack then and will let their guard down.'

Ulf scratched his beard. 'That makes sense.' Ulf knew what celebration they were talking about. The Christians believed that the son of their god had sacrificed himself for their sins and that he had come back to life afterwards. Ulf struggled to understand what the sacrifice was if the son of their god still lived afterwards, but then most things the Christians did made no sense to him. 'That was why he started the raid before the winter was over?'

Jarl Knut nodded. 'Aye, but that celebration is still many days away and much can happen before then.' He glanced at Jarl Hakon and Ulf wondered about the small smile on the Norse jarl's face as a raven crowed from the top of Jarl Ragnar's tent.

Chapter 19

Horns blew deep into the night, waking Ulf from his sleep. As he sat up, rubbing his eyes, he heard men shouting outside.

'We're under attack!'

'The Franks are here!'

Ulf looked to where Thorir was and in the darkness, he could just see the bóndi jumping to his feet and running out of the tent, his axe in his hand, but his leather jerkin left behind. Ulf shook his head and got to his feet. He wondered if he had enough time to put his brynja on, but with all the shouting, he doubted it. So he grabbed Ormstunga and his axe and followed Thorir out of the tent.

Outside, men ran around as the horn continued to blow from the centre of the camp. Ulf frowned at that because if there was an attack, then the horn should have come from the wall that they had built days ago.

'Calm down! There is no attack!' one of Jarl Ragnar's hirdmen roared as he stomped towards Ulf, his fists clenched. Ulf just had enough time to frown at the warrior before he punched Ulf in the stomach.

Ulf bent over as the air was knocked out of him, but before he could do anything, the man grabbed him by his hair and pulled his head up. Ulf was blinded as another warrior held a torch in his face, the flames almost singeing his eyebrows.

'What is going on?' Thorir shouted as the surrounding warriors stopped and stared.

'There's no attack?' someone asked.

'There is no attack,' Jarl Ragnar said as he walked up to Ulf and punched him in the face. Ulf's head snapped to the side, and he tasted the blood in his mouth, but he was too confused to do anything other than stare dumbly at the bloodied knife in Jarl Ragnar's hand.

'By the gods, what's going on?' Thorir asked again.

'This bastard tried to kill Jarl Ragnar again,' Jarl Ragnar's hirdman said and tightened his grip on Ulf's hair. 'But this time he killed one of the Jarl's hirdmen instead.'

Ulf winced as his hair pulled on his scalp and was about to protest when he glimpsed Skadi as the dancing flames of a torch lit up the shadows between two tents. He would have frowned at the smile on her face if his head wasn't spinning with confusion.

'Ulf couldn't have done,' Thorir said. 'We were in the tent, sleeping until the horn blew.'

Ragnar held the bloodied knife up for everyone to see and many of the warriors gasped, but Ulf was not paying attention to the knife any more. His eyes were still fixed on the spot where he had seen the volva and he wondered if she had killed the warrior. 'This is the knife that killed Sigurd! I pulled it from his dead body after I heard men fighting outside my tent.'

Ulf spat the blood from his mouth and glared at Jarl Ragnar. 'That is not my knife.'

Jarl Ragnar raised an eyebrow at him. 'You could have used another man's knife so that I wouldn't suspect you. But I'm smarter than you think, you ugly bastard. Twice you tried to kill me and the gods know I'm not foolish enough to give you a third chance.'

'And twice you tried to kill me!'

Jarl Ragnar's eyes widened, and he punched Ulf again while the others still held him. 'You lie!'

Ulf shook his head. 'You sent men to kill me before the winter, and a Danish arrow almost took my life a few days ago.'

Jarl Ragnar's hand shot out as fast as a striking snake and gripped Ulf around his throat. Ulf glared at him as he squeezed, but he refused to give Jarl Ragnar the satisfaction of begging for his life.

'Ragnar, enough of this!' Jarl Knut said as he arrived with Jarl Hakon by his side, both jarls still in their brynjas and Jarl Hakon hiding his arm behind his back.

Jarl Ragnar turned, his face red in the light of the torches. 'How dare you! I am the leader of this army, not you!' He let go of Ulf's throat and stomped towards Jarl Knut, who stood his ground as Ragnar glared at him. 'You dare tell me what to do, cousin?'

In the dim light of the torches, Ulf saw the anger in Jarl Knut's eyes, an anger he recognised from his own. 'No, Ragnar, I do not. I merely suggest you calm down and think about it before you kill Ulf.'

'And why should I?'

'Because how do you really know it was Ulf?'

'It wasn't the Bear-Slayer,' Ragnvald said, surprising everyone. 'Been sitting outside my tent all night, and not once saw Ulf leave his.'

Ulf stared at Ragnvald and wondered why the one-handed warrior was defending him as Jarl Ragnar's warrior let go of Ulf's hair. Ulf shook his head and straightened as the other warriors let go of him as well.

'Jarl Ragnar, I do not know what is going on here, but I swear on my ancestors' honour that I had nothing to do with the death of your man or the attack on you.'

Jarl Ragnar turned his glare towards Ulf before he glanced around at the surrounding men. Most of them were Jarl Hakon's Norse warriors, although many of the Danes had arrived to see what was going on.

'Jarl Hakon, I know you as a man of honour and good reputation. Ulf Bear-Slayer is your man, oath sworn or not. Do you vouch for his honour?' He turned to Jarl Hakon. 'Would you stake your life on it?'

Jarl Hakon smiled as he glanced at Ulf. 'His name is widely known in Norway, as are his deeds.' Ulf frowned as he wondered which deeds the jarl was referring to. 'As Odin is my witness, I stand by Ulf. If he claims not to have anything to do with the attacks, then I believe him.'

Jarl Ragnar's brow creased, the flickering from the torches casting strange shadows on his face, as he considered what Jarl Hakon had said.

Jarl Knut stepped forward and cleared his throat. 'Why don't I take my men and Jarl Hakon's and we go raiding for a few days? That way, Ulf would be out of the camp and you can relax.'

Jarl Ragnar's lip curled at the implication and somewhere a warrior hissed, but Ulf wasn't paying attention to any of that. He was scanning the shadows around the tents, trying to find any sign of Skadi. He was certain she was there, and the gods knew he wouldn't be surprised if he found out that she had killed the warrior outside Ragnar's tent. Out of the corner of his eye, he spotted Thorir staring at him as if he was trying to work out what Ulf was doing.

'Where will you raid?' Jarl Ragnar asked.

Jarl Knut looked at Jarl Hakon and shrugged. 'There is a large town not far from here. Thought we'd go see what they have to offer.'

Jarl Ragnar nodded. 'Good. Be back in three days' time.' He turned to face the men around him, their faces lit by the torches and the moon. 'Then we will make our way to Paris and bring the king of the West Franks to his knees. Before this summer is over, we'll all be richer than the gods!'

The men cheered, but Ulf noticed how many of them rubbed the pendants they wore around their necks. Even Ulf found his hand going to the Mjöllnir pendant he wore. He had learnt not to anger the gods.

Thunder rumbled through the night sky and Ulf wondered if it was because of Jarl Ragnar's words. Ragnar, though, did not seem quelled by the thunder as he laughed at it.

'The gods are with us! They want us to bring the Christians to their knees. To punish them for what they have done to our brothers and sisters.'

The men cheered again, this time louder than before, and when the thunder stopped, they all went back to their tents and campfires. Jarl Knut and Jarl Hakon lingered for a while, both men staring at Ulf. Behind them, Ulf spotted Ragnvald glaring at him, and he wondered why the old man had defended him as he turned and made his way back to his tent.

'Who were you looking for?' Thorir asked him, his voice filled with suspicion.

Ulf raised an eyebrow at him. 'Nobody.'

'Eldrid warned me to stay away from you. And many of the men say you are cursed.'

Ulf's jaw muscles tightened, and he took a deep breath to calm himself before he turned to face the bóndi. 'And I told you to go back to your farm.'

Thorir stared at Ulf, but then he sighed. 'I don't want to die because of you, Ulf. That's all.'

Ulf glared at Thorir, wondering why the man had lied for him before only to question him later. 'Then you should have listened to Eldrid.'

Thorir nodded and went back to the tent, but Ulf stayed where he was. He looked at the moon breaking through the clouds and scanned the shadows around him. *What game are you playing, volva?*

The following morning, Ulf stood by Jarl Hakon's ship, his cloak wrapped around his shoulders because of the morning chill, as the men loaded their chests and weapons. Shields were placed on the side, facing outwards so they would be out of the way and also to protect the men from arrows while they rowed. Men laughed and birds sang their morning songs, while the smell of wet earth filled his nostrils, but Ulf found it hard to share the men's optimism.

'Your luck will change one day, Bear-Slayer,' Ragnvald said, making Ulf jump because he had not heard the old man approach.

Ulf scowled at him. *I never had any luck*, Ulf wanted to say, but then he remembered the many times he was about to die during battles, only to be saved by his luck. Others had claimed it was Tyr protecting him, but to Ulf, it was the same thing. 'Aye,' was all he could say as he again wondered why Ragnvald had defended him the night before. Ulf turned and saw Thorir talking to some of Jarl Hakon's warriors, laughing at something they said.

Ragnvald followed his gaze. 'Be careful of those around you. Not everyone is the friend they claim to be.'

Ulf turned, his eyes wide at Ragnvald's words. But the old man had walked off before he could say anything. Ulf shook his head, wondering why everyone had to bring him into their games. He turned his attention back to Thorir as he rubbed the hilt of Ormstunga with his thumb. *Tyr, protect me from the dangers I cannot yet see. Odin, turn your eye away from me. I want no part in your games.*

'These games have nothing to do with the All-Father,' Skadi's voice whispered in his ears, but when Ulf turned around, there was no sign of the volva. His heart raced as he scanned the ground for footprints, or even marks left behind by a snake, but there was nothing. He shook his head and looked up to see Jarl Hakon frowning at him.

'Time to go, Bear-Slayer.' He looked at his men around him. 'It's time to show these Christians how weak their god really is!'

The men cheered as they boarded the four ships, Jarl Knut's two ships and Jarl Hakon's two ships. Thorir stopped next to Ulf and slapped him on the shoulder.

'Come Ulf. Let's forget about last night and kill some Christians. At this rate I'll be rich enough to buy four farms when we return to Denmark.' He laughed as he boarded the ship, and Ulf shook his head before following the bóndi to their place at the rear of the ship, near the steering oar.

Jarl Hakon looked at Jarl Knut on his ship and when the Danish jarl nodded, Jarl Hakon gave the order. The ships were pushed away from the banks of the river; the men using their oars to move the ships away from the others and towards the middle of the wide river.

A raven screamed above them and when Ulf looked up, he saw her standing on the riverbank. Her dark eyes fixed on him and her mouth moving, although Ulf couldn't hear her words. He felt the shiver run down his spine and again, prayed to Tyr, asking his ancestor to protect him.

Chapter 20

THEY DID NOT ROW for long. Only half a day until they got to a bend in the river when the signal came from Jarl Knut's ship, and the four ships made for the riverbank. Ulf saw no sign of a town, although he spotted a well-worn path which he guessed led to the town Jarl Knut wanted to attack.

This part of the river looked much the same as most of what he had seen already. The land on either side was flat and mostly empty, although there were patches of forests where oak and ash trees grew near the river. Ulf wasn't sure why, but he felt nervous every time they rowed past those parts. Perhaps it was because he still expected the king of West Francia to send his army to attack them, and the forest seemed like a perfect place to ambush Jarl Ragnar's fleet. But it never happened. It was as if the gods wanted this raid to happen.

'Are you ready to kill some more Christians, Bear-Slayer?' Jarl Hakon asked as he walked past Ulf on his way to the prow of his ship. Some men laughed, including Thorir.

'I know I am,' the bóndi said as he rolled his shoulders and checked the edge of his axe.

Ulf sighed and took his shield from the side of the ship. He glanced up at the sky and saw a few clouds, but not enough to hide the sun. Ormstunga would stay in her scabbard, but Ulf doubted she would be needed.

After the two jarls selected men to stay behind and guard the ships, they led the rest of the army, about one hundred and sixty men, up the path which Ulf guessed led to the town. The men walked in silence, their eyes scanning the trees and grasslands on either side of the path, but all they saw was a shepherd boy when they were close to the town. The boy's face paled when he noticed the raiders and before one of Jarl Knut's men could grab him, the boy turned and raced towards the large town sprawled out in the Frankish countryside as the other warriors mocked the man for missing the boy. Wooden walls protected the town, but the walls were lightly guarded, and in the centre, Ulf saw the tower of a Christian church sticking out over the walls.

'I guess the surprise is over,' Jarl Hakon laughed.

Jarl Knut smiled and gave the signal to the man beside him, who raised his horn to his lips and blew one long note. The Danish and Norse warriors roared as they charged at the town. Ulf did not roar. Neither did he call out to Odin and Thor. He took his axe from his belt and as he ran along with the men of Jarl Hakon, with Thorir running ahead of him, someone kicked his ankle. As Ulf struggled to keep his balance, believing it had been an accident, somebody shoulder barged him and knocked him over. Ulf hit the ground hard and almost lost hold of his shield, when his ancestors screamed in his ears. Ulf obeyed as he rolled over on the ground and lifted his shield to protect himself when he felt a spear striking it. His anger erupted from the pit of his stomach and spread through his limbs.

Ulf jumped to his feet, his heart racing, and tried to see who had attempted to kill him, but all he saw were the backs of Jarl Knut's Danes as they charged at the town, its church bells ringing loud enough to be heard over the war cries. Someone had tried to kill him. Of that he was certain, and as Jarl Knut's men broke through the town gates before they could be closed, he remembered Skadi's warning and knew Thorir was also in danger. Ulf lowered his head and raced after the men while praying to Thor that he was not too late.

By the time Ulf caught up with Jarl Knut's force, the fighting had already started as the Danish and Norse warriors streamed through the open gates and into the town. There was no shield wall as the Danes and Norsemen ran through the streets and hacked down any Frank within reach of their weapons. The only ones not killed were the women, but only the young ones. Old women with hunched backs and grey hair were cut down without mercy, their cries ignored by the men who cared only about gold and glory. Not that Ulf saw much glory in what they were doing. He watched as a Danish warrior stabbed an old man through the back before grabbing the girl the old man had been protecting by the hair and dragging her into one of the houses.

Somewhere, Ulf heard a dog howling and turned in time to see it being skewered by a spear, just like he had almost been. The voices in Ulf's ears were raging at him, telling to kill the bastards who had tried to do the same to him, but Ulf did not know who had stabbed at him. He didn't know if it had been one of Jarl Knut's men or Hakon's. As he walked through the streets, trying to find Thorir, he sensed movement from his side and turned in time to block the pitchfork aimed at his head with his shield. Ulf punched out with his axe and caught the Frank, his face too young to grow a beard, in the chest and as the Frank staggered back, Ulf struck him in the side of his head with his shield, but only hard enough to knock him out. He was certain the young Frank would have a headache when he woke up, but at least he would be alive.

Ulf turned and saw Thorir fighting alongside three of Jarl Hakon's men in the town's market square. All four of them were covered in blood as they hacked down a group of Franks trying to protect the house behind them. Ulf shook his head and was about to run towards them when another Frank attacked him. This one wore a leather jerkin and stabbed at Ulf with a spear, which Ulf dodged and chopped in half with his axe before kicking the man's legs out from under him. As the Frank landed on his back, Ulf buried his axe in his chest. He pulled the axe free and rushed towards Thorir, who was fighting on his own now. Thorir blocked the spear with his shield, but the Frankish warrior jumped back to avoid the bóndi's axe. Ulf wondered where the other three men had gone, the ones who had been by Thorir's side only moments ago. He reached Thorir just before the Frank stabbed at his exposed side and hacked at the man's neck, drenching both him and Thorir in blood.

'By the gods,' Thorir said, his face creased in anger. 'I had him!'

Ulf shook his head and turned when someone screamed behind them. But instead of facing another Frankish warrior, a young man, too young to have been with a woman yet, charged at them armed only with a knife. Ulf was about to trip him up and knock him out when Thorir shot forward and punched out with his shield, sending the young Frank to the ground. The knife fell from his hand and his face turned white as Thorir stood over him, his axe held high.

'Now you die, you Christian scum.'

Ulf saw himself, not much older than the young Frank, charging at the monster who had slaughtered his family and knew he couldn't let Thorir kill the Frank. He shot forward and shoulder barged Thorir before he could bring the axe down and kill the young man. Thorir went sprawling to the ground as Ulf turned to the young Frank.

'Run!' he said, hoping the boy would get the meaning of what he was saying. But the boy just lay there, staring at him with wide eyes. 'Run!' Ulf shouted again.

'Bastard!' Thorir shouted and Ulf turned in time to see the bóndi swinging his axe at his head. Ulf ducked under the swing and resisted the urge to punch Thorir in his exposed stomach. 'They were right about you! You are nothing but a coward! A Christian lover!'

Ulf stepped back as Thorir punched out with his shield. 'Thorir, stop this!'

'Fuck you!' Thor spat at Ulf and shot forward, swinging his axe at Ulf's head again, and again, Ulf ducked under the swing, but this time he punched Thorir in the stomach with his shield and as Thorir bent over, Ulf struck him in the face with his axe hand. Thorir fell to the ground and glared at Ulf, who stood over him, his limbs trembling with rage. 'You just want all the glory for yourself.'

Ulf hawked and spat. 'What glory is there in killing farmers and young boys? Of hacking old women down as they flee for their lives?'

'The gods want us to kill the Christians. They threaten our way of life.'

Ulf shook his head and wondered why Thorir believed the nonsense Hakon's men had whispered in his ears. 'These Christians are not a threat to us. They are not the ones attacking us. They do not raid our shores and kill our people or sell them as thralls. Open your eyes, Thorir. This attack, this raid, has nothing to do with protecting the gods or our way of life. It's about greed. It's about men like Ragnar who want to be more powerful than the rest of the jarls in Denmark.'

Thorir wiped the blood from his face and glared at Ulf. 'I should have told them you left the ship and that you were gone long enough to attack Jarl Ragnar. I never should have lied for you.'

Ulf sighed and remembered what Inga had asked of him. He shook his head and turned. 'No, you shouldn't.'

He walked away and ignored the fighting around him and Thorir cursing him. Ulf glanced at the sky and saw the ravens and other carrion birds circling the sky above the town. Already black smoke mixed with the few clouds above the birds, a signal for anyone nearby that this town had been attacked. But Ulf cared little for any of that as he walked away. Women screamed and children cried around him as the Danish and Norse warriors laughed and killed.

'Thor's balls, would you look at that? The Bear-Slayer is walking away from the fight,' someone said, and Ulf looked up to see the men of Jarl Knut, the ones who were there when the jarl had spotted him in Jelling. Ulf tightened his grip on his axe as he expected them to attack him, but they just laughed.

'You're a coward, Bear-Slayer,' Hallr said as the others laughed. 'I bet your mother wished she drowned you at birth.'

As soon as the words came out of the man's mouth, Ulf rushed at him, his speed catching the man by surprise and there was nothing the Dane could do as Ulf headbutted him. Ulf was glad that neither of them wore helmets as the man dropped to the ground. He glared at the others, his rage spreading through his limbs like the flames on the thatch roofs around them.

'Any of you bastards have anything to say?' The men, all of them stunned by Ulf's attack on Hallr, took a step back and shook their heads. Ulf glared at the bastard on the ground. He gripped his axe as the man stared at him, his beard covered in the blood from his nose. 'Call me a coward again and not even Hel would want you in her hall.'

'Is there a problem here?' Jarl Knut asked, and Ulf turned, surprised to see him standing there, his brynja clean, as with the previous battles. Even his bleached hair was still immaculate as he stood there. Jarl Knut's scowl was not directed at Ulf, but at his man on the ground.

The man shook his head and got to his feet. 'No, Jarl. This bastard just attacked me. All I did was have a laugh with him.'

'That's what you said last time, as well. Perhaps it should be obvious to you that the Bear-Slayer does not appreciate your sense of humour, Hallr,' Jarl Knut said. Hallr opened his mouth to say something when the others around him grabbed him and pulled him away. But as they left, Ulf felt their glares on him and knew that they would come for him at some point. 'You have a habit of not making yourself popular, Ulf,' Jarl Knut said to him, and Ulf frowned.

'I'm not here to be popular.'

'No, you're here because you want to make yourself rich. All so you could free a thrall. That friend of yours likes to talk,' Jarl Knut said when Ulf raised an eyebrow at him.

Ulf looked to where Thorir was, but he could not see the bóndi. 'Thorir needs to learn to keep quiet.'

Jarl Knut laughed. 'Aye, he does. But then it's good to have friends that speak up for you.'

Again, Ulf frowned and wondered what the jarl meant by that. 'I don't think I can consider Thorir a friend any longer.'

This time, Jarl Knut raised an eyebrow. 'He doesn't agree with your point of view?'

'Few do.' Ulf was about to walk away when Jarl Knut said,

'You keep resisting what you really are, Bear-Slayer. Others see it and it makes them jealous of what the gods have given you. They see you as a threat and that makes them nervous when you are around.'

Ulf stopped and turned as he remembered Skadi saying something similar to him. 'Who sees me as a threat?'

But Jarl Knut did not respond. Instead, he turned and walked away, back towards the carnage of burning houses and screaming women. As Ulf stared at his back, he caught sight of Ragnvald watching him, the old man's brynja covered in blood. Ulf glared at Ragnvald, wondering if he was the threat Ulf had been warned about. But if he was, then why did the one-handed man save his life before? Or defended him when he was accused of killing Jarl Ragnar's man? As Ulf wondered about this, Ragnvald turned and walked away, and Ulf decided he needed to do the same. He made his way to a quiet spot far enough so the screams of the townspeople couldn't bother him and sat down to clean his axe.

Perhaps it had been a bad idea to come on this raid. He should have sought a different jarl, one who wanted no part of Jarl Ragnar's raid. But then Ulf looked up as a raven landed on a branch above him. The large bird tilted its head as it stared at him with its beady eyes, and Ulf felt like he had never had any choice. The gods wanted him to return to West Francia, and Ulf wished he knew why.

Chapter 21

Ulf did not join the men as they feasted under the moon and stars after the attack. He did not dance around the flames of the fire by the riverside, nor did he play any musical instruments or sang songs. Instead, he sat by himself and stared at the dancing light from the burning town, wondering if that was what it would look like when Surtr burnt Asgard. His aunt had told him the story when he was a boy and it had always been one of his favourites, as was the story of Ragnarök. As a boy, Ulf wanted to fight alongside the ice giants and Loki against the gods, because Ulf had hated the gods. He almost smiled at the thought as he dragged a whetstone along the edge of his axe. The blade didn't need to be sharpened, but Ulf needed something to take his mind away from what had happened earlier on.

When the attack was over, the captives, mostly women and children, were herded back to the ships, along with carts filled with whatever plunder they could find. There wasn't much gold or silver, not even in the church, which had been emptied long before they had arrived. But there were plenty of barrels of ale and wine, and that had been enough to put smiles on the face of the Danes and Norsemen. Not that many of the men needed a reason to smile. Even Thorir, his face still bloody from his fight with Ulf, was laughing with Jarl Knut's men.

Ulf turned away from the feast when the women they had taken from the town were being passed around and it had annoyed him even more when he saw Thorir take a woman for himself.

'You should take a woman. Enjoy yourself.' Jarl Hakon joined Ulf by the tree he was sitting under and handed him a jug of wine. Ulf took a sip and grimaced. He had drunk Frankish wine before, but preferred ale. The wine was too sour for him and he hated the way his mouth felt like it had grown fur afterwards. 'They're not as pretty as our Norse women, but it's dark, so you won't even notice.'

Ulf shook his head as he drank more wine, but only so that he wouldn't say something to offend Jarl Hakon. It had been a long time since he had been with a woman, but he refused to take a woman against her will. Not after what had happened to his aunt and Eldrid.

'That bóndi of yours is turning out to be a fine warrior, even for a Dane,' Jarl Hakon said when Ulf didn't respond. 'He fought well today.'

Ulf looked at the fire as one man jumped through it, much to the cheers of the others, and then at Jarl Hakon. He wondered why the jarl was here, talking to him instead of feasting with his men. But then, Ulf knew he shouldn't complain. Jarl Hakon had stood by his side and had defended him when Ragnar had accused Ulf of killing his men. He still didn't understand why, but Ulf was glad that Jarl Hakon at least seemed to be on his side. 'He did,' Ulf said. 'But it's easy to fight well when you're attacking farmers.'

Jarl Hakon laughed. 'Aye, you speak the truth. Not all men are warriors. Some just love to kill. Perhaps Thorir is one of those. Perhaps he only wants to be a warrior so he could slake that thirst. You never really know a man, do you, Bear-Slayer?'

Ulf frowned at Jarl Hakon. 'What do you mean?'

Jarl Hakon shrugged. 'I knew Jarl Thorgils when he was a young man and his father was still jarl. Just like I know King Halfdan.' He stared at the stars before he turned and went back to the fire. 'I don't blame you for killing the bastard, Ulf. I wanted to do it myself many times.' Jarl Hakon walked away before Ulf could say anything, his head spinning. He glanced at the jug and wondered if it was because of the wine or because of what Jarl Hakon had said to him. Ulf looked up at the stars and wished that Skadi was there. Perhaps she could tell him what was going on, but then, she rarely made any sense.

***

Many of the men were grey-faced the following morning as they rowed to meet up with Jarl Ragnar's fleet, but they were still talking about the attack on the town and the women they fucked. Birds flew amongst the reeds alongside the river, singing their songs as the sun shone brightly above them. The days were getting longer and Ulf felt that spring had a firm grip on the countryside as flowers washed the riverbanks with different colours. Bees and other insects hopped from one flower to the next, pausing only to take Freya's gift from between the petals. Summer would arrive soon and the farmers would be planting their crops and preparing for the calving season. But not the ones alongside this river. Most of them were dead or had fled and their livestock was slaughtered to feed the army of Jarl Ragnar. Ulf saw an otter slip under the water and wondered if that was an omen. He remembered what Jarl Knut had said to him the day before. Did Jarl Ragnar see him as a threat? Did Ulf make him nervous? Ulf shook his head and dismissed that idea. Ragnar wanted Ormstunga. He wanted another pretty sword to add to his collection of other pretty swords. Men like Jarl Ragnar, who always got what they wanted, couldn't take it when you said no to them. That was why Jarl Ragnar hated Ulf. Because he had said no. But the gods only knew why Ragnar couldn't just let it go.

And then there was Thorir. Ulf glanced at the bóndi, who had not spoken to him since their fight. His face was bruised and he had a cut on his arm, but the man was in good spirits as he joked with the others around him. Ulf, though, was not part of the conversation, but he preferred it that way. Just like he preferred it that Thorir wanted nothing to do with him at the moment. That way, he might survive this raid and make it back to his family. Ulf still didn't understand what dangers he faced and didn't want others killed because of that.

They soon met up with the rest of Jarl Ragnar's fleet and the warriors shouted greetings to each other from across the river. Some asked about the raid, while others asked if there was any ale left. Jarl Hakon waved at Jarl Ragnar, who returned his greeting before glaring at Ulf, who did his best to ignore the Danish jarl. Instead, Ulf watched the riverbank, trying to see if he could spot any more otters. But it seemed like the animals had decided not to hang around as Ragnar's large fleet made its way to Paris. Many of the towns and farms they saw along the way seemed deserted. Like the otters, the people had fled as well. Once in a while, a few ships would break off from the fleet to plunder anything of value left behind.

'There is a large monastery not far from here,' Jarl Hakon shouted to his crew. 'They say it's as large as Valhalla, but with not a single warrior in sight.' The men cheered at this, and Ulf glanced over his shoulder at Jarl Hakon's other ship. As always, Ragnvald was glaring at him, and Ulf wondered why the old bastard could not just leave him alone. 'Do you think we should leave this monastery be, Bear-Slayer?'

Ulf almost dropped his oar as the question took him by surprise and he scowled at Jarl Hakon, who only smiled back. Ulf knew what the jarl was doing, just as he knew he couldn't say yes, because that would turn the men against him, even those who had been good to him so far. 'It doesn't matter what I think,' Ulf said, hoping this answer would not anger the men. 'The Norns have already decided what we do.'

'And what do you think the Norns have decided?' Jarl Hakon asked, clearly not wanting Ulf to avoid answering the question.

Ulf sighed and looked at the river, but he saw no sign to tell him what the gods wanted. But he knew what the surrounding men wanted as they all stared at him, waiting for him to answer. 'They have decided that we attack the monastery.'

The men cheered, and those nearby reached over and clapped him on the back, as Ulf prayed that the Christian priests were smart enough to flee their monastery. But in his experience, they weren't. They believed their crosses and their god would protect him, but Ulf had never seen that happen. Their god was always silent when they plundered the churches and killed the priests, and yet the Christian priests insisted on staying and praying to their god.

Ulf looked at Jarl Hakon, who was still smiling at him. He sensed the jarl was up to something, but couldn't figure out what. If they knew about the monastery, then that meant they had already decided to attack it. The jarls had spent many days in Ragnar's tent planning the raid and the attack on Paris. Where they got the information about the places, he didn't know, but guessed it must have been from traders like Tormod and Ingolfr. Ulf knew they had travelled up this river and traded in Paris, although they hadn't done so while Ulf was with them. They claimed the taxes were too high, but Ulf knew it was more because they didn't want to travel all the way to West Francia when there were good markets in East Francia. The journeys were much shorter, which meant they could stay there longer and do more trade.

'Where is this monastery?' one man asked and Jarl Hakon shrugged.

'Another day's rowing, I think. So we'll not get there today. But the Norns know that tomorrow we'll need to get another ship because there won't be enough space left on any of the ships for the riches we'll get from that place.'

The men's eyes lit up as they looked at each other and discussed what the jarl had said. Another man came to take Ulf's place on the rowing chest and handed him a flask of water, which Ulf drank from before rinsing his face. The spring sun was not as strong as the summer sun, but it was still warm enough to make Ulf sweat while he rowed. Ulf stretched his shoulders and glanced at the captives huddled around the mast and guarded by some warriors. Many of them were bloodied and bruised, and more than a few had ripped dresses, but all of them were broken. Ulf rubbed the Mjöllnir pendant around his neck and prayed to Heimdall, asking the god of thralls to protect these women and children.

Ulf made his way to Jarl Hakon at the stern of his ship, who watched him with an amused grin as he approached. 'You want your men to hate me, don't you?'

Jarl Hakon laughed. 'No, Bear-Slayer. The opposite. I figured you were smart enough to answer the way you did. The men need to see you as one of them. Otherwise, you might find they are not so quick to lift their shields to protect you in the shield wall.'

Ulf frowned and thought about the battle right at the start of the raid. When Thorir had pushed Ulf amongst the enemy in his eagerness to kill the Franks. If it hadn't been for Ragnvald, then Ulf would have been dead and Ulf still didn't know why the old man had done that. He glanced at Ragnvald on the other ship, but this time he was not staring at Ulf. 'But I am not one of them. I swore no oath to you and we both know that as soon as we get back to Denmark, then I will go my own way while they return to your hall with you.'

Jarl Hakon shrugged. 'The gods know that's not important. You are a Norseman, fighting the Christians alongside other Norsemen.'

'And fighting for the Danes,' Ulf added, which made Hakon smile.

'Aye, but we all fight for the same thing.'

'Fame, gold and silver,' Ulf said.

Jarl Hakon laughed again and surprised Ulf by not denying it. 'You know as much as any of us how important fame is. You fought with Snorri Thorgilsson and Ragnar Four-Fingers. Names even the Danes fear. Jarl Thorgils had such a reputation that even King Halfdan of Vestfold was nervous of him. Even you, Ulf Bear-Slayer, the man they say is blessed by Odin and cannot die.'

'Heard they hanged you and Odin broke the tree, a mighty oak that had stood for generations,' one warrior sitting near the jarl said. Ulf saw it was Hjalmar, the old warrior who had identified the Danish arrow that almost killed Ulf.

Ulf's hand went to his neck, where he still bore the scar from the rope Jarl Thorgils had put around his neck, but didn't respond.

'Fame, gold and silver guarantee us a place in Valhalla, amongst Odin's Einherjar. Some of these men need to be told there is a reason other than our own greed for raiding the rich kingdoms of the Franks, but we know the truth. We all want fame and some will go further than others to get that. The question always is, what are you willing to do for your fame?'

Ulf frowned as he watched the river go by. Somewhere a fish splashed out of the water, its silvery scales flashing in the sunlight. 'I never asked for my fame. And besides, Odin only kept me alive because of the oath I had made to him. When Griml died, that oath was completed, so the All-Father has no reason to keep me alive any more.'

'Aye, but he still has his eye on you. Those of us who have been around long enough to see our friends die can feel it,' Hjalmar said, and Ulf couldn't stop the shiver run down his spine.

Chapter 22

The fleet rowed for the rest of the day as Ulf sat near the stern and stared at the Frankish lands. But it was not the trees he was looking at, or the birds and the occasional deer. Ulf was watching the Frankish people flee as soon as they saw Ragnar's fleet approaching. When Ulf had been here with Snorri a few winters ago, many of the people stared at Norsemen as they rowed past along the river. By the time Asgeir's fleet, the Danish jarl they had joined up with, had reached Rouen, the Franks had learnt the danger the ships from the north had brought with them.

This time it was different. The Frankish people knew and as soon as they saw the countless ships with beast heads on their prows, they fled. Ulf had heard that the Christians believed their devil had sent the raiders from the north to attack them, although Ulf didn't know who this devil was and why the Christians feared him. Ingolfr had suggested that the Christian devil was like Loki, but Tormod had disagreed and said he was like Surtr. Ulf had never paid attention when the brothers argued over these things, but as he sat there staring at abandoned farmsteads and empty towns, he decided he agreed with Tormod. The Christian devil was evil, something Loki wasn't. Although Ulf knew there were those who prayed to Loki when they wanted to do evil things to others. Loki was also cunning and a trickster. Kids called out his name when they wanted to play tricks on others. Warriors asked for his help when they wanted to fool the enemy. Loki was both good and bad, just like Odin and the other gods of Asgard. *Just like Thorir*, the words came to him and Ulf looked at the bóndi, who was sitting with Jarl Hakon's men near the prow.

Thorir was not a bad person. He had tried to befriend Ulf and had even stood up for him when others believed he had attacked Jarl Ragnar. But Ulf could not understand his lust for blood. Thorir was no warrior, but he was a killer. The Dane had learnt that on this raid, or perhaps he had always known that and that was the reason he wanted to come on the raid.

'You think too much,' someone said from behind Ulf, and he turned to see Hjalmar smiling at him.

'How do you know I'm thinking?'

The warrior laughed. 'That scowl of yours. If you're not careful, then Loki will make sure your face stays that way.'

'Might be an improvement,' another said, and the old warrior laughed again. Ulf turned away from them and stared at the countryside again.

'By the time we get to this Paris, there will be no one left to fight. They all would have fled,' Hjalmar said as he followed Ulf's gaze. 'Although, as long as they leave their riches behind, that might not be a bad thing.' The other warrior grunted his agreement and even Jarl Hakon nodded as he leaned on the side of his ship by the steering oar.

'You think we are going too slow?' Ulf asked.

Hjalmar shrugged. 'Not my place to say. I go where Jarl Hakon tells me and kill who he tells me to kill.'

'Not that you do any of that very well,' Jarl Hakon said with a smile on his face and the old warrior laughed. Jarl Hakon and his men started talking about other things, but Ulf had stopped listening as he wondered why Jarl Ragnar was taking his time. They had spent many days sitting in their camp, and often stopped along the river for a day or two. Other jarls would take their ships raiding then and would return a few days later, their ships filled with captives and plunder. And Ulf saw the effect it was having on the Franks. Perhaps that was the plan. Perhaps Ragnar wanted enough time for word of their attacks to spread. Then fear would spread amongst the Franks as fire spreads in a dry field. Ulf had to admit it was a good tactic. It meant that there were fewer Franks to fight when they attacked towns, which also meant Ragnar would not lose as many warriors as he would have done if the Franks hadn't fled beforehand.

Lost in his thoughts, Ulf never realised that the sun had lowered and that Jarl Ragnar had decided to make camp. The first he knew of it was when Jarl Hakon's ship pulled up on the riverbank, the vibration of the ship's keel grating along the riverbed, startling him from his thoughts.

'Hjalmar was right. You think too much,' Jarl Hakon said when Ulf shook his head to chase his thoughts away.

'Aye, that's not the first time I heard that.' Ulf stood and stretched his back. He looked around him and saw that the men were already unloading the ships and preparing the camp for the night. Ulf caught Thorir glaring at him and Ulf sighed. He already had Ragnvald and Jarl Ragnar glowering at him every time they saw him, so having Thorir do the same did not bother him so much.

'What happened between the two of you?' Jarl Hakon asked.

Ulf looked at the jarl and wondered if he should tell him. 'Like you said, Jarl Hakon. Some men are warriors, while others are just killers. And I've spent enough time with men who only want to kill those weaker than them so that they can feel strong.'

Jarl Hakon laughed. 'I never thought the Bear-Slayer would be so against fighting.'

'I'm not against fighting. I'm against killing those who cannot defend themselves.' Ulf walked away and jumped off the ship before Jarl Hakon could say anything. As he followed the others to the camp, Ragnvald appeared by his side.

'Your luck will run out soon, Bear-Slayer. And Odin knows that when it does, I'll be there.'

Ulf glared at the one-handed warrior, but he decided not to say anything. Ulf was tired, and all he wanted to do was get his tent up and crawl inside and sleep. So he turned and walked away from Ragnvald, who hawked and spat in his direction.

Later that night, as the army of Jarl Ragnar feasted, Ulf sat brooding by his tent. A large fire had been built, cattle from nearby farms slaughtered and more barrels of ale and wine taken from churches and other towns. The warriors sang and danced, some wrestled, while others bet on the outcome. Men told stories of the battles they had fought, each more outlandish than the other, and laughed at the cowardice of the Frankish people. The jarls all sat together, with Jarl Ragnar in the centre, and drank ale while they watched the warriors enjoy themselves. Jarl Knut, sitting on Ragnar's right, was the only one who was not smiling, but Ulf didn't care about that as he watched Thorir mock attack another warrior, no doubt talking about how he killed an unarmed boy.

Jarl Ragnar's army had good reason to be relaxed, as no one expected an attack from the Franks, even though the jarl still had men guarding the perimeter of the camp. The raid had gone so well that even Ulf was starting to believe that the gods had blessed it. But as much as the warriors and the jarls enjoyed themselves, Ulf could not. Too many dark thoughts and unanswered questions plagued his mind, and all the revelry and joy only irritated him even more. So he took the loaf of bread he had been chewing on, and after making sure he had his weapons with him, Ulf got up and walked to the river. Perhaps the sound of the flowing water would calm him. The smell of the meat roasting on the large fire made Ulf's mouth water, but he did not want to hang around for a slice of beef. He hoped that when he came back there would still be some left, but he had to get away from the noise of people enjoying themselves.

Ulf made his way to the river and knew he would not get much peace there. The waning moon cast a dim light over the river and the ships on the riverbank. And in that faint light, the prow beasts, left on to protect the ships from the Christian spirits, seemed alive with their snarling teeth and flicking tongues. The sounds of the captives crying and mourning not only drowned out the flowing water of the river, but made it sound like the prow beasts were calling out to him, warning him not to come any closer, otherwise they would rip him apart. The image of Jörmungandr from his dreams came to him, and Ulf couldn't help but grip the hilt of Ormstunga as a shiver ran down his spine.

The captives had all been gathered on four of the ships and were guarded by warriors who were already too drunk to perform their tasks, but it was not up to Ulf to do anything about that. Ulf knew that Jarl Ragnar would send the ships with the captives and injured warriors back to the island camp where the other captives and plunder were guarded by men loyal to the jarl. Ulf turned away from the ships, eager to get away from the beasts when he sensed movement nearby. He stopped and tilted his head as he tried to find the source of the noise in the darkness, thinking that it might have been Skadi because she liked to sneak up on him in the dark.

'Skadi?' Ulf turned around, but saw nothing other than the outline of the ships on the riverbank.

'Who is Skadi?' a familiar voice said from nearby and when Ulf turned towards it, he saw three men step out from behind one ship. Ulf recognised the voice as the bastard who had taunted him before. Jarl Knut's man, Hallr, who he had headbutted. The three men fanned out, and Ulf guessed they must have seen him leave the camp and followed him.

'Maybe his mother.' One of the men laughed, and Ulf clenched his jaw as he felt the first spark of his anger in the pit of his stomach as Ulf's hand went to the hilt of Ormstunga.

'Go back to the feast,' Ulf said. 'No one needs to get hurt.'

Hallr laughed. 'See, you're wrong there. Somebody needs to get hurt. You attacked me twice. You really think I'm going to let you get away with that, you Norse scum?'

Ulf took a step back, but then sensed more movement behind him. He glanced over his shoulder and saw two more men standing there, both of them with weapons in their hands. 'So you're going to kill me and throw my body into the river?'

'Hadn't thought about what we would do with your body, but that seems like a good idea,' Hallr said. 'The gods know no one would miss you, anyway. Even the bóndi abandoned you.'

Ulf would have regretted leaving the safety of the camp and coming to the river where these bastards could kill him, but the voices of his ancestors wouldn't let him as they roared in his ears. They wanted blood. They wanted these bastards to die, just like those sent by Ragnar had died when they tried to take his sword from him.

'Go back to the camp, enjoy your feast and leave me be.' Ulf tried again and this time, all the men laughed. Ulf pulled Ormstunga free from her scabbard and thought he could hear her sing with joy as he turned and attacked the two men behind him. In three quick strides, he reached the first one and sliced his throat open, the man's laughter dying with him, before Ulf turned and stabbed the second through the chest. The force and speed of Ulf's attack drove the point of Ormstunga through the man's brynja, and Ulf just saw him gape at the sword in his chest.

'By Odin!' Hallr shouted, and the remaining three men attacked.

Ulf kicked the man he had just stabbed in the chest so he could free Ormstunga, at the same time pulling his axe from his belt. He ducked under Hallr's attack and was forced to dodge the axe of another before he could cut Hallr's leg open. The third warrior stabbed at Ulf with his sword and Ulf used his axe to deflect the blade when his ancestors roared in his ears, forcing Ulf to jump back before Hallr could open his throat.

'You'll die, you bastard!' Hallr said as the axe wielder hacked at Ulf.

Ulf twisted out of the way, but before he could do anything, the third man rushed at him and shoulder barged Ulf to the ground.

Fighting to keep his weapons in his hands, Ulf rolled to his feet, but was forced to jump out of the way of another attack.

'Only the gods know how you killed our friends. You are no warrior!' Hallr said, already panting as he rushed at Ulf, who deflected his sword, but had to twist out of the way of another attack.

Ulf stepped back, wondering how he was going to get out of this. The three facing him were experienced enough to attack him at the same time, and only Ulf's speed had kept him alive so far. But he could not land a blow on any of them, which meant it was only a matter of time before they killed him. He gripped his weapons as his ancestors screamed in his ears when one of the men rushed at him. Ulf stood his ground and let the man come, and at the last moment, he dropped to his knee and stabbed with Ormstunga. But the warrior saw the move and twisted out of the way, while the second man charged. Ulf didn't see him though and if the man hadn't tripped on something, then Ulf would have died.

Ulf didn't waste time thinking about that as he jumped to his feet and faced Hallr when the other man screamed behind him. He turned, expecting an attack, but in the dim moonlight, he saw the man's bulging eyes and the knife in his throat. Ulf frowned and then remembered Hallr. He turned in time to deflect Hallr's sword with his axe and sliced Ormstunga across Hallr's legs. Hallr cried out as he fell, and Ulf was about to stab him when a voice shouted in the darkness.

'Leave him alive! The gods want him!'

Chapter 23

Ulf turned, his weapons still in his hands, as he scanned the shadows cast by the moon, but he still shuddered when Skadi walked out of them, a bloodied knife in her hands and a cruel smile on her face. He glanced at two of the men, both dead but neither killed by him, and his heart raced when he realised she had saved his life, because Ulf doubted he would have been able to defeat the three Danes. And then he looked at Hallr, his legs bleeding as he tried to crawl back to the camp.

Ulf tightened the grip on Ormstunga and stalked the Dane who had tried to kill him.

'I told you to leave him, young wolf,' Skadi said, and the thunder in her voice made Ulf stop in his tracks. Even Hallr stopped and gaped at the volva.

'Wh...who is sh...she?' he asked, but Ulf ignored him.

'Why?' He glared at Skadi. 'Why must I spare his life? Why should I care what the gods want?'

'Because if it weren't for the gods, then you would have died a long time ago.' Skadi moved towards him in her typical serpent-like walk. 'You are important to the gods. To Odin and Tyr. Even Frigg watches you.'

'Is that why you are always there? Watching me? Following me?'

Skadi smiled, but didn't answer his questions. Instead, she walked past him and stood over Hallr, whose face was as pale as a full moon. 'This one, though, the gods want for another reason.'

Before either Ulf or Hallr could say anything, her hand shot out, and she pulled Hallr's brynja and tunic up to expose his stomach, which she sliced open. Hallr cried out, but Ulf doubted anyone could hear him. Not even the men who were guarding the ships. He clenched his jaw as he wondered if they had been asked to look the other way while Hallr and his friends attacked Ulf.

Hallr's cries dragged Ulf out of his thoughts and he raised his brows when he saw what looked like a handful of snakes slithering next to the Dane. Ulf frowned at first, not understanding where they had come from, but then he realised they were not snakes. His head spun as Skadi picked up a coil of Hallr's intestines and wrapped it around the Dane's neck, and then another. She did that until none of his insides remained on the ground and all of it was wrapped around Hallr's neck. Hallr had stopped moving, but in the deathly silence that suddenly surrounded them, Ulf heard his faint breathing. He wanted to ask Skadi what she was doing, but it felt as if his tongue had fled his mouth.

Skadi looked to the sky and closed her eyes as she muttered words he did not understand. As much as Ulf tried to look away from Hallr with his intestines wrapped around his neck, he couldn't. Hallr lifted his head and stared at Ulf. In the darkness, Ulf could make out his eyes, imploring Ulf to do something, but there was nothing Ulf could do.

To Ulf, it felt like he had stood there for a lifetime, staring at Hallr as the volva muttered her strange words. He did not notice her sticking her hand inside of Hallr's stomach. Just like he did not notice her walking towards him. The first he knew of it was when she spat something in his face. Before Ulf could protest, his head spun violently, and he felt the bile reaching the back of his throat. The trees around him blurred until they became one. An old ash tree, dimly lit by the waning moon, its branches swaying and moving as if the tree was alive. Ulf felt the icy fingers of fear grip his stomach, a fear he had not felt for a long time. He tried to turn and flee from the tree, but his legs refused to obey him. He tried to call to Skadi, but his mouth refused to open. And then he saw something move along the branches of the tree. A snake as long as his arm and as thick as his wrist. Its belly was as white as snow, but its back was as black as a starless night.

The snake raised its head and stared at him, its tongue flicking out. It seemed to smile at his fear as it coiled itself around the branch.

Two wolves face each other. The words rang in his head. *The first wolf wants to protect what the second wants to take. The second wolf wants revenge for what the first wolf has done. One wolf will be stabbed in the back.*

Ulf frowned, not understanding what the words meant, but before he could ask, the snake opened its mouth and shot towards him. He lifted his arms to protect himself, but before the snake could bite him, everything turned black and he felt nothing.

***

Ulf groaned when someone kicked his shoulder. He tried to turn away from it, but the kick came again, this time hard enough to make him open his eyes. Bright light blinded him and he felt his head spin, forcing him to lift his hand and block his eyes.

'Looks like the Bear-Slayer can't handle his drink.' Ulf recognised Hjalmar's voice as others laughed.

He moved his hand away from his eyes and took deep breaths until the spinning went away and he could focus on Hjalmar standing over him. Ulf frowned when he realised he was outside his tent. He looked around him, certain that this was another dream, but Ormstunga and his axe were with him. He tried sitting up and groaned as his head pounded.

'How much did the bastard drink?' someone asked.

'I didn't see him drink anything,' someone else said, and Ulf frowned when he saw the group of warriors standing around him, all of them smiling at his discomfort. 'Didn't see him at all, come to think of it.' The man scratched his beard.

Ulf looked over his shoulder, just to make sure he really was by his tent, as he remembered what had happened the night before. *What did you do to me, Skadi?* He wondered to himself as he took in the camp around him. Warriors were folding tents and making sure the campfires were dead, while others were carrying barrels and food back to the ships. Men laughed at those who had drunk too much, while somewhere Ulf heard someone vomit.

He rubbed his head and saw the fresh cut on his arm and then remembered that Hallr and some of the Danes had jumped him by the river. But then how did he get back to his tent? And who had cleaned the wound and his weapons? The axe was clean, and Ulf could only guess that Ormstunga was as well. Did Skadi do all of that? But how? Surely she couldn't have carried him back here without being seen.

'Aye, well as fun as this is, Jarl Hakon told us to wake you up. We're leaving soon.' Hjalmar turned and walked away.

Ulf nodded his thanks while his mind still tried to make sense of what had happened. He struggled to his feet and saw that his brynja was clean as well. As the other warriors walked away, Ulf turned so that his body shaded Ormstunga and half pulled her out of her scabbard. As expected, the blade shone and was free of blood. He shook his head to rid himself of the confusion and regretted it when the headache pounded his skull.

The camp was almost packed up when Thorir stopped beside Ulf and frowned at him. 'What happened last night?'

Ulf frowned back, not sure what the bóndi meant and wondered why Thorir was talking to him. 'Nothing.'

'Nothing? You walked around the camp as if you were draugr and just collapsed outside your tent. Slept so deep, not even the giants could have woken you.'

Ulf, still frowning at Thorir, wondered what Skadi had done to him, because he could not remember any of that. The last thing he remembered was being attacked by Hallr and some other Danes. And the snake on the tree came to him and Ulf shuddered when he remembered the words it spoke to him.

'Ulf?'

Ulf shook his head. 'What?'

Thorir raised an eyebrow at him. 'Nothing. You just went pale, that's all.'

Ulf nodded and when Thorir saw Ulf was not going to explain, he walked away, leaving Ulf to make sense of what had happened and what the warning from Skadi meant. Realising he was one of the last few left in the empty camp, Ulf rushed to catch up with the rest of the fleet before they left without him. When he got to the ships, he saw Jarl Knut talking to Jarl Hakon, the Danish jarl scowling as he rubbed the back of his neck.

'Bear-Slayer!' he shouted when he spotted Ulf.

Ulf sighed and wondered if they had found the bodies of the men he had killed. He thought about running, but knew it was pointless. He had nowhere to go and, with his head aching, he doubted he'd get far before he puked his guts out. 'Jarl Knut.'

'Have you seen Hallr and the group that follow him around all the time?'

Ulf almost looked towards the area where he had fought Hallr, but stopped himself before he did it. 'Not since we raided that town.'

Jarl Knut chewed on the inside of his cheek as he scowled at Ulf. 'Bastards have gone missing, and there is no sign of them.'

'How many are gone?' Jarl Ragnar asked, catching them all by surprise and glaring at Ulf. Ulf resisted the urge to grip Ormstunga and took a step back to distance himself from the jarl.

Jarl Knut shrugged. 'About five of them, I think. Not a big loss, but strange none the less. Hallr is one of my best men. He wouldn't just disappear like that.'

An image of Hallr lying on the ground, his legs cut and his intestines hanging around his neck while Skadi stood over him came to Ulf. He shuddered at the memory and felt his stomach churn.

'Ulf?' Jarl Hakon asked, and Ulf saw the raised eyebrow from Jarl Ragnar, as if he knew something.

'Something I ate,' Ulf lied, but knew that none of the jarls believed him as they stared at him. Ulf turned and went to the ship, eager to get away from the jarls and their scrutiny.

'Here, drink this.' Thorir held out a flask when Ulf reached his place and sat down.

Ulf took the flask and sniffed it before he drank the water inside, which settled his stomach. He looked at Thorir and wondered why the bóndi was being nice to him, but Thorir did not hang around for him to ask. He nodded to Ulf and then went to the group of warriors he had been spending time with. Ulf watched as the warriors pointed at him and laughed and felt relieved that most thought he was hungover. But he still didn't understand what Skadi had done to him as Jarl Hakon gave the order for the men to get the oars ready and row. He groaned as he took his oar and pulled on it when he spotted a raven sitting on a low-hanging branch at the spot where Skadi had killed Hallr, its head following him as the ships went past, and felt a shiver run down his spine.

The rowing was hard at first, but as the sun rose and the fleet continued up the river, Ulf felt his head clear and his stomach settle. As always, the ship was abuzz with the warriors talking and singing songs. Anything they could think of doing to pass the time. Those who weren't rowing were sleeping or playing board games. Ulf rarely paid any attention to any of the warriors on the raid, but this time his ears were strained as he listened to the men talking about the disappearance of Hallr and the others. Even Jarl Hakon and old Hjalmar were talking about it.

'Must have been the Franks,' one man said, glancing at the riverbank as if he expected a Frankish army to appear out of nowhere.

'The Franks?' Hjalmar asked.

'Aye,' the man said. 'They must have snuck into the camp and took Hallr and friends.'

'Why them?' Jarl Hakon asked. 'If the Franks got into the camp, then why not kill Jarl Ragnar, or Jarl Knut?'

'Or you?' Hjalmar added and Jarl Hakon nodded. The warrior shrugged and looked at the riverbank again.

'Perhaps it was the Christian god,' Jarl Hakon said and winked at Ulf. 'Perhaps he plucked them away and made them disappear.'

'Same question as before,' Hjalmar said. 'Why Hallr? The man's a good warrior, but not important. If the Christian god intervened and made men disappear, then why not go for Jarl Ragnar?'

Again, Jarl Hakon nodded. 'To cause fear and uncertainty.' He looked at Ulf again. 'Perhaps someone will disappear every night until we are too frightened to continue and flee back to Denmark.'

Ulf wondered if Jarl Hakon was hinting at something. 'Then why start now?' he asked. 'Why not do that when we started the raid?'

Jarl Hakon shrugged and then one of the other men said, 'I heard that those guarding the ships saw Hallr and his friends on the riverbank. Said it looked like they were following someone.'

Ulf looked away, not wanting to see if anyone on the ship suspected him, but instead found old Ragnvald glaring at him from Jarl Hakon's other ship.

'Who were they hunting, I wonder,' Jarl Hakon said and when Ulf turned his attention back to the jarl, he found Hakon smiling at him.

'Whoever it was, it looks like they got the better of Hallr and his friends, but my old bones tell me the gods have a hand in this affair and I don't like it.' Hjalmar's hand went to the spear pendant he wore around his neck and Ulf noticed those sitting around them all did the same. All of them apart from Jarl Hakon, who was staring at Ulf, his eyes glinting in the afternoon sun.

Chapter 24

Ragnar's fleet continued its way up the river and towards Paris as dark clouds filled the air, promising rain that would drench tunics and rust weapons, but the warriors of Denmark and Norway were unconcerned. They laughed and told stories as they rowed and rested, their moods defying the dark clouds sent by the Christian god to slow them down.

High above them, a lonely eagle soared on the strong winds, its screeching cry reaching the ears of the raiders and making them smile even more as they believed that the All-Father was watching them. All of them, apart from Ulf, who brooded as he pulled on his oar. For most of the day, men had talked about the disappearance of Hallr and his friends, until they had got bored and moved onto something else. What didn't help was that every time Ulf looked up, he saw Jarl Hakon watching him, as if he knew Ulf had something to do with it. Ulf wondered again what the gods had planned for him and whether he could trust Skadi. He knew she only cared about the will of the gods, but she had saved his life.

Jarl Hakon called one of his men to take over the steering oar and then walked towards Ulf. He stood beside him, his hands on his waist, as he took a deep breath. 'Christian air. Some believe that if we breathe it in, then the Christian god poisons us with his words and makes us turn our backs on the gods of Asgard.' He grimaced. 'To me, it just stinks. Or perhaps it's all you dirty bastards I'm smelling.' He smiled, and those nearby laughed, but Ulf only frowned as the jarl leaned on the side of his ship so that he was closer to him. 'Ragnvald thinks you killed Hallr and his friends.'

Ulf glanced to the other ship, where Ragnvald was staring at him. 'Ragnvald can think what he wants.'

The jarl smiled. 'He said you and Hallr had a falling out after we attacked the town.'

Ulf shrugged as he rowed. 'I had nothing to do with what had happened to Hallr or his friends.'

'Just like you had nothing to do with the attack on Jarl Ragnar?' Ulf stared at the jarl, who smiled at him. 'Relax Ulf. I know you had nothing to do with the attack on Ragnar or whatever happened to Hallr and his friends. But there are those who see things differently. Jarl Ragnar being one of them.'

'Why are you telling me this?' Ulf asked and glanced at Thorir, who was watching the two of them talk.

'Because us Norsemen must stick together. You can't trust the Danes. Just like they don't really trust us.'

Before Ulf could respond, the warriors cheered, and they both looked up to see the top of a large Christian church on the horizon. Jarl Hakon smiled and pointed to it.

'Look at how proud it stands! The house of the Christian god, built to intimidate us. To make us believe that the Christian god is more powerful than our gods.' The warriors jeered at his words and Jarl Hakon waited a few heartbeats before he continued. 'We will show these Christians how weak their god is. We will kill their priests and take all the gold they like to hoard in their churches for ourselves. For Odin! For the gods of Asgard!'

'For Odin!' the men echoed as a group of ships, including Jarl Ragnar's, broke away from the fleet and went towards the large church.

The ships stopped on the riverbank and the warriors jumped off, weapons ready, and raced towards the large church. Ulf realised that the church wasn't just one building. There were many buildings connected to the large church in the centre and the land surrounding them was filled with fields which had recently been worked. But there was nobody working the fields, neither were there people running towards the safety of the church.

'They're long gone,' Ragnvald said beside Ulf, whose hand went to Ormstunga's hilt. Ragnvald smiled when he saw that. 'You really think that pretty sword will save you?'

'It has done before.' Ulf glared at the old warrior as he wondered what he wanted, but Ragnvald only smiled before he looked at the large church again.

'It's what they call a monastery. Many priests stay here and farm the lands when they aren't praying to their god. They make good mead, though.' He turned his attention back to Ulf. 'You better watch your back, boy.'

Ulf gritted his teeth as Ragnvald walked away, leaving him trembling with rage. All he wanted to do was to free Eldrid, and he didn't understand why others had to make that difficult for him. Why Ragnvald had to threaten him every chance he got and why Jarl Ragnar was accusing Ulf of attacks he had nothing to do with.

'Something strange is going on,' Thorir said suddenly from behind Ulf. Ulf frowned at him. 'Did you kill Jarl Knut's men?'

Ulf stared at him, not sure if he could trust the bóndi any more. Whatever friendship they had was gone now, and Thorir must have seen that as well, because he shrugged when Ulf didn't respond. 'Doesn't matter to me, but Inga will not forgive me if something happens to you.'

Ulf almost laughed at the fact that a bóndi on his first raid believed he could protect him. 'I can take care of myself.'

Thorir nodded. 'Aye, I'm sure you can.' With that, he followed the others as they made their way to the monastery.

Ulf was about to follow when he felt someone's eyes on him. He turned and saw Jarl Ragnar glaring at him. Ulf clenched his fists as Ragnar, his hirdmen not far behind him, turned away and walked towards the monastery. He thought about the warning he had in the vision and wondered if Jarl Ragnar was the second wolf. Then he remembered the first warning and reminded himself that he needed to keep an eye on Thorir. They might have fallen out, but Ulf still didn't want the bóndi to die because of him.

By the time Ulf got to the church, the looting had already started as warriors rushed inside all the buildings, while others scoured the fields around the buildings. Ulf stood back, doing his best to ignore the glances from the other warriors. He was used to people staring at him because of the scars on his face, but this time, it was different. Now they stared at him because they believed he had killed Hallr and his friends. Word had spread of his altercation with Hallr after the raid on the town a few days before. Many kept their distance, though, apart from Jarl Hakon's men. The Norse warriors weren't exactly friendly towards him, not like they were with Thorir, but they didn't treat him like he had the plague.

'It's empty!' Jarl Hakon said as he came out of the main church. 'The whole bloody place is empty.'

'What you do mean, empty?' Jarl Ragnar asked, his frustration clear in his voice.

'No gold, no silver. Only four priests.' Jarl Hakon stood aside as his men dragged the four priests out of the church. Three of them were old and thin, their faces heavily lined and their hair grey, while the fourth and younger priest kept coughing and could barely stand on his feet. Ulf rubbed the Mjöllnir pendant around his neck and prayed that the man didn't have anything dangerous, and saw many others do the same.

'There has to be gold,' Jarl Knut said, and Ulf caught the glance he directed at Jarl Ragnar, whose jaw muscles were working hard under his red beard.

'You can look for yourself,' Jarl Hakon said. 'The place is empty. Only a few candle holders and silver spoons. Not enough even for draugr to want to attack here.'

'Question the priests,' Jarl Ragnar said. 'They must have hidden their treasure somewhere nearby.' He turned to the rest of the warriors. 'Spread out and search everywhere! Find where they hid their gold.'

The men did what they were told, and Ulf was about to do the same when Jarl Hakon called him. 'Bear-Slayer. You stay here. Your face should be enough to get the bastards to talk.'

Those nearby laughed as Ulf swallowed his anger down. He had never liked being the butt of others' jokes, but knew he had to keep quiet and take it. There was too much trouble around him already, and he didn't want to add to it. A group of Jarl Ragnar's warriors surrounded the four priests, while others went to fetch a barrel of water. Ulf frowned as he wondered what they were going to do with that while Jarl Hakon spoke to the priests in their tongue. He pointed to Ulf as he said something, and the faces of the priests all paled. One of them shook his head and said something which made Jarl Hakon smile.

'He said he would rather die in the name of his god before he tells us anything!' Jarl Hakon said and the men laughed as two warriors grabbed the old priest and pulled his head back.

The old priest wailed as one man forced his jaw open while another took a ladle and filled it with water from the barrel.

'I hope you're thirsty, you old bastard,' the warrior said as he tipped the ladle into the priest's mouth and forced him to drink the water. The surrounding warriors all swore at the priest, a few even beating and kicking him, while the warrior with the ladle kept pouring more water down the priest's throat.

Ulf felt the flames of his anger ignite as the old priest shook his head and desperately tried to close his mouth, but the Danes kept forcing it open and making him drink even more water. Already, Ulf could see the priest's stomach swell and he glanced at Jarl Ragnar, who stood there, as cold and hard as a mountain in the middle of winter, wondering how the jarl could allow his men to torture the old man.

Jarl Hakon turned to the second priest while the first was still being forced to drink water. His eyes bulged as he coughed up the water being forced into his mouth, but the Danes kept his head facing upwards, so the water he was coughing up had nowhere to go but back down again, along with the water the warrior was forcing him to drink. The old priest's bulging eyes were filled with panic as he choked on the water when his body tensed for a moment before he went limp and collapsed.

'The bastard is dead,' the warrior with the ladle said and Ulf fought hard not to strangle the man because of the disappointment in his voice.

Jarl Hakon looked at Jarl Ragnar, who nodded, and Ulf had to resist the urge to pull Ormstunga from her scabbard and cut the bastard down. But instead, he stood there as they grabbed the second priest and forced him to drink water until it came out of his nostrils, before he too choked on the water and died. The surrounding warriors started taking bets on how long the last of the old priests would last, before he too was tortured. The last old priest did not last much longer than the other two and soon only the ill priest was left alive. He was much younger than the others, and Ulf wondered why they had been left behind. Ulf rarely thought about the Christians, but he couldn't understand how they claimed they were better than the Norse and Danes when they left their old and ill behind to be tortured and killed. Unless they had done it to slow Ragnar's army down.

Jarl Hakon grabbed the young warrior, who looked like he was about to faint, and asked him something, but the young priest shook his head as he gaped at his dead companions. 'He claims not to know anything, either.' The Norse jarl shoved the young priest towards the men with the barrel when Jarl Ragnar held a hand up.

'What's wrong with him? Why was he left behind?'

Ulf frowned at the question, as did Jarl Hakon, before he asked the priest.

'Says he has a fever and was too weak to follow the others, so he offered to stay behind. As did the other three.'

'Bastard wants to die for his god,' Jarl Knut muttered and the others grunted. Jarl Ragnar smiled, though.

'So he has nothing too serious? Good. He looks strong enough. Tie him up. We'll take him with. We can ransom him back to the Franks. At least get something out of this disappointment.' Jarl Ragnar turned and called for his men to return to the ships as Jarl Hakon spoke to the priest. Ulf thought he'd be happy that he wouldn't be tortured like the others, but then the priest screamed and started undressing himself.

'What, in Odin's name, is the bastard doing?' Jarl Knut asked, as Ulf wondered the same.

'He wants us to fuck him.' Someone laughed as the priest, naked now, lay down on the ground and chanted something in a language that sounded different to the Frankish tongue.

'He wants us to kill him. Says he wants to join his god in their heaven,' Jarl Hakon explained and Knut shook his head. He grabbed a spear from one man and struck the priest on the back with its butt.

'Get up, you bastard! You're not joining your god just yet.'

The priest stayed on the ground, his pale skin bruising where Jarl Knut had struck, and kept chanting the same thing over and over again.

'Well, if he wants to join his god, then let's help him,' Jarl Knut said, and some of the other warriors struck the priest with the end of their spears. The priest cried out in pain and soon tears were streaming down his cheeks, but he refused to get up as the warriors struck him harder and harder.

Ulf winced at the cracking noise as one of the priest's ribs broke and couldn't understand why the man didn't just get up. Surely living was better than dying like this. He knew many warriors wanted to die in battle so that they could go to Valhalla. But the Christian priests, it seemed, also wanted to die for their god, and Ulf wondered what they had been promised in their afterlife as another sickening crack made the priest scream loud enough to irritate even the gods.

In the end, Ulf could not take it any more and grabbed a spear from one of the warriors. Before the man could protest, Ulf struck the priest on the skull. There was a loud crack, and the priest shuddered before his body lay still and his bowels emptied.

'You killed him,' one man complained, his disappointment all over his face.

Ulf shrugged. 'I must have hit him too hard.'

He saw the knowing glance from Jarl Knut and before he turned to walk away, Jarl Hakon said,

'So you don't kill farmers and old men? Only warriors and Christian priests.'

Ulf ground his teeth as a raven flew overhead and the voices of Ulf's ancestors drowned out the laughter of the warriors behind him.

Chapter 25

'By Odin, I knew this was going to happen!' Knut raged as he walked around the empty monastery. He ignored the large stone columns that supported the tiled roof that stood so high he'd have to crane his neck upwards to look at it. He barely looked at the coloured windows, filled with images of people he knew nothing about, as he made his way to the altar where he guessed the head priest would preach to the Christian sheep. The altar where a large golden cross was supposed to be, but stood empty. And not because it had been taken by the raiders, but because the Christian priests had been warned of their arrival and had enough time to hide their treasures and flee.

Jarl Hakon walked behind him, his head lazily turning as he looked at the images on the windows and those painted on the walls. 'They are very creative, these Christians. I always admired that about them. I imagine Kvasir would have enjoyed spending time with them.' Kvasir was the god of poetry and the most intelligent of the gods. That was, until the two dwarfs, Fjalar and Galar, killed him and used his blood to create the mead of poetry. Knut had always wondered how intelligent Kvasir could have been if he didn't realise the two dwarfs were planning to kill him. But he did not think about that as he turned and grabbed Hakon by his brynja.

'You admire the Christians! After they made us look like fools!' His face turned red and he felt his temples throb, which only worsened when Hakon shrugged, his expression almost looking bored.

'The Christians didn't make us look like fools. They did what they always do when they know we are coming. They ran. You can't blame them for that.'

Knut let go of Hakon and growled. 'You're right. We can't blame the Christians. This is Ragnar's fault. I warned him about this. I told him he was taking too long to get to Paris.' Knut kicked the stone altar and winced as he hurt his foot. 'By the gods! By the time we get to Paris, we'll have to face the entire Frankish army. That must be the reason King Charles has not sent anyone to stop us. He is waiting for us in Paris.'

Hakon sat down on one bench and leaned back so he could look at the roof above him. 'How do you think they built that? Did the giants help them?'

Knut glared at Hakon. 'How, in Thor's name, can you be so calm? Ragnar still lives and this raid will fail!' He paced around the front of the church. 'We will return to Denmark a laughing stock, and no one will join my army when I make a move for the throne.'

Hakon lowered his head and smiled. 'Knut, we have more ships filled with plunder and captives than I can count. We've bled the lands around this river dry and we've barely lost a man doing that.' He stood up and walked towards Knut before putting a hand on his shoulder. 'There is still time to deal with Ragnar and even if we don't take Paris, then it only means the Norns didn't plan for us to. We just move on and attack another town and then another town. The summer has only just begun. Let King Charles keep his army behind the walls of his city.'

Knut frowned at Hakon, wondering why the man made more sense than he should have done. And why he couldn't see the same? But he knew why. Some of his most trusted men were gone, and no one knew why or where. Knut knew Hallr wouldn't just ran away. The man owed him everything. Knut also knew he hated the Bear-Slayer because Ulf had humiliated him twice in front of the other warriors and Knut could only pray that Hallr had not gone after the scarred warrior. Although, he struggled to understand how Ulf could defeat five of his men. He glanced at Hakon.

'Have any of your men befriended Ulf?'

Hakon raised an eyebrow at the question and then shrugged. 'Most tolerate him, but there are a few who have warmed to him. Thought he'd be a better warrior, though.'

'And those who have warmed to him, would any of them fight to defend him?'

Again, Hakon raised an eyebrow at him. 'No. Ulf might be Norse, but to my men, he is still an outsider. It doesn't help that he makes no effort to speak to any of them. Unlike the Dane, who chases after my warriors like a virgin desperate for his first fuck.' Hakon smiled. 'Ulf made himself even less popular when he killed the priest. Didn't think he had it in him, though.'

Neither did Knut. So far, he had struggled to see how the scarred warrior had earned his reputation. 'We need to find a way to push Ulf to attack Ragnar and soon.'

'You really think he could kill Ragnar?'

Knut shook his head. 'If Hallr failed, then Ulf stands no chance, but he doesn't need to kill Ragnar. The warriors just need to see him attack Ragnar and then, when we kill the bastard later, then they will believe it was him.'

'We need to keep Ulf alive long enough for that. If others see him attack Ragnar, what's stopping them from killing the Bear-Slayer?'

Knut turned and stared at the coloured glass in the windows as he wondered the same. 'I don't know yet, but I'll think of something.'

Both men turned when they heard footsteps in the church as Ragnar approached them with a smile on his face. *What are you smiling about, you bastard*? Knut thought as he smiled back.

'There might be no gold or silver, but the Christians didn't leave us with nothing.' Ragnar glanced around the church before he reached Knut and gripped his shoulder. 'The men found the room where they keep their wine and it is still full.'

'See, Odin does smile on us,' Hakon said to Knut, who had to ignore the raised eyebrow from Ragnar.

'Aye, so he does.' Knut turned to Ragnar. 'The men will be pleased, I'm sure. But cousin, I believe we need to hurry and get to Paris before King Charles reinforces the town. If he hasn't already.'

Ragnar shook his head. 'You worry too much, Knut. King Charles is hiding in one of his churches. And besides, the Christians won't expect us to attack on one of their holiest days.'

'We will show them how weak their god is.' Hakon grinned and Knut wasn't sure if it was because of what Ragnar had just said, or because of the room full of wine Ragnar had told them about.

'Aye, their churches will be full and the walls will be empty. It's the best time to attack them.' Ragnar smiled at Knut.

Knut still disagreed, but he kept those thoughts to himself as he returned his cousin's smile. Ragnar did not like people questioning him, and even though Knut was older, he still didn't want to be at the wrong end of Ragnar's wrath. That spot he was saving for Ulf Bear-Slayer. 'The Bear-Slayer killed the priest you wanted to ransom,' he said, which took the smile from Ragnar's face.

'I still don't understand why that bastard is here, or why you had to let him join your army.' Ragnar looked at Hakon.

'Odin knows if I had known about your history with him, I wouldn't have done.'

'Aye, so you keep saying. The man tried to kill me and you tell me I shouldn't hang him.'

'The gods are with him, that is well known in Norway. They say Odin won't let him die and if anyone tries to kill him, then they die instead.'

'Like your men?' This question was aimed at Knut, who clenched his fists as he responded,

'I don't know what happened to my men.'

'Aye, but Hallr has been part of your army for a long time. Your champion almost. I doubt he would just leave you like that.' Ragnar stepped closer to Knut. 'I'm telling you, cousin. The Bear-Slayer needs to go. I know it was him who attacked me that night, and that it was him who killed my man. And now Hallr and a handful of your men just disappear. Ulf is behind it all. I can feel it. If we can't kill him because of the gods, then we send him away. But I'm telling you now, if that bastard comes near me again, I will kill him. The gods might favour him, but they favour me too.' With that, Ragnar turned and left, leaving Knut smiling behind his back because he knew Ulf was getting to his younger cousin.

'Should we send Ulf away?' Hakon smiled and Knut shook his head.

'We keep him even closer. It will be easier to kill Ragnar while he is distracted by the Bear-Slayer.'

***

Ulf's head pounded as he pulled on the oar and felt the ship moving along the river. He had drunk too much of the Frankish wine the night before as the men feasted again. The priests had been dumped in the river, their corpses feeding the fish as the men feasted on the food and wine left behind by those who had fled. There had been no gold or silver, even though Ragnar's army had searched the entire area, but the raiders did not care. They were already rich from what had been plundered and there was still the prospect of Paris, the city richer than the gods of Asgard.

But Ulf cared for none of that as he thought about the priest he had killed. Ulf had expected the man to haunt his dreams, but no dreams had come, and that unsettled him even more. Ulf didn't understand why the priests wanted to die for their god. It was another question he wanted to ask Skadi, but every time he saw her, he couldn't ask any of them. Skadi was not there to answer his questions. She was there to warn him, but she refused to tell him what the danger was. Unless it was in the riddles that she gave him, but Ulf could not make sense of them. Lost in his thoughts, he did not hear Thorir approach.

'So you get angry at me for killing farmers who charge at me with pitchforks, but then you kill a naked Christian priest?' Ulf heard the contempt in his voice, which only angered him.

'I only killed the priest to put him out of his misery. They would have broken every bone in his body and left him suffering from the pain.'

'They were having fun. Making him pay for all the things the Christians have done to us.'

Ulf's oar almost faltered as he glared at Thorir. 'What have the Christians done to you? How have they made you suffer?' Ulf had never understood that argument. He had heard the stories of what past Christian kings had done to those who had refused to abandon the gods for the Christian god. But that was a long time ago. Thorir returned Ulf's glare, but said nothing as those nearby stared at them, including Jarl Hakon. 'Don't fall for the lies of others. We raid the Christians because they are richer than us. We raid them because we want their gold. Like Fafnir killed his father for his gold. That is the truth of it, Thorir. There is no battle of the gods.'

'You say that, but the Christian kings send men who tell us that our gods are not real and that we should only believe in their god and his words,' Jarl Hakon said, and many grunted in agreement. Ulf couldn't really argue with that because he had seen the same. He knew the Christians wanted everyone on Midgard to follow their god. But Ulf had learnt to ignore them and didn't understand why others couldn't do the same.

'And that gives us a reason to attack their farms and kill their farmers?'

'Why does that upset you so much?' Thorir asked. 'By the gods, all you do is complain about the poor farmers being killed.'

'Do you think they wouldn't kill our farmers, men like Thorir, if they raided our lands?' Hjalmar asked him. Ulf growled because he knew they would.

'I know they will. We live in a cruel world where the gods provide with one hand and take with the other. But that doesn't mean that I have to agree with it or kill those who only try to survive, regardless of which god they follow.'

Thorir leaned in closer. 'Eldrid was wrong about you. You're nothing but a coward.'

Ulf snapped and let go if his oar before he even knew what he was doing. He punched Thorir in the face and sent the man falling on others as they tried to row. Those not rowing grabbed hold of Ulf before he could jump on Thorir and pulled him back, while another grabbed his oar. All the while, Jarl Hakon laughed.

'Jarl Hakon, is everything alright?' Ragnvald shouted from the other ship and the jarl raised his hand to show that it was.

'Just a minor disagreement,' he said before he turned to Ulf. 'There's a beast inside of you, Bear-Slayer. And I pray to the gods I'm not in the way when you let go of it.'

Ulf glared at Thorir as Jarl Hakon's words penetrated the voices of his ancestors. And in those voices, he heard the gods laughing at him because Jarl Hakon was right.

Chapter 26

They rowed in silence after Ulf had punched Thorir, although Jarl Hakon never took his eyes off Ulf. Ulf did his best to ignore him, but he couldn't. Just like he couldn't understand why the jarl had to keep staring at him like that. Thorir was sitting near the prow, his beard red with blood from his busted lip, while the men near Ulf kept glancing at him. He knew they all resented him, but he didn't care. He was tired of having to explain himself to Thorir. Just like he was fed up with trying to make the bóndi see that what he was doing did not make him a warrior.

'A dog can't be a wolf, even if he has sharp teeth and growls like one,' Hjalmar said, and Ulf's eyes widened as he stared at the old warrior. He remembered what Skadi had said to him about the wolf and the dog. *Who dies first?* Her words came to him as if she was sitting next to him while Hjalmar continued talking. 'Sure, he can bite others and maybe kill a deer, but he won't be a wolf.'

'What's that got to do with anything?' one warrior asked.

'Hjalmar had his wits stolen by Loki again. You should have left him in Sygnafylki,' another said to Jarl Hakon, who smiled.

'Hjalmar is smarter than all of you combined. If you don't understand what he is saying, then you are the ones I should have left behind.' The jarl stared at Ulf again, who wanted to look away as he rowed, but had nowhere to look to. So instead, he focused on his hands as he pulled on the oar.

'Is Ulf the dog?' someone asked a while later and Ulf felt his irritation grow.

'No, Ulf is not the dog,' Jarl Hakon said. 'Ulf is a wolf who pretends to be a dog.'

'Aye, I can see it too,' Hjalmar said. 'Been around long enough to recognise those who try to be something else.'

Ulf glanced at the old warrior. Everybody seemed to tell him that recently. Ingolfr, Eldrid, Skadi and now Hjalmar. But Ulf did not think that he was pretending to be something else. He accepted he was a warrior and that he could never be anything else. That didn't mean he needed to enjoy killing others. Wolves didn't kill because they enjoyed it. They did it to survive.

The men rowed in silence after that until the signal was given that they were to make camp for the night. Ulf was about to follow the others when Jarl Hakon called out to him.

'You stay with the ships, Ulf. After what had happened today, I don't think you should be around the rest of the men. Not after they get drunk, anyway.'

'And what happens when they come looking for me?' Ulf asked, wondering what Jarl Hakon was up to.

'I'll stay here with you to make sure that nothing happens,' Hjalmar said and Jarl Hakon nodded.

Ulf shrugged and made himself comfortable as he watched the men unload some chests and prepare the camp. The sun lowered in the sky and insects seemed to appear out of nowhere as they flew around his head, but Ulf ignored them as he sat on Jarl Hakon's ship and stared at the river.

'One day, Thorir will see that you are right. That there is more to being a warrior than just killing others,' Hjalmar said, his eyes still closed. Ulf thought he had been sleeping and had been enjoying the silence.

'No, he won't. He believes this is what being a warrior is. That and getting rich. He spent his whole life living on a farm and believes that there should be more to life than that.'

Hjalmar opened his eyes. 'You sound like you understand him.'

Because I do, Ulf thought, but didn't say. He had hated living on his uncle's farm when he was a boy because he had felt that there should be more to life than growing crops and milking cows. Hjalmar stared at Ulf for a while and when Ulf said nothing, he asked.

'Why did you do it?'

Ulf raised an eyebrow. 'Do what?'

'Kill that jarl? They say he treated you like a son and then you just cut him down.'

Ulf's heart thudded in his chest as he fought to control his anger. 'Jarl Thorgils never treated me like his son. He hated me.'

'Is that why you killed him?' Hjalmar held his hand up to show he meant no offence when Ulf glared at him. 'A bard travelled north. Told us about it and how his son had you banished.'

'So everyone knows about it?' Ulf wondered why he cared about that.

Hjalmar nodded. 'They call you the Jarl-Slayer behind your back.'

'Why are you telling me this?'

Hjalmar shrugged. 'My brother struggled to control his temper. He was a good man, a fierce warrior. But he struggled to control his anger.'

Ulf glanced at Hjalmar, wondering what any of this had to do with him. 'What happened to your brother?'

Hjalmar looked at Ulf, who saw the tears in the old man's eyes. 'He let others control his anger, and it killed him.'

'That won't happen to me,' Ulf said, although even he doubted his own words. His anger had caused him more problems than he needed, but it was always others who died because of it while he walked away.

Hjalmar smiled a sad smile. 'My brother thought the same.' The old man looked towards the camp as a large fire was started where the men would cook their evening meal. 'I am loyal to Jarl Hakon, just like I was loyal to his father. I watched him grow into the man he is today and I know when he is up to something.' Hjalmar looked at Ulf before he got to his feet and stretched his back. 'Watch your back, Ulf. Someone is planning something and you're in the middle of it.' He walked away and found a spot to sleep before Ulf could say anything, not that Ulf knew what to say. He knew who was planning something, and he was certain he knew why he was in the middle of it. Jarl Ragnar wanted Ormstunga, and he wanted Ulf dead. But for a reason Ulf did not understand, Ragnar kept his distance from Ulf.

Ulf's hand went to the Mjöllnir pendant around his neck and he wondered if there was more to what was happening. Maybe it wasn't about Ragnar wanting Ormstunga. His head started hurting, and Ulf took a deep breath as he leaned back and stared at the darkening sky. He watched as birds flew in random patterns as they chased insects, which made him think of the patterns the Norns weaved. Were they random, like the path the birds flew as they reacted to the movement of their prey, or was there a purpose in their weaving, a goal they were aiming for? Many believed that the Norns had already determined their fates. Ulf believed the same, even though he had spent much of his youth fighting that idea. But he couldn't explain how things that appear random at first seemed to have a purpose later on. Ulf had attacked a man in Jelling while he was drunk and because of that fight, he had found Eldrid. That was the reason he was on this raid, led by the man who he had fought with, a man who wanted to take his sword. At first, the fight with Ragnar had seemed like a random event, but with everything that had happened since, it was obvious that it was meant to happen. Ulf was meant to find Eldrid again. He fell asleep as these thoughts raged through his mind and dreamt of the tree again, with the snake on the branch hissing at him as she repeated her warning. *One of them will be stabbed in the back.*

A kick to the stomach woke Ulf from his dream and as his eyes snapped opened, someone punched him in the face. Instinct made Ulf roll out of the way before one of his attackers stomped down on where he had been, and, still dazed from the punch and sleep, he jumped to his feet and raised his arms in time to block another punch. But it was too dark for Ulf to see who was attacking him, as someone hit him in the stomach. Ulf bent over from the blow and was shoved to the ground before he was kicked more times than he could count.

'What's going on here?' Ragnvald's voice forced the kicking to stop, and Ulf heard his attackers run away as he lay on the stomach, coughing as he tried to breathe.

'What's going on?' Hjalmar repeated the question in a sleepy voice.

Ulf opened his eyes and saw Ragnvald standing over, the flames of his torch casting shadows in the lines on his face.

'I had a bad dream.' Ulf spat the blood out of his mouth before he sat up.

Hjalmar frowned at him. 'Must have been a very bad dream.'

Ulf nodded as he and Ragnvald glared at each other.

'You should be watching the ships, not sleeping!' the one-handed warrior said.

But Hjalmar waved a hand at him. 'The ships are fine. No one's going to do anything to them. And even if they do, what can the two of us do to stop them?'

Ragnvald grunted, but his glare was fixed on Ulf. 'I told you to watch your back.'

Ulf struggled to his feet. 'Why? So I can see you coming?'

Ragnvald smirked. 'Boy, I won't be coming from behind.'

'Enough you two,' Hjalmar said. 'We've had enough excitement for one night.' He turned to Ulf. 'Did you see who attacked you?'

Ulf shook his head. 'Only that some of them wore leather boots, while others had strapping around their legs.'

'Well, that's helpful.' Hjalmar smiled, then turned to Ragnvald. 'What are you doing here?'

Ragnvald shrugged. 'I couldn't sleep, so I went for a walk when I heard the scuffle.'

Both Ulf and Hjalmar frowned at Ragnvald, before Hjalmar said, 'Well, I guess Ulf can thank the gods you can't sleep. Otherwise, he might have been dead now.'

Ulf shook his head again. 'They didn't want to kill me. They would have stabbed me instead of kicking me.' Ulf glanced at Ragnvald and wondered if he was behind the attack, because he didn't believe that Ragnvald just happened to be there because he couldn't sleep. Just like when Ulf had seen Skadi for the first time, Ragnvald had also been there. *Is he following me?* Ulf thought and then wondered why Ragnvald would need to do that. Was it because he wanted to kill Ulf and was looking for an opportunity, or because Jarl Hakon had asked him to? But why would the jarl do that? To protect him from men sent by Ragnar? Ulf felt his head throb at all the questions, and it angered him that he didn't know the answers to any of them. And those who did refused to tell him what was going on. Again, he wished he had gone to another town to find a jarl to raid with. But the Norns had taken him to Jelling and only they knew why.

Hjalmar scratched his cheek. 'I'd ask why they wanted to attack you, but we all know the reason.' Ragnvald growled at him, but Hjalmar only shrugged. 'What? We all know there is something between Ulf and Jarl Ragnar.'

Ragnvald grunted as Ulf glanced at Hjalmar and wondered if the man knew more than he was letting on. 'It doesn't matter,' Ragnvald said and turned his attention back to Ulf. 'This time, don't sleep.'

Ulf clenched his fists. 'You really expect me to stay awake all night? Why can't the jarl send men to replace me if he wants his ships guarded?'

Again, Ragnvald grunted before he turned and went back to the camp.

Hjalmar stood beside Ulf, who wiped the blood from his face. 'Jarl Hakon doesn't want you to protect the ships. He wants to keep you away from the others.'

'Why?' Ulf raised an eyebrow.

'Thorir has become popular amongst the men. The Dane is vicious and they like that. He is also not very smart and they like that even more. And many of them are upset that you attacked him today. So the jarl is worried that someone might attack you in your tent.'

'So he keeps me here, alone on his ship?'

'I'm here,' Hjalmar said.

'Aye. A lot of help you were when I was getting my head kicked in.'

Hjalmar laughed and went back to his spot where he made himself comfortable and within moments, the old man was snoring. Ulf growled as he stared at the camp. He was about to go back to his spot, but then decided against it as he took his cloak and looked for somewhere else to sleep. He got off the ship and found a tree near the river and made himself comfortable. But Ulf knew he would not be able to sleep. Not with all the questions distracting him. And the more he thought about it, the less sense anything made to him. Why would Ragnar go through all this effort just because of a sword? As Ulf watched the moon move across the night sky, he wondered if any of his ancestors ever had people try to kill them just to get to the sword.

Chapter 27

'Well, Loki just fucked us,' Jarl Hakon said a few days later as the fleet continued up the river. Ulf, his face bruised and with a cut on his lip, stood up and his heart raced when he saw the huge Frankish army on the riverbanks. Hundreds of flags fluttered in the wind as the Frankish army stood on both sides of the river. Over the sounds of the oars slapping the water, Christian priests could be heard praying to their god as the Frankish warriors stood in grim silence and waited for the Danish warships to approach. Ulf guessed there must have been thousands of Franks.

A horn blew from Ragnar's ship, followed by horns from the other ships to warn those at the rear of the one hundred and twenty ships of the threat. Those, like Ulf, who were not rowing, all stood and stared at the enemy, who almost blended in with the trees along the riverbank.

'What do we do?' one warrior asked and many of the Norsemen looked at Jarl Hakon, who smiled despite the danger the fleet now faced.

'We trust the gods and do what Jarl Ragnar tells us to do.'

'Aye,' Hjalmar said as he stood beside Ulf. 'And we pray Odin has enough benches available in Valhalla.'

Ulf nodded as his hands trembled, and he remembered the last time he had faced such a large force. He glanced at Thorir, the bóndi who was eager to be a warrior, and almost smiled when he saw the man's pale face. It was one thing facing badly armed farmers who were only trying to defend their homes. But facing a large army was something very few had the courage to do. And Ulf knew he wasn't one of them, as his bladder suddenly felt full. The voices of his ancestors, though, seemed to relish the prospect of the battle, and Ulf thanked Tyr that dark clouds blocked the sun.

'We're not going to fight them, are we?' Thorir asked.

'Are you afraid?' Hjalmar asked the bóndi, who puffed his chest out.

'No,' he said, but Ulf noticed the quiver in his voice as he stared at Jarl Ragnar's ship. Would Ragnar risk his forces in a pitched battle against the Franks? Or would he run? But even Ulf looked over his shoulder at the ships behind them. He knew they would fight. There were too many ships on the river. Even if Ragnar wanted to, he wouldn't be able to turn his fleet around. And sailing past the army, which was spread out on both sides of the river, put them at risk of archers who could shoot flaming arrows at the ships. Ulf's hand went to the hilt of Ormstunga and he saw from the smile on Jarl Hakon's face that the jarl saw the same thing he did. That the river would be red with blood before the sun set.

***

Knut growled as he stared at the Frankish army. He cursed the Norns and Ragnar as he scanned the army on either side of the river for any sign of the Frankish king, but they were still too far away to see the bastard. This was what Knut had been afraid of. He had wanted to get to Paris as quickly as possible, but Ragnar wanted to take his time. He wanted to smell the spring flowers and watch the bees feed on them. And that had given the Frankish king time to muster his army and prevent them from getting to Paris. Knut had known this would happen. He had tried to warn Ragnar, but the bastard wouldn't listen.

Knut was surprised, though, that the king had decided to meet them here and not in Paris. He frowned as he wondered what the Frankish king was trying to protect that was more important than Paris. Traders had told them that there were important churches near Paris, but Knut had thought that King Charles would want to protect his city. It seemed that Knut had been wrong about that. And he had also underestimated the Frankish king, who had been smart enough to split his army in two and have them on both sides of the river. It meant that Ragnar couldn't avoid a fight. He glanced at the sky as his hand went to the spear pendant he wore around his neck and prayed that the dark clouds were not a bad omen from the gods as the horns of war echoed in his ears.

***

Jarl Hakon's warriors, like those on the other ships, prepared for the battle they all knew was coming. No order needed to be given. Nothing needed to be said to break the grim silence as men checked their weapons to make sure their edges were sharp and the blades were clean. Armour was readjusted, so it sat comfortably and the warriors could move freely, while belts were tightened to help carry the weight of brynjas and to make sure they stayed in place.

'You should say something to him.' Jarl Hakon pointed at Thorir, who looked like he was about to faint.

'What can I say to him?' Ulf asked, and Jarl Hakon shrugged.

'It's not good going into battle with bad feelings between friends. You know as well as I do that not everyone walks away from them.'

Ulf scowled and knew that the jarl spoke the truth, but he couldn't think of anything to say to Thorir other than don't die. And Ulf doubted Thorir would find that comforting. He tried to remember any words of comfort that might have been said to him before a battle, but the only thing that came to him was the line Snorri used to say to his friends. *See you after the battle or in Valhalla*. 'He's not my friend,' Ulf said after a moment and again, Jarl Hakon shrugged.

Hjalmar started singing a war song which sounded familiar to Ulf, but he didn't know the words. Jarl Hakon joined in, as did the rest of his crew, and those on his other ship. Some men stomped their feet on the deck of the ship in time with the words, and Ulf felt it vibrating up his legs and into the pit of his stomach. The voices of his ancestors stirred, and Ulf glanced at the clouds again to make sure they still blocked the sun. He spotted Thorir staring at him, and not knowing what else to do, he nodded at the man. Thorir nodded back and Ulf whispered a silent prayer to Thor, asking the thunder god to protect Thorir so that he could return to his family.

Gripping the hilt of Ormstunga, Ulf watched the lead ship and again wondered what Jarl Ragnar was going to do. As the warriors of Jarl Hakon sang their song, Ulf frowned when Ragnar signalled for all his ships to turn to the right riverbank.

'Clever bastard.' Jarl Hakon smiled. 'The king of West Francia is not a smart man, not like our leader. He split his forces, but they are not equal. The force on the right riverbank is smaller than one on the left. And there is nowhere nearby where the larger force can cross the river.'

Ulf stared at the Frankish army, close enough now for him to see that most of them wore no armour and only a few had leather jerkins. Only a small group of warriors on the left riverbank wore brynjas and they all surrounded their king. He also saw that Jarl Hakon was right and understood what Ragnar was doing. He was sending his five thousand strong army against the smaller force on the right, while the larger force on the left could do nothing to stop them. Ulf didn't know what was further up the river, but Jarl Hakon was right. There was nowhere to cross down the river. He couldn't help but smile at the cleverness of Jarl Ragnar, but his smile soon disappeared when Jarl Hakon roared, 'Prepare for battle!'

The warriors cheered and sang their war song again as the men who weren't rowing beat their weapons on the back of their shields. Someone offered Ulf a shield, which he took and strapped on to his back. He ignored the raised eyebrows from Hjalmar and the others. Ulf doubted there would be a shield wall. The Frankish army would not want the Danish and Norse warriors to get a foothold on the riverbank and form a shield wall. So they would charge as soon as the first ship reached the riverbank and hope to stop the other ships from doing the same.

Ulf's heart raced when he realised that Jarl Hakon's ship would be one of the first, and his ancestors started whispering in his ears in anticipation of the coming bloodshed. Even Ormstunga felt like she was vibrating with excitement in her scabbard as Jarl Hakon gave the order and the rowers sped up while he positioned his ship so that it was next to Jarl Ragnar's.

Tyr, lend me your battle skill, Ulf prayed as he freed Ormstunga from her scabbard and took the axe in his left hand. He took a deep breath and made his way to the prow, where he stood beside Jarl Hakon and his hirdmen. Hjalmar was there as well and smiled at Ulf.

'Looks like we finally get to see the real Bear-Slayer,' Jarl Hakon said and his men laughed, but Ulf ignored them all as he gave himself to the voices of his ancestors.

They want to see the Bear-Slayer, Ulf thought, as he remembered how they had mocked him ever since they had attacked the first town. *I will show them the Bear-Slayer.*

As soon as the keel of Jarl Hakon's ship struck the riverbank, Ulf followed the jarl and his men as they jumped overboard, all of them calling out to the gods and silencing the Christian priests. Ragnar's ship hit the riverbank moments later, as did the rest of the ships at the head of the fleet. Before the Franks could form their defence, more than three hundred Danish and Norse warriors stormed at them.

'Tyr!' Ulf roared as he charged at the shocked Frankish warriors, their faces pale and their eyes white. More than a few had vomit stains on their padded tunics and leather jerkins, but Ulf blocked all of that out of his mind as he swung his axe at the first Frankish warrior. The man reacted too slowly and Ulf's axe cleaved his face in two. He rushed past and stabbed another in the side. Ormstunga found a gap in the Frank's leather jerkin and tore through his insides. The man shuddered as Ulf pulled his sword free and was already attacking the next Frank before the man fell to the ground.

The Frankish king, along with his army, on the other riverbank could do nothing but watch with pale faces as Jarl Ragnar's ships landed and more Danish warriors charged at those on the right riverbank. Men cried out as they were cut open and trampled on while the Danes and Norse warriors called out to the gods and roared in ecstasy. Ulf, his battle lust driving him on, ducked under a spear thrust and sliced his attacker's stomach open with Ormstunga before he kicked another Frank to the ground and buried his axe in the man's skull. He turned in time to avoid another spear and found himself standing next to Jarl Ragnar. His heart skipped as they stared at each other, the battle around them almost forgotten. Jarl Ragnar bared his teeth as his eyes went to the bloodied blade of Ormstunga and, for a moment, Ulf thought the jarl was going to kill him for the sword. It was the perfect time for Ragnar to do it. In the middle of a battle when everyone would think that he was killed by the Franks. But then somebody knocked Ulf to the side and as Ulf struggled to stay on his feet, he turned and saw Ragnvald, his face covered in blood, glaring at him.

Ragnvald tensed and Ulf expected him to attack when a Frank stabbed his spear at the one-handed warrior, forcing him to turn and face the man. Ulf shook his head, trying to make sense of what was going on when he saw a Dane creeping towards Jarl Ragnar, who was fighting a large Frank. At first, Ulf thought the Dane was there to help the jarl against the giant man, but the voices in his ears told him something was wrong.

The Dane straightened up and pulled his sword arm back as the noise of an axe striking shield nearby made Ulf remember the warning Skadi had given him. *One of the wolves will be stabbed in the back.*

Ulf, certain now that Skadi had meant Jarl Ragnar and not him, attacked before the Dane could kill Ragnar. He chopped at the Dane's arm with his axe, cleaving through muscles and bone, and before the Dane could react, Ulf stabbed him through the neck. Warm blood wet his face as he pulled the sword free and the Dane, his eyes still wide in shock, dropped to the ground. Jarl Ragnar, unaware of what had happened, turned and glared at Ulf, who stepped back when he saw the fire in the jarl's eyes.

'You trying to kill me, Bear-Slayer?' Ragnar said, confirming what Ulf had thought.

Ulf hawked and spat. 'No, but someone is.'

Ulf turned when he sensed movement nearby and deflected a spear aimed at his head, before someone else killed the Frank. Ulf rushed at another Frank, who dropped to his knees and let go of his spear. The man screamed something in his language, and even though Ulf could not understand the words, he knew the man was asking for mercy. Not that he got it as Jarl Hakon stepped in and hacked at the Frank's neck with his sword. Blood squirted in the air as Jarl Hakon glared at Ulf, but before the man could say anything, a horn blew to sound the end of the battle.

Chapter 28

The battle song was replaced by different noises, some familiar to Ulf and others not. Injured and dying men called for mercy and prayed to their god. The Norse and the Danes prayed to Odin, asking the All-Father to let them into Valhalla, while some called for their wives or their mothers. The Christians begged for mercy and asked for forgiveness for what they believed were their sins. Ulf knew it was important to them, but he never understood it. All men made mistakes. Why should where you go after you died depend on that?

The cries of ravens and other carrion birds filled the sky, almost drowning out the other noises as the birds came to feast on the dead. Some swept down and landed on the corpses of the dead warriors and pecked out their eyes while the raiders from the north stared at the Frankish army across the river. They always went for the eyes, the ravens. Someone had once told Ulf that they were searching for a new eye for the All-Father who had given his right eye to Mimir's well so that he could drink from it and gain its wisdom. But Ulf had never believed that. His uncle had told him that the ravens just enjoyed eating the eyes.

The other noise, the one that Ulf had never heard after a battle, came from the other side of the river. Like most of the Danes and

Norse warriors, Ulf watched the remaining Frankish army as they stared impotently at their dead comrades. None of them shouted insults at the raiders or waved their weapons in the air. There was no threat of retribution from the Franks or their king. Instead, many of them were on their knees, their hands clasped in front of them as they prayed, although Ulf did not know what for. Did they expect their god to come down from wherever he was to help them? Or were they praying that Jarl Ragnar didn't send his army across the river to fight them as well?

The king of the West Franks, a man who looked to be close to Ulf's age, sat on his horse, his face pale as the Danish and Norse warriors taunted him and his army. They waved their weapons in the air and banged them on the back of their shields, the thunderous echoes drowning out the praying and the wailing of the Christians and sending some of the carrion birds back to the skies. The men from the north were still filled with their battle lust. Ulf could feel it even though he had lost his. They wanted to wipe out the rest of the Frankish army and, more than that, they wanted to get their hands on the Frankish king. Ulf watched a few of the Danish warriors pull their pants down and bend over, while one warrior gripped his cock and swung it in circles while pointing at the king of the Franks. But King Charles's eyes were fixed on Jarl Ragnar as he stood a short distance away from Ulf, grinning at the king who had thought he could bring his army to this river and stop him. Instead, Jarl Ragnar had outsmarted him, and now Ulf doubted the Frankish king had enough men left to stop Ragnar's fleet.

'There's nothing the bastard can do, and he knows it. He also knows we know it,' Jarl Hakon said, his teeth almost too white against his dirty face when he smiled. 'He should have kept his army together and waited for us in Paris.'

'Or forced us into a land battle,' Ragnvald said, for once not glaring at Ulf. Ulf nodded as he agreed with both men. The king of the Franks had made a mistake by splitting his army, especially in a place where he could not cross the river easily. And that was another thought that bothered Ulf.

'Why here? Why bring his army here and not somewhere where he had the upper hand?'

Jarl Hakon shrugged. 'If the Christians knew how to fight battles, then we wouldn't be raiding them.' Jarl Hakon then smiled as he glanced at Ulf. 'You fought well, Bear-Slayer.' Ulf nodded, but wasn't really paying attention as he scanned the battlefield for Thorir. His heart raced as he saw no sign of him and Ulf hoped the bóndi didn't fall. 'I see how you've earned your reputation and why Ragnar wants that sword of yours so much.'

Ulf broke from his search for Thorir and glanced at Jarl Hakon, wondering why the jarl had said that. His mind went back to when he and Ragnar faced each other on the battlefield. The moment when Ulf had wondered if Ragnar was going to cut him down and take his sword. But Ragnar had only glared at him. And then he remembered something else. The Dane who had tried to kill Ragnar. His head spun from the confusion and without his battle lust to keep him going, Ulf felt exhausted. His hands trembled, as they always did after a battle, and Ulf glanced at Ormstunga and the axe. Both weapons were covered in blood, but Ulf knew he couldn't clean them. Not with the rest of the Frankish army facing them from across the river.

'Round up the survivors!' Jarl Ragnar ordered and turned his back on the Frankish army.

Ulf frowned as he watched Ragnar's men push and shove the surviving Frankish warriors towards the trees along the riverbank not far from where they had fought the Franks.

'Now you'll see why men fear Jarl Ragnar.' Jarl Hakon smiled at Ulf's confusion. But there was something else in that smile, something that sent a shiver down his spine. Ragnvald, still standing beside Jarl Hakon, shook his head, and Ulf turned his attention back to the Frankish men as they were lined up in front of the trees. More than a hundred men, Ulf guessed as their hands were tied with rope the Danes had retrieved from the ships. A few of the Franks were resigned to their fate, while others cried and begged for mercy. Ulf didn't need to know the words they spoke to know that was what they were doing. His brows creased as he tried to make sense of the unease he felt, and in the shadows of the trees behind the Frankish warriors, he thought he glimpsed thick black hair. But it disappeared before he could make sure, as Skadi's words came to him. *The wolf brought a dog with him. Who dies first?*

Ulf's heart raced as he scanned the Danish army. 'Can anyone see Thorir?' he asked, but no one responded. He glanced over his shoulder to make sure they were still there and saw both jarls staring at the captured Franks as Jarl Ragnar's men tied ropes around their necks and threw the other ends of the ropes over the branches of the trees. 'He's going to hang them? All of them?'

'King Charles's grandfather did far worse to the Saxon people before we were born,' Jarl Hakon said before he spat to the ground. 'The Christians will get what they deserve.'

Ulf had stopped listening to Jarl Hakon as he searched for Thorir amongst the Danish and Norse warriors. There were some dead Danes and Norsemen, but without walking amongst them, Ulf could not tell if Thorir was one of them. He prayed to Thor that the bóndi wasn't, but he still felt uneasy. Like something was about to happen. Something Skadi had warned him about, and Ulf had been too blind to see it. His eyes went back to the Frankish men about to be hanged as Jarl Ragnar stepped to the edge of the river again and faced the Frankish king.

'Odin!' the jarl roared to the dark clouds. 'Odin, cast your eye on us as we sacrifice these men to you!'

As the warriors of Denmark and Norway roared and the Frankish army wailed, Ulf ran his eyes along the men about to be hanged. And then his heart skipped a beat when he spotted Thorir amongst them, dressed like a Frankish warrior. Thorir's eyes were wild with fear as he stared at Ulf, while blood streamed out of his mouth and into his beard as he struggled. Ulf heard the gods laughing at him, mocking him in the cries of the ravens as he watched the men behind Thorir pull on the rope. Thorir's eyes bulged as his feet were lifted off the ground. He opened his mouth to call out, but only blood came out and Ulf realised they cut his tongue out. The old scar around Ulf's neck seemed to burn as he remembered when he was hanged, and Ulf knew he couldn't let the bóndi die like that.

'Thorir!' Ulf roared and was about to rush towards Thorir when someone struck him from behind. Blinding light flashed in his eyes, and then everything went dark.

***

Jarl Knut nodded at Jarl Hakon, who smiled. He only hoped that the blow Jarl Hakon had delivered didn't kill Ulf. Especially because Ulf wasn't wearing a helmet. And then he looked at the bóndi, his bulging eyes fixed on him as his legs kicked and he pissed himself. Just like most of the Franks that were being hanged. A growl escaped from Jarl Knut's lips because he knew this would be spoken about long after Ragnarök and that Ragnar's name would never be forgotten. Unlike his. *That should have been me*, he thought. It would have been if Ulf had not killed the man he had sent to kill Ragnar during the battle.

Knut had believed the gods were smiling on him when Ulf and Ragnar were fighting close together, especially when they faced each other. He had thought that was a sign from the gods and had sent one of his hirdmen, one of the few left he could trust, to kill Ragnar. But Ulf had killed him before he could stab Ragnar in the back.

'A pity we had to kill the bóndi,' Hakon said as the man finally died. 'Was starting to like him.'

Knut grunted. He did not care about the bóndi. The man was fated to die the moment Knut had first laid eyes on him.

'What do we do with the Bear-Slayer?' the one-handed warrior asked and Knut glanced at him. He did not like the look in the man's eyes, but the old bastard was not important.

'You don't get to kill him. Not yet,' Jarl Hakon said, and Ragnvald shrugged.

'No, we still need Ulf.' Knut glared at Jarl Ragnar as he stared at the Frankish king across the river. 'What kind of fool splits his army into two and picks a spot on the river with nowhere to cross?'

'A fool who doesn't know how to lead an army,' Jarl Hakon said. 'So what do we do with Ulf?'

'Take him to your ship. When he wakes up, make sure he believes Ragnar was behind his bóndi's death.'

'What's the point?' Ragnvald asked, and Knut growled at the old man, who only stared back at him. 'Even if you kill Ragnar now and take over the fleet, everyone here will tell stories of what the man had done here.'

Knut clenched his fists, and even though he knew Ragnvald was right, he still wanted to kill the bastard. 'Now I just want Ragnar dead.' Knut turned away from Hakon and his one-handed man, and his eyes fell on Ulf's sword. He picked it up and was surprised at how balanced the sword felt. Knut ran his finger along the edge, which was still as sharp as a new blade, as a smile parted his lips. Ulf owed him something for ruining his plans, and his sword would be fair compensation.

'Bad luck to take someone's sword while they still live,' Ragnvald said.

'Hakon, silence your dog before I do it,' Knut said, his patience for the old bastard gone. He watched as Ragnar ordered his men onto the ships. It seemed that Ragnar had decided to finish the Franks off. But the Franks on the other side of the river did not have the stomach for a battle. Not after watching Ragnar hang their companions. They turned and fled before Ragnar's ships had their oars out, their king not far behind them. The Danes cheered, the noise chasing the ravens and crows away from their meals as

Knut cursed the gods and Ragnar. And more than that, he cursed Ulf for ruining his plan.

Chapter 29

Ulf groaned as he opened his eyes. He lay on the ground and waited for them to come into focus, wondering how many more times he would wake up like this. His eyes focused on the stars in the sky and Ulf frowned as dull pain throbbed at the back of his head. He tried to remember what had happened, but everything after the battle on the riverbank was a blur.

'Drink this,' a familiar voice said and Ulf looked at Hjalmar sitting next to him by his tent while holding out a cup. The old man looked exhausted and had a fresh cut on his forehead. 'Not as fast as I used to be.' He smiled when Ulf glanced at the cut. Ulf nodded as he took a cup and grimaced when he drank the ale. 'Aye, the ale is not good, but it's all we got.'

'What happened?' Ulf asked as he tried to sit up, which only made his head throb even more.

'Steady now.' Hjalmar reached out to help Ulf. 'A Frank must have clobbered you during the battle. We found you afterwards lying near the riverbank.'

'A Frank?' Ulf frowned. It couldn't have been a Frank. Ulf remembered the battle and the end, and he remembered Jarl Ragnar hanging the surviving Frankish warriors. And then his heart raced as he remembered Thorir, his legs swinging as his bulging eyes pleaded with him. 'Thorir.'

Hjalmar looked away. 'Sorry, lad. He didn't make it.'

'I know he didn't make it! They hanged him!' Ulf growled as the memory ignited his anger and pushed the headache away. 'They cut his tongue out and hanged him!'

Hjalmar frowned at Ulf. 'I think that blow was harder than we thought. Thorir died in the battle.'

Ulf shook his head. 'No, they hanged him. I saw it before...' He rubbed his head as he still tried to make sense of what had happened after the battle.

Hjalmar was about to say something, but then he glanced to the side as Jarl Hakon and Ragnvald appeared.

'Ulf is right,' Jarl Hakon, who wasn't wearing his brynja any more, said. Ulf glared at them as he remembered talking to them and Jarl Knut when the hanging was happening. 'Ulf—'

'Who did that to Thorir?' Ulf cut the jarl off. 'Why did they do that?' He looked at Ragnvald and clenched his fists. 'Who hit me?'

'One of Ragnar's men struck you when you ran to help Thorir,' Jarl Hakon said, and Ulf noticed how Ragnvald looked away, but he thought nothing of it.

'Why do that to him? Why cut his tongue out?'

Jarl Hakon shrugged. 'Punishment.'

Ulf frowned as his mind reeled. 'Punishment? What did Thorir do to deserve that?'

'He lied,' Jarl Hakon said. 'He lied to protect you, and Jarl Ragnar found out about it. So he had his men grab Thorir during the battle. They cut his tongue out for lying and dressed him as a Frankish warrior. Jarl Ragnar wanted you to watch him hang because he lied to protect you.'

'What are you talking about?'

Jarl Hakon stared at Ulf for a few heartbeats. 'The night Ragnar was attacked. Thorir said you never left the ship. But he lied. You left the ship and Ragnar found out about it.'

Ulf glared at Ragnvald, remembering how the old warrior had seen him in the forest that night. Before anyone could stop him, he jumped to his feet and launched himself at Ragnvald. 'You bastard!' He grabbed Ragnvald by his brynja and punched him in the face. Ragnvald's head snapped to the side and before he could do anything, Ulf punched him again, causing him to drop to his knees. But Ragnvald did not fight back. Instead, he stayed on his knees and glared at Ulf.

'I warned you. I told you to—'

Jarl Hakon grabbed Ulf and pulled him back before Ragnvald could finish his sentence. 'Ulf, it was not Ragnvald's fault. Someone else must have seen you.'

Ulf turned and grabbed Jarl Hakon by his tunic. 'You lie!'

Jarl Hakon shook his head. 'No, Ulf. I swear to the gods, I'm not lying. Ragnar hates you, but he can't do anything to you because men say you are blessed by the gods. So he killed Thorir instead.' Ulf, still holding the jarl by his tunic, glared at him as he tried to make sense of everything. And the more he thought about it, the more it made sense. Only Ragnar could have done that. Ragnar believed Ulf had tried to kill him. So he must have had Thorir killed because of that. He thought of the other times Ragnar had been attacked. Ulf had been blamed for those attacks. 'I liked Thorir, Ulf. You know that. I would never do that to him.'

Ulf let go of Jarl Hakon and stepped back. 'Ragnar did this?' Jarl Hakon nodded and Ulf clenched his fists as the heat from his anger spread through his limbs and his arms trembled. 'Where is he?' Ulf said through clenched teeth. His hand went to his side, but his eyes widened when he didn't feel Ormstunga there. Ulf turned before Jarl Hakon could respond and scanned the area where he had been lying and his heart felt like it stopped when he couldn't see his sword. 'Where is Ormstunga?'

Jarl Hakon shook his head. 'Jarl Ragnar took it. You know how he wanted your sword.'

Ulf's temples throbbed as his anger burnt inside of him. 'He killed Thorir and took my sword?'

Jarl Hakon nodded again. 'We tried to stop him, Jarl Knut and me, but he refused to listen to us. He wanted us to leave you behind so the Franks kill you, but we couldn't.'

'Where is he?' Ulf had stopped listening to Jarl Hakon, not that he could hear anything over the voices of his ancestors raging in his ears. Ragnar had taken his ancestral sword from him and they wanted blood. Ragnar's blood. Ulf turned and stomped towards the centre of the camp before Jarl Hakon could answer his question. He could make out Ragnar's large tent, which stood above the rest, and clenched his jaw as he marched towards it. In his mind, he replayed the image of Thorir hanging from the tree. It was like kindling added to the flames of his anger as he walked past warriors celebrating the victory over the Franks. Few paid him any attention, and those who saw him were too drunk to notice the rage on his face. Not that any of them could stop him.

'Who—?' one of the warriors guarding Jarl Ragnar's tent started asking when Ulf punched him in the mouth. Before he dropped to the ground, Ulf turned and kicked the other warrior's legs out from underneath him. As the man landed on the ground, Ulf kicked him in the side and stormed into the tent.

'Ragnar!'

'Ulf!' Jarl Knut jumped to his feet and knocked the stool he had been sitting on over.

'What is the meaning of this?' Jarl Ragnar asked, a cup of ale in his hands and his eyes wide with shock.

Ulf ignored Jarl Knut and launched himself at Jarl Ragnar, who threw his cup at him. Ulf ducked under the cup and tackled Ragnar to the ground as Jarl Knut jumped back and rushed out of the tent.

'I'll fetch help!' Jarl Knut shouted, but then Ulf forgot about the man as he threw a punch at Jarl Ragnar.

Jarl Ragnar twisted his head out of the way and kneed Ulf in the side before throwing him off of him. Both men rolled to their feet before Ulf attacked again, his rage refusing to let him stop. Ragnar batted his punch away, and Ulf ducked under one from Jarl Ragnar before he pulled his sax-knife from his belt and swung it at Ragnar's stomach. Jarl Ragnar was not wearing his brynja and was forced to jump back, and Ulf rushed at him. He stabbed at Ragnar's head, who tried to twist out of the way, but Ulf was too fast and he sliced the jarl's cheek open. Ragnar ignored the cut to his cheek and punched Ulf in the side, winding him and sending him a few steps back with his strength. Ulf was gasping for air as Ragnar launched his own attack. He swung a punch at Ulf's head, which Ulf ducked under, but then Ragnar caught him with a knee to the face. Ulf's head snapped up and Ragnar grabbed him by the throat and threw him to the ground. Ulf landed hard, but still kept hold of his knife as he rolled to his feet.

'So you try to kill me again? After all your failed attempts, you still think you can kill me?' Ragnar's face was red as he paced in front of Ulf, who shook his head to clear it.

'I never tried to kill you!'

'You lie!' Jarl Ragnar launched himself at Ulf again. Ulf twisted out of the way of his fist, but could not bring his sax-knife around to stab Ragnar in his exposed side.

'You are the one who sent men to kill me so that you could take Ormstunga!'

Ulf had just enough time to see the frown on Ragnar's face as he threw a punch with his left hand. Ragnar was too slow to move out of the way, and Ulf caught him on the cheek. The jarl staggered backwards and shook his head.

'I never sent men after you!' Ragnar stepped back to avoid Ulf's sax-knife as he swung it at his stomach. Outside the tent, men sang and cheered as they feasted, unaware of the fight in Jarl Ragnar's tent. And in that noise, Ulf heard the gods laughing at him.

'You're lying! You sent men to kill me after our fight in Jelling.'

Jarl Ragnar shook his head again and moved back to create space between him and Ulf. 'I didn't send anyone after you! I made the traders you were with pay the mangæld you owed me and told them to leave Jelling. The gods know I'd forgotten about you until I saw you on Jarl Hakon's ship.'

Ulf hesitated as the voices of his ancestors still raged in his ears. 'I never tried to kill you! I did my best to avoid you!' Ulf tightened his grip on his sax-knife as he remembered Thorir. 'You killed Thorir!' He attacked again, swinging the sax-knife at Jarl Ragnar, who stepped out of the way and tripped Ulf. As soon as Ulf hit the ground, he turned and raised the knife as he expected Ragnar to jump on top of him, but the jarl just stood back and glared at him.

'I don't know who that is.'

The voices in Ulf's ears screamed even louder as the image of Thorir hanging from the tree, his beard red from the blood from his mouth, came to him. 'You killed him. You cut his tongue out and hanged him like he was a Frank!'

'What in Odin—' Ragnar didn't get to finish his question because Ulf attacked again. But before Ulf reached the jarl, a voice he never expected to hear said,

'Ulf, stop. Jarl Ragnar speaks the truth.'

Both men turned to the centre of the tent, their eyes wide as Skadi stood there. Her hair was the same as before, dark and wild with twigs and bones tied in, as was the deerhide she wore with the snakeskin around her neck. But this time, she had black lines running down the side of her face, similar to Ulf's scars, but on both sides and with a black band painted over her eyes. Ulf wasn't sure what the purpose of that was, but it made him hesitate as he glanced at Ragnar again, who was gaping at the volva. Ulf sensed that was his moment to kill the jarl and avenge Thorir, and get his sword back, but before he moved a muscle, Skadi said,

'Kill him and the gods will curse you, young wolf.'

Ulf growled while tightening the grip on his sax-knife. 'The gods have already cursed me. He killed Thorir and took Ormstunga from me.'

'Who is this woman?' Ragnar asked as his hand went to the spear pendant he wore around his neck.

'He did neither of those things, young wolf. Look around you. Do you see her anywhere in the tent?' Ulf glanced around the tent and saw no sign of Ormstunga. Only Jarl Ragnar's sword by his armour in the corner of the tent. 'I tried to warn you, but you were too blind to see it.'

Ulf turned his fury to her. 'Too blind to see it! You spoke words that made no sense. Nonsense about wolves and hounds.'

Skadi smiled, which only angered Ulf even more. 'I told you what the gods allowed me to tell you. I spoke their words, so don't blame me if you didn't understand them.'

'I don't care whose words they are! I want my sword back and I want this bastard to die for killing Thorir!' Ulf turned and was about to attack again when Skadi moved faster than he thought was possible and stood between them.

'Then kill me first, because that is the only way you get to kill Jarl Ragnar.'

Ulf glared at Skadi, the whites of her eyes even brighter because of the black paint around her eyes. He lowered the sax-knife and took a step back, not really prepared to anger the gods by killing a volva. For a moment, he wondered if he could kill her when he heard her voice in his head. *No, you can't.*

On her face, all he saw was her smile before she turned to face Jarl Ragnar, who was still gaping at her.

'Who is this woman and how did she get in my tent?' he asked again.

'She is a volva,' Ulf said and glanced at the entrance of the tent as he, too, wondered how she had got in without any of them noticing. He looked at the snakeskin she wore around her neck and wondered if she had changed into a snake and slithered in.

'A volva? Why is there a volva in my tent?' Ragnar, still gripping the spear pendant hanging around his neck, took a step backwards. He glanced at the entrance to the tent.

'No one is coming to help you. No one will enter until the sun rises.'

Both Ulf and Ragnar frowned at her and Ragnar asked, 'What did you do?'

'I did nothing. I do nothing. I go where the gods tell me to go and deliver the messages they want me to deliver. That is all I do.' She glanced at Ulf, who remembered how she had manipulated him in the past for her own revenge and knew that she was lying to Jarl Ragnar. What he didn't know was whether what she was doing now was for her own gain or if it was for the gods.

'I am here to protect you, young wolf,' she said, as if reading his mind, which sent a shiver down his spine. 'I told you that before.'

'I don't need protecting. I can kill him.' Ulf nodded towards Jarl Ragnar, who bristled while the smile on Skadi's face made him wonder if she thought that was true.

'Why do you want to kill me? Because of the traders?' Jarl Ragnar clenched his fists as if he was about to attack Ulf.

Ulf glared at him. 'You killed Thorir,' he said. 'You took my sword.'

'I told you, young wolf. He did neither of those things,' Skadi responded before Jarl Ragnar could.

'Just like he didn't send men after me?'

'By the gods, I already told you I didn't.'

Ulf frowned at Jarl Ragnar and Skadi as he tried to remember the men who had attacked him the winter before. He tried to remember if any of them had said that Jarl Ragnar had sent them, but he couldn't. He couldn't remember anything they had said. But then, why did Ulf think it was Jarl Ragnar?

'Three wolves face each other,' Skadi began. 'One is the alpha, another wants to take his place while the third is too blind to see that he is being used.'

Ulf looked at Skadi and then at Jarl Ragnar, whose brow was creased.

'What is she talking about?' Jarl Ragnar asked him, and Ulf sighed as he understood. He thought back to everything that had happened since the raid had started. The person who had attacked Jarl Ragnar had a sword with a golden hilt, so that Jarl Ragnar would think it was him. The arrow that almost killed him and that he had been told was a Danish arrow. The other attacks on him. It all made sense now, and Ulf cursed himself for not seeing it.

'Someone wants you dead and they're using me to do it.'

'What, in Odin's name, are you talking about? Who wants me dead?'

Ulf glanced at Skadi, who was smiling at him as if she was waiting for him to see it. Which he did when he thought about who had told him that Jarl Ragnar wanted him dead.

'Jarl Knut.'

***

Jarl Knut went back to his tent, unable to keep the smile off his face. This time, the gods had smiled on him and his plan had worked to perfection. He had his men, who were hidden behind Jarl Ragnar's tent, replace the two that Ulf had attacked. They had orders to wait a while and then to go into the tent and to kill whoever survived the fight between Ulf and Ragnar. They would blow a horn and he would go running to his cousin's tent and play the grieving cousin. Ragnar would be given a funeral fitting his station, with his main ship and some of the plunder from the raid, while Ulf would be dumped in the river.

Knut glanced at the moon and his smile grew wider. After Ragnar's funeral, he would take the fleet and attack Paris. He would burn the city to the ground and erect a large stone monument in his own honour. He already knew the words he would put on the stone. *The kingdom of the West Franks was brought to their knees by Knut, son of Torgeir and descendant of Odin. King Knut of the Danes did what the All-Father could not. He defeated the Christians.*

Attacking Paris would be much easier after Ragnar had defeated half the army and sent the others running for their lives. Even the king of the Franks had run off to a monastery instead of going to Paris to defend the city. Knut would make sure Ragnar would be remembered for the small part he played, but he would be remembered for the success of the raid.

'So?' Jarl Hakon asked as Knut entered his tent. He was not surprised to see the Norse jarl there, sitting on a chair and drinking ale.

'The Bear-Slayer stormed into the tent like a raging bull and attacked before Ragnar could get a word in.' He helped himself to some of the wine they had taken from the monastery they had raided a few days ago and savoured it before he emptied the cup. When he became king of Denmark, Knut would make sure he had plenty of the stuff because he was starting to enjoy the taste of the Frankish wine. 'What did you say to Ulf?'

Jarl Hakon shrugged. 'What we agreed on. Ragnar was behind it all and that Ragnar took his sword.' Hakon took a sip of his ale. 'So now we wait.'

Knut picked up Ulf's sword and marvelled at it. 'How did he get a sword like this?'

Hakon shrugged again. 'Killed for it, I guess.'

Knut rubbed his finger along the runes on the thick guard as he read them. Not for the first time since he had the sword cleaned after the battle against the Franks. *I am from a place of darkness. Do not draw me in the light of the sun.* A shiver ran down his spine, but Knut ignored it. He was not a superstitious man, so he doubted the words meant anything as he drew the sword and looked at her name on the blade. Ormstunga. *A dumb name*, he thought and decided that he would rename the sword when he returned to Denmark. Putting the sword back in her scabbard, he rested her on his lap and drank more of his wine. 'Now we wait.'

Chapter 30

Knut woke up as someone grabbed his shoulder and frowned when he opened his eyes and saw Hakon's worried face. His heart raced when he glanced at the entrance of his tent and saw the bronze and orange colours of dawn as the sun chased the moon away. Knut jumped to his feet, his mind reeling from all the wine he and Hakon had drunk the night before, and he staggered for a moment as Ormstunga fell to the ground. 'What happened? Where is the horn?'

Hakon, his brow wrinkled, shook his head. 'There was no horn.'

'Are you sure?' Knut rubbed his face. His mind was muddled, and he struggled to make sense of what was happening as Jarl Hakon shrugged.

'We fell asleep, so we might have missed it.'

Knut cursed himself for being too arrogant. He had been too confident that his plan was going to work and allowed himself to drink more of the Frankish wine than he should have done. He looked around him, not sure what he was trying to find when his foot struck something. Looking down, he saw Ormstunga and picked her up. But the movement made his head spin, and he had to wait for a few heartbeats for his head to settle before he rushed out of the tent with Hakon behind him.

The morning sun blinded Knut, and he cursed himself again for drinking so much wine. Perhaps he wouldn't have it delivered to him in Denmark. The camp was still waking up as the sun sat just above the horizon. Men were crawling out of their tents, many of them with their eyes half-closed as they went to empty their bladders. Others still had jugs of ale in their hands, and there were more than a few of his men sleeping outside in the dirt. But Knut ignored them all as he rushed towards Ragnar's tent, praying that he was not too late. He had to be the first one there so he could take control of the fleet, because Knut knew there were others who would take advantage of the situation and name themselves the new leader. And if Knut's men had blown the horn when they were supposed to, then he was already too late. As he and Hakon raced towards Ragnar's tent, he wondered why none of his men had come to collect him when he didn't respond to the horn. He would hang them both if they had ruined his plan, he thought as he ignored the frowns and stares from the warriors as he rushed past their tents.

Knut reached Ragnar's tent, his heart racing and his brows sweating, and wondered where his men were when he saw two of Ragnar's men guarding the tent.

'Perhaps they're inside waiting for us,' Hakon suggested, his voice uncertain, and Knut nodded as he hoped that was true. He took a deep breath as he composed himself before he straightened the stolen sword around his waist and fixed his tunic. He was about to take a step towards the tent when Ragnar walked out, his face bruised and his eyes dark with fury. And before Knut could think of what to say, the Bear-Slayer walked out behind him. Like Ragnar, his face was bruised, and Knut shivered at the rage he saw on the scarred warrior's face when his grey eyes fell on Ormstunga around his waist.

'Jarl Knut,' Ragnar said, his voice dripping with anger. 'How good of you to come. I was just about to send for you.'

Knut swallowed back his fear and thought he could hear a raven laughing at him, but he saw none of the birds. He glanced over his shoulder and his heart skipped when Hakon wasn't there. He fumed at the Norse jarl for abandoning him, but then, he had been warned not to trust the Norse.

'Cousin,' Knut said, his eyes flickering to Ragnar's tent as he sensed another presence inside. But he couldn't see anyone there. 'You survived. Men, grab that traitor! He tried to kill your jarl!' Knut said, hoping he could still get out of this.

'The traitor you sent to kill me by poisoning his mind with your deceit?' Ragnar said and Knut's heart thudded in his chest, because he knew he had lost.

Knut took a deep breath to calm himself and straightened his back. He was a jarl and the cousin of the king and if he was going to die, then he would do it with pride. The gods valued those who took their chances, and he was certain that Odin would still accept him in Valhalla. 'All I did was try to take what should have been mine,' he said with as much conviction as he could.

'What should have been yours?' Ragnar raised an eyebrow at him.

Knut nodded as his hand gripped the hilt of Ormstunga.

'That is my sword,' Ulf said, and Knut tensed when it looked like the young warrior was about to attack him. But then the

Bear-Slayer tilted his head and nodded, as if someone behind him said something. Again, Knut tried to peer into the tent, certain that someone was there but couldn't see anyone standing behind Ragnar and the Bear-Slayer.

'You couldn't kill Ragnar, so you talked it out?' Knut glared at Ulf as his own anger took hold. Anger that the man Jarl Hakon had boasted about couldn't do the one thing he was supposed to be good at. Killing a jarl.

'Something like that,' Ragnar said as the Bear-Slayer shrugged. 'Now tell me, what is yours that I have to die for?'

Knut tightened his grip on the sword and looked around him as Ragnar's men formed a large circle. 'These men! This fleet! I should have led the raid, not you!'

'Why?' Ragnar asked, his arrogance only irritating Knut even more. 'Why should you lead the raid?'

'Because I am next in line to the throne!' Knut shouted before he could stop himself. But he didn't regret those words, because he knew it was true. King Horik had no named heirs and Knut had the support of many of the jarls, so he knew he would be chosen as the next king of Denmark when Horik died. But Knut did not want to wait that long.

Ragnar shrugged. 'No one told me that.' His men laughed, which only annoyed Knut more, as did the Norse bastard glaring at him. 'But then why did Horik ask me to lead and not you if you are to be our next king?'

'Because you convinced him to name you.' Knut jabbed a finger at Ragnar. 'By Odin, I don't know how you did it, but somehow you convinced him to make you the leader of this raid. A raid that never would have happened if it wasn't for me!'

'Aye, you did much to make this raid happen. You paid jarls for their support. Made promises you had no intention of keeping and offered them much of the spoils. And Horik knew about it all. That was why he made me the leader of the raid. And you tried to kill me for it. But instead of facing me in the open, you hide in the shadows and use others to do your bidding. It was your man who attacked me that night, but you made sure that he had a sword with a golden hilt so that I believed it was Ulf.'

'And it was you who sent men after me when I left Jelling before the winter. Just like you sent Hallr and others after me.' Ulf sneered at Knut, who scowled back at him.

'I never sent Hallr to kill you. I needed you alive, you dumb bastard. What did you do to Hallr?'

'I killed him. Just like I killed all the other men you sent after me.' Ulf took a step forward. 'Just like I'm going to kill you.'

Knut smiled and pulled the sword he had taken from the Bear-Slayer out of her scabbard. Her blade glinted in the morning sun and his smile only grew wider when Ulf's eyes widened, no doubt imagining the shame of being killed by his own sword.

'You shouldn't have done that,' Ulf said, the tone of his voice sending a shiver down Knut's spine as he glanced at the words written on the guard. But he pushed them out of his mind and reminded himself that he was not a superstitious man. Ulf took a step forward when Ragnar stopped him.

'No.' He glared at Knut, who knew what Ragnar was about to say. 'Jarl Knut wants to kill me so he can take my place as the leader of the raid.' Ragnar walked towards him, his sword still in her scabbard as his men all stepped back to give them some space. Everyone, even the ravens circling above them, knew what was about to happen. Knut glanced at the ravens and wondered if one of them was Odin's. 'So here is your chance, Knut, to show that you are the one who is meant to lead this raid. Kill me and the fleet and all the glory is yours.'

Knut glanced at Ragnar's warriors surrounding him and wondered if they would accept him as their leader if he killed Ragnar. Most of his men had arrived as well and had mixed in with Ragnar's, their confused voices adding to sounds of the ravens calling from the skies above. He looked at the ravens again and wondered if Odin was giving him a chance to change his fate. Kill Ragnar and lead the fleet as they burn West Francia or die and be forgotten. Those were his options, although the Norns had already decided which one it would be, so there was no point in him worrying about it. Still, he prayed it was the first one and not the second.

Knut looked at Ragnar, who stood a head taller than him and wore his brynja. His hand was on the hilt of his sword, but she was still in her scabbard. The anger in Ragnar's eyes was enough to make any man tremble, but not Knut. He had seen it too many times before. Knut glanced at the ravens one more time. He did not like to fight battles. He did not stand in the shield wall and only joined when the enemy was broken and all that was left to do was to kill them. But that was not because he didn't know how to fight. He had bested Ragnar before in sparring sessions and even though that had been when they were much younger; he believed he could do it again. Especially with a sword that felt as if it weighed nothing in his hand.

The men fell silent as Ragnar pulled his sword from her scabbard and one of his men gave him a shield. Knut stepped towards his men and took the shield offered to him. He glanced around, wondering where that worm Hakon was. The bastard should have been here. He was as much part of this plan as Knut was and Knut swore if he survived this, he would hang the Norse bastard and all of his men. But not the Bear-Slayer. Him, Knut would feed to a bear after cutting his feet off so he couldn't run away.

Pushing the thoughts from his mind, Knut held his shield in front of him and moved towards the centre of the circle the warriors had created. Ragnar did the same, his dark eyes glaring at him from over the rim of his shield. They stared at each other for a few moments, the surrounding men as silent as the frozen North. And in the silence, a raven crowed and both men roared as they charged at each other. Ragnar stabbed with his sword, which Knut blocked with his shield, before he swung his sword low, hoping to cut Ragnar's leg. Ragnar jumped back and Knut charged with his shoulder behind his shield, but Ragnar saw it coming and pressed his own shoulder behind his shield and they came together in a loud crash, which rung in Knut's ears.

Both men grunted as they tried to push each other back, and Knut's heart leapt when Ragnar pushed him back a few steps. He stabbed around the shields and felt the tip of the sword strike Ragnar's brynja, forcing him back as Knut's warriors cheered. But Ragnar only smiled.

'You really think you are going to win this?' he said as he shuffled around Knut.

'Stop talking and fight!' Knut charged, cutting high with the sword and forcing Ragnar to lift his shield to block the blow. Knut brought his shield around to punch Ragnar with its rim, but Ragnar jumped back before stabbing at Knut's face. Knut was forced to duck under the blade, but then Ragnar pulled his sword back and Knut felt it slicing his cheek open. Ragnar's men cheered and his hissed as he stepped back, doing his best to ignore his burning cheek and the blood soaking his beard. He glanced at Ulf as the words on the sword's guard came to his mind. The Bear-Slayer stood there, his face unreadable as he watched the fight and Knut got the sense that the bastard was just waiting for him to die.

Distracted by Ulf, Knut didn't know of Ragnar's attack until his men cried out a warning. He turned and saw the sword coming for him and got his shield up to block the blow, but the sudden movement unbalanced him and there was nothing he could do as Ragnar punched out with his shield and sent him sprawling to the ground. Knut panicked as the sword almost slipped out of his hand, but he kept hold of her as he rolled to his feet and tried his best to ignore the fear crawling in his gut.

Ragnar stabbed at him and Knut ducked under the blade and cut at his exposed side, but the links of Ragnar's brynja prevented his sword from doing any damage. Knut cursed as Ragnar turned with a backhanded cut that narrowly missed his face. But his fear had gripped him and as hard as Knut tried, he could not stop glancing at Ulf instead of focusing on the fight.

Knut roared as he tried to push the fear away and stabbed at Ragnar, who ducked under his sword and, before Knut could react, sliced his leg open. He cried out as he dropped to his knee while Ragnar's men cheered and his warriors fell silent. Knut did not look at them, though. His eyes were fixed on the grim face of Ragnar as he walked around him.

'Get up,' Ragnar said. 'We're not done yet.'

But Knut knew he was. He could hear it in the cries of the ravens and in the silence of his men. His leg was bleeding heavily from the deep cut and Knut knew it was only a matter of moments before he lost too much blood to fight. So why prolong the inevitable? The Norns had decided that he was going to die, so why waste time?

'It should have been me,' he said through clenched teeth, but Ragnar only smiled as he stood in front of him.

'No, Knut. It was never going to be you.' He raised his sword for the killing blow, but before he brought it down, Ulf shouted,

'Wait!'

Ragnar glared at Ulf, and Knut wondered if he could still kill Ragnar. He would still die, but at least that way neither of them got to lead the raid. But before he could lift his sword, Ragnar stepped out of reach as Ulf approached.

'What do you want?' Ragnar asked.

Ulf walked past Ragnar. 'He doesn't get to die gripping my sword.' Ulf lowered himself and ripped the sword from Knut's hand. Knut panicked at the thought of dying without a blade in his hand, but then Ulf leaned in closer and said,

'You should have listened to the sword. You are cursed and will never reach Valhalla.'

Knut felt the blood drain from his face as Ragnar stepped forward to deliver the killing blow, Knut heard a voice whispering in his ears.

Do not draw me in the light of the sun.

Chapter 31

Ulf gripped Ormstunga as Ragnar plunged his sword through Knut's neck and into his chest. Knut's eyes bulged as Ragnar's sword tore through his lungs and his body shuddered as his life left him. And as Ulf glanced at Ormstunga, he wondered if Knut would go to Valhalla. Did Knut deserve to be there? He frowned at the question as it came to him. Knut had been a powerful jarl, and he had sought to take what he had believed was his. But the way he had done it made Ulf hope he would never see the Danish jarl in Odin's hall of the slain. Ulf pushed the question out of his mind and glanced at his sword again. He was glad he had her back, but was unsettled that her curse claimed another life. A curse many refused to believe was real until it was too late for them.

Ragnar stepped back as Knut's body dropped to the ground and faced his cousin's men, who were all stunned into silence by the death of their jarl. The atmosphere was tense and Ulf knew that the smallest of sparks would do what the Frankish king and his army could not do. Stop Ragnar's army from reaching Paris.

Jarl Ragnar stared at his cousin's men, his jaw set as he ran his eyes over them all. 'Your jarl, my cousin, betrayed me! He plotted to kill me from the shadows like a snake instead of facing me in the open.' Many of Jarl Knut's men looked away, embarrassed by what the man they had sworn oaths to had done. But some glared at Ulf as if it was his fault their jarl was dead. 'I see the anger in your eyes,' Ragnar continued, seeing the same thing. 'The gods know the anger in your hearts, just as they know I did what I had to.' Ragnar took a step towards Knut's men, who all took a step away from him as he scrutinised them. 'You have a choice. You can draw your weapons and avenge your jarl, but you will all die.' Jarl Ragnar waited a few heartbeats as if to see if any of Knut's men would attack him, but apart from the ravens flying circles over their heads, no one moved. 'Or you can swear an oath to me and be welcomed with open arms. Knut's deeds will stay with him and him alone. You will all still get a share of the plunder you have fought hard for.' He paused again as Knut's men glanced at each other. Ragnar's men waited, and Ulf sensed them holding their breaths as they waited to see what Knut's men would do. 'Choose now or die,' Ragnar said, his voice showing that the men of Knut had no real choice.

One of Knut's men stepped forward and glared at Ulf before he looked at the body of his jarl. 'We had no knowledge of our jarl's plans and cannot be held responsible for what he did. But if we turn against him, then those at home will curse us and cast us out for abandoning him.'

Jarl Ragnar nodded. 'I understand your concern and I swear to the All-Father that when we return to Denmark, I will send men to all corners of Midgard so they can tell everyone of what Knut did.'

The man glanced over his shoulder at the rest of Knut's warriors, who nodded at him. He turned back to Ragnar. 'Then we will swear an oath to you, Jarl Ragnar.'

Jarl Ragnar nodded as his men relaxed. Ulf felt the tension leave the air around them as one raven turned and flew away and Ragnar turned to him. 'Your volva friend was right, Ulf. She's a good ally to have.'

'Aye,' Ulf said as he glanced at the tent, even though he knew she was not there any more. Skadi had snuck off soon after the fight between Jarl Ragnar and Knut had started, but he still sensed her eyes on him.

'You don't seem pleased.' Jarl Ragnar raised an eyebrow at him. 'Knut is dead and you have your sword back.'

Ulf frowned. 'Thorir still died a death he did not deserve.'

Jarl Ragnar glanced at the ravens flying above them. 'The Norns decided it was his fate. There's nothing you can do about that.'

Ulf tightened his grip on Ormstunga. 'I can kill those responsible.'

Jarl Ragnar stared at him for a few heartbeats. 'It was my men who hanged him.'

Ulf nodded. 'It was, but they were not the ones who cut his tongue out and dressed him as a Frank.' He glanced at Jarl Knut's men as they all stood there, waiting to swear their oaths to Jarl Ragnar. Many of the warriors were still glaring at him, and Ulf resisted the urge to grip the Mjöllnir pendant around his neck as Skadi's words came to him. *One of them will be stabbed in the back.* Even with Jarl Knut dead, he sensed that the danger lurking over him was not gone yet.

'You think it was one of them?' Jarl Ragnar asked, and Ulf saw the jarl staring at him.

'I don't know.' Ulf turned and looked towards Jarl Hakon's camp. 'Jarl Knut and Jarl Hakon were good friends. They were always together, whispering things to each other.'

'Aye, they were.' Jarl Ragnar scratched the back of his neck. 'Hakon was with Knut when they approached my tent. And he ran away quickly when they saw I was still alive.'

Ulf's brows creased as he thought of the Norse jarl. 'He treated me like a friend, so I would drop my guard. Made me think he was protecting me from you.' The flames of his anger ignited in the pit of his stomach as he thought of something else. 'It could not have been Knut's men who grabbed Thorir. He was fighting alongside Jarl Hakon's men. Only they could have done that.'

Jarl Ragnar signalled to one of his men before he turned to Ulf. 'It's time we cut the rest of this rot out of my fleet before it can spread any further.' A large force of Jarl Ragnar's men gathered around them and many more went to their tents to collect their armour and weapons. Ulf even saw some of the other jarls also gathering their men and prayed this would not end in a battle that would ruin the raid. He still needed to make enough plunder to free Eldrid.

Ulf walked beside Jarl Ragnar as they went to the Norse camp. He glanced at Ormstunga in his hand, her blade glistening in the sunlight, and prayed that the curse would not get him. He had not drawn her, but that didn't stop Ulf from rubbing the Mjöllnir pendant around his neck. As they passed the other tents, many of the warriors jumped to their feet and frowned at what they were seeing, before they followed and by the time the short walk to Jarl Hakon's tent ended, they had a large army following them.

To Ulf's surprise, Hakon's camp was still there, and so were his ships. He had expected the jarl to flee as soon as they had been found out, but instead, he stood in front of his tent, wearing his armour and with his hirdmen behind him. Ragnvald was there as well, his sword in his hand, as he scowled at Jarl Hakon.

Jarl Hakon stared at Ulf and at Jarl Ragnar beside him. 'Knut is dead, then?'

Ulf nodded. 'Jarl Ragnar killed him.'

Hakon glanced at Ormstunga. 'I thought as much when I saw you with your sword back. He was a good man, just tried to be too smart.'

Ulf tightened his grip around the hilt of Ormstunga. 'He used me. You used me.'

Jarl Hakon shrugged. 'I never liked it. You're well known back in Norway, Jarl-Slayer. Knut thought he could use your anger to kill Ragnar.'

'You don't deny it, then?' Jarl Ragnar asked and Jarl Hakon smiled at him.

'The gods know that I have no reason to deny it. You standing here with your men behind you already tells me you have figured it out and besides, the Norns have already decided my fate.'

Ulf glared at Hakon, a man he almost considered a friend. 'Jarl Knut sent men after me to make me think that Jarl Ragnar was trying to kill me?'

'Aye. We had to push you.'

Ulf growled. 'And Thorir? You killed him.'

Hakon laughed. 'No, Ulf. Ragnar hanged him. You saw it for yourself. But my men grabbed him during the battle and dressed him in the armour of a dead Frank.'

'And cut his tongue out.' Ulf felt his heart racing in his chest.

'He lied to me, his jarl. That's what he deserved.'

Ulf felt his anger take hold of him as he took a step forward. 'He swore no oath to you.'

'He sailed on my ship. Fought in my shield wall.'

'So did I.'

'Aye, but you were always going to die.' Hakon shot forward, his sword in his hand, and jabbed at Ulf's chest.

Ulf deflected the sword and punched Hakon in the face. Jarl Hakon staggered back a few steps and Ulf rushed at him as Jarl Ragnar raised his hand to stop his men from interfering. The Danish jarl had had his fight, and it was time for Ulf to have his.

He cut at Hakon's chest, hoping to end the fight quickly, but the jarl recovered in time to block Ormstunga and punched Ulf in the side. Ulf grunted from the blow and was forced to duck under Hakon's sword as the jarl sliced at his neck. The voices in Ulf's ears raged at him as he stabbed at Jarl Hakon, who twisted out of the way of Ormstunga and kicked Ulf's legs out from under him. Ulf landed hard on his back, but he quickly rolled out of the way of Hakon's sword and jumped to his feet.

The surrounding men watched in silence, and Ulf spotted Hjalmar amongst the Norse warriors, who were all nervously glancing at the Danes, but had no time to wonder about the look on the man's face as Hakon rushed at him again.

Ulf deflected Jarl Hakon's stab, but Hakon pulled his arm back faster than Ulf expected and turned the stab into a backhanded cut which grated along his brynja. Gritting his teeth at the pain in his chest, Ulf took a step back to get away from Jarl Hakon, but the jarl rushed forward and swung his sword at Ulf's head. Ulf deflected the blade, the noise of the two swords clashing ringing in his ears, but he could not block Jarl Hakon's punch, which sent him staggering backwards and blurred his vision for a few heartbeats.

'Pathetic.' Jarl Hakon spat to the ground. 'And to think of all the stories they tell of the Bear-Slayer. The warrior who is descended from Tyr and who killed a bear with his bare hands. The warrior who defeated an army by himself. The gods know I expected more from you.'

Ulf growled as his ancestors raged in his ears. They did not like being mocked and neither did he. He pushed himself to go as fast as he could as he attacked and hoped to catch Jarl Hakon off guard. But the jarl had enough experience to step out of the way of Ulf's attack before he threw another punch, one that Ulf saw coming and twisted away from before pulling Ormstunga back in a backhanded cut which struck Hakon in the chest, copying Jarl Hakon's attack from moments before. Unfortunately for Ulf, Ormstunga didn't break any of the links on Hakon's brynja, but the blow still sent Hakon back a few steps. Enough for Ulf to follow up with a punch of his own, which drove Jarl Hakon to the ground.

Hakon rolled to his feet and smiled. 'That's better.' He charged at Ulf, jabbing with his sword and forcing Ulf a step back. He swung his sword at Ulf's head, but Ulf ducked under the blade and stepped to the side. Ulf stabbed at Hakon's exposed back and was about to land the killing blow when something struck his head. His vision blurred as he dropped to his knee, and before Ulf could make sense of what had happened, Hakon jabbed his sword at his face. Ulf's ancestors screamed in his ears and Ulf obeyed their command as he rolled out of the way. But Ulf knew he was in trouble. Whatever had struck him had muddled his mind, and he struggled to concentrate on the fight. He heard Hakon charging again and lifted Ormstunga in time to deflect Hakon's sword, but he didn't see the punch until it landed and sent him reeling backwards to the ground. Ulf rolled to his feet and regretted it as his head spun and his legs wobbled under him. He heard Hakon's laughter, which fed his anger and strengthened his legs. 'This is the man that killed Griml Troll-Face and yet he can barely stand.' Ulf wondered if Jarl Ragnar was going to step in and end the fight. But it seemed the Danish jarl was content to stand back and let Ulf and Jarl Hakon fight it out. Ulf couldn't blame him, though. They were not friends nor were they allies.

Jarl Hakon rushed at Ulf, who snapped out of his stupor and twisted out of the way of Hakon's sword, but he still felt the edge of the blade cut along his brynja. Hakon's momentum brought him closer to Ulf, who punched the jarl in the face and as his head snapped back, Ulf punched him again, breaking his nose and sending him to the ground. Ulf rushed at Jarl Hakon and kicked him to the ground again as he tried to get back to his feet, but as he raised Ormstunga for the killing blow, Jarl Ragnar stepped forward.

'Enough!'

Ulf hesitated and glanced at Jarl Ragnar, wondering why the man had intervened now when Ulf finally had the upper hand. Had Jarl Ragnar hoped that the Norse jarl would kill him? Distracted by his thoughts, Ulf did not notice Jarl Hakon pull his sax-knife out of its scabbard.

'Ulf, watch out!' Ragnvald shouted as Jarl Hakon stabbed at him. The voices in his ears raged and Ulf twisted before swinging Ormstunga at the jarl's arm. Her sharp blade sliced deep into Hakon's muscle and Ulf felt it grate along the bone in Hakon's arm as the jarl dropped his sax-knife and blood sprayed from the wound. But as Ulf raised Ormstunga to kill Jarl Hakon, Jarl Ragnar's hirdmen rushed forward and pointed their spears at him.

Ulf glared at Jarl Ragnar, who stared back at him. He tightened his grip on Ormstunga as the voices of his ancestors demanded Jarl Hakon's blood. For a heartbeat, Ulf glanced at Jarl Ragnar's hirdmen around him and wondered if they would kill him if he ended Hakon.

'I understand why you want to kill him, Ulf, but Jarl Hakon was part of the plot to kill me. I let you fight him, but he is mine to punish.' Jarl Ragnar took a step towards Ulf. The Norse warriors were all tense as they watched the scene in front of them, their hands near their weapons and their eyes burning with anger. But who that anger was directed at, Ulf couldn't tell. Only Ragnvald did not seem angry as the one-handed warrior scrutinised Ulf. 'Step back, Bear-Slayer.'

'Thorir begged for mercy when my men grabbed him,' Jarl Hakon taunted Ulf. 'He begged for his mother to come rescue him and squealed like a pig when my men cut his tongue out.' Ulf glanced at the Norse warriors and wondered which of them had grabbed Thorir and cut his tongue out. His eyes landed on Ragnvald, and the old bastard squinted as he stared back at Ulf. Ulf was certain he was part of it, but then why did he warn Ulf before? Ulf then glanced at the large stone on the ground near him and wondered if Ragnvald had thrown it.

'Ulf?' Jarl Ragnar said and moved closer as Ulf kept Ormstunga raised, ready to bury it in Jarl Hakon's skull.

Jarl Hakon glared at him. 'Kill me, Ulf. Show the gods that you are not the coward we all know you are. The coward Thorir thought you were. He never called for you to help him when my men grabbed him. He thought his mother was braver than you.'

Ulf screamed and was about to bring his sword down when a firm hand grabbed his wrist. Ulf turned his fury on the person and was shocked to see Ragnvald standing there.

'No, Ulf. You already defeated him. There's no honour in killing an unarmed man.'

'Ragnvald! You treacherous bastard!' Jarl Hakon shouted, his face red with fury.

But Ragnvald only looked at him and shook his head. 'No, Hakon. You are the one who betrayed us all when you risked the lives of your men on this witless scheme with Knut.' He turned back to Ulf, who was still glaring at him. 'If you kill him now, then these men will kill you.'

Ulf glanced at the surrounding Danes, their eyes on him and not Hakon. 'And you wouldn't want them to kill me, would you?'

Ragnvald shook his head. 'No, I wouldn't.'

Before Ulf could respond, Jarl Ragnar stepped between them. 'Ulf, listen to Ragnvald. Walk away and cool down.'

'And what about Hakon?' Ulf asked.

Ragnar glanced at the Norse jarl, who was glaring at them. 'He'll be hanged under the moon.'

CHAPTER 32

JARL HAKON STOOD UNDERNEATH a large tree, his face expressionless, like a man who had accepted the fate the Norns had given him as they tied a rope around his neck. Flies buzzed around the open wound on his arm, while dried blood caked his hand and his tunic. The flames of the torches fluttered as the wind swept over them, while Jarl Ragnar stood beside the condemned Norse jarl. Three other Norse warriors were there as well, like Jarl Hakon, with ropes around their necks. But unlike their jarl, their faces were contorted with anger. They were part of Hakon's hirdmen and had tried to free him while they waited for nightfall. But the men had failed and now they would be hanged with their jarl.

Jarl Ragnar stared at the Norse warriors in front of him, all of them surrounded by his Danish warriors, his mouth set thin and his brows creased. A handful of the other jarls stood with him, all of them as stern-looking as Ragnar. Ulf knew it was to send a message to the Norse warriors as he stood there, his jaw clenched as he took in the scene. They were outnumbered and surrounded. If any of them tried to stop Jarl Ragnar from hanging Hakon, then they would all die.

'It's a pity,' Hjalmar said as he stood next to Ulf, who had to fight the urge to rub the aching lump on his head. Ulf had spent the day avoiding the Norse warriors, especially Ragnvald, worried that they would attack him for his part in this. He doubted that any of them would care that he had wanted none of this. He never wanted to be part of the plot to kill Jarl Ragnar and had even done his best to avoid the man. Just like he never wanted to be part of the games the gods liked to play, but unfortunately for Ulf, Odin seemed to be amused by him. Ulf glanced around the shadows cast by the many torches held by the Danes and wondered if Skadi was there, watching them. He couldn't feel her presence, not like he usually did, but he was certain she'd want to watch this. 'Jarl Hakon is a good jarl. His greed just got the better of him.'

Ulf glanced at the older warrior who had sought him out after his fight with Jarl Hakon, but said nothing. Ulf was too angry and confused to speak. He would have preferred to be on his own, but Hjalmar had insisted on staying near him. And he was not the only one as Ragnvald stood not far from him, his eyes on Ulf and not Jarl Hakon.

Ulf turned his attention back to Jarl Ragnar, who had not spoken to him since the morning as he faced Jarl Hakon. 'Jarl Hakon. You plotted with my cousin against me. You made me believe another was trying to kill me while you and my cousin attempted to stab me in the back like the cowards you are.'

There was a hiss from the Norse warriors, which angered Jarl Ragnar and he turned to face the Norse warriors, his nostrils flared.

'Do you deny it is cowardly to kill a man from behind from the shadows?' He waited for a response they all knew was not coming. 'Do you think it is honourable to stab a man in the back while he fights beside you in the shield wall?' Some of the Norse warriors looked at their feet, but many still glared at Jarl Ragnar as he turned to face Jarl Hakon and the other three Norse warriors. 'I welcomed you to my fleet. I gave you the honour of sailing at the front and fighting by my side. I treated you as a brother and still you plotted my death. All so that you and my cousin could take over my army.' Jarl Ragnar glared at Jarl Hakon as if he was waiting for him to say something, but Hakon only spat at his feet. Ragnar grunted. 'I pray Odin bars the doors of Valhalla so that you cannot enter the hall of the slain.' He gave the signal to the warriors holding the other end of the rope. As one, they all pulled and the Norse warriors wailed as Jarl Hakon and the other three men were pulled off the ground.

Ulf watched, his fists clenched by his sides, as he thought of Thorir dying the same way. The man had not deserved that, but Hakon did, and Ulf's only regret at that point was that he hadn't thought of cutting Hakon's tongue out. Just like they had done to the bóndi.

Jarl Hakon's eyes bulged as his face turned purple and his swollen tongue stuck out of his mouth. Ulf knew how that felt and as with every time he saw someone being hanged, the scar from his own hanging started tingling. It was as if Odin was reminding him of how he had saved Ulf that day.

After what felt like a long time, the four men stopped jerking and their bodies went limp as they hanged from their necks. All four had pissed and shat themselves, and Ulf saw how the jarls all crinkled their noses at the smells that the wind blew over them. That was why no warrior wanted to be hanged. It was humiliating going to the afterlife knowing that that was the last image everyone would have of you. Ulf guessed that was why Hakon had goaded him. He wanted to die by the sword, not this way. But Ulf felt no sympathy for the man who had pretended to be a friend. He felt Ragnvald's glare on him, but kept his eyes on the corpse of Hakon. 'Do you know who helped Hakon grab Thorir? And who cut his tongue out?'

He felt Hjalmar shake his head beside him. 'No, I was close to the jarl, but not that close. He trusted others with things like that.'

'Others like Ragnvald?'

Hjalmar shrugged and when Ulf looked at him, he saw the fresh tears on the man's cheeks. 'Possibly. The gods know there's a reason Ragnvald's son was the monster he was.'

Ulf turned his attention to Ragnvald and swore an oath to the gods that he would kill the one-handed man for his part in Thorir's death as Jarl Ragnar said,

'Tomorrow we reach Paris. A city richer than Asgard and unguarded because the king of the Franks is hiding in one of his monasteries.' He glared at the Norse warriors. 'You would have been richer than the gods themselves, but because of your treacherous jarl, you will return to Norway empty-handed. I will not fight with men I do not trust and the gods know I do not trust any of you.'

There was a cry of dismay from the Norse warriors, and even Ulf felt bad for those who did not know what Jarl Hakon had been doing. To his surprise, though, Ragnvald stepped forward.

'Jarl Ragnar, these men have fought bravely from the start of the raid. They have shed blood and lost friends against our enemies and deserve to be rewarded for that.' There was a howl of anger from the Danes, but Jarl Ragnar raised his hand to silence them so that Ragnvald could continue. 'None of these men had any knowledge of what Hakon had planned with Jarl Knut and they should not be punished for his wrongdoing.'

'You expect me to believe that not a single one of them knew about your jarl's plot to kill me?' Jarl Ragnar asked, and Ragnvald shrugged.

'Some might have done, but I do not know who they are.'

'Fucking liar,' Hjalmar hissed beside Ulf, who wondered what the one-handed warrior was up to.

'But I ask you to let these men continue on this raid. They have risked as much as you Danes.'

One of the other jarls stepped forward. 'And who will lead them? You, a one-handed old man?' Some of the Danes laughed, but Jarl Ragnar's face showed nothing other than his anger.

Before Ulf knew what was happening, Hjalmar stepped forward. 'I say the Bear-Slayer should lead us!'

Ulf gaped at Hjalmar, as did many of the surrounding warriors. Even Jarl Ragnar was stunned by this as he raised his brows while staring at the old warrior standing beside Ulf.

'Bullocks, no!' Ragnvald said and many of the Norse warriors protested as well. As Ulf had expected them to. Ulf had not been popular with them before the fight with Jarl Hakon, and he was sure that he was even less popular now.

'Why not?' Hjalmar said as he turned to the Norse warriors. 'The Bear-Slayer has a reputation and we've all seen he can fight. And more than that, Jarl Ragnar trusts him.'

Ulf frowned at Hjalmar and wondered what the old warrior was up to as a raven called out nearby. He turned his attention to the large black bird as it sat on the thick branch Hakon was hanging from and wondered if this was what the gods had wanted.

Is she behind this? He wondered, but as he scanned the shadows beyond the reach of the torches, he saw no sign of Skadi and neither did he feel her presence.

'He killed our jarl!' someone shouted.

'He's a miserable bastard!' another said as there was an explosion of noise, like thunder, as the Norse warriors argued amongst themselves.

'What are you doing?' Ulf asked Hjalmar, who seemed to enjoy the chaos he had unleashed.

Hjalmar glanced at Ulf. 'Making sure that Ragnvald doesn't lead us.'

'Why?' Ulf scowled at Ragnvald, who was glaring at him and Hjalmar.

'Because you can't trust that bastard, Ulf. Remember who his son was.'

Ulf's heart raced in his chest as he thought of Griml, but before he could say anything, Jarl Ragnar raised his hand.

'Silence!' His voice cut through the noise like a sharp blade through flesh and the Norse warriors all fell silent as they stared at the Danish jarl. 'Ulf Bear-Slayer, would you be willing to lead these men?'

Ulf's hands trembled as everyone stared at him, while the lump on his head where the stone had struck him seemed to hurt more than before. He glanced at the raven and felt like even the gods had their eyes on him before he took a deep breath. 'Forgive me, Jarl Ragnar. But I am not a leader of men.'

'See, he can't lead us!' Ragnvald said and many of the Norse warriors agreed with him. But to Ulf's surprise, there were some that supported him as they called out his name.

Jarl Ragnar's brows creased as he stared at Ulf for many heartbeats. 'The Bear-Slayer might not believe that he is a leader of men, but the gods have their eyes on him. We have all seen that.' Jarl Ragnar glanced at Ormstunga around Ulf's waist before he turned to the rest of the Norse warriors. 'And the gods also know that right now, I trust the Bear-Slayer more than you, Ragnvald. Or anyone you might suggest. So this is your choice, warriors of Sygnafylki. Accept Ulf Bear-Slayer as your leader for the rest of the raid or return home empty-handed.'

'Do we have time to think about it?' Ragnvald asked, and Jarl Ragnar shook his head.

'The Christian Easter is two days away. Tomorrow we leave for Paris, so you need to decide now.'

There was a stunned silence from the Norse warriors as they stared at each other before a small group broke away from the rest and walked towards Ulf.

Many of the Norse swore at this group, but slowly, more and more broke away and walked towards where Ulf and Hjalmar were standing, while others turned and walked towards the ships.

In the end, only Ragnvald stood where he was, as most of the Norse warriors had decided to stay. The one-handed warrior glared at Jarl Ragnar and then at Ulf, and just when Ulf thought he would go to the ships, he walked towards him. No one moved or said anything as Ragnvald stopped in front of Ulf, whose heart was racing as he scowled at the old warrior. Hjalmar's hand went to his axe and a handful of other warriors stepped closer. Ragnvald smiled as he glanced at them before he turned his attention to Ulf.

'I'm staying, but I warn you, Bear-Slayer. You better watch your back.' Skadi's warning came to Ulf as Ragnvald glanced at Hjalmar before he turned and walked away.

'The bastard was never happy that Hakon took his jarldom from him,' Hjalmar said, but Ulf barely heard him over his heart racing in his ears.

Jarl Ragnar signalled to one jarl standing with him and the man took his warriors and followed the Norsemen who had decided to leave back to the ships. 'Tomorrow at sunrise, we set sail for Paris.' The Danes cheered as Jarl Ragnar turned and went to his tent, with many of the jarls following him.

Ulf's eyes went to the raven that was still sitting silently on the branch Hakon was hanging from, watching him with its beady eyes. *Tyr, guide me.*

Chapter 33

The city of Paris sat on a large island in the middle of the slow-moving river. Thick stone walls, which stood taller than three men, surrounded the city and the only way to enter was by two bridges on either side of the island. Towers loomed over the bridges while more towers stood on the wall, all of them filled with archers to protect the city from attack. Church bells rang while a thin trail of white smoke lazily drifted towards the sky and, as Ulf stared at the city of stone, he wondered how Jarl Ragnar was going to take a place that even the giants would find difficult to attack.

It was the day after the deaths of Knut and Hakon, and as Ulf stood on the prow of Hakon's ship, with Hjalmar by his side, he felt the eyes of many of the Norse warriors on his back. Ulf had not slept the night before. Not because of his dreams, but because he worried that someone might kill him in his sleep. So instead, he had spent the entire night awake in his tent, with Ormstunga in his hand. But no attack came, and now Ulf was exhausted.

More than half of Hakon's men had stayed while the rest had taken his second ship and had left during the night. But Ulf knew that those who had stayed were only there for the plunder, so he still avoided them, especially Ragnvald, who never seemed to be far from him. Like he was waiting for a moment to strike, which made

Ulf's neck hurt from all the tension he felt. Ulf was glad, though, that Hjalmar stayed near him as they had prepared to leave that morning.

'Makes you wonder why King Charles didn't bring his army here and defend the walls. The gods know we never would have been able to take the city if he had,' Hjalmar said, and broke Ulf from his thoughts.

'And we can now?' Ulf scrutinised the walls and tried to think of how he would attack the city, but he couldn't think of a way.

'Aye, we just need to find a way over the walls.'

Ulf glanced at Hjalmar and saw the smile on his lined face. The old warrior seemed to relish the idea of attacking Paris, as did many of the warriors on the ship. 'You've attacked cities like this before?'

Hjalmar nodded. 'A fair few, although most of the ones we attacked had wooden walls. But the idea is still the same.'

Ulf gripped Ormstunga's hilt and stared at the stone walls. 'And how do we do that?'

'Ladders,' Hjalmar said. 'Lots of ladders.'

'Aye,' Ulf said as Jarl Ragnar's ship gave the signal for them to land the ships on the riverbank opposite the city.

'He wants them to know we are here for them,' one warrior said, and Hjalmar grunted his agreement.

'It'll drive them to their churches where they will pray to their god to save them.' Hjalmar looked at the towers. 'And the poor bastards defending the walls won't get any sleep because they'll spend the entire night wondering when we will attack. By sunrise, they'll be too tired to fight properly.'

Ulf glanced at the towers and knew how the defenders felt because he doubted he'd get much sleep himself that night. He looked over his shoulder at Ragnvald by the stern and wasn't surprised to see the one-handed warrior glaring at him. Ragnvald then took his eyes off Ulf and pulled on the steering oar as he aimed for a spot on the riverbank. Ulf braced himself as the ship's keel struck the ground and the ship came to a halt. Other ships did the same, and Ulf noticed they weren't as close to Jarl Ragnar's ships as they had been before. That didn't surprise him, though. Jarl Ragnar didn't trust the Norsemen any more, and they didn't trust him either.

Even though the sun had just reached its peak, Ulf knew that Jarl Ragnar wanted to wait until the next day before he attacked. That was the day that the Christians would celebrate their Easter and Ragnar believed the city would be easier to take. But Ulf couldn't help but wonder if Jarl Ragnar wanted to strike on a holy day to show the Christians that their god was weak.

Hjalmar gave the order and the Norse warriors unloaded the ship and prepared their camp while Ulf stood back and watched them work with practised ease. These were experienced men, and they all knew what they needed to do. And besides, Ulf was not their leader, despite what Jarl Ragnar had said.

Ulf saw Ragnvald, still on the ship as well, glaring at him and wondered why the man had stayed behind. Was his need to kill Ulf that strong? But if that was so, then why hadn't he done it yet? While Ulf struggled with these questions in his mind, a Dane approached and called for him. 'Jarl Ragnar wants to see you in his tent.'

Ulf nodded and glanced at Ragnvald as he jumped off the ship and followed the Dane. His hands trembled as they walked past the many other warriors of Jarl Ragnar's fleet and he felt all of them watching him. If Ulf had been unknown to most of them before, he wasn't any more. Word of what had happened the day before had spread through the fleet like the plague, and everyone knew Ulf's part in it. Although, Ulf was certain the truth had changed as different mouths retold the story. That was what usually happened and so he doubted that many knew what had really happened. Still, he did not like having so many eyes on him.

'In there.' The Dane pointed to Ragnar's large tent and Ulf nodded his thanks before he entered and saw the other jarls were there already. Many of them scowled at Ulf and grumbled to each other as they wondered why he was there. Ulf wondered the same. He was no jarl and had nothing he could add to any conversation about how to attack Paris.

'So you're the bastard that caused the death of Knut and Hakon?' one jarl asked, and Ulf clenched his jaw as he glared at the dark-haired man.

'Heard he took both of Hakon's hands off,' another said and the jarls all broke out in conversation like birds fighting over berries on a shrub.

'Enough,' Ragnar said as he stood in the centre of his tent. 'My cousin and Hakon caused their own deaths by plotting against me. The Bear-Slayer is not responsible.'

'Aye, that may be so,' the dark-haired jarl said. 'But why is he here? He is no jarl.'

Jarl Ragnar looked at the man who kept his eyes fixed on Ulf. 'I asked Ulf to be here because he leads the Norsemen.'

'Should have sent them all back to Norway,' another added, but Ulf couldn't see who.

Jarl Ragnar shrugged. 'Those who wanted to leave have left. But Ulf knows as well as I do that if any of the Norse cause any more problems, then they'll all be hanged.'

'We'll need a lot of trees for that,' one jarl said, and the others laughed, but Ulf struggled to see the funny side.

'The Norsemen are here to fight. They will not cause any problems,' Ulf said with an urge to defend the Norse warriors.

'Aye, but fight who?' the dark-haired jarl asked.

'Who I tell them to,' Jarl Ragnar said and the look on his face showed that that conversation was over. 'Tomorrow the Christians celebrate their Easter. They believe that on this day, the son of their god returned from the dead to lead them to a life of eternal glory. That all their sins have been forgiven and that they will all go to their heaven.' Jarl Ragnar paused as the other jarls smiled at him. They all knew this already, even Ulf did. 'The people of Paris will flock to their churches and they will pray to their god. They will make offerings and the treasure chests in the churches will be full of gold and silver. More treasure than we have ever seen. And while they do that, while they pray and give their gold to their priests, we attack.' Jarl Ragnar smiled as he turned and looked at the walls of Paris outside his tent. 'We will show them how weak their god is and those who feel brave enough, we will send them to their heaven. By sunset tomorrow, my friends, we will be richer than the gods themselves and the king of the West Franks will beg us for mercy.'

Most of the jarls in the tent cheered and clapped each other on the backs, but like Ulf, there were a few who remained quiet, their furrowed brows betraying their doubts.

'How do we know that King Charles isn't marching towards us with his army?' one of those jarls asked.

Jarl Ragnar smiled at the jarl. 'What army? We killed half of them and the gods know the rest of them are too scared to face us now. No, Jarl Egil, King Charles is hiding in one of his monasteries with his tail between his legs, like a whipped dog. The only thing that is a danger to us now is the weather and tonight we will make an offering to Njord to ask for good weather tomorrow.'

Jarl Egil, with a frown still on his face, glanced at the other jarls before the dark-haired jarl said, 'You doubt Jarl Ragnar, Egil? Are your ships not already full of plunder and captives?'

Jarl Egil's cheeks burnt red as he shook his head. 'I do not doubt Jarl Ragnar.' He glanced at Ulf. 'I just wonder why Jarl Knut and Hakon turned against you.'

The other jarls cried out and threatened Jarl Egil, but Ulf admired the man for asking what he was certain many of the others were thinking. Jarl Ragnar seemed to sense the same as he raised his hand and the jarls fell silent.

'My cousin and his Norse friend did not turn against me, Jarl Egil. They were never with me. Knut had been plotting against me even before the raid started, because he believed that he should have led the raid. That was the reason he got Jarl Hakon to bring the Bear-Slayer with him.'

'Why? What's so special about the Bear-Slayer?' one jarl asked and Jarl Ragnar hesitated before he responded.

'Ulf and I had a run-in last winter and Jarl Knut thought he could use that to his advantage.'

'He is the one who gave you the bruised face?' one of the jarls said, and Jarl Ragnar clenched his jaw as he nodded. Ulf looked away, not wanting to see the way the other jarls were staring at him.

'Must have been a lucky punch,' the dark-haired jarl said, and Jarl Ragnar nodded.

'Aye, it was.'

Again, Ulf kept quiet. His new alliance with Jarl Ragnar was still fragile, and he didn't want to endanger that. Not when he still needed to make enough to free Eldrid. So he kept quiet and ignored the stares from the other jarls.

'Now, do we want to talk of the past or do you want me to tell you how we are going to take Paris?' Jarl Ragnar asked and all the jarls turned their attention to him. 'Good. Jarl Egil, you will lead your men and attack the bridge on the east side of the city. Jarl Bjarni, you will do the same with the bridge on the west side.'

'That will get us all killed,' Jarl Egil said and Ragnar shook his head.

'There won't be enough defenders to stop either of you because the rest of us will attack the walls around the city at the same time. Those defending Paris won't know where to defend and that is how we will take the city in one day.'

'And how do we do that?' one jarl asked.

'Ladders,' Ulf repeated what Hjalmar had said to him before and knew that was what Ragnar was planning when he smiled at Ulf.

'Aye, lots of ladders.' Jarl Ragnar turned to the rest of the jarls again. 'Get your men to make ladders. As many as they can. The gods have blessed us because there are plenty of trees in the area.'

'What if those in Paris see what we are doing?' Jarl Egil asked.

Jarl Ragnar shrugged. 'What are they going to do?' The other jarls laughed when Jarl Egil couldn't respond. 'And one more thing. Tell your men not to kill their priests.'

'Why?' one jarl asked and many others, including Ulf, frowned at that.

'Because their priests are very important to them, we all know that.'

'And that is why we like to kill them.' The other jarls nodded in agreement, but Ragnar shook his head.

'Not this time. We keep them alive and then ransom them back to King Charles.' Jarl Ragnar smiled at the jarls, who all slowly started smiling back when they realised what that would mean for them. Untold riches.

'You really think he would pay to spare the priests?' one jarl asked.

'They have done before,' the dark-haired jarl said and others nodded in agreement. 'Like Jarl Ragnar said. Their priests are more important to the Christians than their wives.'

'That's why we get to keep the wives,' another added and the jarls laughed.

Jarl Ragnar waited for the jarls to have their moment before he sent them back to their men, and as they left, Ulf stayed behind and stared at the walls of Paris. His hands trembled at the thought of attacking the city and he couldn't say which prospect he feared the most. Climbing the ladders or charging the bridges.

'Your Norsemen will be the first to scale the walls on the south side of the city. Just ahead of my men.'

They're not my Norsemen, Ulf wanted to say, but knew there was no point. Just like he knew there was no point arguing about Jarl Ragnar's order, so Ulf just nodded.

'Your volva friend would be useful to have around right now.'

Ulf glanced at Jarl Ragnar as he scratched his red beard. 'Skadi only appears when she needs something. Not when you need her. And the gods know, I'd rather not have her nearby when we attack Paris tomorrow.' Jarl Ragnar frowned at Ulf, who remembered the last time she was around when he attacked a large city like Paris. 'The last time didn't end well for me.'

Jarl Ragnar smiled. 'But you still live.'

'Aye,' Ulf said. *And only because of her*. He was about to leave the tent when Jarl Ragnar asked,

'Can we trust the Norse warriors?'

Ulf scowled as he thought about it. 'As much as we can trust snakes in a snake pit.'

CHAPTER 34

CHURCH BELLS RANG AND horns blew as warriors cried out to the gods and the people of Paris prayed to theirs. Already, large ravens and crows circled the sky and Ulf wondered if Odin had sent his ravens to watch the assault on Paris as he stood by the prow of Hakon's ship, with the Norse warriors behind him. Most of them were rowing towards the island which Paris sat on, while the rest held the six ladders they would use to attack the walls. Jarl Ragnar's fleet had worked hard to build as many ladders as they could and there had even been a competition between the jarls to see whose army could build the most. Ragnar won, but only because he had the largest army of all the jarls, but the warriors had enjoyed the competition, so no one really cared about that.

As with every battle, Ulf's hair was braided, and he had a thick braid in the centre of his beard. But this time, Ulf had no helmet to protect his head. And that made his stomach churn as he stared at the walls of Paris. But even if he had a helmet, Ulf knew he couldn't wear it. Not with the lump on his head from the stone which had been thrown at him during his fight with Hakon. He resisted the urge to glance at the Norse warriors as he wondered if the bastard who had thrown the stone was still there or if he had returned to Norway with the others. Ulf took a deep breath and grimaced at the pain in his chest from the bruise Hakon had given him as he tried to calm his nerves.

'Row, you bastards! Show the Danes why we are better than them!' Ragnvald roared and Ulf felt the ship surge forward as the rowing warriors grunted in an effort not to be outdone by Ragnar's Danes. His hands trembled as he glanced at the sun, which glistened off the water and meant that Ormstunga would stay in her scabbard. Both Ragnvald and Hjalmar stood beside Ulf by the prow of the ship and as much as Ulf didn't want Ragnvald standing there, he knew he couldn't send the man away. The Norse warriors respected him and many saw him as their leader, not Ulf.

Ulf tested the weight of the shield on his left arm, which felt heavier than what it did when they had boarded the ship. But Ulf knew that was only because of his nerves, as was the desire to piss. Ulf was too tired to care about that, though. The Norse warriors might have been pleased that they'd be the ones who had to scale the wall first, as they saw it as a chance to earn Odin's favour, but Ulf couldn't sleep. Every time he closed his eyes, he saw two wolves staring at each other. *One of them will be stabbed in the back*. The words were whispered from the darkness, and Ulf feared that the threat Skadi had warned him about still loomed over them. Ulf was about to glance towards Jarl Ragnar's ship when he heard the unmistakable sound of arrows being released.

'Shields!' Hjalmar and Ragnvald both shouted, and Ulf lifted his shield above his head as arrows landed amongst the Norse warriors. Ulf gritted his teeth as arrows struck his shield and some warriors cried out in pain behind him.

Tyr, lend me your battle strength. Odin, lend me your rage. Thor, protect me. Let me survive this so I can fulfil my oath to Eldrid.

The defenders of Paris released another volley of arrows, and as Ulf glanced over his shoulder, he saw the Norse warriors were prepared this time. Those carrying the ladders had dropped them and were holding their shields above their heads to protect themselves and those rowing. But Ulf's heart raced as he saw the arrows on the deck and three dead warriors while another four were injured.

'Bastard archers!' Ragnvald growled and for once, Ulf agreed with the one-handed warrior, who had his shield above his head.

'Brace!' Hjalmar roared, and Ulf turned back to the front to see that they had reached the island. He tensed his legs and felt the timber tremble under his feet as Hakon's ship grounded itself. Before the ship came to a stop, Ulf straightened and punched his one-handed axe in the air.

'Warriors of Sygnafylki! Charge!' Without looking behind him, Ulf jumped off the ship and stormed at the wall. In the silence filled by his racing heart, he prayed that the Norse warriors would follow him and not stay on the ship and wait for him to be killed by arrows. But to his relief, he heard them shout to the gods and storm the city walls. The voices of his ancestors came alive in his ears as the defenders shot arrows and threw stones at him and the Norse warriors. Behind him, men cried out in pain, but soon he reached the wall and was surprised to see Ragnvald right behind him, while Hjalmar was further back. Ulf, though, had no time to think about that as the rest of the Norse warriors arrived with the ladders.

'Ladders up!' Ulf roared as he looked behind the ladder carriers and saw dead and dying warriors on the ground. Jarl Ragnar's ships had also landed, and the jarl, dressed in all his war glory and wearing shaggy trousers he liked to wear when fighting battles, led his men as they raced to the walls of Paris before the defenders could kill them. As soon as the first ladder was up against the wall, Ulf moved his axe to his left hand, behind his shield, and started climbing. His sweaty hands made it hard for him to grip the ladder, and Ulf was barely a few rungs up the ladder and was already panting. But he had to be the first one up if he wanted the rest of the Norse warriors to fight. So he forced his fears out of his mind and held his shield above his head as he pushed himself to climb the ladder while arrows and stones whizzed past him. Below him, warriors cried out in agony and called out to the gods as jarls urged their men on, while above him the defenders cried out in dismay as more ladders were pushed onto the wall.

As Ulf climbed, the ladder trembled, and Ulf's heart skipped a beat as he thought it was being pushed over. But then he glanced down and realised it was only the Norsemen following him up. He glanced to the side and saw a Dane skewered through the eye by an arrow, while another ladder was pushed off the wall. The Danes screamed as they fell on top of their comrades before Ulf turned away and kept on climbing. It was chaotic, and it was terrifying, and Ulf knew the gods must have been laughing as another warrior's head was crushed by a large stone dropped from the top of the wall.

'For the go—' the warrior below Ulf shouted, but his words were cut off as an arrow pierced his throat and sent him tumbling down. He took the man below with him and all Ulf could do was pray that he did not piss himself as he struggled to climb while holding his shield above his head.

It felt like he had been climbing for a lifetime and he almost let go of the ladder in fright when an arrow struck his shield, but when Ulf looked up, he realised he was almost at the top of the wall. *Odin, don't let me die now.* He prayed as one of the Norsemen on the other ladder near him made it to the top as well, only to be thrown over again. His screams were drowned out by the sounds of thousands of warriors roaring as more charged up the ladders to get at the Frankish defenders.

Ulf pushed it all from his mind and with one final prayer to the gods, he held his shield above his head and rushed up the final few rungs of the ladder. A Frankish warrior turned to face him, his face pale and his eyes wide with shock, as Ulf reached the top of the wall. Ulf wasted no time and punched the man in the throat with the rim of his shield. The Frank clutched his throat, his eyes bulging as he struggled to breathe before Ulf kicked him off the wooden platform.

He shifted his axe to his right hand as he gave himself to the voices of his ancestors, which were raging in his ears. 'Tyr!' he roared as he hacked at a Frankish warrior, sending him off the platform as well, before he lifted his shield and blocked the spear from another. Behind him, more of the Norse warriors climbed onto the wall and formed a loose shield wall as they pushed the defenders back. The Danes were also on the wall now, and Ulf spotted Ragnar fighting with his men. Ulf scanned the Danes around Ragnar with Skadi's warning in his mind. But he saw no one trying to kill Ragnar from behind and knew that he had to trust that Ragnar's hirdmen would protect him. Unfortunately, Ulf could not do the same and could only pray that none of Hakon's former warriors stuck a knife in his back.

Blood sprayed over Ulf, bringing him back to the fight in front of him. He tried to ignore the metallic taste of the blood as he deflected a spear from a Frankish warrior, but as Ulf lifted his axe to kill the Frank, someone pushed him from behind. Ulf's heart stopped beating as he fell towards the edge of the fighting platform and before he fell over the edge, someone grabbed hold of his brynja and pulled him back.

Ulf turned, his ancestors raging in his ears, and caught sight of Ragnvald, glaring at him as he backed off. Believing it was the one-handed warrior who had pushed him, Ulf was about to rush after him when a scream made him turn to his left. Ulf saw the axe at the last moment and twisted out of the way before he buried his own in his attacker's leg. The Frank screamed as Ulf shoved him off the platform, but then Ulf cursed as there was no sign of Ragnvald.

More of the Danes and Norse made it up the ladders as the fighting on the wall continued. The platform below their feet was as hazardous as the weapons they wielded as both defenders and attackers tripped over dead bodies or slipped on blood. But soon, the Franks had no choice but to fall back. They were heavily outnumbered by Jarl Ragnar's fleet and too thinly spread as the rest of the ships had reached the other walls. The Danes cheered as the Franks fled, but Jarl Ragnar cut their celebration short.

'To the streets!' he ordered and his warriors roared as they chased the Franks into the streets of Paris. Jarl Ragnar pointed his sword at Ulf. 'Take your men to the eastern gate and open it for Jarl Egil.'

Ulf nodded as he took a moment to catch his breath. His heart was racing faster than it had ever done, and Ulf didn't know if it was because he had to scale the wall or because someone had almost pushed him off the platform. *Not someone, Ragnvald*, Ulf corrected himself as he tightened his grip on his axe. As he stood on the wall, Ulf took in the sight of Paris in front of him, and he didn't like what he saw. Too many houses squashed into the city walls, some looking like they were built on top of each other as a handful of church towers reached to the clouds over the houses. Already dark smoke drifted towards the skies as houses burnt, while the church bells rang as if the Christian priests were summoning their god. Ulf shook his head and turned to the Norse warriors.

'You heard Jarl Ragnar. To the eastern gate!'

The Norse roared and stormed down the stairs of the platform and ran towards the eastern gate, while cutting down anyone within reach of their weapons.

As Ulf ran with the Norse warriors, someone shoved him hard from behind, and he almost lost his axe as he fell. Ulf turned and saw one of Hjalmar's friends looming over him. He smiled as he thought the man was there to help him up, but then frowned as the warrior raised his axe and snarled at him.

'This is for Jarl Hakon,' the man said before he chopped down with his axe.

Ulf lifted his shield to block the man's axe. He felt it bite deep into his shield and knew the axe was stuck. He twisted his shield, hoping to unbalance the bastard, but as he did that, the warrior let go of his axe and pulled his sax-knife from its scabbard. Before Ulf could react, someone shoulder barged the warrior and stabbed him in the throat with his sword.

Ulf blinked as he struggled to make sense of what was happening when he saw it was Ragnvald. But then his anger ignited when he remembered Ragnvald had almost pushed him off the platform on the wall. Gripping his axe as his rage spread through his limbs, he glared at Ragnvald.

'Want to kill me yourself? Is that it?'

Ragnvald shook his head, which only confused Ulf even more. 'You fool. I'm not trying to kill y—'

Ragnvald's eyes widened as he was stabbed in the back and Ulf gaped at Hjalmar standing behind the one-handed warrior with an ugly snarl on his face. Ragnvald turned and punched Hjalmar in the face before he collapsed to the ground with Hjalmar's sword still in his back.

Ulf jumped to his feet and was about to thank Hjalmar for helping him when something made him hesitate. Skadi's words came to his mind again, and he glanced at Ragnvald, whose beard was red with blood as he pulled himself onto his elbow.

'I...I'm not your enemy, Ulf.'

Ulf's hands trembled as more of Hjalmar's men circled around him. The same ones Ulf had thought were there to protect him from those who wanted him dead for his part in Hakon's death. Ulf cursed himself for being so blind, and he resisted the urge to rub the lump on his head as he stared at Hjalmar.

'You threw the stone at me when I was fighting Hakon.'

Hjalmar shrugged as the men behind him laughed. Ulf glanced at Ragnvald, whose face was turning pale, before he looked towards the eastern gate where the rest of the Norse warriors were fighting the few Franks defending the gate. But even if they were nearer, Ulf wondered if he could trust any of them to help him. He stepped back to put some distance between himself and Hjalmar's men, but then they just took a step towards him.

'I told you, Ulf. I served Jarl Hakon's father loyally for many winters. Just like I served Jarl Hakon loyally, even if I didn't always know what he was up to.'

Ulf's brows furrowed as he struggled to make sense of everything. 'You tried to push me off the platform.'

'That was me,' one man next to Hjalmar said. 'Should have pushed you harder, but then that bastard had to grab you before you could fall off.'

Ulf looked at Ragnvald as he cursed himself again. He took another step back as Hjalmar and his men moved closer to him.

'I thought you were my friend,' Ulf said to Hjalmar, who laughed at him.

'Jarl Hakon told me to get close to you. To make you think the Danes were trying to kill you. But you know, I actually liked you. Until you got my jarl killed.'

'Aye, and now you will die for it,' one warrior said as he moved closer to Ulf, who was backed up against the wall of the house behind him.

Hjalmar smiled. 'Your luck has run out, Bear-Slayer. Today you die and Jarl Ragnar will think it was during the battle.'

The others laughed, but Ulf wasn't listening as he had realised something. He dropped his shield and moved the axe to his left hand when he saw he stood in the house's shadow. The voices of his ancestors exploded in his ears as Ulf pulled Ormstunga from her scabbard.

'You really think that pretty sword of yours is going to save you,' Hjalmar said as Ulf's rage coursed through his veins and heightened his senses. 'Kill —'

Hjalmar never got to finish his sentence as Ulf shot forward and stabbed him through the mouth. Broken teeth and blood sprayed through the air as Ormstunga burst through the back of Hjalmar's head. And before any of the others could react, Ulf turned and pulled Ormstunga free. He buried his axe in the chest of one of Hjalmar's men, his anger giving him the strength to drive the axe head through the man's brynja. Before this man died, Ulf sliced another's throat open, but then had to duck when one of the men swung his sword at Ulf.

Ulf moved behind the man and cut his leg open, before the voices of his ancestors screamed at him to turn. He deflected the axe of the man attacking him and kicked him in the stomach. As the man bent over, Ulf chopped at his neck with his axe and took the man's head off.

Ulf turned and saw that only one of Hjalmar's men was left, the one whose leg he had cut. His face was as pale as Ragnvald's as he stared at his dead companions around him before he looked at Ulf.

'Please, don't kill me. It was Hjalmar's idea. He said we had to kill you to avenge Jarl Hakon.'

Ulf stood in front of the man, his limbs trembling with rage, and without saying a word, he buried Ormstunga in the man's chest as the rest of the Norse warriors opened the eastern gate and Jarl Egil's men stormed into Paris.

Chapter 35

'Hang on, you old bastard. We'll get you some help.'

Ulf dragged Ragnvald through the streets of Paris as the city burnt. People screamed as they fought for their lives while the invading force of Jarl Ragnar killed and raped at will. Everywhere Ulf looked, he saw Danish warriors breaking doors down and rushing into the houses, while dead Franks littered the streets. More often than not, the Danes came out of the houses looking disappointed, but occasionally they came out dragging a woman behind them or with barely enough trinkets to fill their blood-covered hands.

Ragnvald's breathing was ragged and his face was too pale, but Ulf was determined to help the one-handed warrior. Even if he didn't know how. Ulf had removed Hjalmar's sword from his back and had done what he could to stop the bleeding, but he was no healer. He scanned the streets, praying that Skadi was there somewhere. If anyone knew how to help Ragnvald, it was her, but there was no sign of the volva and that didn't surprise Ulf. She only showed herself when she wanted something.

'Ulf, by the gods, put me down.'

Ulf glanced at Ragnvald and saw the pain in his creased face. 'No.' Ulf shook his head. He looked around him, trying to see if he could spot any of the Norse warriors. Some of them were still loyal to Ragnvald, but he had lost sight of them after they had opened the eastern gate.

Ragnvald grunted as he pulled himself free from Ulf's grip and collapsed. And when Ulf went to grab him again, he slapped Ulf's hands away. 'Stop it, you fool!'

Ulf's anger sparked, and he had to bite it back. 'I'm trying to help you!'

Ragnvald sighed as he looked at Ulf. 'Why?'

Ulf opened his mouth to respond, but then he realised he didn't know. He guessed it was because he felt guilty. This entire time, he had believed that Ragnvald had wanted to kill him. He looked around him at the chaos and the frustrated faces of the warriors as they found little to plunder and even fewer women to rape. With his own sigh, Ulf sat down next to Ragnvald. His hands trembled as they always did after a battle, and Ulf was exhausted. He glanced at Ormstunga, her blade red with the blood of Hjalmar and his men, and Ulf wondered how he had been fooled once again by those who pretended to be his friends. 'Why did you do it?'

Ragnvald took a strained breath. 'Do what?'

'Help me. This whole time, I thought you were keeping me alive because you wanted to kill me.'

Ragnvald laughed, and then he coughed before he looked at Ulf. 'I was angry at you first when I heard you killed my son. But then I realised you did me a favour.' Ulf raised an eyebrow at the old warrior. 'The gods know I could never kill my son.'

'But he took your hand.'

Ragnvald shrugged. 'He was still my son. I've always known there was a cruel streak in him and I prayed to the gods that it would disappear when he became a man. But when it didn't, I sent him away so that others could deal with him.' Ragnvald looked at the stump on his left arm. 'The gods took my hand as punishment for that. So, Bear-Slayer, you killing Griml freed me of that guilt.'

Ulf shook his head as he watched the surrounding carnage. The Danes had moved on to another part of Paris, but there were still some warriors around having their way with those unfortunate enough to be found. Somewhere, Ulf could hear a woman scream in pain as a horn blew in the distance. Paris had fallen, and it had taken them less than half a day. 'That day on the training ground in Jelling. Why did you fight me?'

Ragnvald coughed again. 'I wanted to test the man who killed my son. You disappointed me.'

Ulf looked at Ragnvald and scowled at how pale his face was. The old man had lost a lot of blood and Ulf knew he needed to stop the bleeding, but Ragnvald refused to let him do anything. 'I told you, I had help. I could never defeat Griml on my own.'

'No one could. The gods cursed us when my wife pushed that monster out. She was his first victim.'

Ulf nodded, because he didn't know what to say to that. 'So, you following me, always telling me to watch my back. You knew Hakon was up to something.'

Ragnvald's eyes fluttered as he nodded. 'Aye. I didn't know what at the time, but I knew it would not end well for you. You ended my curse, so I saw it as my duty to protect you.' Ragnvald stared at the clouds as the smoke of the burning houses mixed with them. 'Do you think Griml is in Valhalla?'

Ulf frowned at the question. 'I pray he isn't. That isn't a face I want to see again.'

'Neither is yours.' Ragnvald smiled.

Ulf rubbed the scars on his face and returned the old man's smile. 'Aye.' He turned and saw a house near them was untouched and struggled to his feet, hoping that he can find something inside to stop Ragnvald from bleeding to death. 'Come, old man. You're not dying yet. I need you to rein the Norsemen in.'

Ragnvald groaned as Ulf pulled him to his feet and led him towards the house. Ormstunga still in hand, Ulf pushed the door open and peered inside. The house was dark and, from the looks of it, empty. Sensing no danger, Ulf went inside. He was about to help Ragnvald onto a stool when he heard a movement in the corner of the house. As his eyes adjusted to the darkness, Ulf saw a woman cowering from him, but it was the small boy that caught his attention as he stared at Ulf with wide eyes and tear-stained cheeks.

Ulf lowered Ragnvald to the ground and took a step towards the woman and boy. The woman gripped her son tighter as she pressed herself deeper into the corner.

'I'm not going to hurt you,' Ulf said, even though he doubted the woman understood what he was saying. He noticed something that looked like a Christian cross in the woman's hand as the boy started crying again. She shushed the boy without taking her eyes off Ulf, who backed off. He would get what he needed and then leave the house. All he could do then was pray that none of the Danes came to this house.

He rummaged around the house, trying to find something to help Ragnvald when he heard a scream behind him. Ulf turned, expecting to see a Dane in the doorway, but instead he saw the woman standing over Ragnvald, her hand on the knife in his throat. The knife he had thought was a cross.

'No!' Ulf screamed as he rushed at the woman. His anger took hold of him and he raised Ormstunga, but then the woman cried out as she dropped to the ground and covered her head with her bloody hands. The boy's scream broke through Ulf's red mist and as he stood over the woman, Ormstunga still raised, he saw Ragnvald was dead. What surprised him, though, was the peace he saw in the one-handed warrior's face. Ulf lowered Ormstunga and stepped back so the woman could run back to the corner where her son was. She stared at Ulf, her face pale with fear, and all Ulf could do was look at her.

'We weren't going to hurt you,' Ulf said as he dropped to the ground beside Ragnvald. He pulled the knife out of his throat and looked at it, before he threw it towards the woman. She screamed as the knife landed on the floor in front of her, but Ulf ignored her as he stared at Ragnvald. Another person dead because of him. 'Go to Valhalla, old man. And thank you.'

Ulf sat there as the sun moved through the sky, ignoring the woman and her boy in the corner of the house. At some point, the boy fell asleep, but the woman never took her eyes off of him. Occasionally, a Dane would stick his head into the house and Ulf would tell them the house was empty before sending them away. He wasn't sure why, though. Perhaps it was because he knew that the woman was only protecting her son. Or perhaps it was because he knew Ragnvald was going to die anyway. The wound to his back was deep and was bleeding heavily. Ragnvald knew it as well. Perhaps that was why he didn't stop the woman.

After a long while, Ulf struggled to his feet and walked to the door of the house. The sun was sitting low and Paris had gone quiet. Over the houses, Ulf could see some fires, but most of them had been put out or had died out themselves. The sounds of fighting were replaced by the sounds of carrion birds as ravens and crows fed on the dead and Ulf watched as one raven fed on the tongue of a Frank in front of the house. He wondered if it was the husband of the woman before he turned to her.

'Wait until nightfall and then run as fast as you can. If your god is with you, then most of the men will be too drunk to catch you.' Ulf didn't know why he had to say that. He knew she wouldn't understand as he walked out of the house and towards the centre of Paris, where he thought he might find Jarl Ragnar.

Ulf gripped Ormstunga tightly as he walked through the streets of Paris. His axe was tucked into his belt, and Ulf didn't know where his shield was. Most likely where he had killed Hjalmar. But Ulf did not want to go back there to retrieve it. He did not want to see Hjalmar's body because it would only remind him of what a fool he had been. Was he that eager for friends that he ignored the signs that he was being fooled? Ulf didn't know the answer to that. Only the gods did, and Ulf wanted nothing to do with them.

Ormstunga's blade was still dirty, even though Ulf could have cleaned her and put her in her scabbard. But he didn't want to. Not until he was certain that the threat against him was gone. Ulf didn't know how many more of the Norse warriors wanted to kill him because of Jarl Hakon. And what about the Danes, those who had fought for Jarl Knut? How many of them wanted to kill Ulf for what had happened to their jarl? Ulf's back tensed as the thought came to him, and he couldn't help but glance over his shoulder to see if anyone was behind him. Neither could he stop himself from slowing down every time he neared the corner of a house just for in case someone was waiting to ambush him. And then he remembered that many of those Danes fought with Jarl Ragnar now. Ulf had to believe that Jarl Ragnar's hirdmen would have kept him safe as he walked past warriors more concerned about finding plunder than him.

As Ulf made his way to a large church where most of the warriors were congregating, he noticed men carrying jugs in their hands and with large smiles on their faces. Some warriors leaned against walls and sang songs while others boasted of the men they killed. Ulf ignored them all as he pushed past men towards the door of the large church. Some men complained and one pushed him back, only for others to recognise Ulf and clear a path for him. Ulf nodded his thanks to the men, but could not relax, as he expected to feel a knife in his back at any moment. Those concerns stayed with him as he entered the church and made his way to a group of men standing near the altar. To his relief, Jarl Ragnar was there, his face dirty and his brynja red with blood, as were the others around him.

'By the gods, he still lives,' one jarl said, and they all turned to Ulf, who ignored the upturned benches and broken windows of the church. Just like he ignored the large dome roof and the brightly coloured pictures painted on the walls.

'Jarl Ragnar,' Ulf said as he stopped by the group.

Jarl Ragnar smiled at him. 'Ulf Bear-Slayer. We were told you died taking the eastern gate.'

Ulf clenched his jaw as he thought about how true that could have been and then shook his head. 'No, although they came close.'

The other jarls frowned, but Jarl Ragnar seemed to understand as he nodded. 'I thank the gods they didn't succeed.' *The gods and Ragnvald*, Ulf thought, but didn't say as Jarl Ragnar raised his arms and smiled at Ulf. 'But enough of that. It's time to celebrate, Ulf. Paris is ours!'

Chapter 36

'Paris might be ours, but the bloody city is empty,' one of the jarls said, and a few of the others grunted in agreement. The smile fell from Jarl Ragnar's face as he stared at the jarl while Ulf glanced around the large church they were in.

Apart from the richly coloured paintings on the walls, there was nothing else. No large golden crosses studded with gems or candle holders. No books decorated with precious stones or with golden covers. And more importantly, none of the masses Jarl Ragnar had said would have filled the church on the sacred Christian day.

'Aye, you said the churches would be full of wealthy people. That we'd be richer than the gods!' Jarl Egil, with a fresh cut to his forehead, said. Again, a few of the other jarls grunted in agreement. 'Jarl Knut was right. You took too long to get here and now Paris is empty.'

Jarl Ragnar grabbed the younger jarl by his brynja and almost lifted him off his feet as he growled into his face. Jarl Egil paled as he realised his mistake while the other jarls took a step away from him. 'You agree with my cousin? Perhaps you were part of his plot to kill me?'

Jarl Egil shook his head, but Ulf had to admit the man was right. Paris was empty. Most of the houses Ulf had walked past were empty. His mind went to the woman and the boy, and he wondered why they had not fled. Perhaps they believed their god or their king would save them, but both were too busy to concern themselves with the lives of those on the bottom. Ulf clenched his fists at the thought as Jarl Egil responded.

'No, Jarl Ragnar.' He looked to the others for support, but even Ulf saw that he wasn't going to get it as Jarl Ragnar glared at him.

'Then what is it?'

Ulf sighed and said, 'The people fled and took everything they could with them. Even this church is empty.'

Jarl Ragnar curled his lip at Ulf, who wondered if he should not have kept quiet. But Ulf was exhausted and did not care any more. If Jarl Ragnar wanted to be angry at him for saying the obvious, then so be it. Ulf would just leave and find his way back to Denmark. He was sure he had enough in his pouch to buy Eldrid's freedom.

'Not empty,' the dark-haired jarl said with a smile. 'My men have found some priests too stubborn to flee and a room with more barrels of wine and ale than I can count.'

'Plenty of people still about. Half my men are fucking Frankish captives as we speak,' another jarl said as Jarl Ragnar let go of Jarl Egil, but kept his eyes on Ulf.

'Paris is ours,' he said again. 'It doesn't matter that the churches are empty or that the people have fled. We hold the jewel of the king of the West Franks in our hands. A city that gets more trade than Jelling and the rest of the markets in Denmark. King Charles will not want us to stay here.'

'He'll raise an army to chase us out,' one jarl said, and Jarl Ragnar shook his head.

'He doesn't have enough men. And even if he finds more, we hold the city.'

'He can starve us out,' Ulf said. He had heard stories of how some walled cities were taken that way. Instead of losing men to take the gates, the attacking army just surrounded the city and starved the defenders out.

Jarl Ragnar nodded as if he considered that an option. 'But that will take time and the longer we stay in Paris, the weaker he looks. He'll want us gone quickly.'

The dark-haired jarl frowned at Jarl Ragnar. 'So what will he do?'

Jarl Ragnar smiled at the jarls surrounding him. 'He'll come with carts filled with treasure and beg us to leave. Gather your men, get them to stop the fires and stop raping the women. Bring all the priests here and make sure all the gates are guarded. As Odin is my witness, before the next full moon we'll be sailing back to Denmark with our ships so full of plunder, they'll barely stay afloat.'

The jarls cheered, but Ulf noticed that many of them still seemed unsure.

'Until then, we have enough ale and wine to even challenge Thor.' The dark-haired jarl raised his arms and Jarl Ragnar nodded.

'Pass it out amongst your men. Tonight, we feast and we celebrate. Tomorrow, we bleed the lands around Paris dry.'

The jarls cheered louder at this and left the church as Ulf and the dark-haired jarl stayed behind.

'Where are your Norsemen?' Jarl Ragnar asked, and Ulf shrugged. He was too tired to argue that they weren't his men.

'Doing the same as everyone else is. Plundering and raping.'

'You don't seem too pleased about that,' the dark-haired jarl said, and Ulf tightened his grip on Ormstunga.

'Because the people of this city do not deserve their fate.'

'It's not up to us to decide if we deserve our fate or not, Ulf. That's what the Norns are for.' Jarl Ragnar gripped his shoulder, and Ulf could only nod as he wondered why the Norns had decided that Ragnvald deserved to be stabbed in the throat by a Frankish woman. 'Your Norsemen have gathered near the eastern gate. I have men watching them, but there seems to be some confusion over who is leading them.'

Ulf scowled before he sighed. 'I'll go to them.'

'And keep those dogs under control,' the dark-haired jarl said and Ulf had to take a deep breath to calm his anger down as Ormstunga seemed to tremble in his hand. Or perhaps that was just his hand.

'You did well, Bear-Slayer. So did your Norsemen,' Jarl Ragnar said as Ulf turned to leave the church.

'You mean we survived when you thought we'd be slaughtered taking the wall?'

Jarl Ragnar smiled, and Ulf sensed a warmth in it, which surprised him. 'Aye. It seems that Odin has blessed you, after all.'

Cursed, more like, Ulf thought as he walked out of the church and towards where Ragnar had said the Norse were.

Ulf avoided the area where he thought the house was where Ragnvald had been killed as he made his way back towards the eastern gate. He didn't know if it was because he didn't want to see Ragnvald's body or because he didn't want to see that the woman and her boy had been killed. He kept Ormstunga in his hand and his eyes on every warrior he walked past. Skadi's warning was still in his head and Ulf was certain there were more men out there that wanted him dead. And walking alone through the streets of an unknown city was the perfect opportunity to kill him. But despite the danger hanging over him, Ulf was happy that he was on his own. He did not want to deal with anyone trying to talk to him as he tried to calm the storm in his head. What he had hoped would be a simple raid to earn enough to free Eldrid had been anything but, and all Ulf wanted to do was to leave Francia and never return to these lands.

He heard the Norsemen before he saw them. Their songs reached his ears while he was still a short distance away, as did their laughter. They were in good spirits, and Ulf wondered if that would make it easier to face them. Because somehow, he had to get the Norsemen to agree to let him lead them until they left Francia. Something even Ulf didn't want to do because he still didn't know if any more of them had plans to stick a knife in his back.

Ulf rounded the corner of the house and scowled at the large fire the Norse warriors had built in the middle of the street. Benches and tables, as well as bed frames and other furniture he could not recognise any more, were piled on top of each other as flames leapt towards the cloudless skies and warriors danced around them. Barrels stood to one side, away from the fire, and Ulf guessed they had also found the wine cellars of the churches in this part of Paris.

Ulf took a deep breath and made his way towards the Norse warriors. His heart was racing in his chest and Ulf felt more nervous than what he did when he stood in a shield wall. *Thor, protect me*, Ulf prayed as he stopped in front of the Norse warriors and waited.

One of the warriors spotted Ulf and tapped the man beside him on the shoulder. One by one, the Norse warriors fell silent as they turned to face him, until all Ulf could hear were the flames and a woman crying somewhere.

'It's the Bear-Slayer,' one man said.

'I thought the bastard was dead,' another added as they all stared at Ulf.

'Where's Ragnvald?' Another man stepped forward and glared at Ulf. Ulf looked up at the warrior, who stood almost a head taller than him.

With Ormstunga still in his hand, Ulf said, 'Ragnvald is dead. And so are Hjalmar and his friends.'

'Aye, I saw Hjalmar's body,' someone said, but Ulf didn't see who as he stared at the large warrior in front of him. Ulf was taller than most men and felt uncomfortable when he came across someone bigger than him, but he would not be cowed by the man.

'You killed Ragnvald,' the large warrior said, and many of the warriors grumbled at that. 'We all know you hated him.'

Ulf shook his head. 'Hjalmar killed him,' Ulf lied. He didn't think these men needed to know that a Frankish woman had killed the one-handed warrior.

'Why?' The large warrior took a step towards Ulf, as did some of the others.

Ulf stood his ground as he tightened his grip on Ormstunga. 'To protect me.' He glared at the man in front of him and then turned his attention to the rest of the Norse warriors. Men who had sailed with Jarl Hakon for many winters. Men who had become rich fighting for the jarl from Sygnafylki. 'Hjalmar and his friends tried to kill me. Men I had believed were trying to befriend me attacked me from behind as we stormed the eastern gate.'

'You're lying!' someone shouted and others agreed.

Ulf scanned the Norse warriors as he tried to work out who had spoken, but all he saw was a sea of angry faces. He had accused one of their own of being dishonourable, and they didn't like it. At that moment, Ulf wondered if he would make it out of Paris alive. He pushed the thought out of his mind as he faced the Norsemen. 'As Odin is my witness, I am not lying. Hjalmar blamed me for the death of your jarl, as I am sure many of you do.' He waited to see what the warriors would do, but no one said anything. Ulf spread his arms wide as he stared at the Norse warriors. Most of them were older than his twenty-two winters. They had raided more lands and had fought more battles than he had, but their names were unknown while his was spoken throughout the lands. Ulf beat his chest with his fist. 'I am Ulf Bear-Slayer! Descendant of Tyr. If any of you doubt my word, then step forward and face me! If any of you hold me responsible for the death of your jarl, then now is the time to avenge him.' Ormstunga trembled in his outstretched hand as his anger coursed through his veins and warmed his limbs.

In front of him, the Norse warriors glanced at each other, but no one stepped forward to face him as the fire raged behind them. Somewhere, a raven called out and many of the men gripped the Mjöllnir pendants around their necks.

Eventually, the large warrior in front of Ulf said, 'Hjalmar was always a sly bastard. We all know that. He was constantly sniffing at Hakon's behind, like a dog looking for scraps. Ragnvald saw that as well and never trusted the man. If you say Hjalmar tried to kill you, then I believe you.' Some of the Norse grunted their agreement, but many stayed silent. 'But you are not our leader. It doesn't matter what Jarl Ragnar says. We will not be led by the man that killed our jarl.'

'Or is from Vestfold,' someone added.

Ulf nodded and took a deep breath to calm his anger. 'I accept that. But someone needs to lead you.'

'I'll do it,' the large warrior said, and Ulf noticed how no one disagreed, so he shrugged.

'What's your name?'

'Halstein Ericsson,' the large warrior said, and Ulf nodded.

'Well, Halstein Ericsson. Keep the men out of trouble and soon we'll all be going home richer than we've ever been.'

'How?' someone shouted. 'Paris is empty.' Others agreed, and Ulf had expected this.

'Jarl Ragnar has a plan.'

Halstein grunted. 'So what do we do now?'

Ulf sighed as he glanced at the moon. 'We wait.'

Chapter 37

Ulf crinkled his nose as he walked towards the large hall which belonged to the king of the West Franks. Jarl Ragnar had taken it for himself, and his army had taken most of the houses around the hall. The other jarls had taken large houses which Ulf guessed belonged to important people. Ulf had been offered a house which was almost as large as the hall back in Thorgilsstad, but Ulf had refused. He preferred to sleep out in the open, especially now that they were midway through spring and the weather was improving.

Most of the days were sunny and warm, although there would be the occasional rain. There was a light breeze that would carry the scent of five thousand men cramped together behind the walls of Paris through the streets and all that caused another problem.

Ulf glanced at one warrior lying on the ground, too weak to move. The man was thin and reeked of shit, and the bloody stain on the back of his trousers showed the cause of his state. Ulf held his breath as he walked past the man, whose pleading eyes stared at him, but even the man must have known there was nothing Ulf could do.

And the Dane wasn't the only one who was suffering from the flux. At least half of the Norsemen were, and one had died a few days ago. Another two looked like they didn't have long left. The Norsemen were angry, and it was hard for Halstein to keep them calm. And Ulf knew he wasn't the only one who had these problems as he reached the large hall. The building looked similar to the halls they had in Denmark and Norway, but it was built with stone and had windows in the walls. The glass in the windows was broken during the attack, but the building still looked impressive as Ulf walked past the men guarding the door. One of them looked pale and could barely stand straight, while the other looked like he wanted to be anywhere but standing near the ill man.

'The bloody flux is killing more of our men than the Franks did!' One jarl waved his arms in the air. 'Many of my men are too ill to stand and the others don't want to go near them!' some of the other jarls grunted in agreement as Jarl Ragnar sat on a large chair on a raised platform. Jarl Ragnar had aged in the time they were in Paris. His face had more lines than before and his eyes were red and puffy, but there was still the same fierceness in them that Ulf had seen before. Even Ragnar's hair seemed to have lost some of its colour.

Ulf glanced around the hall, glad that he did not have to lead this army. The walls were decorated with brightly coloured images showing women with wings, a young man leading others somewhere, and even a mother with a baby. Ulf knew the images were from their religion, but he never understood any of them. There had been banners hanging from the rafters, but Jarl Ragnar had them removed and burnt on the day after they had taken Paris.

'Ulf,' Jarl Leif, the dark-haired jarl, greeted him. The man had warmed to Ulf over the spring, as Ulf had spent most of his time in the hall with Jarl Ragnar and his jarls. The Norsemen didn't need

Ulf to watch them, and neither did they want him to. Halstein was their leader now and Ulf wondered if the man would try to make himself a jarl when they returned home.

Ulf looked at the jarl and scowled when he saw how thin he looked. But then they were all thinner. Food had run out and the hunting parties could not find enough in the forests around Paris to feed the five thousand men camped in the city and neither did there seem to be enough fish in the river. The barrels of wine and ale from the churches had run out many days ago, and all that was left to drink was the water from the river around the city. The same river they had thrown the dead Franks into. The same river the men shat and pissed in. 'There are fewer jarls than yesterday,' Ulf said, and Jarl Leif nodded.

'Jarl Egil has the flux. The poor bastard has been shitting blood all night, or so I've been told.'

Ulf grimaced and turned his attention to Jarl Ragnar, who nodded a greeting to him.

'You said we'd be gone by now, Jarl Ragnar!' the jarl who was speaking continued. 'You promised us untold riches and instead we're dying while bleeding out of our arses!'

Ulf grimaced again as the other jarls all spoke out. He had thought that hanging was the worst way to go for a warrior, but the flux was worse than anything he had ever seen before.

'And to make things worse,' Jarl Leif whispered to Ulf. 'We've heard that King Charles is riding around his kingdom to gather more men. He means to fight us.'

Ulf scowled at that news. 'The men are too weak to fight.'

'Aye, they are. That's why everyone is complaining. They all know it.'

Ulf scrutinised the jarls and saw from the creased eyebrows and thin lips that none of them were pleased. 'So what is he planning?'

Jarl Leif shrugged. 'I don't know. Only Ragnar and the gods know that.'

Ulf turned his attention back to Jarl Ragnar as he raised his hand to silence the jarls. One by one, they fell silent and watched Jarl Ragnar, who was still sitting on the raised chair as if he was a king. Ulf wondered if that was what his ambition was.

Jarl Ragnar sighed before he stood and faced the jarls in front of him. Ulf noticed how some of them tensed, but knew they wouldn't attack. Not with Jarl Ragnar's hirdmen nearby. 'My friends, the gods know I share your anger. My men are also suffering from the flux and just yesterday, I found two of them dead. One by his own hand.' He looked around the jarls, perhaps hoping for some sympathy, but he got none. 'You've all heard that King Charles is gathering more men. He seems to think that he can defeat us and chase us out of his city.'

'He doesn't need to. The bloody flux will do that for him,' one jarl said and a few of the others grunted. Ulf saw a flash of annoyance on Jarl Ragnar's face before he nodded.

'It won't come to that.' Jarl Ragnar stared at the jarl.

'How can you be so sure?'

Jarl Ragnar smiled. 'Because what I know is that King Charles is facing a rebellion from within his own family and, even though he is trying to raise more men, he is in no position to fight us.'

Ulf glanced at Jarl Leif, who shrugged. Many of the jarls seemed surprised by this, as well as they frowned at each other.

'How do you know this?' one jarl asked.

Jarl Ragnar nodded to someone behind them and when Ulf looked over his shoulder, he saw one of the jarl's men bring an old priest towards them. 'This man speaks our tongue. Says he learnt it from Danish traders.'

'And he told you this?' Jarl Leif asked and Ragnar nodded.

'Aye, that and many other things.' Jarl Ragnar put his hand on the shoulder of the old priest, who seemed to shrink as he stared at his feet. Apart from his dirty clothes and face, the old priest was unharmed, but the man looked thinner than a draugr and Ulf wondered how he had the strength to keep standing. 'Tell them what you told me about the flux, priest.'

There was a moment's silence and Ulf doubted the priest would say anything until he raised his head and with a firm voice, he said, 'The bloody flux is a punishment from God on you heathens! Where iron and wood have failed, our Lord will succeed. He has damned all of you to suffer and to die a slow and agonising death, just as your evil souls will suffer in the flames of hell for all eternity.'

The jarls all gasped in shock and many grabbed the pendants they wore around their necks as Jarl Ragnar smiled. Ulf resisted the urge to do the same as he glanced at the image of a man leading others on the wall of the hall. He thought of warnings Skadi had given him, but since the fall of Paris there had been no sign of the volva and neither was his sleep plagued by dreams of snakes and wolves. He thanked the gods for that every day, as it meant that the threat to him and Ragnar must have been over. But he couldn't help but wonder if they had not underestimated the Christian god.

'And what must we do to save ourselves from the punishment of your god?' Jarl Ragnar asked the priest.

The priest glared at the jarls before he spoke. 'You must fall to your knees and pray for mercy! You must denounce your false gods and accept our Lord the Saviour as the one veritable God!'

The jarls all shouted out and Ulf felt the violence in the air as they swore at the priest and demanded his head. To Ulf's surprise, the priest stood his ground and glared at the jarls, perhaps believing his god would protect him.

'And what else did you say?' Jarl Ragnar asked as the jarls fell silent again.

'You must fast to show penance.'

Ulf glanced at Jarl Leif, who shrugged before Jarl Ragnar explained. 'He means we can only eat once a day and no meat or ale and wine.'

'We already don't have any ale or wine,' someone said, and the others agreed.

Jarl Ragnar nodded. 'Aye, we don't. All we have is water to drink.'

'And that's probably what's causing the flux,' Jarl Leif said, and again Jarl Ragnar nodded.

'That and the streets covered in shit. What is happening is no punishment from the Christian god, but we will take the advice of the priest. Ration what food we have, only one meal per day, and make sure the men only drink boiled water. Our priest friend informed me it kills the evil in the water.'

'The men will not like that,' one jarl said.

'Then tell them it's that or dying of the flux,' Jarl Ragnar said and the jarl nodded.

'And that will get rid of the flux?' Ulf asked, which startled some of the jarls, who didn't seem to know he was there.

'So the priest says,' Jarl Ragnar said.

'And what do we do about King Charles?' a jarl asked.

Jarl Ragnar looked at the jarl and then said, 'We talk to him.'

'Talk to him?' The jarl frowned.

'Our priest friend has sent a letter to King Charles on my behalf. King Charles has agreed to meet to discuss terms.'

'What terms?' the jarl asked as the others frowned.

'To surrender Paris to him.'

'It could be a trap,' Ulf said before anyone could respond, as he thought again of Skadi's warning.

'Aye, which is why I'm not going.'

'Then who is?' Jarl Leif asked.

'You.' Jarl Ragnar looked at the dark-haired jarl. 'You will meet King Charles at a monastery not far from Paris and give him my terms.'

'So if it is a trap, then Jarl Leif dies and not you?' one jarl said and Jarl Ragnar scowled at the man.

'Do you want to go in his place?' The jarl looked away as those around him laughed. 'For what it's worth, we have King Charles's word that my men will be unharmed.'

Jarl Leif puffed his chest out. 'I'll do it, Jarl Ragnar.'

Jarl Ragnar smiled at Jarl Leif. 'Good man.'

'And what are your terms?' Ulf asked, not caring if it was his place or not. The other jarls all nodded to show that they also wanted to know as Jarl Ragnar smiled at Ulf.

'Simple. Pay us for the priests and allow us to leave with all our plunder or we burn Paris and the lands around it.'

Chapter 38

A few days later, Ulf rode out of Paris with Jarl Leif and his men. Ulf had been surprised when Jarl Leif asked him to join and had considered turning him down, but then decided against it. The Norsemen did not need him to watch over them and he didn't want to stay in Paris. Not with the stench of the flux still in the air.

They had done what the priest had suggested, apart from praying to the Christian god. Large pots they had found in the houses were filled with water from the river and were placed over large fires until the water boiled. The men had been told not to eat vegetables or meat, only the grain from the grain stores in the city. Although there wasn't much left as they were still in spring. The men had complained at first, but they knew the alternative was to get the flux and no one wanted that. Not after seeing how the others had suffered from it. The hardest part was only eating once a day, and Ulf had struggled to sleep as his rumbling stomach kept him awake at night. And seeing the tired look on Jarl Leif's face, he knew he wasn't the only one. It had only been a few days, but each day there were fewer men with the flux. But there wasn't much they could do for those already ill. Those men would either get better or die. It was up to the Norns.

The horses they rode were found in the stables behind the main hall, and Jarl Ragnar had given strict orders that they be left unharmed. Along with any other horses they found around the city. That meant they had enough horses for thirty men, but the hardest part was finding men well enough for the journey. The old priest rode with them as well, his lined face set in a scowl as if he thought this was beneath him. Or perhaps it was just because he had failed to convert the Danes.

'Where is this monastery?' Ulf asked to distract himself as they rode along the river. Bloated bodies littered the riverbanks, and many more had stomachs ripped open and mangled faces as foxes and wolves feasted on the dead.

Jarl Leif glanced at the old priest and smiled as they rode north. 'Near where we fought his army.'

Ulf almost pulled on the reins of his horse as his heart thudded in his chest. 'Where we fought his army?'

Jarl Leif nodded. 'Aye. The gods do like their games.'

And they enjoy making me a part of their games, he thought as he clenched his fist around the reins of his horse.

They rode in silence for half a day before the priest pointed to a large monastery made of white stone dominating the landscape. Ulf looked to where he guessed the river was and wondered if Thorir's body was still hanging from the tree with the Franks, or if they had been cut down and buried. His hands trembled at the thought and he focused on the monastery to take his mind away from that day.

The monastery looked like any other Christian church he had seen in Francia, but this one was surrounded by a black smudge which Ulf guessed was what remained of King Charles's army. White tents were scattered amongst the smudge and the smoke from campfires drifted to the sky and almost obscured the monastery. The old priest tutted at the sight before them as Jarl Leif glanced at the men behind him.

'You still think it could be a trap?' Ulf asked him and the jarl scowled.

'We best pray for the thunder god's protection because we will not leave here alive if it is.'

'Your false god will not protect you,' the old priest said with a creased brow as Ulf rubbed the hilt of Ormstunga. 'And besides, King Charles will not spill the blood of heathens near this sacred monastery.'

Ulf and Jarl Leif raised an eyebrow at the priest. 'Why not?' Jarl Leif asked.

'This monastery is very important to King Charles. It is his favourite, and he was determined to protect it from you heathens.'

'So he abandoned the people of Paris to protect a building?' Ulf felt the sparks of his anger in the pit of his stomach as he remembered the woman who had killed Ragnvald and her boy. He had often wondered what had happened to them. A few days after the attack, he had taken Halstein and some of the Norsemen to the house so they could retrieve Ragnvald's body. It had been untouched, and the house was empty, so Ulf hoped the woman had got out with her son.

'God works in mysterious ways,' the priest said, and Ulf almost punched him off his horse. Jarl Leif must have sensed his anger because he moved between Ulf and the priest.

'What is so important about this monastery?' the jarl asked.

'Saint Denis is buried here.' The priest beamed with pride as Ulf and Jarl Leif frowned at each other, but before they could ask who that was, the priest continued, 'He was the first bishop of Paris and was decapitated by the Romans. They say he carried his head for four leagues to here and pointed to the spot where he wanted to be buried. Some time later, the monastery was built to remember Saint Denis and what his faith in God allowed him to achieve.'

Jarl Leif laughed, which only seemed to annoy the old priest. 'And I thought our stories of the gods were strange. Sounds like one of Loki's tricks, if you ask me.'

Ulf didn't know who the Romans were and didn't really care, but he had to agree with Jarl Leif. It did sound like something Loki would do.

The men tensed as they neared the camp and Jarl Leif had to tell them to keep their hands away from their weapons. They might have been dressed for battle, with their brynjas and helmets, apart from Ulf, who still didn't have one, but they were not here to fight.

The Frankish warriors, their faces stained with dirt and looking gaunt, stood up and glared at the small party of Danes that rode through their camp towards the monastery. The old priest raised his hand and spoke to the Franks in their tongue and to Ulf, it sounded like he was repeating the same words over and over again.

'What's he doing?' one of the Danes asked.

'He is blessing them in the name of their god,' Jarl Leif said as he scrutinised the Franks. 'And they'll need it because if their king does not agree with Jarl Ragnar's terms, then most of them will feed the crows and it'll take a lifetime to wash their blood from these lands.'

Ulf frowned as he studied the Franks and realised that Jarl Leif was right as they stopped in front of the church. Most of these men looked like farmers, with their wiry limbs and bleak faces. None of them had any armour other than the thick tunics they wore and what surprised Ulf the most was that behind the glares directed at the Danes, Ulf saw the fear they were trying to hide. The Franks might have heavily outnumbered Jarl Leif's little party, but every single one of the Danes looked like a warrior. They all wore brynjas and had swords on their hips, along with the shields on their backs. They were tall and broad-shouldered and had the eyes of men used to killing. And then there was Ulf with his scarred face. He saw one man cross himself the way Christians liked to do when he saw Ulf, and Ulf glanced at Jarl Leif and wondered if that was not the real reason he had asked him to come along.

Ulf turned his attention towards the group who waited for them and saw the first proper warriors of the West Frankish king's army. Six tall men stood behind three priests and scowled at the Danes. They wore brynjas as well, although theirs were longer and went to their knees. Each man had a spear and a sword on their waist, but still there was a hint of fear in their eyes even as they tried to look imposing. Ulf wondered if they had been on the other side of the river when Jarl Ragnar slaughtered half of their king's army as the old priest greeted them.

The priests spoke while the warriors glared at each other as warriors did. Ulf glanced around and spotted a raven sitting on the roof of the church. He rubbed the hilt of Ormstunga as he wondered what that meant. Was Odin making sure that no deal would be struck because he wanted more bloodshed?

'Ulf?' Jarl Leif's voices broke Ulf from his thoughts and he realised they had all dismounted apart from him. He nodded and got off his horse before he followed them into the church.

'Told you the Norse were strange,' one of the Danes said and another laughed, which made the priests scowl, but Ulf ignored them. The Norse thought the same of the Danes and they both felt the same of the Swedes and the Geats, who most likely thought the same of them. That was just the way of things.

'So where is this headless priest buried?' one warrior asked, and even Ulf glanced around the church as the old priest shushed the man. The noise made a group of people by the altar look up and the old priest quickly apologised before he bowed towards the group.

He said something to the group, who parted to reveal the king of the West Franks. The man looked older than he had done after the battle by the river. His face also seemed thinner, although it was hard to make sure from where Ulf stood. King Charles had thick black hair and, despite his current situation, was still dressed in a fine tunic and with a fur-trimmed cloak around his shoulders. His fingers were covered in golden rings with large stones on them and he wore a thick gold band on his head, which, like the rings, had a large gemstone in it.

Jarl Leif gave a soft whistle as he must have noticed the same. 'Looks like he is wearing all of Paris's wealth on him.'

'Aye, we should just kill the bastard and take it so we can go home,' one of the Danes said, and Ulf noticed the smile in Jarl Leif's beard.

'Tempting, but no. We are here hunting a larger price, don't forget that.'

The priest said something to the king before he turned to the Danes. 'Before you sits King Charles of the West Franks, son of Louis the Emperor and grandson of the great Emperor Charles. You must bow before his greatness.'

Jarl Leif hawked and spat. 'We bow before no man.'

There was a hiss from the Franks and Ulf felt the tension rise inside the church as King Charles spoke. His voice was softer than Ulf thought a king's should be, but then the man had narrow shoulders and, as the battle at the river had shown, was no warrior.

'The mighty King Charles says he will forgive your disrespect only this once, but the next time you defile the house of our Lord, he will have your head cut off.'

Jarl Leif smiled. 'Tell him that if he wants my head, then he needs to come get it himself. Not send someone else to get it.'

The old priest paled and when he spoke, what he said seemed much shorter than what Jarl Leif had said. King Charles nodded and then grimaced as he glanced at Ulf, who didn't react.

'The king says you have brought nothing but death and misery to his lands,' the old priest said after his king spoke at length. 'You are a curse from the devil. You have killed innocent priests and destroyed churches along the river. Stolen sacred artefacts and pillaged anything of value. Why should he make a deal with you now?'

'Innocent priests and churches,' Ulf growled, unable to hold his anger. 'What about the people who work the lands to feed your precious priests? The people of Paris who died while he cowered in this place? Is he not their king? Is it not his duty to protect them as a jarl must protect those who pay landskyld to him? Like Thor protects us from the giants.'

Jarl Leif put a hand on Ulf's chest to calm him as the priest paled and the king of the West Franks glared at him. He might not have understood Ulf's words, but Ulf's tone was unmistakable. The Frankish warriors' hands went to their swords as the old priest pleaded in their tongue.

'The Bear-Slayer wants to make sure we all die here,' one Dane said, but Ulf didn't care. He was tired of seeing those deemed less worthy die for someone else's greed. The least this so-called king could do was pretend to care about them and not just his priests.

'Calm yourself, Ulf. Do not anger their king.' Jarl Leif glanced at him, and Ulf nodded as he took a deep breath to calm the flames of his anger. The old priest said none of that to his king. Instead, he said,

'My King wants you to leave Paris, as well as his kingdom.'

Jarl Leif nodded as he thought about it, and then said, 'Why should we leave? Jarl Ragnar has become quite fond of Paris.'

The old priest translated this to his king, who scowled as he listened. Those around him, wealthy men Ulf guessed, were his jarls and other important men, shook their heads, but they stayed silent.

Jarl Leif smiled, and Ulf knew the Franks were not going to like what they were about to hear. 'But the gods know he is keen to go home as well, so if you want him to leave, then you must pay Jarl Ragnar ten thousand pounds of gold to leave Paris.'

CHAPTER 39

ULF HEARD THE GODS laugh in the eruption of noise as the priest translated Jarl Leif's words with a trembling voice. The Frankish king looked like he was about to collapse, one of the priests with him did, and the Danes all tensed as they prepared for an attack. Even Ulf's hands went to his weapons as one of the Frankish nobles shouted something.

'He wants to know how you dare to ask for such a sum.' The old priest looked like he wanted to sit down as he translated the words.

'Jarl Ragnar holds Paris. He has an army of five thousand warriors, and he has already defeated your king in battle. That is why he dares to ask for such a sum.'

The tension inside the church increased as Frankish and Danish warriors glared at each other. The voices of Ulf's ancestors stirred in his ears and he realised he wanted the Franks to attack. He wanted to cut them down and spill their blood in their church for not defending the people of Paris.

King Charles barked an order and stood up. The man was taller than Ulf had thought as he glared at them with his fists clenched by his sides. If he was trying to look imposing, he failed as he spoke in a strained voice.

'The king says his army has grown since that battle and he knows that many of your warriors are too ill to fight. That God is punishing them for their crimes.' The priest crossed himself as he translated the words, but Jarl Leif only smiled.

'Peasants and farmers are no match for our warriors, even if many of them are ill.' Jarl Leif waited as the priest spoke his words to King Charles. 'And besides, the gods know you can't afford to have them all killed as they attempt to chase us out of Paris. And neither can you sit around and wait for us all to die of the flux. Summer is on us and most of your so-called army need to work the land, otherwise you'll have no food to feed your people.'

King Charles and his nobles glared at Jarl Leif as the old priest translated his words and just when Ulf thought he was going to have them killed, the king sighed and sat down. With that, the tension left the church as if the gods had swept it away and they all knew Jarl Ragnar's gamble had paid off.

The king stared around the church for a long time as if he was debating something with himself, and when he finally spoke, Ulf could hear the defeat in his voice. Not even the priests or the nobles protested as the old priest translated King Charles's words to the smiling Danes.

'My king cannot pay such a large sum, but he will give Jarl Ragnar six thousand pounds of gold and silver and will allow him to leave his kingdom unmolested.'

Jarl Leif pretended to think about it, even though Ulf knew he would accept. This was far more than Jarl Ragnar had hoped for, but Ulf knew that instead of saving his kingdom, King Charles had doomed it. 'Jarl Ragnar accepts.'

Before the old priest could translate the words, King Charles said something. The old priest nodded and turned to Jarl Leif. 'The king says he needs some time to collect the payment and that he will have it delivered to Paris.'

Jarl Leif nodded. 'Tell your king not to take too long. Odin knows there's only so long we can stop five thousand men from killing his priests.'

The old priest started translating but then paused and carried on as if he chose not to mention something. When he was done, the king of the West Franks glared at the Danes before he nodded.

Ulf guessed the meeting was over and was glad for it. He wanted to get away from these Frankish nobles who cared little for those they were supposed to protect. They left the church and mounted their horses in silence, the Danes tense as if they expected an attack from the Franks. But none of the Frankish nobles inside the church or the men outside said or did anything as they rode out of their camp.

'How much is six thousand pounds of gold?' one Dane asked and Ulf wondered the same.

'That must be more than what Fafnir is guarding,' another added to the nods of the others.

'Then we better hope the dragon doesn't hear of this or we might face his wrath.' Jarl Leif glanced at the sky as if he was searching for a dragon amongst the clouds. 'And he will definitely have more bite than these Franks.' The jarl hawked and spat, and the Danes rubbed the Mjöllnir pendants around their necks.

Ulf also glanced at the clouds, but not to look for a dragon. He doubted Fafnir would care about their gold. Not when he already had so much of his own. He glanced at the clouds and prayed that the king of the West Franks did not take his time to collect the payment for Ragnar. Ulf was tired and had had enough of this kingdom. He wanted to go back to Denmark so he could free Eldrid and then... Ulf frowned. He did not know what then.

***

The Danes cheered as the four carts loaded with large chests approached the eastern bridge. The stone walls of Paris rattled at the noise and birds from all the trees which surrounded the city took to the sky. Even the gods must have wondered what the noise was.

'Well, if Fafnir didn't know about this, he will now,' Jarl Leif said as he stood beside Jarl Ragnar and Ulf on the wall overlooking the bridge. Jarl Ragnar, looking thinner than he did when they had taken Paris, frowned at Jarl Leif before he turned his attention back to the carts. It had been a month since the meeting with King Charles and Ulf knew that many of the jarls had questioned whether the Frankish king would keep his word. Even Ulf had wondered the same, but Jarl Ragnar had been firm in his belief that King Charles would deliver the payment.

The flux had lost its grip on the warriors, but not before many more men had died from it. The priest's advice had worked. But the men were hungry, and so was Ulf. The Norse warriors had got into a fight with some of the Danes over a deer they had caught and ten men had been hanged. Five of the Norse and five of the Danes. Halstein was struggling to keep the Norse contained to their camp by the eastern gate, but he had not been the only one. The Danes were getting restless as well. They couldn't go out raiding nearby farms because Jarl Ragnar did not want to do anything that would cause King Charles to change his mind. So every day, as the flux lost its grip, the tension between the men only grew. Ulf rubbed the Mjöllnir pendant around his neck and thanked the gods that the payment from King Charles had finally arrived.

'The man is a bigger fool than I thought,' Jarl Ragnar said with furrowed brows.

Jarl Leif nodded. 'Aye, he doesn't realise that by paying us to leave, he is only going to encourage more jarls to bring their ships to his lands.'

Jarl Ragnar scanned the surrounding land as he gripped the stone wall. Ulf did the same, but saw no sign of an army hiding amongst the trees or any other signs of a trap.

'It's quiet,' Jarl Leif said as Ragnar glanced at Ulf.

'How many Norsemen have you got left?'

Ulf sighed and looked over his shoulder at where the Norse were standing. Like everyone else, they were thinner than before and Ulf knew they were all ready to go home. 'About forty, I guess.'

Jarl Ragnar nodded again. 'Send them to collect the carts. Tell them to chase the Franks away. I don't want them to enter the city.'

Ulf scowled. He knew why Jarl Ragnar was sending the Norse instead of the Danes. 'I'll go with them.'

'You don't have to, Ulf.' Jarl Ragnar looked at him with raised eyebrows.

'I'm not sending my countrymen to their deaths without facing it with them.'

Ulf turned before Jarl Ragnar could say anything and walked towards the Norse warriors, who were all staring at him. Over their time in Paris, they had warmed to Ulf. He defended them against accusations from other jarls and had fought hard to get them enough food. He knew they would never accept him as one of their own, but at least Ulf slept better at night.

'Jarl Ragnar wants us to bring the carts in.'

'Why us?' one man asked and glanced at the surrounding Danes.

'Because if there is a trap, then he'd rather us Norse die than any of his Danes,' Halstein said, and Ulf nodded.

'And I bet the Bear-Slayer gets to stay behind,' one warrior said.

Ulf nodded. 'Aye, but I'm coming with.' He went to his sleeping mat and picked up his brynja. It shone brighter than the stars, and Ulf knew his weapons were sharper than anything the dwarfs of Svartalfheim could make. Most days there had been nothing to do. So, like most of the warriors, Ulf had spent his time sharpening his weapons and cleaning his armour.

'Why?' Halstein asked him and Ulf shrugged as he pulled his brynja over his head and tightened his belt around his waist. Around him, the other Norsemen were busy putting their armour on as well, but they all watched Ulf as they waited for his response.

'Someone needs to make sure you don't steal one of the carts,' Ulf said and was glad that some of the Norsemen smiled at his response.

Halstein, smiling as well, nodded at Ulf. 'Everyone knows Danes can't count higher than one, so they won't notice if one cart goes missing.'

Ulf grabbed his shield and when the rest of the Norse were ready, he led them out of the eastern gate. He glanced at Jarl Ragnar, who nodded at him before he disappeared from view.

'What are the chances that the Danes will rush out to help us if this is a trap?' one man asked and Halstein smiled.

'We all know they'd just stand here and watch as we kill anyone dumb enough to attack us. Odin favours the Norse. That is why we are the better warriors and why the Danes hate us.'

Ulf raised an eyebrow at Halstein, who had his eyes fixed on the four carts in front of them. The drivers of the carts sat and waited as the Norsemen walked towards them at a comfortable pace. Not too fast to be caught out by anyone, but not too slow so the Danes would think they were afraid, while Ulf watched the driver in the first cart, certain that he would give the signal to spring the ambush. The Norse warriors had their shields in front of them as they scanned the area around the carts. Ulf felt their nervousness. He was nervous himself and struggled to stop his shield from trembling in his hand, but as they reached the first cart, they all breathed a sigh of relief. The drivers on the carts were pale as they stared at Ulf's scarred face and after he glanced at the trees in the distance, he gave the order for the Norse to throw the drivers from the carts.

The Franks wasted no time and bolted for the safety of the trees and Ulf waited a few more heartbeats. His limbs trembled in anticipation as his grey eyes scanned the surrounding landscape, while his ears strained as he listened out for any noise that would warn of an attack. But all he heard were the birds singing from the branches and the water splashing over rocks in the river.

'Nothing,' Halstein said with an incredulous look on his face. 'There really is no trap, no ambush?'

The other Norse warriors moved around the carts and shook the chests or hit with their shields, but all the chests sounded full as Ulf glanced back at the walls of Paris. He felt Jarl Ragnar's eyes on him, as well as the tension from the Danes.

Taking a deep breath, Ulf turned to the Norse. 'Let's get these carts into the city.'

Halstein, his eyes still scanning the surrounding landscape, nodded and gave the order. Four Norse warriors got onto the front of the carts while others jumped onto the back, their weapons ready. Ulf, along with Halstein and a handful of men, waited as the carts were taken over the bridge and only when they reached the gates did Ulf and the others turn and run back to the safety of the walls.

Inside the city, the Danes were cheering so loud that Ulf thought his head was going to explode as they surrounded the carts. Hands reached out for the chests as if the men wanted to make sure they were real when Jarl Ragnar's voice boomed over the noise.

'I promised you all riches far greater than anything you have ever seen!' He spread his arms wide as he stood on the wall. 'The gods know I am a man of my word!' He gave the signal, and Jarl Leif jumped onto one cart and opened the chests to the gasps of everyone around.

Ulf had to blink a few times before his eyes adjusted to the bright contents inside the chest. Gold coins and jewellery shone brighter than the sun, while gems of different colours glistened like the stars on a clear night. The men had to step back, so they weren't blinded by the treasure inside the chests. Ulf glanced at the Norsemen on the other carts and nodded at them. They cheered as they opened the chests to confirm that those were also filled with gold and silver, as well as different-sized gems.

Ulf couldn't help but rub the hilt of Ormstunga as he prayed that this didn't draw too much attention from the gods. Loki loved nothing more than to pluck a man's dreams from under his nose, and even Odin liked to ruin a man's plans just to amuse himself. But as before, he could not sense Skadi's presence to warn him that the gods were up to something.

'Do we get to kill the priests now?' one jarl shouted over the noise and his men around him cheered, but Jarl Ragnar shook his head.

'No, the priests will remain unharmed.'

'Why? We got what we wanted!' The jarl scowled at Ragnar, who scowled back.

'Because the All-Father knows I am a man of my word, and I told King Charles that his priests will not be harmed if he pays us to leave. He has kept up his part and now I must uphold my part. Any man who is caught or suspected of hurting any of the priests or people of Paris will be tied to a stone and thrown into the river.' He glared at the men as a tense silence fell over them all. Many of them shook their heads at the jarl who had spoken out, and even Ulf wondered why the man had done that. After a while, Jarl Ragnar smiled again. 'Load the ships, men. It's time to go home.'

CHAPTER 40

ULF STOOD ON THE prow of Jarl Ragnar's ship and savoured the sea air as they approached Jelling. Sea birds hovered above the ships, screaming at the men for scraps of food while men swore at the birds when they were shat on. Small fishing ships moved out of the way before waving their greeting to the warriors who sang songs of past battles and made new songs and poems of this raid.

Jarl Ragnar's victory over the Frankish king by the river was a popular topic for the men to sing about, but every time they did, all Ulf could think of was Thorir and how he would have to tell his parents that their son was dead.

The men were in good spirits, and even Jarl Ragnar had a smile on his face. And the gods knew they had good reason to be. They had left Paris as soon as the ships were loaded with chests and anything of value they had found in Paris. King Charles had stayed true to his word, and the ships were left alone as they rowed downriver towards the sea, but that had only encouraged the Danes to raid farmlands and small towns along the river. Jarl Ragnar did not stop any of the ships from doing that and had even sent one of his own to attack a large farmstead. There weren't many riches to be taken from these places, but the ships came back filled with food and wine, something more valuable to the hungry men of Jarl Ragnar.

At night, they camped along the river and feasted, and even Ulf had to admit that he had enjoyed the first sip of ale he took. Once they reached the island camp, the spoils of the raid were shared out amongst the jarls, although Jarl Ragnar kept the largest share for himself. True to his word, Jarl Ragnar had allowed the Norsemen to keep their share of the plunder and had even rewarded them with more treasure for their part in taking Paris. The Norse warriors had cheered and Ulf had been thanked, but as they departed for Norway, he had stayed behind.

'You could come with us to Sygnafylki,' Halstein had said and many of the Norsemen agreed, but Ulf shook his head.

'Not yet. I'll return to Norway when the Norns decide it's time for me to.'

'And how do you know this is not that time?' Halstein had frowned at him.

Ulf had only shrugged. 'It doesn't feel right.'

Halstein nodded and the two men had gripped each other's arms. 'I hope we meet again, Ulf Bear-Slayer.'

'So do I,' Ulf had said with a smile before watching their ship leave the island and row towards the sea.

Lost in his thoughts, Ulf did not realise that Jarl Ragnar's ship had docked and shook his head to clear his mind before he turned to see Jarl Ragnar smiling at him.

'Has anyone ever told you you think too much?'

Ulf smiled. 'Aye, many times.'

'And yet you still do it. That is why men feel uneasy around you.'

Ulf shrugged. 'I was raised on a small farm away from everyone else. I'm not used to being around other people.'

Jarl Ragnar nodded. 'And yet you have accomplished much for a warrior so young. No wonder people say you are blessed by the gods.' Ulf shrugged again. He never felt blessed by the gods, but he knew there was no point in trying to convince others of that. 'So what now for the great Bear-Slayer?'

Ulf glanced at the sky and watched as seabirds flew in circles or hovered over fishing boats. The smell of fish and sweaty men filled his nostrils as the noise of shouting fishermen and warriors assaulted his ears. 'I have some business to take care of and then I don't know. Whatever the Norns have decided for me, I guess. What about you?'

Jarl Ragnar glanced towards the centre of Jelling and smiled. 'First, I'll tell my cousin, the king, of the raid and of how weak the Franks are. Maybe convince him to allow more raids.'

Ulf nodded as he looked around the ship. Most of the men were busy unloading the chests and captives and weren't paying any attention to them. 'And if he refuses?'

This time, Jarl Ragnar glanced around his ship before he shrugged. 'My cousin is old. He has been a great king, but perhaps it's time for someone younger to take his place.'

'Someone who just led one of the largest raids and defeated the king of the West Franks?'

Jarl Ragnar smiled, but did not respond to the question. Instead, he said, 'You should join me, Ulf. The gods know you and me could do many great things together.'

Ulf scratched his beard as he thought about it. A part of him wanted to say no, but he had nothing else to do and nowhere else to go. And Ulf would not make the same mistake again by trying to be something other than what he was. A warrior and a wolf. 'Perhaps, but first there is something I need to do and a favour to ask of you.'

Jarl Ragnar raised his eyebrow. 'A favour?'

'The brothers, Ingolfr and Tormod. Allow them to trade in Jelling again. They do not deserve to be punished for my mistakes.'

Jarl Ragnar rubbed the side of his face where Ulf had punched him the previous winter before he smiled. 'Done. I'll send men out to every known market in Denmark and tell the brothers they are welcome back in Jelling.'

Ulf nodded his gratitude to the jarl. 'Thank you.'

They left the ship and walked towards the centre of Jelling, each man enjoying their own thoughts as the townspeople stepped aside to give them space. Jarl Ragnar greeted those he knew, and many took his arm in a forearm grip and smiled warmly at him. Some asked about the raid and others about family members, while Ulf looked around the large town and wondered if he could ever live in a place like that. As someone bumped into him, he decided he couldn't. Ulf preferred the open space and the fresh smells of the countryside.

Ulf and Jarl Ragnar reached the large hall of King Horik, and both men stared at the wooden building as the king's banners fluttered in the breeze. Four large warriors in full armour and carrying spears and swords guarded the door, and Ulf was certain there were more warriors inside the hall.

'You want to join us inside? Meet the king?' Jarl Ragnar asked.

Ulf scowled at the hall, with its carved timber posts and the dragon head on the roof, and shook his head. He had had enough of kings.

Jarl Ragnar smiled as if he expected the answer, before he handed Ulf two large pouches. Ulf grunted at their weight in his hands and knew there was enough in those pouches not only to free Eldrid, but to buy the old folks' farmland and have enough to spend the winter comfortably. 'Go take care of your business, Bear-Slayer. And when you're done, come find me so we can plan our next raid. I hear Britain is ripe for the plucking.'

Ulf nodded his thanks as he gripped Jarl Ragnar's forearm. 'Thank you, Jarl Ragnar.'

He left the jarl at the king's hall and made his way to the nearest stables, where he bought himself a horse. Ulf hated the animals, but he did not want to walk to the old folks' farm. Especially not after what had happened last time.

As he left the stables with his new horse, Jarl Leif stood there smiling at him.

'The Bear-Slayer is leaving us? So you decided not to join Jarl Ragnar?'

Ulf raised an eyebrow, but knew he shouldn't have been surprised. Warriors liked to talk more than their women did, and news always spread fast amongst them. 'I haven't decided yet.'

The dark-haired jarl nodded, but his knowing smile suggested he believed Ulf would be back. And perhaps Ulf would. 'Well, Ulf Bear-Slayer. I'll pray to the gods that you return and join us.' He gripped Ulf's forearm. 'I know we didn't start off on the right foot, but Thor knows it was an honour to fight beside you, even if you're still growing your first beard.'

Ulf smiled, even though he was about twenty-two winters old and he guessed not that much younger than Jarl Leif. 'Aye, it was an honour, Jarl Leif.'

Jarl Leif nodded and before he left, he said, 'May the gods be with you, Bear-Slayer.'

'And you, Jarl Leif.' Ulf mounted his horse and rode out of Jelling. He was glad to get away from the crowded town and its smells, even if he was only there for less than half a day. But Ulf was eager to get back to the farm and pushed his horse as fast as she would go. The animal was placid, which Ulf preferred and obeyed his commands, and ran at a good pace for most of the day.

Ulf camped out in the open at nights and made a small fire, even though it wasn't really needed. The summer days were long and warm, and even when the sun went down, his cloak was enough to keep him warm. He ate food he had brought from the market in Jelling while his horse seemed content to graze on the land every time they stopped to rest.

Two days after leaving Jelling, Ulf saw the farmstead in the distance. A thin trail of smoke drifted towards the clouds from the house as two goats chased each other around the farmstead. The old man was sitting on his bench outside, perhaps enjoying the early afternoon sunshine, while near him, Ulf saw Eldrid emptying a bucket out. His heart raced when she straightened and seemed to stare in his direction, and he felt the weight of the pouches around his waist.

'You could turn around right now and live a comfortable life for many winters before you run out of coin,' Skadi's voice said from beside him, and Ulf almost fell off his horse. He turned to her and furrowed his brow as she stood there, her eyes fixed on the farmstead. Ulf never understood how she did this, but neither he nor the horse had sensed her approach. He looked around him and wondered where the volva had come from. The nearest forest wasn't close enough for her to walk from in the short time he had been standing there, but then he shook his head. He knew he would never understand.

'I owe her a debt.'

'Do you?' He heard the smile in Skadi's voice. 'Was it your hand that sold her into slavery?'

Ulf turned his attention back to the farmstead and saw Eldrid had not moved from where she was. 'No, but it was my hand that led to her being sold into slavery.'

'Be careful with her, young wolf. She has bigger teeth than you.' Skadi was about to turn and walk away when Ulf said,

'You were wrong.'

Skadi raised an eyebrow at him as the corner of her mouth curled into a smile, revealing some of her blackened teeth. 'Was I?'

'You said someone would be stabbed in the back. Either me or Jarl Ragnar, but neither of us were. We both survived.'

Skadi's smile grew larger as she tutted at Ulf as if he was still a young boy. 'Ah, young wolf. But Jarl Ragnar was stabbed in the back, and so were you. The gods are never wrong and neither am I.'

'But—' Ulf started before Skadi cut him off.

'Jarl Ragnar was betrayed by his cousin. A man he had trusted and thought of as an ally. And you, young wolf, wanted so much for Jarl Hakon to be your friend that you closed your eyes to how he was using you.' Skadi laughed as she walked towards the forest in the distance. 'We will meet again, young wolf. And remember, I am never wrong.'

Ulf frowned as he watched her walk away, her laughter being carried over the breeze, before he took a deep breath and nudged his heels into his horse's sides and rode towards the farmstead.

By the time he reached the farmhouse, both Asketill and Inga were standing outside, their hands covering their eyes from the sunshine. Eldrid stood behind them, her arms crossed on her chest as she scowled at him.

'See, woman. I told you it was him,' Asketill said as he grinned at Ulf. 'I told you he'd be back. Didn't I, Eldrid?' The old man glanced over his shoulder at Eldrid.

Ulf dismounted his horse and for a few heartbeats stood there, not sure of what to do. He had never returned to others from a raid before and did not know how to act. With one glance at Eldrid, he took one of the pouches from his belt. Ulf wasn't sure how much they had paid for her as he handed the pouch to Asketill.

'This is for Eldrid's freedom.'

The old man's eyes lit up like a hound who was given meat from the table as he opened the pouch and saw the gold and silver inside.

'That is much more than we paid for her,' Inga said after she gasped at the contents of the pouch.

'Quiet, woman.' Asketill closed the pouch and gripped it tightly as he looked at Eldrid. 'You hear that, girl? You are no longer a thrall. Ulf has freed you, like he said he would.'

To everyone's surprise, Eldrid only turned around and walked into the house. Ulf stared at the spot where she had been, not sure if he should follow her inside or wait for her to come out again.

'Give her time, Ulf,' Inga said. 'She worried about you, even if she won't admit it.'

Ulf nodded before Asketill asked, 'And where is Thorir? Did he go to his family's farm?'

Ulf shook his head, and the smiles fell from the old folks' faces. 'Thorir didn't make it. But he fought bravely and died a warrior's death,' Ulf lied. They did not need to know of what had happened and neither did Thorir's family. Let them believe he had done well and that he went to Valhalla.

'I'll let his family know,' Asketill said. 'They'll be glad to know that at least he went to Valhalla.' Ulf doubted that was true, but kept quiet as the old couple walked back into their home, their heads low as they digested the news of Thorir's death.

Ulf stood outside and stared at the clouds as they drifted overhead. Birds danced through the clouds as a large bird circled high above, and goats bleated from behind the house. He took a deep breath and savoured it as a calm settled over him.

'So now what? You expect me to become your wife now that you've freed me?' Eldrid said and the calm Ulf felt moments before was replaced by an annoyance that he had been snuck up on again.

He kept his eyes on the clouds as he said, 'I'm not expecting anything from you, Eldrid. I only wanted to free you from this place.'

Eldrid's laugh made him turn towards her. 'And where do I go? I have no home and no family. My mother is most likely dead and only the gods know where my brother is. This *place* is the closest I have to a home now.'

Ulf looked at the farmhouse behind Eldrid and shrugged. He had never thought of what would happen after he freed Eldrid.

Not only had he caused her to be here, but he had killed most of her family. Even if she didn't know it. 'I don't know, Eldrid. You can stay here, I guess.'

Eldrid stared at him and shook her head before she took a deep breath and crossed her arms. 'Thank you, Ulf. I might not have anywhere to go, but at least my fate is my own again. For that, I should at least be grateful.' Ulf nodded and guessed that was the best he was going to get. 'So now what for the mighty Bear-Slayer? Settle down and become a bóndi?'

Ulf shook his head before he turned and looked at the forest Skadi had disappeared into. He had spent a long time running away from what he was, and that had only caused him more problems. He might not enjoy killing and violence, but Ulf knew it was time he accepted who he was. 'No, the life of a bóndi is not for me. We both know that.'

'So what will you do, Bear-Slayer?' Ulf heard the smile in her voice as he glanced at the sky and followed the path of a hawk as it glided in the wind.

'I'll rest for a short while and then return to Jelling. Jarl Ragnar offered me a place in his army.'

'So no more pretending not to be a warrior?'

Ulf shook his head. 'You said it yourself, Eldrid. That's what I am.'

A warrior and a wolf.

Historical Note

When I first started writing the Ormstunga Saga, one thing I wanted to do was to have Ulf join legendary Vikings on their exploits across Europe and Britain. So, after a brief hiatus from the series, I decided to start with one of the best-known Vikings of the period. Ragnar Lothbrok. (He was also the first chronologically that Ulf could join.)

Ragnar Lothbrok is well known to anyone who has watched the Viking TV series or has read the Vǫlsunga saga. What makes Ragnar Lothbrok such an interesting character is that, much like Robin Hood and King Arthur, historians don't know if he really existed or not.

What they know, though, is that in 845 a Viking leader named Ragnar, or Reginherus, took a fleet of 120 ships and sailed up the Seine River to besiege Paris. Whether this was the legendary Ragnar Lothbrok or just another Viking named Ragnar is up for debate, but what happened during the raid and its impact on Europe was very real.

Ragnar's fleet entered the Seine in the beginning of March and rowed up the river, plundering settlements and towns on both banks. Even cities like Rouen and Carolivenna (modern day Chaussy) weren't spared. They did not appear to face much resistance, most likely because there wasn't much resistance to offer. King Charles of West Francia had been involved in a civil war with his brothers, which only ended two years earlier (a topic covered in my other series), and I doubted West Francia had much of an army to stop the Vikings. As they continued upriver, enriching themselves, news had spread of the attack which had sent many of those living alongside the river Seine fleeing the area, including the monks from the Abbey of St Denis, who took their relics and riches with them, and not leaving anything of value for the raiders other than wine, which I'm sure Ragnar's warriors enjoyed.

I came across the story of the four monks being found in an abandoned abbey in Chapter 24 during my research and although I can't know for certain if it really happened, as I only found in it one source; I added it to the novel. What I did not add, though, was that Ragnar punished the men who killed the monks and had even compensated the monastery for the death of the monks by paying them a large sum of silver.

King Charles did eventually muster an army and confronted Ragnar, but not on the walls of Paris, where he might have repelled Ragnar's attack. Instead, he chose a spot along the river Seine, near his favourite monastery, the Abbey of St Denis, which he was desperate to protect from the Vikings. Two things probably counted against King Charles. One was his lack of military experience. King Charles was only twenty years old at this point and had only been king for two years. The other thing was that Vikings avoided pitched battles and would often flee as soon as they spotted an approaching army. So, King Charles split his army in two and had them posted on both sides of the river, most likely to force Ragnar into a battle. King Charles, though, made one colossal mistake. The place he chose had no crossing nearby, which meant that the two halves of his army could not support each other. Ragnar must have seen this as well, because he attacked the smaller half of the Frankish army, killing most of them. After the battle, Ragnar hanged the 110 surviving Frankish warriors in front of King Charles and the rest of his army. Ragnar then boarded his ships with his army, planning to attack the other half, but they fled before Ragnar's ships could cross the river. Not to the safety of Paris, though, but to the Abbey of St Denis.

This left Ragnar with a clear path to Paris, and on the 28th of March, the day before Easter Sunday, his fleet of 120 ships, over five thousand warriors, reached the undefended Paris. Ragnar most likely planned this. He would have known that the churches would be full of people celebrating Easter and so would the church coffers. Perhaps there was a religious element to this as well by attacking a Christian city on one of the most important religious days.

What he might not have known, though, was that word of his fleet had reached Paris and by the time he arrived, most of the inhabitants had fled, taking with them most of their valuables, as well as any relics in the churches. So, when Ragnar's army attacked and captured the city on the 29th of March, Easter Sunday, they found it largely empty.

And it got little better for the Vikings after that, although it's not hard to imagine that they enjoyed the wine they had found in the wine cellar of the Abbey of St Germain. Ragnar was effectively trapped in Paris, while King Charles was busy gathering reinforcements for his army. To make matters even worse for Ragnar, dysentery had broken out amongst his men, most likely because of the filthy and cramped conditions they were living in. All this left Ragnar with no option but to reach out to King Charles.

What King Charles did next most likely changed the nature of Viking raids, not only in Europe but in Britain as well. Instead of taking his army and surrounding Paris, therefore trapping Ragnar and his five thousand men behind the walls of Paris and letting the dysentery and lack of food take care of them, King Charles offered to pay Ragnar nearly 6000 pounds of gold and silver to leave Paris. Not only that, but they could leave Paris and West Francia unmolested, as well as taking their plunder with them. King Charles effectively rewarded the Vikings for raiding his kingdom. It took King Charles about two months to collect this vast sum, which meant that the dysentery took a serious toll on the Vikings, but this was the first recorded case of Danegeld.

Why King Charles did this instead of fighting the Vikings would only really be known to him, but as I mentioned earlier, he was new to the crown and had other problems to deal with as well. He most likely wanted to get rid of the Vikings so that he could deal with a rebellion that was brewing against him in Aquitaine. But what he did was show the Vikings how they could make their raids even more lucrative, and they employed this tactic across Europe and in Britain after this. Attack a place and then demand Danegeld so that they would leave.

Ragnar returned to Denmark, sacking Hamburg along the way, and boasted to King Horik of Denmark about how weak the Franks were and how easy it was to raid them. There is a tale from a Christian witness who was in King Horik's court of how Rangar dropped to his knees and wept that the only resistance he met was from the dead St Germain, who supposedly caused the dysentery outbreak.

Unfortunately, we don't really know what happened to Ragnar after this. Some believe that Ragnar died soon after his return to Denmark and that he may have been poisoned by King Horik. King Horik might have seen Ragnar's newfound glory and wealth as a threat to his throne. Or perhaps it was to appease the Frankish Kings, especially Louis the German, who was furious about the attack on Hamburg. Others believe he went on to raid Britain and died in a pit of snakes after being captured by King Ælla of Northumbria, as mentioned in the sagas.

What we do know is that even to this day, his legacy inspires many, even historical fiction writers like me. I hope you enjoyed this novel and my take on the events of the Paris raid. I tried to stay loyal to the available facts, but of course I took some liberties where it was needed for the plot.

Thank you for reading *The Bear Slayer* and I hope to see you on Ulf's next adventure.

Glossary of Terms

Asgard: the home of the Norse Gods

Einherjar: Odin's army of fallen warriors who live in Valhalla, they will fight for him during Ragnarök

Fafnir: legendary dragon that guards a great treasure

Fenrir: giant wolf and offspring of Loki

Gjallarhorn: the horn of Heimdall which he sounds to warn the gods of the coming of Ragnarök

Gleipnir: the magical chain forged by the dwarves of Svartalfheim and used to bind Fenrir

Godi (pl. Godar): a chieftain, a priest

Hel: the underworld where most of the dead dwell, also the name of the ruler of Hel and offspring of Loki

Hirdmen: a retinue of household warriors

Holmgang: a duel between two men

Huginn and Muninn: Odin's ravens, they inform him of events in Midgard

Jörmungandr: giant serpent that encircles the world's oceans while biting its own tall and offspring of Loki

Mangæld: a or as paid to the person's family if that person was killed or injured by another.

Midgard: the world inhabited by humans

Mjöllnir: Thor's hammer

Niflheim: the world of primordial darkness, cold, mist, and ice

Norns: the three sisters who control the fate of men and women

Skjaldborg: a shield wall

Surtr: a fire giant who leads his kin into battle against the gods of Asgard during Ragnarök

Svartalfheim: the world inhabited by the dwarves

Valhalla: Odin's hall where those who died in battle reside

Valknut: a symbol made of three interlocked triangles, also known as Odin's Knot. It is thought to represent the transition from life to death, Odin, and the power to bind and unbind

Valkyrie: Odin's female warriors, they choose who goes to Valhalla

The Gods

Æsir: the most prominent of thetwo tribes of gods

Odin: chieftain of the gods, alsothe god of war, poetry, wisdom and magic

Frigg: Odin's wife

Thor: god of thunder and fertility

Tyr: god of war, law and justice

Vidar: god of vengeance, also knownas the silent god, will avenge Odin at Ragnarök

Vali: god of vengeance, avengedhis brother Baldr's death

Baldr: son of Odin and Frigg, godof the summer sun and light

Loki: the trickster god

Heimdall:the ever-vigilant guardian of Asgard

Ran: mother of waves, those whodie at sea reside in her hall

Vanir: the second tribe of gods

Njörd: god of wealth, fertility andthe sea

Frey: god of ecological fertility,wealth and peace, son of Njörd

Freya: goddess of love, fertility

Ullr: god of hunting and winter

Hodr: son of Odin and blind. Ismainly known for killing Baldr

About the Author

Donovan Cook is the author of the well-received Ormstunga Saga series, which combine fast-paced narrative with meticulously researched history of the Viking world and are inspired by his interest in Norse Mythology.□His second series, The Charlemagne's Cross Series, was published by Boldwood Books, as well as his new series, The First Kingdom Series.

Donovan was born in South Africa but raised in England, where his fascination with Medieval History, especially the Vikings and Norse Mythology, took root. In his free time, Donovan spends time with his family, watches rugby whenever he can, and takes their Frenchie out for long walks.

Feel free to contact him on Facebook, X, Bluesky, Goodreads and Bookbub to talk about history, rugby or anything else.

Visit Donovan's website: donovancook.net.

We hope you enjoyed reading *The Bear Slayer*. If you did, please leave a review.

Also by Donovan Cook

Ormstunga Saga

Son of Anger

Raid of the Wolves

Chaos of the Gods

The Bear Slayer

The Charlemagne's Cross Series

Odin's Betrayal

Loki's Deceit

Thor's Revenge

Valhalla's Fury

The First Kingdom Series

Woden's Spear